# MOUNT EROS

EROS CRESCENT TRILOGY VOLUME THREE

## RICHARD LEE

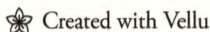

*Dedicated to a world in need of
love and imagination*

Imagine a retired writer, living in a bush hut in a forest beside a river in rural Australia. He gets lonely sometimes. Drawing on the memories of an active life in long gone days in a big city, he sets out to write a simple fantasy, populated with events and people that he remembers and others that he invents. Welcome to *Mount Eros*.

— THE AUTHOR

# CONTENTS

# PREFACE

It should go without saying, that relationships between people are, as always, the essential elements of any romantic story. But equally important are the settings in which the characters act out their parts.

In Mount Eros, we introduce you to The Club, a newly styled female friendly venue that had its origins in the old and shabby blue movie cinemas of New York, London, Berlin and Amsterdam.

The two women, Jackie and Miranda are home in Australia from London at last and happily ensconced in the house at the end of Eros Crescent and looking to start a family.

Life has changed significantly for Helen and Mary and many of the others, all of whom are more than happy to share their lives and loves with each other.

———

*Mount Eros* is the third and final volume of the Eros Crescent Trilogy which includes volume one entitled *The Fifi Code* and volume two, *Eros Crescent*.

## RELATIONS & RENOVATIONS

THE PROPERTY at number twenty-one Eros Crescent had likely never seen more feverish building activity since the time it was first built in 1903.

Rogers step-sister, Jackie had visited from London to survey their newly inherited property, and with her professional organisational abilities and helped by her very deep pockets, she reached out to architects, interior designers and builders and in less than a month she had set in motion the biggest home makeover the locals had ever seen.

Jackie was "camping" as she called it, in the cottage with her brother.

Roger was at first a bit self conscious about having a house mate but he soon settled down to enjoy his sisters company. Jackie didn't once nag him like she did when he shared her London apartment with her and Miranda, and he figured that his newly formed relationship with Jackie's close friend and occasional lover Caroline, had a lot to do with it.

In between Jackie's busy daily schedules, Roger managed to introduce her to Caroline's mother and father, Rosa and Bertie and it was satisfying to see her so excited about meeting them. Rosa knew that Jackie was among her daughter's lovers which probably made their meeting especially significant and the two women enthusiastically agreed to meet again soon.

Then Roger organised a visit to Helen and Freddy and the excitement that both women tried to hide but without success was apparent to both men who responded graciously by excusing themselves to take a blokes only tour of Freddy's amazing workshop.

Caroline had told Helen about her close friend Jackie and her partner Miranda who would be moving in to number twenty-one later in the year. And when Caroline arrived in London a couple of weeks before Jackie's trip to Sydney, she had told Jackie and Miranda about Helen; even the story of their unrequited love and how it had at last been fulfilled.

Roger made an earlier than usual appearance for a late breakfast the morning after their evening with Helen and Freddy and found Jackie at the kitchen table with her large notebook and her telephone.

"Hi sister! Sleep well?"

Jackie looked at Roger, meaningfully, he thought.

"Yes, wonderful, thank you, big brother. And thank you for last night. Meeting Helen and Freddy was great."

"Glad you enjoyed it Sis. I really like them. Couldn't wish for better neighbours really. I meet up with Freddy and Caroline's dad, Bertie for coffee at a cafe once a fortnight. I hadn't realised how much I missed contact with thinking men. It's wonderful."

Jackie continued looking at him.

"Helen has asked me to come and see her studio this afternoon."

Roger smiled back and buttered a piece of toast.

"I'm supposed to be meeting a friend for a long walk on the Mount this afternoon. What say I won't tell if you don't tell?"

Jackie burst out laughing.

"Does Caroline know this person Bro? Should she be worried? She has indicated to me and Miranda that she thinks she's falling in love with you so that she might not appreciate you have anything 'on the side' in her absence. Do I need to meet this person so that I can assess the potential threat?"

It was Rogers turn to laugh.

"Well, Sis. Caroline is the only person I've been with since we first met in London. I've kept myself nice just for baby making and as you can imagine, your dear girlfriend's baby making itinerary kept me happy and sufficiently busy. I thought that now we are comfortably pregnant and she is far away, maybe I should take the horse for a trot for old times sake, so to speak, and to check everything is working as it should. Is it different for blokes, I wonder?"

In a highly unusual move, Jackie came over to Roger and pulled a chair around beside him and took his hand. She looked lovingly into his eyes.

"You've come a long way darling brother and I'm so proud of you. Yes, I think you can take the horse for a trot, as you put it. You deserve it. But there is something I must tell you. What you and Caroline have done has impressed both me and Miranda, especially as Caroline has so energetically emphasised your good points to us.

"Miranda and I both want to have babies when we return to Australia. Caroline has recommended you to us as a dad and her enthusiasm has rubbed off on us. Miranda and I would like you to consider donating sperm when the time comes. It's still a while away yet, but I thought we should let you know what we have in mind. Would you consider this proposition Roger? We would very much appreciate it."

Roger was understandably surprised and momentarily tongue-tied.

"If you agree now, then I can register us at the in vitro clinic before I leave so that they can be ready to receive you as a donor and Miranda and I can both be ready to go as soon as we get back here."

Jackie squeezed Roger's hand then leant forward and kissed him on the cheek.

Rodger's brain was buzzing. He knew what he wanted to say but he didn't know how to say it. He didn't want to hurt Jackie and however he put it, she might also see it as being creepy.

"It would be an honour to father your babies dearest step-sister. However there is just one obstacle."

Jackie looked at him studiously. Then she collected herself and asked the obvious question.

"What is that obstacle, Roger?"

"I'm against the use of the in vitro method of making babies for non essential reasons. I won't bore you with my organic reproduction philosophy right now but I could only agree to father your children if we did it naturally. I'm sorry. I know that having a sexual relationship with a man does not fit with your's and Miranda's philosophical views, but resorting to medical science to make a baby when it isn't necessary, does not make any sense to me. I'm so sorry, Jackie. I believe you should still go and register at the clinic and find out what the donor options are. It should all be pretty straight forward. From the little I know, they will provide full details and health checks for the men on offer."

Jackie was unable to respond. She had accepted that Roger might not want to father children for other reasons but never the one he just gave. Jackie let go of Roger's hand and sat back, looking down at her hands in her lap.

"And I want you to know that I promise I'm not being creepy about this. This is nothing to do with wanting to fuck you or Miranda. I think you know that I find you both very attractive and sexy anyway, but I completely accept who you are. I just can't allow myself to stand by and watch nature be constantly subverted by science."

Jackie continued looking down at her lap. Then she spoke in a whisper.

"Thank you Roger. I respect your viewpoint. I will discuss it with Miranda. Thank you for your honesty. Caroline was right. You are a man of principle and I must respect you for it."

Jackie rallied herself and leant forward, taking Roger's hand in hers and moving her face towards him. Then she put a hand up and turned his face towards her and moved forward and put her lips on his and kissed him tenderly. Roger was confused and hardly responded, only just enough to let her know that he wanted that reassuring kiss as much as she did.

"I guess we sometimes need to change our viewpoint dear brother. And I'm talking about mine, not yours."

———

Jackie's hectic preoccupation with the renovations meant that Roger rarely saw her until much later in the day. He continued to rise in the early afternoons. Jackie was out and about from early in the morning.

Roger was impressed with her organisational abilities, be it appointments with bathroom fittings companies or dealing with tattooed men that looked like murderers or pirates and who seemed to populate the world of floor lifting and re-stumping. And of course there were the council permits and inspections not to mention the beautiful interior designer, Natalie.

Roger couldn't help but notice this super-attractive older woman.

"Natalie coming around this week Jackie?" Roger asked casually but with a cheeky smile while making a salad in the cottage kitchen.

"Well, Roger, I hope so. Do I get the feeling that we would both like to know her better, Bro?"

"Oh, I just thought that if she had a spare moment, she could come in and give me some suggestions for updating the cottage although I'm sure Caroline will take care of all of that if and when she decides to move in. It would still be handy to have Natalie's opinion though so that I can better talk to Caroline about it when she gets home. Might get points if I sound as though I know what I'm talking about."

Jackie stared at her brother studiously and with a wry smile.

"Perhaps we should invite Natalie to dinner one evening, darling Bro. The lovely lady has more or less indicated her willingness to let me explore her sensitive side, and she has twice commented on my 'very spunky brother'. She's single, I know that much. She has a couple of kids in their twenties."

Roger brought over a plate of cheeses and ham and sat down at the table.

"Let me unpack what you just said Sis. Are you talking about sharing or have I got it totally wrong?"

A hand reached over and took hold of Roger's spare hand. Jackie was looking at him as she often did lately. It was as though she was trying to get the measure of the man; looking for something that she sensed was there, but she hadn't yet really quite understood.

"It would be a start, Roger. Who knows? An enjoyable two-in-one might lead us to a one-on-one Bro. I've been thinking about things and I've decided I should consider the offer you've made and on your terms when the time comes. So Roger, can I invite the sexy lady to a candle lit dinner? And if she agrees, would her lovely personality entice you to join me in discovering her charms?

"It will be Natalie's last visit to the project tomorrow. She has pretty much finished what had to be done before the builders get started with the rebuilding, and she's off overseas next week, to Italy I think. We will see her next when I return from London in a couple of months."

Roger put down his fork and moved his hand over. Clasping Jackie's hand he looked back at her lovingly.

"One small step at a time sounds good to me dear sister. Yes, lets ask Natalie to dinner. I'll impress her with a fish dish then tell her fascinating stories of my time in Italy."

The pair couldn't help but laugh and Jackie seemed genuinely pleased with their plan.

"One more thing, Roger. If you do saddle up and take your horse for a trot today as you said you planned to do, please don't exhaust yourself. Natalie might just be very demanding once she gets the bit between her teeth, and as for me, well, we'll find out how I perform in harness, trotting or, if I get really excited, at a gallop."

———

Jackie answered the door the next evening and ushered Natalie into the tiny lounge room.

Natalie was the usual self-assured professional woman that Jackie had got to know well over the past month and who was about to leave to attend a design convention in Italy.

"Oh what a lovely little cottage Jackie, although I do have to say that a tiny make-over could be in order. Maybe when I finish your big project next-door later in the year, I will get invited in to wave my magic wand. A possibility, do you think?"

Jackie eyed the beautiful older women intently, admiring Natalie's firm and shapely legs and backside. She wore a bright red lipstick and red and silver drop earrings.

Jackie wasn't sure why, but in the last day or so she had felt particularly turned on whenever she met up with Natalie. In fact if she stopped to think about it, she had been turned on by whoever stood in front of her, including Roger. And Laura, the horticulturist in charge of sorting out the extensive vegetation in the property grounds along with Milly, her hot little nubile short-shorts assistant seemed so responsive when she gave them each a peck on the cheek when she met them at the summer house to talk about the tangle of trees and shrubs blocking the light and access. Both wrapped their arms around her and hugged her as though they hadn't seen her for ages. And did she imagine it, that Laura had pushed herself suggestively forward during that hug.

And Jackie felt sure that the four men re-stumping the kitchen floor had stared at her legs much more than usual this morning when she inspected what they'd achieved this week.

Jackie returned to the matter at hand.

"That could well happen Natalie. I've mentioned Caroline to you. I expect she will be the one who leads Roger into making some changes in the cottage and now that I think about it, I'm sure she will get even more excited by the idea once she's met you."

Natalie looked at Jackie with a saucy smile.

"Is she as gorgeous as you Jackie? Would she be able to motivate my inner creativity the way you do?"

"I'm certain that you would find working for Caroline very pleasurable. Now, come and say hello to my kitchen slave who wants to impress you with his culinary prowess. I suspect that he's working on a special dish with which to seduce you so be warned."

Roger had finished and was ready to serve at any time and suggested that if the two women would like to make themselves comfortable at the little round table he'd laid out in the alcove off the sitting room, he would take delight in being their slave and serving their meal.

"Oh Roger, You're going to spoil me. I hope I deserve this and I hope you will find it was worth your while, you lovely man."

"I've had a great day and now I'm blessed with the company of two beautiful women so I'm in the mood to spoil both of you. Go and sit down and get comfortable. Oh, and Jackie, would you mind taking those two bottles of Pinot Grigio with you."

Jackie saw how much effort Roger was putting in and inhaled the wonderful smells of fresh herbs.

"I'm so impressed dear brother. Right now I think I'd do anything you asked."

The two women smiled mischievously at each other and Jackie collected the wine and a corkscrew and led Natalie out of the kitchen.

"He is so sexy Jackie. Not sure how you manage to keep your hands off of him. Maybe you don't, unless of course you're a girls only person?"

Jackie put the wine bottles on the table. Then she turned and put an arm around Natalie and playfully pulled her close.

"You will find out soon enough dear lady but I'm a little shy so I will need a drink to give me courage."

Natalie turned and embraced Jackie and lovingly placed a lingering kiss on her lips and Jackie melted into the warmth of this welcoming woman. Jackie had left London a few weeks ago and this length of time without her lover was beginning to weigh on her.

"I can't wait darling. We could have a quick pre-dinner drink now if it would help?"

Jackie uncorked a bottle and poured three glasses of wine just as Roger arrived with a tray of food.

"I understand that you are about to visit Italy, Natalie. This mediterranean pan-roasted salmon is a dish I enjoyed regularly last year while living in a small town on the Amalfi coast. I later had plenty of opportunities to practice cooking it when I moved to a hillside cottage that was a bit too isolated and far away from the town eateries of Positano. I hope you both like it."

Everyone settled down to feast on Roger's masterpiece and enjoy the wine and the good company. Natalie sat in the middle of the three. The round table was very small but just big enough for three people.

Jackie asked Natalie about her planned trip.

"Well, I'll be in Rome for about five days at a conference then I'll move on to Madrid for a week, then Paris then back home."

"Oh, so you won't get to London then? That is such a pity. I will be back there in a week or so and I would have loved you to have met Miranda. And of course, you could have stayed with us. Now that we've sent Roger here to the colonies, there's plenty of room in our flat. I'm sure she would love to meet you. I've mentioned you to her. I won't say what I said, but she certainly got excited."

Natalie wriggled in her seat and giggled and put a hand out and stroked Jackie's arm.

"Oh dear, I wish I'd known. Maybe I could rearrange my itinerary."

Roger refilled their glasses and proposed a toast to absent lovers, thinking of his Caroline and his sister's Miranda.

"Absent lovers!" echoed Natalie as she swallowed more wine.

The trio had just about finished eating and Natalie was rapidly emptying the third fill of her glass. She leant closer to Jackie and smiled lovingly.

"This is so lovely Jackie, being here with you two. I'm already in love with both you."

Natalie gave a tiny hiccup and leant her head forward towards Jackie and puckered her lips, seeking to be kissed. Jackie obliged with a prolonged lip to lip sensuous exchange which ended only because the two became breathless. Taking another deep breath, Natalie repeated her gesture and the two women were again glued to each other.

Roger took advantage of their mutual affectionate outpouring to quickly glance beneath the table, confirming what he suspected. Jackie's hand had disappeared up Natalie's skirt and Natalie's hand was similarly exploring somewhere at the top of his sister's legs. Both skirts were pulled up indecently high. The view of two beautiful women's legs spread wide as they touched each other was exciting beyond belief and roger wished he could have stayed looking at them for longer.

Only moments later, just as Roger was about to clear away the dishes, he felt a hand on his leg. Natalie's free hand moved quickly up as far as it could go, far enough to be able to grope Roger's already stiffening cock safely hidden in his trousers. He felt the hand looking for his zip and as he contemplated helping Natalie locate the object of her desires, Jackie stood up, a little unsteadily on her legs, lifting

Natalie by her hand and announcing quietly that Natalie should follow her to somewhere more comfortable.

Natalie rose and followed, just managing to turn and flash a come hither smile and gesture with her hand for Roger to come too, before being half dragged towards Jackie's bedroom door. At the doorway, Jackie stopped and turned and looked at her brother.

"We want you to come too, Roger. We'll need a chef just incase we get hungry. Don't you think Natalie?"

Natalie giggled, "Definitely darling. We'll definitely need Roger won't we darling. I mean how could a girl not want Roger in her bed? Come along you darling man. Don't be shy."

"Thank you ladies. You go ahead and get comfortable. I'll just clear these dishes and be right there."

———

Natalie was lying face down on the edge of the bed and Jackie was peeling the woman's skirt down over her noteworthy buttocks and down over her legs and feet.

"Oh yes, Jackie, do whatever you want you naughty girl. I haven't felt this excited, ever."

Then Jackie rolled Natalie over and pulled her properly onto the bed, running a hand up between her legs while bending over to kiss her neck and lips. Then Jackie removed her own frock and bra and Natalie reached out and pulled down her underpants.

"Oh you really are a proper blond. What a beautiful little pussy, you have. I must kiss it Jackie."

Roger watched as the two women explored one another. It was a most erotic picture and he knew it was time for him to join the party.

If there was anything holding Roger back, it was a feeling of doubt about touching Jackie. He had never ever touched his step-sister's body except for those recent hand holding moments and kissing episodes. He had always felt attracted to her but he had conditioned himself to put Jackie out of his mind in respect to all things erotic in deference to her and Miranda's rigid lesbian beliefs. Now it seems that this was about to change. But he still felt awkward about it. Hopefully, he would feel differently once he joined the two women on the bed.

Roger slipped out of his trousers and the rest of his clothing, and with his member standing at attention, he moved onto the bed.

Roger fears were allayed by Jackie the moment she felt him arriving. In the most sensuous welcome a man could possibly have received, Jackie turned to him and smiled and put her arms around him and drew him close while covering his lips with hers. Then she slowly pushed her tongue into his mouth and at the same time moved a hand down, wrapping all of her fingers around his cock.

Roger was in heaven. Jackie's welcoming him to the bed was one thing, but importantly it brought to an end years of his needing to repress his deeper feelings for her.

Roger put his arms around Jackie and lifted a hand to lightly feather her bare shoulders and neck with his fingers. Her delicate milky white skin had alway excited him and now she was giving him access to something that had until now been totally taboo. The two continued to lightly kiss and tongue each other. It was a blissful moment for both of them and when they stopped kissing and looked into each others yes, they both smiled and each gave a little laugh, acknowledging this historic event.

"It's okay Roger. I love you Bro," Jackie whispered.

"Thank you Sis. Love you too."

Natalie had watched the two kissing tenderly and was now totally randy.

"My turn, darling."

One of Natalie's hands encircled the base of Roger's cock while the other gently fingered his balls.

"Oh all right Natalie. If you insist."

Jackie smiled at Roger then let go of him and rolled over and pushed Natalie back down, opening the woman's legs wide and burying her head in Natalie's very verdant valley. Natalie gave a little scream.

"Oh yes, you sexy bitch. Yes please."

As she called out, Natalie reached for Rogers member, dragging it down to her large lipsticked lips and engulfed him in wet warm softness, moving her tongue around him as she began to thrust herself upwards to meet Jackie's mouth.

Roger sat back on his knees revelling in the sensations of what Natalie was doing to his cock while he stared at Jackie's rear end. It was truly a sight to behold. Her small perfectly shaped bottom and the tiny bunch of yellow curls surrounding a just visible glistening vulva were mesmerising and Roger reached forward and put his face and tongue where it longed to be. Jackie's body shook ever so slightly and she reached back and grabbed his hair and pulled him closer to her.

Knowing that Jackie wanted him there caused Roger's cock to twitch inside Natalie's mouth and the excited woman sucked him even more energetically and then, reaching up to where his face was imprisoned she put fingers on Jackie's clit. Jackie's back arched as she had a tiny orgasm, and Roger responded, pushing his fingers hard into her at a spot just below her shoulder blades.

All three lovers were ecstatically absorbed in satisfying their mutual longings. Only the sounds of sucking and gasping along with the odd utterance denoting great pleasure, could be heard.

Roger's mesmerising vision of Jackie's beautiful rear end combined with Natalie's loving attention was suddenly interrupted. Natalie removed Roger from her mouth and pulled it up to rest agains Jackie little yellow brush.

"Now you two, satisfy my fantasy of seeing you both fucking each other. Slip it into her Roger, darling. I'm sure Jackie will love it."

As Roger began to panic, Jackie turned her head to look at him and in a super soft voice said, "Do as she asks, Roger." And as she spoke, she wriggled her rear back against his cock where it rested hard up against her.

"There darling. Be a good boy and do as Jackie says."

Natalie took hold of Roger's cock and testicles with both hands and pointed him at Jackie's glistening pussy. Then she rubbed the head of his penis against all the wetness, and fed him in between Jackie's pale pink lips. Roger hesitated for only the shortest moment before he slowly slid his whole member into the passageway that led him to heaven.

"Now fuck the bitch. She really wants it. And you must fuck me too so don't stay in her forever."

But neither Roger or Jackie were listening. Once he was right in, Roger stopped for a moment. Then his cock twitched and then twitched again and each time, his step-sister gasped and trembled. Then the two settled down into a slow steady rhythmic shagging mode, both knowing that they now belonged to each other for ever.

"Is it my turn yet, Jackie," came a whisper from behind. Natalie had watched the two fucking while she fingered herself, excitedly coming regularly as a result of all that was happening.

"Please fuck me now, Roger. She's being greedy."

Jackie reached back and took hold of Roger and slowly moved him out of her. Then she swung around and faced him. The two stared lovingly at one another and kissed. Then Jackie leant and whispered in Roger's ear.

"Don't come inside her whatever you do Roger. Come in me. I so want that. Come back and have more of me my darling Bro. Love you."

Roger kissed Jackie again then moved around to face the beaming smile of Natalie.

"Now give it to me, master chef. Cook up a storm in my cunt, you sexy bastard."

Jackie smiled lovingly at the two shagging figures on her bed, still feeling the effects of Roger having her, her very first ever penetration by a man. And after Natalie had exploded a couple of times, throwing herself about in her excitement, Jackie leant forward and whispered something in her ear.

"Yes, alright darling. If I can have him again before I leave for overseas then yes, I'll pass him over."

Jackie was now interested in trying Roger while laying on her back. She laid down beside Natalie and pointed her head towards him and smiled, puckering her lips to indicate that she was available. Jackie lifted up her legs to signal her willing submission.

"Don't think this is the last you'll see of me master chef. I will book you again when I return home. Now the greedy bitch beside me wants more."

Roger moved across and Jackie took hold of him, dragging him swiftly into her and arching up to meet him. They stared into each other's eyes, a faint smile on their faces. Having done so much with the two women for the past hour, Roger knew that he had to come very soon, and he did. In a sudden flurry of hard shagging, first Jackie and then Roger came, climaxing together. As Roger collapsed on top of her, Jackie whispered 'You wonderful man.'

"Well, you two! That was worth buying tickets for. Congratulations and I hope that will be on the menu on my next visit."

———

When Roger and Caroline talked on Skype one evening a couple of weeks after she had arrived at Jackie and Miranda's home, he mentioned Jackie's suggestion of she and Miranda having his babies and he went on to tell Caroline about his reply.

She was slightly taken aback as was Jackie, but she quickly recognised that what Roger believed was earnest and heart-felt and she could think of no reason to try to persuade him otherwise. In fact in the back of her mind Caroline registered that having principles like this was just one more reason to appreciate him.

"So how did Jackie react, darling?"

"Very well really, now that I think about it. She seemed to accept my response and said she thought that she might have to rethink things and maybe change her viewpoint. I wasn't quite sure what she meant but that's okay.

I was conscious that you had put a lot of effort into recommending me so I felt a bit guilty saying what I did. Still, it was better to be up front I guess. She hasn't mentioned it since and we are getting on very well."

While the two talked, they played silly games with their hands and fingers and even tongues, making rude gestures suggesting they would dearly like to get their hands and mouths on each other. Skype made possible other layers of communication to frustrated lovers, not just sound. Caroline giggled when Roger mimed lifting her skirt up and pulling down her panties.

"I love the idea darling but I'm wearing jeans. I might dress up for you next time. Would you like the librarian look sweetheart?"

The two continued to make rude banter then Caroline became serious.

"Now, it might not be the right time to tell you but I'm feeling sufficiently pregnant with our baby that I'm suddenly feeling confident in us being a couple, whatever that entails. We'll explore that when I get back.

"I told Helen before I left that I wasn't yet prepared to share you. Well, I've decided now that I can share you, but only for worthwhile causes of course, and with your approval.

Alice approached me before I left. She wants to have a baby and she fancied you as the dad. I explained that whilst I hoped that you and I would eventually adopt the Helen and Freddy model of sharing, I wasn't quite up for it yet, and sent her away.

"I do love her and I now believe that if you were up for it, she would be more than willing to let you be the father of her child. And I want you to know that I would welcome it too. What do you think darling? No, that's not fair. You need time to think about it. Let me know later."

Roger stared at the screen and at Caroline.

"Wow! I never knew that a man could do so little and still be in such demand. I wonder if all my fellow males are having this sort of upsurge in popularity? But no, I can give you an answer right now my love. The answer is yes, with your blessing

I am able to offer myself as a daddy donor. And how did you come to this decision so quickly you might ask? Simply because having you in my life is a blessing and strangely enough, things aren't as complicated as they were before I met you.

"Oh! Just one thing, Caroline. I cannot guarantee that I can do the deed on demand. You are already aware that I need to be attracted to someone, so it would be wrong to advertise me far and wide. I need to be sufficiently moved before I can plant the seed. I know you understand that but thought now was a good time to mention it again to avoid disappointed clients in the future.

"So there, you sexy bitch. Now! Get out of Miranda's bed and come home soon. I miss you."

Caroline giggled and looked lovingly at Roger and blew him a kiss then made a tube with her hand and her fingers and moved the hand up and down suggestively.

"There is no one like you darling man. Oh how I wish I was there to tug you. I've only just realised that now you have introduced me to giving proper hand and blow jobs, I'm constantly fantasising about unzipping you and having my way with you.

"Now, I'll immediately add you to my register of volunteer donors and circulate the list amongst my hundreds of single girl friends with ticking clocks and also mentioning that you will require them to take personality test beforehand. Oh yes, I'll also give them a complete list of Agnes's successful seduction wardrobe, just to help them along and help ensure that you are sufficiently moved.

The two laughed lovingly and blew kisses and murmured loving thoughts and prepared to finished the call.

"Keep your phone handy darling, eat properly and exercise. I won't call Alice. I'll tell Helen who will then pass on the news to Alice. Game on!"

———

That evening over dinner, Roger told his step-sister about the conversation he'd had the night before with Caroline.

"So Jackie, I just wanted you to know in case you discover an obviously horny women wandering around the property looking for me."

Jackie laughed and indicated that she would watch out for such women with great interest.

"I hope this doesn't mean that when Miranda and I get back to Australia we'll find that you have a long waiting list.

"My God! I can see it now. There will be a waiting room and you will have a big titted lesbian assistant inspecting and warming up waiting horny on-heat women and inspecting their apparel to make sure that you are turned on quickly when they get ushered in and thrown to you on your giant bed. And just when I was thinking that my brother was at last going to lead a normal life at last and happily settle down with our darling Caroline."

When their laughing subsided, Roger reminded Jackie that as far as he knew, in the short term, there would only be one person looking for him as a result of Helen passing on the news that Caroline had announced that his services were now available.

"I don't think you've met Alice. She's around your age. Freddy was married to Alice's mother who died quite young. So when he married Helen, Helen happily became the wicked stepmother. All of the afore-mentioned names are 'intimates', if you get my drift."

"Well dear brother, can I assume that this super attractive young Alice will be in search of your body, and that if your wicked sister finds her first, she will be allowed to look after her every need until my randy Bro shows up?"

"Yes, Jackie, that is about it except I'm assuming that Alice will make contact to arrange a pre-ovulation check-in so to speak. I've met her a few times but I've never really had a proper conversation with her. We need to get to know each other just a little, don't you think?"

"Oh yes, of course you do, Roger. After all, you're not the commonplace evil zipless fucker striking women down in a bowling-alley-row of pussy's, are you? Or are you?"

The two had descended into a whirlpool of hilarity and they were enjoying each other immensely.

"I really am on your side Bro. I think you know that. Whilst I might energetically pursue my interests, I promise I won't jeopardise yours."

Jackie did what she seemed to be doing more and more, she leant across and kissed Roger, not on the cheek but on the lips and looked deep into his eyes.

"I'm looking forward to coming to live on Eros Crescent Roger, knowing we will all be settled in this place together. What a wonderful thing to have happened."

———

Her preoccupation with planning how she would have a child was placing Alice on the borderline of being an obsessive. Her analytical mind had served her well up till now both as a student and in her work. But Alice's attempts to chart a course of action for what she realised would be a significant and life changing event, was causing her a lot of anxiety. Her inability to choose a path was crippling and she was not happy.

"But I thought you'd decided that Freddy should be the one, my love. What has changed?"

Freya was bearing the brunt of Alice's anxious moments of self-doubt and felt powerless to advise her knowing as she did how her lover was capable of overthinking most things before coming up with the solution.

"It just seems too much to ask. Freddy and Helen have done so much for me over the years and wanting them to fix this seems like a step too far; the easy way out. It would be like I was refusing to grow up, or at least, to me it would. No! I have to move on and that means finding someone else. One option is finding a donor and going through a clinic but I cannot get my head around that at the moment. It just doesn't seem right."

Freya stood behind her love and gently massaged Alice's neck and shoulders and Alice reached up and took Freya's hand in hers and kissed it.

"Sorry, sweetheart. I'll work it out."

And strangely, suddenly it did.

Alice's phone rang.

"Hello! Hi Helen, what? Oh my God, Freya and I are just sitting here going over my dilemma and you ring in the middle of it. What a coincidence.

"She did? Oh my goodness. I'm more confused now. Had you already mentioned it to Freddy? Oh, that's good. Better we don't worry him with it until I work out what to do. Alright, darling. We'll see you tomorrow. We both love you."

"What was that about?"

"Caroline just called Helen and told her that she was making Roger available to me. She thought it better that Helen tell me so Helen is coming around tomorrow evening to give us the details."

"Great news! And it sounds as though she has appointed Helen as Roger's agent?"

"Well if she has, then I'd best get my order in early to avoid the rush. Oh Freya! So much to think about."

Alice was now suddenly struck with the idea that she was planning to make love and hopefully a baby, with a man she'd met only once or twice and hardly knew. It was time for her to get serious about her feelings and her intentions and importantly, how her relationship with Roger should be approached and ultimately consummated.

The more she thought about it, the more Alice realised that wanting a baby was a selfish thing if she didn't also want to know about her child's father. If she hoped for a successful conception, she needed to also hope for some sort of positive relationship with the man who was to provide the wherewithal.

Alice would talk to Helen first, the fount of all womanly wisdom. Then she would call Caroline in London and talk to her.

———

"Caroline is fine with it darling. She explained that her main concern was that Roger might fall in love with another woman just when Caroline was thinking more positively about their relationship and planning a future together. I can well understand what she was going through. I did point out to her that mine and Freddy's sharing agreement helps avoid that situation arising simply because we are both so aware of each others other interests. But she is right. One does need to have forged a strong relationship as well. And I suppose that your step dad and me being older than Caroline and Roger must make a difference."

Helen was visiting Alice and Freya at Freya's house. It was her first visit since Alice and Freya had started living together. Alice wanted Freya to be there so that she was a party to all that transpired or was discussed as things moved along. All three women were lovers together so that they didn't need to keep secrets and were there for each other in moments like this.

"Thank you Helen. So that side of things seem to be okay given that Caroline has approved me. So now the reality is that I don't know what I should do next. I'm thinking that I should call Roger and suggest we get together for a 'get to know each other' moment. Am I right?"

Alice looked at Helen and then at Freya, looking for their opinions.

"Well, I'm certainly not the one to ask considering how I arrived at where I am, happily pregnant by accident."

Alice and Helen laughed, both jokingly agreeing that Freya had had it too easy.

"Of course, we did benefit from your wicked stepmother's wise words on how to get the best out of a man; letting them decide how and when to do the deed. I'm sure we could easily have messed it all up if we hadn't had her advice and by simply expecting Freddy to do what he was asked to do. Keeping that in mind in this situation is important I think. Don't frighten Roger."

"Yes, sweetheart, I think you are right and best I not try to hurry things along. Getting to know Roger and him already knowing from Caroline what is being asked of him, is all I can do. I mustn't over-think things. Am I right?"

Helen and Freya smiled and rolled their eyes at each other, then nodded at Alice in agreement.

"We have one other ally in this situation. Freddy now has regular contact with Roger and they get on very well. Freddy knows about what we have all discussed and he has given his step-fatherly stamp of approval on the situation. Having him on side so that if needed he could casually mention something to Roger will be very useful. I'm so glad they get on well. Hate to think how it would have been if they didn't like each other."

All three laughed and someone mentioned the old days and shotgun weddings.

"So I'm thinking that I should call Roger and ask if we could meet up for a chat. How does that sound?"

"Yep! I think that sounds like the way to go, Alice. Do you agree Freya? Anything to add darling?"

"Nothing except will I sometimes get a little bit of attention from one of you sexy bitches, or will I need to call and just hope you can fit me in? Or should I just look elsewhere for comfort?"

Alice and Helen looked at each other, amused at their long-legged loves perceived predicament. Then, as one, they stood up and reached forward and lifted a surprised Freya from her chair.

"I can feel a sudden fancy for a prego lady coming on, Alice. Are you feeling it too?"

"I certainly am Helen. Come with us Freya. There are a few little things Helen and I would like to talk to you about in the bedroom."

Frey sighed and smiled.

"Only if get to lick and nibble all four tits."

"Be our guest while we remove your panties, you slutty little bitch. Let us ravish you until you beg for mercy."

"Or ask for more?"

———

Alice braced herself and made the call to Roger. It was mid afternoon. She had been reminded by Helen that he worked late and wasn't available until later in the day.

"Hello! Roger Roberts phone. Roger's not available at the moment. You can call back in half an hour or perhaps I can help you? My names is Jackie. I'm his sister."

This wasn't something the already slightly apprehensive Alice hadn't foreseen and she hesitated a little longer than she wanted to. The silky voice at the end of the phone also rang other bells which confused the single minded Alice.

"Aah, hmm! Hello Jackie. My name is Alice. We haven't met but Caroline and Helen have mentioned you. I do hope you are enjoying your visit. I understand you will be returning to London soon. Hopefully we will meet up when you come back."

"I would hope that we'd see each other before I leave in ten days time, Alice."

Jackie's voice had softened and now carried a sensuality that Alice could not ignore.

Oh, here comes Roger, darling. I'll put him on. Bye, Alice."

"Hello, Alice. Roger speaking. I'm thinking you may be calling to arrange for us to catch up? I've spoken to Caroline so I guess we both know what needs to happen. I must admit, this is all a bit new to me so I might seem a little nervous but I'm sure things will work out. So when would you like to come over, or would you prefer that we meet somewhere?"

"Hello Roger. I'm on holidays at the moment so that anytime that suits you will be fine with me. And I'm more than happy to come to your place, preferably sooner rather than later, Roger."

"Okay then. How about tomorrow, at around two o'clock. Come to the cottage behind the main house? Does that suit?"

"Thanks Roger. That sounds fine. I look forward to seeing you then."

———

Alice felt a twinge of expectation when she knocked on the front door of the cottage but it wasn't the thought of meeting her hoped for sperm donor that caused it. The silky voice of Jackie had resonated with her, upending the normally guarded feelings that Alice maintained and triggering a mix of anticipation and expectation far exceeding any thoughts she had about her planned activities with Roger. And when the door opened and a stunning looking woman around her own age greeted her, Alice new that things were going to work out a little differently.

"Alice? Do come in. Roger has been called away and apologises. His solicitor called and told him that some papers relating to this property hadn't been fully signed off and that it was urgent that the matter be attended to before I returned to London and any renovations took place at the main house. He should be back from the city a little after three o'clock.

Roger suggests that you wait or make another time. I told him that

I was sure that you and I would have things to chat about and that hopefully you would stay until he returned."

The two women stared at each other in the dimness of the hallway, appraising the delightful vision that both were a party too.

Alice's mind raced through everything she knew about Jackie, visualising both Caroline and Helen naked before Roger's very beautiful sister. As she was doing that, Jackie was also thinking about her about her two lovers and their explicit recommendation of the slender shapely Alice.

"I Skyped Caroline yesterday morning, London time, Alice. She asked me to give you a big kiss from her. Can I deliver the kiss now, please?"

Jackie's voice carried both authority and pleading mixed together to make an irrefusable request. In an unaccustomed move, Alice moved a step backwards and leant against the front door, positioning herself in anticipation then she reached out with both arms giving a positive and reassuring response to Jackie's offer.

"Yes, Jackie, please kiss me."

In just moments, the women had their lips slowly and gently touching. Then Alice pushed out her tongue and Jackie sighed and took it in and lovingly slid her own tongue around it. Then she pushed her tongue into Alice's mouth, feeling a tremor run through Alice's body. Then two hands ran down Jackie's back. Alice grasped Jackie's buttocks and pulled her closer and the two women slowly rubbed the lower parts of their bodies against each other, and while they lovingly gyrated, Jackie let her hand move in between their bodies and feel for Alice's pussy hidden beneath her cotton frock and undies.

———

Unbeknown to Alice, Jackie was still running hot from the previous nights loving moments with Roger and Natalie and still feeling the sensation of Roger's beautiful cock in her pussy.

Sex was uppermost in her mind and Jackie now suspected that she had been ovulating but foolishly hadn't realised it, and the voice in her head and her genitals suggest that she probably still was in baby-making mode.

Jackie felt a sudden urge to talk to Alice about ovulating and perhaps discover more about it. But the creature in her arms was now breathing deeply and was completely involved in communicating with Jackie in a physical way and only for her own sexual enjoyment.

It wasn't really the time for a discussion about fertility.

With their arms around each others waists, Jackie guided Alice into her bedroom where the two collapsed onto the big bed, throwing their phones and shoes onto the floor and kissing and touching each other until they both succumbed to anticipation and each began removing the others dress and panties. They spent a long time kissing and gently groping their magic special spots, occasionally calling out 'yes' and gasping with excited delight.

When Jackie's phone beeped indicating the arrival of a message, she wanted to ignore it but given that at any time she might get an urgent communication regarding the building project, she knew she had to check it. She murmured 'Sorry darling. Don't move'. Jackie rolled over and leant down and reached for her phone laying on the carpet beside the bed. It was from Roger; 'Did she arrive? Ten minutes away, see you soon'

Jackie texted back very quickly, 'Join us in my bed' then rolled back up from the floor helped by Alice dragging her by the shoulder then lovingly wrapping herself around her and burying her head between her breasts and pulling the woman's hand back down between her legs.

"Roger should join us in a few minutes, darling," Jackie gasped. "It will be an excellent way for you two to get to know each other. Trust me. I love him dearly. It will be just fine."

Alice felt strangely excited about something she might normally have regarded as a bit sudden or maybe inappropriate. Having Jackie's step-brother in bed with them couldn't be a bad thing, surely? And given how she was adoring the woman's every movement, how could Alice ever doubt her.

Roger arrived and quietly let himself in. He had showered and shaved only a couple of hours ago and he had finalised the paperwork at the solicitors as requested. He was feeling happy with himself and looked forward to meeting Caroline's friend Alice and from Jackie's text, the meeting was going to be a lot different to what he had expected.

Roger smiled down on the two loving women. He had removed his clothes and now stood like an extra player waiting to be called onto the field. He was already semi erect and when Jackie turned and smiled up at him and took his cock in her hand and squeezed him, it jumped into life. Jackie's startled smile broadened and she whispered, "Come and join us, Roger."

Alice raised herself on one elbow and looked up at Roger long and hard then she stared at Jackie's hand holding his cock then put out her hand and took Roger away from Jackie, holding it while still staring up at the two of them. Then, as the two watched, Alice first smiled at Roger then drew his stiff cock into her mouth and moved into a comfortable position and began a slow sucking, moving her head backwards and forwards.

Jackie remained sitting up on her knees and looked lovingly at Roger while lightly running her fingers over his modestly haired but well muscled chest.

"I want your sperm darling Bro. I've realised that I'm ovulating. Please be sure to give it to me. Alice doesn't need it yet, not until she comes on heat in a week or so, I think she said. And if everything works out, me being pregnant will be a lovely present to take back to London for Miranda."

The admiring Roger smiled back.

"Our adventures last night with Natalie and you ovulating must be the reason I've been in a permanent horny state ever since, remembering fucking your beautiful cunt at least every three minutes. I'll give it to you good and proper very soon, my love."

"Oh God, Roger, how we ever got to this point is a mystery. I just love it that you want to fuck me on a regular basis, you sexy bastard. I'm sure I can feel the excitement permanently in my vagina. I so hope that we'll want to do it for ever, Roger. It's so wonderful!"

The two were interrupted by a quiet little voice from below.

"I want you to put your cock in my cunt now please, Roger."

Shagging the beautiful Alice was very exciting as well as oddly fascinating, especially when the unusually straight laced and academically inclined young woman moved into a different persona, uttered strange words and sentence fragments from her psychology studies. "Oh yes, yes, I'm sure this is the right section." And "Could it be lordosis?" And "Oh yes Sigmund, of course I'm going crazy." "No, professor. Don't stop," along with a more regular "Yes, yes, fuck me silly, Roger."

After a good ten minutes, Jackie decided it was time for her to take control, kissing Alice while softly licking her ear and whispering "my turn now darling".

"Lay on top of me please Jackie," pleaded the sexually charged Alice.

Jackie lay on top of her, lovingly rubbing her pussy and clitoris until the girl threw herself upwards, causing Jackie to move backwards, planting her own wet cunt onto the end of Rogers slippery wet and at the ready, cock.

Jackie gasped as Roger pushed into the randy woman's vagina. In an instant, Jackie arched her back and pushed herself against Roger, screaming Alice's name as she came. Moments later, Roger came with such force that he yelled, momentarily slumped forward, but then moved straight away into a second course of thrusting causing the overwrought Jackie to scream expletives.

"You randy fucking bastard, Roger. Fuck me again then, if you can. Go on! Try!"

Roger quickly came again and Jackie screamed and Alice screamed too and the two women embraced, kissing and crying.

When Roger opened his eyes a few minutes later and looked up at two beautiful smiling faces, he felt that all was well with the world.

"Don't leave town Mr Roberts, sir. I will want what Jackie just had in about a week I think. Promise you will give it to me, Roger?"

"I will, Alice. It's a firm booking."

"I've invited a couple of old school friends - Coco and Nico - around for dinner tomorrow night, Caroline."

Miranda and Caroline were lying in bed on a bleak rainy London Saturday morning. Caroline was staying at Jackie and Miranda's flat while she sold her apartment and settled her affairs before returning to Australia. She had just brought in a tray of coffee and vegemite toast.

"That sounds good Miranda. I take it that I've not met them before. Where are they from?"

"Coco and Nico – short for Colette and Nicolette – enrolled at my old school, Twigs, or Tunbridge Well Girls Grammar School, the year after me. They were some of the first West Indian girls to arrive there."

Caroline had forgotten that Miranda's father had accepted a posting at the Australian Embassy in London when she was around twelve and that the family hadn't returned to Sydney until he retired and Miranda was seventeen. Her father was quite a bit older than her mother who was from an Anglo Indian family and who he met when working in the foreign service in what was then Madras but later to become Chennai.

"So you've stayed in touch, obviously."

"Yes. They both work as programmers in a medical research company in the same building as me so we'll often have lunch together. They are a little different but great fun. I'm sure you will like them.

"The interesting thing is that they have both recently announced that they are pregnant and although they aren't saying much about it, gossip around the water coolers say that they are pregnant to the same man. They will tell me about it if and when they want to."

"So do they live together Miranda?"

"Yes, they do. Their grandparents on their mother's side did very well in the food business after they arrived here from Jamaica in the first wave of immigrants in the late nineteen forties, eventually buying a large older house in Tunbridge Wells. Coco and Nico still live there with their mother, their dad having passed away a few of years back. I think their father might have been from India.

"They're bringing a Caribbean takeaway so be prepared for a surprise. They're both vegetarians so don't expect curried goat or the like.

"There is one more thing, Caroline. They are very singleminded about every thing. It's not a problem, just interesting and sometimes downright amusing. Some say the girls are "on the spectrum" but I don't like using labels. Whatever they do, and however weird, simply pretend it's all very normal. Their eccentric behaviour could also be related to the reason they are both regarded as the best systems analysts in any organisation in London. They are super intelligent. Both have extensive foreign language skills. As well as all the major european languages and from memory, they also speak Russian, Swahili, Japanese, Urdu and Icelandic. In so many ways, they are truly extraordinary."

The arrival of Coco and Nico was memorable for a number of reasons. The two girls were staggeringly beautiful. Both were slim and stood tall in their bright coloured coats and frocks and stylish high heels. Their dark skin shone so that Caroline easily understood what she meant when Miriam had earlier in the week mentioned her friends the Glow Sisters, and for all the wrong reasons, Caroline couldn't believe that they could be anything other than models; never nerdy computer programmers and systems analysts.

"Hello, Caroline. So pleased to meet you."

The sisters passed cardboard containers to their host then stood in the hallway removing their coats and putting their matching wet brollies in the stand. Then, to Caroline's amazement, they removed not just their shoes but each hitched up their frocks and divested themselves of their panties, hanging them carefully over the upright brolly handles. Not a word was said about it and the two beauties continued with their a conversation about the food they had handed to Miranda when they arrived.

"It's only mildly hot, Miranda. Hope you both like it."

Caroline ushered the women through to the lounge room while Miranda went back into the kitchen. The sisters made themselves comfortable on the sofa and looked across at Caroline, both smiling and radiant.

"Caroline is a real blond Nico. Nordic I suppose?"

Coco rose and came over to where Caroline was sitting and reached down and lifted her skirt, then pulled the crotch of her panties aside and stared.

"Yep! A proper blond all right, oh and guess what, she's got tiny curls, and guess what else? Her middle toe on her right foot is about an quarter of an inch bigger."

Coco returned to her seat and looked at her sister.

"If she's curly as well then there must be a smidgen of Icelandic although there is some evidence that a few Vikings carried it in their DNA."

Both women turned their faces towards Caroline and smiled.

"You are very beautiful Caroline. We would love to know more about you. Tell us about your lineage. Where were your parents from?"

Caroline pulled herself together and attempted to answer the question.

"Well, umm, yes. My mother was English – from Cornwall – and my father's family were from Denmark but they met in Australia when they were teenagers. Does that help?"

"What colour hair did your mother have, Caroline?"

"She was auburn, almost ginger."

"Miranda said that you are pregnant. What do you know about the father?"

Caroline was not sure that she was happy about the rapid-fire questioning of these two energetic women. But Miranda had warned her that they were different.

"Well, he's what you would usually call an Anglo Celt I suppose. The truth is, I don't know much about his genetic background. Should I be worried?"

"Not at all Caroline. Unless he's from a continuous line of native residents of Schleswig Holstein, but even then it wouldn't be really serious. Just a possibility of two different coloured eyes, one grey and the other hazel. Right Nico?"

The sisters laughed out loud then turned to watch Miranda bring in the food tray and park it in the middle of the room.

"Now come and eat and stop going on with your genetic research nonsense girls.

"I'm from Welsh stock with a smattering of Spanish on one side and Anglo Indian on the other and I'm thinking of using Roger, the same father Caroline chose, for my first baby. He writes crime novels and gets up late and takes long showers, and from what I hear, he's a good lover. That's all I need to know.

"Help yourselves to water. It's over there on the dresser."

Caroline looked at Miranda. With her small stature and jet black hair and red cheeks she fitted the Welsh stereotype except she didn't have the blue eyes.

The food was delicious and when eventually Caroline helped to carry out some of the dishes she was more than surprised when Miranda told her in a quiet voice that things might change once she presented their visitors with after dinner drinks.

"You won't think they are the same girls once they've downed a couple of gin and tonics, Caroline. Be ready is all I can advise. This is where chemistry outsmarts genetics, darling. They will be begging for attention with our strap-ons in no time. And while I'm thinking about it, they are in the bottom draw of the dresser in case you suddenly needed them. The girls like to wear the pink ones and will want us to wear the black ones, at least that is what has happened when they've visited Jackie and I in the past. Not sure why."

When the four had settled and each was on their second gin and tonic, Miranda asked about the girls being pregnant.

"Nico, there is a lot of talk about you both being with child, as we used to say. Is this true?"

Nico and Coco both looked at each other and giggled.

"Yes, it is true. We spend so much time studying human reproduction we think we might have caught something. Not sure how it happened.

"Coco says it was because we invited a visiting super sexy and brilliant Japanese scientist home for dinner, but I still can't see the connection and I have no memory of any talk about Japanese mating habits."

Caroline and Miranda just couldn't contain themselves.

"You're telling us that you didn't notice anything happening? You didn't see a telltale sign like the gentlemen had removed his trousers or perhaps his zipper had accidentally opened?"

"No, we didn't see any behaviour as random as that. The lovely man had brought bottles of saki as a gift in appreciation of us helping him during his visit to London and Nico and I had found the drink very satisfying and it wasn't long before we had removed his clothing; in the name of research of course.

"Penis size isn't regarded as particularly important but we both decided that while we had Akira at home and away from the office, we should take the opportunity to measure his instrument for statistical purposes and add the results to the Japanese files in our databank. The Japanese file was in dire need of more information, He was very obliging and didn't object, did he Coco?"

Coco was downing her third G & T.

"That is so true sister. He suggested that we take turns in holding it until he thought it was the right size for measuring and that is what we did. He complimented us on our fine fingering, and applauded our dedication to science.

"Eventually, Nico commented that she thought it was a lot bigger than she expected and also that she thought it might be too big for the characteristically small Japanese woman to be able to mate with him, at which point he replied that she might be right and it would allay his fears if he could put it somewhere that would give sufficient feedback for him to decide whether he should arrange to have the size surgically reduced, just in case he was lucky enough to find a Japanese wife."

Miranda and Caroline were in fits, laughing.

"Just hold it for a moment dearest ladies. Let me just get something from the dresser and you can perhaps indicate better, the size of Akira's problem."

Miranda went to the dresser and brought back four dildos and laid them on the carpet. Coco immediately slid from the sofa onto her knees and picked one up.

"It was definitely bigger then this wasn't it Nico?"

Coco then put the end of the dildo to her mouth and licked it.

"Yes Coco, much bigger than that.

"Well, we wanted to help him and we suddenly realised that

perhaps we could. We both took off our panties, got down on our knees and turned so that our rears faced Akira and suggested that if he wanted to try us for size then we would welcome the opportunity to help him and that the information learnt would also be useful for our data bank records."

Nico leant down and picked up a dildo and began the licking motion that her sister was enjoying.

Miranda and Caroline couldn't believe what they were hearing.

"And did Akira manage to fit his penis in, Nico?"

"Yes, fortunately, there was a cruet-stand on the dinning table nearby which included an olive-oil bottle. With his instrument well oiled, he thanked us and took advantage of our offer. He tried us each in turn, going from one to the other and then back again, saying that he wasn't quite sure which was the better fit.

"He took quite a long time about it, didn't he Coco, and sometimes he got very excited about things, making a lot of noise and shouting out, which made us both happy knowing that we were helping out with proper in-the-field research.

"Interestingly, Coco and I found his enthusiasm for what he was doing was contagious and we found ourselves yelling out too, didn't we sis? Right through the night in fact. His thirst for knowledge was insatiable. Anyway, Akira told us that the new information he was gaining about his penis was invaluable, so much so that he rescheduled his flight back to Japan and came to see us the next night and repeated the experiment, saying he just needed to double check the results.

It was quite exhausting but also very rewarding having this opportunity to work with such a renowned scientist."

"And he thanked Nico and I and said he would be very happy to have us stay with him in Tokyo if we ever found ourselves there. He said we so inspired him he had thought of other projects that he would dearly love us both to help him with. He was a real gentleman wasn't he, Nico?."

Nico was now down on the floor with her sister and each was fitting a strap-on around the other's waist. Miranda returned from the kitchen with more gin and tonic and slices of lemon and everyone downed another G & T.

Then both Caroline and Miranda removed their dresses and Caroline became panty-less with Miranda's help as they both attached their strap-ons, and it wasn't long before all four women were laying on the floor laughing and groping and licking each other's big rubber cocks.

Four mouths found willing vaginas and nipples and necks and buttocks and thighs and feet and mouths and lips and ears and tongues and toes and fingers.

Then the Glow sisters knelt and leant over the sofa seat beside each other and Coco called out.

"Now, Akira. It is time you continued your research, you dear man. Please see if you can fit into either of these. My sister and I are more than happy to help should you run into difficulties."

Miranda and Caroline accepted the offer on behalf of the absent father-to-be, Akira. And after they had taken turns each shagging each of the girls, they took over the positions of Nico and Coco and had their rear ends seriously shagged, joining in the happy excited chorus of the orgasmic research being studiously enjoyed by all. All in the name of science, of course.

———

Alice was delighted when a Skype call came from Caroline in London and Caroline said she'd called to give Alice some emotional support.

"You will ovulate in the next few days, Alice. Is that right?"

"Yes, probably next Tuesday I hope, Caroline. And Caroline? How are you progressing? It must be almost a couple of months now?"

Caroline assured Alice that all was well and she felt very comfortable being pregnant.

The two talked briefly about their situations. Alice told her how Helen was very well and looked forward to Caroline's return home.

Then Caroline mentioned how Jackie had spoke highly of her encounter with Alice and Alice found herself blushing which fortunately Caroline didn't notice on the less than perfect medium of Skype.

"Well, I hear you accepted the kiss I sent you, and apparently, it came with extras. Jackie is hard to not fall in love with. I should know. I've been in love with her for the past six years."

Caroline's thoughtful but sensitive commentary put Alice at ease and she laughed, saying that Jackie was a joy and that she looked forward to her eventually coming to live back in Australia.

"Now, Alice, one of the reasons I called was because I wanted to help make sure things worked out. Helen might have mentioned that I had told her how Roger's lovers - apart from me of course, and well, maybe a couple of others - have mostly been older than him. In his words, they have a look about them.

"I won't even try to explain what I think he means but I do know a little bit about what he responds to in a woman as regard her appearance."

Caroline then told Alice the story of how she was in the middle of volunteering to wear whatever Roger would like to see her dressed in that might help excite him when the time came to plant the seed, and his unexpected revelation about an ex lover named Agnes and what she wore that so excited him.

"Oh my God, Caroline. That must have been a shock."

"Only that he was so specific, Alice. Even noting the denier of her tan stockings. Actually, by the time he'd finished telling me, I was totally horny for his bespectacled Agnes and everything worked out very well.

Alice laughed, "My goodness, Caroline. I'm turned on just by you telling me about it. So can you suggest what I should be wearing when I go to him? That would be really handy."

"That is why I called you, Alice.

"Now I figured that if Roger and I failed to get pregnant on that first occasion - although as it happened, everything ended up working perfectly - I should take out insurance by collecting together all the clothing that Roger said that Agnes wore. Unbeknown to Roger, I did that and I'm calling to tell you where they are. They are inside a dry cleaning clothes bag at the righthand end of Rosa's dress-up cupboard in your old flat. There is also a small bag with it, containing stockings and smalls, and another containing shoes.

"I never did find a pair of glasses but if you can find a pair of heavy horn-rimmed glasses, that will help a lot."

Alice laughed at the last bit of the instructions.

"Well, I wear glasses a lot of the time for study and work and as it happens, I believe I have a pair that Agnes would have liked. Thank you so much, Caroline. I will call Edith, the new tenant who I know quite well and ask her if I can call in and collect them."

The two women said their goodbyes and blew kisses and then Alice spoke in a quiet shy voice.

"Caroline, can we get together when you get back, if you know what I mean?"

Caroline offered a naughty smile, "I'm hornier being pregnant than I ever was before. Miriam says I'm exhausting her and she is so thankful that Jackie is back. In fact, darling woman, if you could just open your shirt and show me your breasts, then I'll happily remember what I'm coming home to. Do you mind or is that being just too vulgar?"

Alice reached for the buttons on her blouse and began to undo them.

"Oh my, God, Alice. This is better than a blue movie."

Alice removed her top altogether then took off her bra. Then she unzipped her skirt and let it drop to the floor.

"Oh, Alice. Stay there while I have a quick touch-up. I'm sure I'll cum straight away."

Alice responded by smiling seductively and putting her hands inside her panties and slowly rubbing herself while Caroline watched. Then Alice watched as Caroline's face contorted and she arched her back and gave a little scream."

"Oh, you dear, dear girl. I'll love you for that forever. Now I have even more than Roger to come home to."

———

Edith invited Alice to call in to the apartment the next evening after she had finished work. Alice didn't give the details of what she wanted out of the wardrobe, simply that she had left something behind and would like to collect it.

Alice had met Edith a few times, the last being when she handed over the flat when Alice vacated it to go and live with Freya. Alice had met Edith's young lover, Jessica, just once at Maude's house-warming party. She suspected that Edith had Jessica had only recently come out and got together. And in the back of her mind, Alice suspected that Rosa might have had something to do with it. But be that as it may, Alice didn't need to know about peoples private lives unless of course, they wanted to tell her.

Alice was very familiar with the property and was soon chatting to Edith about living there, and Edith said how she loved it. She also mentioned that leaving her husband and moving here from the country, had been the most liberating of things and how life for her now was quite wonderful.

Having Alice visit was exciting for Edith, especially as Alice knew the property and the owners Rosa and Bertie Bennett, very well.

Edith wanted to talk and in the conversation she mentioned that she and her lover, Jessica had decided to live independently.

"Much as we care for each other, so much has happened for both of us that we've realised that living alone was preferable at this stage."

Edith hinted that Jessica was very young and had a lot of living to do before settling down and that she, Edith, wanted the best both for Jessica and herself.

When Alice asked Edith if she ever felt lonely, Edith smiled and said that life now was so different to when she was in a repressive and lonely marriage, that being alone hadn't so far been a bother.

After a cup of tea and a piece of rich fruit cake, Edith accompanied Alice to the spare room to assist should Alice needed help finding her stuff. Alice soon found it and laid it on the table ready to take with her when she left.

Then the two women started looking through Rosa's dress up outfits, laughing and joking as they took out hangers holding different outfits.

"Rosa put the nun's outfit on when I first came to see the flat. It was a bit confronting, me being the ex wife of a Church of England minister and also a Sunday school teacher and only just beginning a new life with a young woman as my lover. But it turned out well."

The two women looked at each other, each inspecting the other from head to toe. Then Alice reached for the schoolgirl outfit and held it up and told that she'd worn this once to seduce someone.

Edith laughed and jokingly suggested that if she had to guess who, she would say it was probably Rosa's friend Maude who owned number nineteen where Jessica lived. And when Alice coloured up in one of her embarrassing blushing sessions, Edith laughed and put her arm around Alice's waist and squeezed her.

"That's fine, darling. I can't think of anybody who hasn't been with, or been approached by Maude. From what I know, if your seduction worked, it was probably worth while. She's a vibrant woman."

"Now you've got me imagining all sorts of things, Alice and I'm feeling quite enlivened. I could see that that same outfit would do it for me too, although I should not admit to it."

Alice noticed that Edith had coloured up a little and was avoiding looking directly at her for some reason. Alice had a hunch that Edith would like to see her in the schoolgirl outfit.

"Let me slip it on, Edith. It might even make me feel a little more chirpy. And dressing up can be such fun."

Edith watched furtively as Alice quickly slipped off her dress and donned the tartan skirt and the regulation school blouse. Then, with the ribbon that also hung on the hanger, she managed to tie her hair back in short pony tail tufts.

"Will that do, Edith? I don't feel like taking off my shoes and stockings. Oh hang on, I remember now. There are school shoe's in the shoe cupboard and I think there are also a pair of white ankle socks."

Alice pulled off her tights and slipped on the little ankle socks and the school shoes.

"There, Edith, does that look like the real thin or am I just too old to play the part?" And then in a quieter more intimate voice, "Interestingly, it's doing it for me right now. In fact I'm more than happy for you to be the school mistress, Edith," Alice whispered, turning red faced yet again.

Alice stared longingly at Edith. "Can I come and sit on your knee, please miss?"

Edith face was a picture of excited lust and she quickly went and sat in the big armchair, pulling her skirt up well over her knees. Then she quietly instructed Alice to walk over to her and sit on her exposed thigh.

Play acting wasn't really necessary and as soon as Alice sat on Edith's stockinged legs, the two had their arms around each other their lips pressed together and in just moments, their tongues were dancing in each others mouths.

Almost as one, both Alice and Edith reached a hand down under the others skirt and two sets of fingers played with two already wet pussy's.

Alice lifted herself up long enough to push Edith's legs apart then she brazenly put her bum on the chair between Edith's legs and lifted her own legs up to rest on Edith's shoulders, exposing the fact that Alice was not wearing knickers and that her almost hairless little cunt was craving Edith's attention. Edith gently fingered the puffy outside of Alice's vagina and gasped excitedly as Alice shuddered and whined in a way that begged Edith for more. Edith groped Alice's vagina then made her stand up and step over to the bed.

Moving to the bed meant that the two loving women could come together as one. Each removed the other's clothing and in a leisurely fashion, they made love. And when they finished they got into bed and cuddled up and a little later, Edith went to fetch cheese and biscuits and more fruit cake and a jug of fruit juice.

"Edith?"

"Yes, Alice?"

"Can we do this again one day?"

"I would love you to come here again, Alice. Just give me an hour or so's notice, darling, in case I want to dress up as a slut or a nun or something."

"Will do. Yes, of course! You as a slut, that could be fun and I could call you dirty names and threaten to abuse you. I could dress as a slut too. Now I wonder what sluts are supposed to get up to? Probably the same as what everyone does, I suspect."

"Careful young lady, you're getting me excited again."

Alice gently caressed the top of Edith's legs and in a very quiet little girl voice replied, "Kiss my pussy again like you did before. I dare you."

———

Alice had called Roger the day before she expected to begin ovulating, they laughingly joked about him fitting her in and in an official and pompous voice he told her that tomorrow would be fine.

"Yes, Alice. Looking at my diary, I can see that there are no other baby making appointments until the week after next, so tomorrow will be fine. I can't really make an early start, given my nocturnal habits. Can we say eleven?"

They agreed not to start until late morning, given Roger's normal sleeping hours, and that attempting anything earlier could be disastrous.

"Thank you, Roger. I will come knocking at eleven."

———

Alice had lots of fun dressing up for her date with Roger. Everything fitted almost perfectly and given that she and Caroline had joyfully compared body sizes and shapes on the morning after Caroline had visited Alice in her bed earlier in the year, Alice expected everything would fit just fine. Even the low-heeled brown serviceable shoes felt comfy and Alice thought how much she liked them and how she could happily wear them all the time.

Alice couldn't help but begin to feel horny as she dressed for Roger. Not only was she planning a date in which she knew she was going to have a sexual rendezvous while wearing the clothes that a her lady lover had purchased and tried on, but there was also the shadowy figure of Agnes watching her over her; a woman Roger had lusted after. And added to that of course, was the fact that Alice was ovulating. There was also the anticipation of enjoying the attention of a man she had made love to only the week before, admittedly with the extra benefit of Roger's step sister being a part of the event.

Everything was in place and Alice admired herself in the mirror, noting that the heavy rimmed glasses totally made the librarian image authentic. Alice thought to herself how she could easily identify with this significant woman in Roger's life and unconsciously decided that today she would happily be the erotically inspiring Agnes.

The look on Roger's face when he opened the door was one of almost deep shock. He was speechless and when Alice smiled and said hello, he spluttered and just managed to ask her in.

Alice knew where things were in the house because she had been to there before, so feeling quite comfortable, she made herself at home and did everything possible to hide her nervousness. She sat down on the sofa and chatted to Roger about anything other than the reason she was there. But then Alice realised that the normally confident Roger was being very quiet, simply staring at her, constantly scanning her from top to toe. And, having run out of things to say and seeming increasingly more agitated each the moment, he came and stood and looked down over her.

There was a long silence. Alice felt a wave of panic and found herself thinking that this might not work. She could feel a sexual tensions but couldn't work out what Roger was thinking.

Roger was silent and about to have yet another epiphany, this time with dramatic results.

———

It was a book signing for Roger's second book at the book department at Selfridges, in London. Things were going well and the publisher's publicity manager, Eleanor, had just arrived back from the carpark with more stock. She was accompanied by a friend also carrying books.

"Roger Robertson, this is Agnes Watford, a friend who has called to say hello and see how things are going. She works at the local branch of the city library." Agnes looked at Roger and smiled and said hello.

Eleanor excused herself to go and talk to the shop manager, "Back in about twenty minutes. Text me if you need me."

Roger smiled at Eleanor's friend and realised that he would like to just stare at Agnes for the rest of the day. She was his idea of the ideal beautiful woman. Poise, mystery, looks, and a smile he would have happily died for. She was dressed in a tweed skirt and a warm looking shirt covered by a grey pullover. Her legs were sufficiently of the solid shape that always excited him and she wore old-fashioned heavy tan stockings and brown brogues.

Roger couldn't stop looking at the woman who, in turn couldn't help noticing his attentive gaze. She decided to rid him of his obvious fantasy.

"A pity I'm only into girls, Mr Robertson. You are a very attractive man. Maybe we could catch up in another life." Agnes turned to open a box of books to lay them out on the signing table. As she did so, a woman approached and picked up a book and asked if she might get it signed.

"Would you write, To Annabelle", please.

This broke the spell, although with Agnes's comments running through his brain, he found it difficult to concentrate.

"I so loved your first book, Mr Robertson. Particularly the lesbian love affair. I never imagined that a man could write something that sensitive and beautiful about something he would know so little about. Does that couple appear in this book?"

Roger listened as he signed the woman's book and noted the irony of the situation he suddenly found himself in. He had only moments earlier fell in love with a woman who very quickly let him know that she was not available.

"Well, I shouldn't really say, madam. Spoiler alert and all that stuff I suppose. Lets just say that one of them decides to take a different path. Probably not a good idea given that People can't usually change who they are very easily."

The customer left happily clutching her Selfridges paper bag.

Agnes had been watching and listening to the conversation.

"I think from what I just heard you say, that you are stereotyping non heterosexuals, Mr Robertson. That is unfortunate.

Roger had had enough of managing his emotions near this remarkable creature and before he could stop himself, he replied.

"Well, Agnes. If you would have dinner with me we could talk about it, otherwise I suggest you simply read my books and better form your opinions that way.

"And I should say that I make a very nice mediterranean pan-roasted salmon. It is a dish I enjoyed regularly last year while living in a small town on the Amalfi coast, finishing this book."

Agnes was taken aback by Roger's bold invitation and before she had thought it through, she was telling him in a somewhat defiant voice that she would love to try his pan-roasted salmon and asking him where he lived and what time should she arrive?.

Agnes found the address and Roger welcomed her, trying not stare or show how much she affected him.

"I stay here with my sister Jackie and her partner Miriam when I'm in England. It's handy to the library and bookshops.

"Now, can I get you a wine or a soft drink or something else. Coffee is not the best here but I've mastered Jackie's magic machine at last."

Agnes watched Roger closely. She wasn't used to socialising with straight men other than her dad and her brothers and brothers in laws. She's had not yet met a man that seemed to know what the real world was on about and bloke culture was the last thing she wanted to know about. But as she watched and listened to Roger, she found him most appealing and even endearing.

At the end of the meal and with the lights dimmed, Agnes did something she had never in life thought she would ever do. Sitting on the sofa with Roger, she lifted her skirt up above her knees and reached for his hand and slipped it between her legs, looking at him defiantly and yet lovingly at the same time.

In just moments, Roger's hands were stroking those wonderful legs in tan stockings and reaching up to discover Agnes's sensible knickers which he deftly slid down and over her shoes.

Agnes was usually the dominant partner in lesbian relationships so that she could not help but want to lead Roger to wherever she wanted him to go. She took off her pullover and was unbuttoning her blouse when she was interrupted by another hand and a voice asking if she minded if he did that. She quickly realised that she didn't mind at all, enjoying the novelty of watching someone else undress her. She delighted in looking at Roger's face and seeing his extreme desire for her.

But then Agnes thought of something that she wanted to try and she reached out to the bulge in Roger's trousers.

For a dedicated lesbian, this was an odd thing to want to do but the situation she now found herself in was exciting her. Perhaps it was because of the unusual circumstance that had led up to her being there on the sofa with a man, but whatever it was, she was enjoying it. Roger was so different to both the sweet young sensitive first-timer girls Agnes was used to seducing and her hard nosed professional women who wanted to be slapped about and ravaged with a dildo. Suddenly, Agnes was free to do whatever she wanted with a real live cock. Or so she thought.

Agnes's ankles were suddenly grasped firmly and her whole body was dragged forward so that her back was lying on the sofa cushions. Then she watched as Roger lifted her legs into the air, exposing the fact that she was not wearing any knickers. She wore them only rarely and then usually just to hold in a strapless dildo when she wanted to be 'at the ready'.

Feeling Roger's cock pushing into her wet vagina was at first a shock. There was no preamble or foreplay. Roger just wanted to fuck her.

From mentally and emotionally sauntering along like she always did when she was in charge, Agnes's world was upended, literally. She gasped as he held her legs up and rammed and filled her cunt with his rock-hard cock. Any thought that his actions might be inappropriate or violent, didn't occur to her or if they did, were put aside.

Roger looked down on the beautiful woman. He simply couldn't not want to fuck her senseless, as the some are want to say. And he did. The more he fucked the beautiful Agnes, the more she pleaded for him to keep going. Her strident screams urged him on.

Agnes was suddenly in a full shagging mode unlike she had ever experienced with her other lovers. She simply wanted Roger to have all of her, and when he leant and bit her neck and her breasts and when he stuck a finger up her arse and when he dragged a foot to his mouth and tried to eat her toes and when he pulled her head up to his face by her hair and kissed her, she threw her arms around him and wouldn't let him go free.

Roger came in Agnes's cunt like an exploding fire hydrant and the woman joined him, coming with screams she never new she could utter. And just when things slowed and Agnes thought their love-making was at an end, Roger rallied for another round and the two did it all over again.

In the sudden silence, Roger stopped and focused. It was Alice and not Agnes who lay on the sofa, her eye closed and her legs wide apart and with her small wet blond busy open and enlarged and staring up at him. Her bare breasts pushed upwards and showed the red marks of his teeth. Her hair was a mess and the suspender on one thigh had become disconnected from her stocking which was now down around her knee.

Roger put a hand on Alice's chest and bent down to kiss her on the lips. Alice opened her eyes and looked up at him and smiled weakly and whispered, "Thank you Roger."

Roger smiled down at Alice.

"I trust you will let me do it to you again soon, Alice?"

Alice stretched and sighed.

"Whenever you want to, Roger. If this is the way a girl gets pregnant, I think I will want you to make many babies with me. Unless, of course you are happy to have me just because you like me?"

"The last idea makes sense to me. And with Caroline's consent, you will be welcomed in our bed at any time, Alice. Now we had better make arrangements for our next coming together. When would you think would be the right time?"

———

Catherine arrived back in Australia just in time for her mothers seventy-fifth birthday, much to everyones excitement.

Her mother, Rosa, announced that they would have everyone at their house for lunch on the weekend. This would include husband Bertie, Helen and Freddy, Mary and Sophie, Alice and Freya along with Edith and Jessica, and of course, Caroline and Roger. Maude wanted to come but had to attend her mum's ninetieth birthday on the other side of town. She said she's drop by on the way home.

Caroline couldn't wait to get Roger home when he picked her up from the airport. And Roger couldn't wait to inspect Caroline's big tummy although in truth, it wasn't really very big at all. A hardly noticeable pregnant tummy.

After Roger deposited her suitcases in the bedroom, Caroline followed him and began to unbuckle his trousers. When she liberated his cock, she stared at it and smiled, saying, "I'm so pleased to see you again at last. I've really missed you," and then immediately putting him into her mouth and slowly beginning to suck him, savouring the moment while looking up at Roger with bright smiling eyes. And when eventually they finished making love and lay back and held hands, Roger lifted himself and inspected Caroline's tummy.

"Ah, yes. All my own work," he muttered.

"Not quite, darling man. I did offer you a randy few days when I constantly pestered your tadpoles to come and meet my eggs. Remember that?"

———

On a midwinters day, the happy crowd at Rosa's birthday mingled and expressed how pleased they were to see each other, variously saying it had been such a long time between catch ups.

Helen and Freddie were a popular couple, as always, and all seemed well in their world, despite misgivings that Helen was having about the amount of time Frederico was spending with the now very obviously pregnant Freya and Sophie.

At first Helen, along with her neighbour Mary, had been excited at the prospect of babies coming into their world. But then Helen realised something she should have anticipated earlier - that both the girls would be feeling the need to bond with the father of their child.

Mary had mentioned to Helen that Sophie had gone through a

stage of feeling depressed and how she had confided in Mary that she would like to see more of Freddie.

Then Alice had reported a similar story from Freya and Helen realised that it hadn't just been about getting them with child. There was a lot more going on.

Helen also acknowledged that, not having a child of her own was probably the reason she had failed to foresee this situation.

After consultation with Freddy, Helen reached out to Sophie and Freya and invited each of them to spend a night a fortnight in the matrimonial bed instead of her. Sophie had broken down and cried, thanking her and embracing her in a great show of feeling which ended up with both of them naked on the sofa in the drawing room. And Freya reacted by immediately unbuttoning Helen's shirt and begging to be allowed to suck her breasts.

So readily had the three taken to the arrangement, Helen was now wondering how long or even if ever the time would come when they stopped enjoying her husband.

Helen looked across at where Caroline and Alice and Roger were talking and laughing.

Helen thought how different it must be for Caroline, she becoming pregnant only a month or two before Alice and both being around the same age. The fact that the two had been lovers - as had Helen and Sophie and Freya - was made different to Helen's situation because of their ages and both being with child. Sharing each other with Roger was unlikely to be a problem.

Helen brooded about getting older and losing touch with all her lovers. She was even seeing less of Polly now that she was at vet school full time and plus she was spending more time with her horsey friend Belinda. This liaison had also moved into a new phase where both girls were now members of an exclusive dressage group. And Polly even let slip that her new horsey friend, Clifford, had asked her to visit his parents farm in the Hunter Valley for a weekend.

On the face of it, Helen's world was turning upside down and she was feeling insecure.

When Helen eventually talked to Freddy about how she felt, he told her not to see things so negatively and that everyone loved her.

For Freddy, life just moved on and he did his best in every way he could, attending to what he thought was needed most. Now it was babies and their mothers that took up a lot of his thinking.

Helen thought how this wonderful man had become two other women's wonderful man. She knew, deep down that it was her fault for seducing the two girls in the first place and so she was denied the chance to blame something or somebody.

If this feeling of things being lost to her wasn't enough, her neighbour, Mary, seemed less keen to visit her and when Helen asked Mary to pop over the next day for some time together, Mary had begged her to change the day as she had something else on, although she wouldn't say what.

Helen couldn't help wondering what was happening to the world.

It was a week or so after Rosa's birthday and it was after dinner one night, that Frederico dropped a booklet on the coffee table in the lounge and asked Helen if she knew about The Club.

"No, darling. I've no idea what you are talking about my love. Should I know? Are we going to be selling raffle tickets for it?"

Freddy laughed. He had spent the afternoon with Roger and Bertie at their fortnightly coffee and cake session upstairs at the Ampersand Cafe in Paddington.

"Roger told us all about it today. He was employed to write up and design this booklet for the owner. I must say that I was shocked when I heard about it, especially when I found out where it was located. I'm still a bit shocked but I'm starting to sort it out in my head."

Helen looked at her husband quizzically, "What on earth are you taking about, darling. Not much shocks you. The last time was when you discovered you were going to be a father for the second time in a month. Should I be worried?"

Freddy spent the next thirty minutes filling Helen in on what he knew about The Club. While he did this, she inspected the booklet he'd brought home.

"I suppose the biggest shock is that it's all happening just down the road," Freddy said.

Helen was intrigued that such a thing existed and begged her husband for more details and asking questions that he didn't have answers for such as "Did husbands and wives go together sometimes or did they just meet up accidentally at The Club?"

They talked about The Club for the rest of the evening. Freddy related and often repeating all that Roger had told him and said how Bertie had mentioned that he and Rosa knew Desley, the owner and her brother Arnold quite well and that he had also met her mother, who was instrumental in getting Eros Crescent renamed. He said she was a fine woman and he wished her well.

Helen, as did Freddy, had more questions than she or he could possibly think up answers for. But as the night drew on and Freddy opened a second bottle of red wine, the two began to see the funny side of things and make jokes.

"Well, darling. I think we should join and then I will put on a wig and enjoy pretending to be somebody else and letting you seduce me, thinking I was the woman in the next street you've always had the hots for."

Freddy giggled.

"I wonder if she is a member?"

Helen punched him but missed and he caught her in his arms and kissed her.

"I suppose membership would fit into our sharing and caring philosophy. What do you think? I guess it's a matter of how much caring and how much sharing we are prepared to get involved in. As you know, darling. In matters of where one expends energy, I'm a bit stretched at the moment," Freddy managed to say with only the slightest hint of an alcohol inspired slur.

Freddy looked at Helen intently, searching for clues of how she thought about it, knowing full well that she was uneasy about him spending so much time with Freya and Sophie.

Helen smiled at her lovely husband and chose her words carefully.

"Well, I seem to have a lot of time on my hands lately Freddy. My lovers all seem to be pregnant or otherwise engaged. Even Mary is making excuses not to see me and Polly is about to be raced off by a young aristocratic polo-playing lad from the Hunter Vally.

"In truth, my love, I do have a small space in my daily routine for a caring and sharing dalliance. But if we joined, it should be as a couple, don't you think. You might just need an occasional change of scenery? I think the daddy-to-be deserves that. We would need to coordinate our club activities so as not to clash, of course."

Freddy leant back on the sofa and smiled at his true love.

"You know that you will always be the most important woman in my life, Helen. I am sorry if you are going through a difficult period with everyone, including me. I'm not against you joining The Club and if they have a special rate for couples, I'm happy to become a member."

There was a silence as the two considered the situation.

"I'll check it out darling."

"Oh yes, Helen. I forgot to mention that we have to be nominated by an existing member. I suspect Roger can help us there. Check with him first."

———

Roger and Caroline had long discussions. They needed to catch up on each others live and both felt that the world had moved on in many ways. Both were really happy to be in the relationship, but now that Caroline was happily pregnant and healthy, did they both expect life to continue as it had been before Caroline's nearly three months away in London?

Caroline told Roger about her deepening relationship with both Miranda and Jackie.

She told him how Jackie had confessed to having different feelings towards Roger now that she too was carrying his child. Jackie had asked Caroline how she would feel about her sometimes sleeping with Roger when she returned. And in all of this, Miranda remained interested in both women's situations and claimed that she would be looking for access to Roger too, once she got here.

"I realised that you were going to be public property number one, Roger, and I'm still working out how I feel about it. I haven't talked to Alice yet, but it wouldn't surprise me if she was looking for a closer relationship with both of us, and not just me.

"I have recently had a conversation with Helen, and although our circumstances are very different - me and Alice being the same age and both pregnant - Helen has alerted me to the possibility of Alice wanting to be a part of your life just as she is of mine.

On the subject of Roger's other escapades, as Caroline liked to call them, she was less concerned than Roger expected, reminding him that woman had a different take on things. They seemed to take sexual activity as a separate thing to relationships and many regarded a fling or momentary shag on the carpet of some other woman as relatively unimportant. Just as long as he came home to their bed.

As the conversations surrounding dalliances' that they had both had began to wind down, and Roger thankfully rejoiced in being released of any feelings of guilt, he broached the subject of The Club. Caroline was first shocked, then appalled and then intrigued.

"And all of this is within walking distance from here? And you say that the seating makes provision for women to be exclusively with women if they chose to be? My God! Wait till Jackie and Miranda find out about this. It will become home away from home. No more trips abroad. The will be just too busy."

Roger was again relieved that Caroline was responding positively to the idea, and when he showed her the booklet he'd written and told her how much Desley had paid him, Caroline hugged him and said how clever he was. Then, without raising an eyebrow or indicating an emotion she said simply, "I hope you gave this Desley a good shagging, Roger," then continued with her questioning as though she hadn't said a thing.

"When will you be taking me to The Club, Roger? I don't know whether I'm up for a bit of fun or not, but I would certainly like to go in and see what its like."

Roger explained that Caroline was too young to be a member but he would be able to take her there as a guest. It also raised the question in his mind about allowing pregnant women into The Club and while this was unlikely to be something that women over fifty would be concerned about, he did see it worthy of a mention in the fine print of the next edition of the booklet. He decided that he would talk to Desley about it when next he saw her.

It was coincidental that Helen phoned Roger about the club as he and Caroline were talking about it. Helen told him that Freddy had shown her the booklet and they had talked about joining The Club.

"He suggested I call you, Roger. He thought you might be able to take me there as a guest. Is that possible? Would you mind?"

Roger was a little surprised to receive Helen's request, but he told her that he wold be happy to show her around and would tomorrow, Wednesday, at 2 o'clock be okay? Helen said that it would be a good time and then she asked him how Caroline had responded to the subject of The Club and Roger was able to say that the two of them were discussing it when she called.

"Well, I'd better leave you to it. Love to Caroline. Tell her that we will have much to talk about when I see her after our adventure."

Caroline had heard all that Helen had said and was much amused.

"Well, Roger. I'm only away for a short time and you have successfully impregnated someone, shagged the home help, and written a manifesto which could revolutionise western culture as we know it. A girl has to be impressed. Now! When do I get to go to The Club?"

Roger quickly thought about it and replied, "Tomorrow at 2 o'clock be okay with you? You and Helen can share the experience."

———

Helen and Catherine were excited to see each other. Since Caroline returned from London they had only seen one another at Rosa's birthday so they had much to talk about. But those conversations would have to wait.

Roger opened The Club door and ushered his lovely ladies into the foyer. Alvie looked up and smiled and Roger introduced her to his two accomplices.

"So good to see you, Roger. I see you've brought your own ladies. Aren't those you meet here good enough for you?"

Everyone laughed and Caroline suggested that now she was back, she would expect that Alvie might see less of him. Alvie went along with the ruse and said how Roger was rather particular and now, having met Caroline, she understood why.

Caroline thanked her and said that because she was now pregnant, Alvie might see him more frequently over the coming months.

Roger acted the tourist guide part perfectly, fielding question after question. Even though he had and Freddy had explained much to their partners, as so often happens, things don't sink in so that they both asked how many men could be entertained in the Home Delivery rooms, and both asked him to explain the twelve rows of seating and their designations to better understand how one learnt to shop for whatever it was you were looking for.

Going inside the theatre was the most exciting moment for both of them.

As Roger walked them slowly down the side aisle and their eyes grew accustomed to the reduced light, both Caroline and Helen would touch each other to draw attention to something. Then they watched in awe as a man pushed down the bra on the woman in the seat in front of him and gently levered her breasts out, one at a time before fondling them.

"My God, Caroline. Imagine this on daytime TV."

Just moments later they were looking at a woman who was staring at the movie screen and seemingly absorbed in the movie. She wore a top coat which was pulled back and exposing her naked breasts, suggesting that the coat was her only piece of clothing. On either side sat a man each with his hand on one of her breasts. But of greater note was the fact that both men's cocks were exposed and erect and being slowly rubbed by the woman in the coat.

"Astonishing! And I thought I'd seen it all. My God. No woman need want for anything every again," said Caroline, holding Helen's hand for reassurance.

When they eventually managed to get further down, the two gasped in unison as they saw two women cuddling each each other in row eight while blatantly exposing themselves to the world.

That was when Helen and Caroline both exclaimed as one, that they wanted to try rows eight or nine to see if they could get some attention.

Roger looked and listened and laughed and then realised that the two were being serious.

"Why don't I leave you here for a little while then? Even if you don't get any takers, you will at least be able to relax and feel the vibes of the place and understand it all a bit better.

Helen and Caroline looked at each other and smiled. Then they told Roger that they thought that this was a good idea. And as they hadn't had any time alone together since Caroline's return, this would be as good a place as any for them to start.

Roger smiled at the two beauties, and said how he would try to find something to do for the next half-hour or so, to which Caroline replied, that she thought she had seen an attractive woman arriving in row six and maybe he should check her out.

Roger turned to retrace his steps and rejoiced that Caroline and Helen had so readily settled into the idea of The Club.

When Roger glanced along row six, he recognised someone. It was Jasmine who he'd met a while back at The Club. Roger slid into the seat beside her and Jasmine looked and gasped. "It's you. Number 28. I've so been looking forward to seeing you again.

At that moment another man sat down on the other side of Jasmine and she immediately turned and whispered "No thank. We're busy." Then she turned to Roger and touched his cheek and said that she would like to take him to The Parlour where they could be alone and much more comfortable. Roger agreed and took Jasmines hand and led her to a cubicle in The Parlour where they spent a wonderful hour together, both agreeing that what they had done, "Was the best."

Roger explained to Jasmine that he had brought two visitors who he had left in row eight and that he should now go and collect them.

Jasmine laughed and when he mentioned which row, said that she was glad they were in row eight which meant that he would not be expected to perform again soon. Roger chose not to answer the question directly, knowing that Caroline would no doubt have plans for him once they returned home.

Roger returned and as he approached row eight, he realised that his visitors had indeed attracted their own visitors. It looked as though the couple who were already there when Caroline and Helen arrived, had moved over to join them.

Helen was on her knees with her head buried between the legs of a woman who was bare breasted. The other woman was between Caroline's legs, moving her head rhythmically up and down. Caroline's breasts were also uncovered and each of the sitting woman had a hand on the others breast. It was indeed a restful but exciting scene and Roger didn't want to interrupt it.

Then Roger heard a familiar voice.

"Would you like to hold my hand, Roger."

Roger turned to see the petite Veronica standing behind him. He was jolted into an unexpected state of mind. Despite his recent activities with Jasmine, he could not stop himself rapidly rising in his trousers as he looked on the divine and most desirable Veronica. She seemed to be on her own and not going anywhere in particular.

"Yes I would but if you are available, I'd also like to fuck you, Veronica."

Roger couldn't quite believe what he'd just said. But it was too late to change anything.

Veronica's large mouth opened even more, then she reached out and took him by the hand and quickly led him to The Parlour, where, in a cubicle next to the one he'd only recently vacated, Veronica smiled at him and took out his cock and sucked him.

"Well, I can tell by the flavour that I'm not the first here today, Roger. I should have got here earlier. But I'm very happy to have you anyway."

Veronica stood up and stripped off her dress and stood in her sexy underwear. Then she took of her panties and pulled Roger to the bed.

"I must first warn your Roger, that I cum very easily and as often as I want, so don't panic but more importantly, don't ever think I want you to stop. Now give it to me, darling man. I've so looked forward to us making love."

Roger went to heaven for the second time that day.

Veronica was a beautiful little dynamo and he met her every which way. She came on his face, she came on his chest and she came on his cock, a few times. She even rolled him over and came on his buttocks then she pushed between his legs and came on his testicles. What an extraordinary joy she was and it crossed Roger's mind that he would want more of her in the future.

Roger met Caroline and Helen as they were slowly making their way up the aisle from where they had been sitting. They were stopping regularly to look at what was going on and when Roger approached, they were silently witnessing an event in row three, The Jungle.

"Oh my God! How many men has she got behind her now?"

"I think it must be four plus the one laying on the seat under her. He's already made his entrance, from what I can see, so I can only guess where the others might be putting theirs."

Roger stood and watched unnoticed as his two companions stared at what was usually a once-a-day event, if that. He thought how good it was that they had seen so much on their first visit.

"Anyone for a cup of tea or coffee?"

Caroline and Helen looked around and laughed at Roger's bald attempt to bring them back to the so called real world.

The two unexpectedly reached out and kissed him, indicating their welcome to him and their old world.

"Take us home you super stud. We've been keeping an eye on you. Don't you think we don't know what you've been up to. That last little doll was delicious. We both want to meet her. What's her name, you Casanova, you.

"Her name is Veronica. Maybe I'll introduce her to you one day. She is Maria's close friend. Maria introduced us."

"You didn't tell us that Maria was a member of The Club, Roger."

"Well its probably because there is a lot to pass on to you both. I suppose I can mention that Maria and Veronica meet up here once a month with a couple of much older ladies who they both do house-work for. The older women like Maria and Veronica to dress up as slutty as possible, then they take them to the Gals Room for a session."

Caroline looked at Helen and commented that Roger was right and that there was much here still to be explored.

They handed back their badges to Alvie who said she hoped they had enjoyed their visit. Then they left the building to walk the few hundred meters to home.

"Well, I'm going to recommend to Freddy that we join. Except we need someone to nominate us. Can we ask you to for help in that regard, Roger."

Roger indicated that he would be happy to nominate them.

Then Caroline bleated out that she was going to miss out on all the fun because she was too young. She added that she thought that they should lower the joining age for lesbians as that wouldn't really upset the balance of men and women.

Roger kindly pointed out that proving your credentials as a dedicated lesbian would be a little difficult.

Caroline pulled a face.

"I would like to go back there. Helen and I enjoyed ourselves very much, didn't we Helen?"

Roger looked at his beloved and smiled. I'll see what I can do. In the meantime, I'm allowed three visitors a year. And if Helen joins she might invite you along as a guest.

"Yes, cuddle up to Desley and plead my case, you animal. I can see how you are the dark horse around here. Mr Nice Guy who fucks all the nice girls and more. You need to come up with a solution for your nearest and dearest."

Roger waited for Caroline to settle down.

"Well, there is one way for you to become a member, but it's not one that you would be happy with, I'm sure."

"Tell me, you promiscuous person of low repute, how would you know if I'd be happy about it?"

Helen was enjoying this pantomime. If nothing else, it took her away from the thing that was bothering her at that moment; sharing her husband with two other women.

"Well, Caroline. If you were married to a member, you would be entitled to membership. Old fashioned sexist rules, I know, but that's not something I can do anything about."

Caroline stopped in her tracks and stared at Roger. Helen also stopped and looked at him.

"If you and I were married, I could be a member of The Club. Is that what you are saying?"

"Well, yes. But of course, it doesn't have to be me. It could be any member. You simply need to get out and meet more people."

Caroline stared at Roger, unbelievingly.

"Are you now telling me - the mother-to-be of your child - that you don't want to marry me. Is that it?"

A thought flashed through Roger's mind that some women are supposedly subject to irrational outbursts during pregnancy.

"I didn't say that."

"Yes you did."

"No I didn't"

"Yes you did."

"But Caroline. You've always been against all that sort of thing."

"That was before I got pregnant, you silly man. Don't you understand anything."

Helen cringed inwardly as Caroline wrought her wrath on the poor Roger. She could see that he didn't stand a chance.

"Well then, would you?"

"Would I what?"

"Marry me."

Caroline stared at the hapless man in a way that would frighten an army.

"Not in a thousand bloody years would I marry you. Now sod off."

With that, Caroline stormed off, leaving the other two standing and wondering what had just happened.

"I'm obviously not very good at these things," Roger muttered, more to himself than to the world at large.

"Well, Roger, for what it's worth, I can tell that yes, she does want to marry you and yes, your not very good at these things. I think you are going to have to reword your invitation. Best of luck."

They had reached the gate to number seventeen and Helen said farewell and headed off up the driveway to her house.

# 2

# NINETEEN EROS CRESCENT

EROS PARK IS a large two hundred hectare hill often called Mount Eros, that runs up behind homes on the Crescent. Each house has a rear gate giving access to the Mount.

There is a long stretch of Paperbarks, Banksias and Tea-tree at the foot of the hill running alongside the narrow footpath that separates the park edge from the road which stretches for around four hundred metres. This bushland gives a wide divide between street numbers fifteen and thirteen so that the neighbours from those houses and others nearby rarely saw each other unless they were walkers and frequented the park.

The main entrance to the park walking track runs up beside number thirteen. It also leads to a car park hidden behind the bushes.

The Mount has a number of huge older orange barked Sydney Red Gums on the lower slopes, above the Banksias and below the sandstone outcrops. Smaller Sydney Red Gums grow above the rocks at the top. This walking path meanders up the slope of the hill and round in a circle at the top. Another track branches off and down to the rest of the suburb at the back of the mount.

Edith enjoyed her morning walk on Mount Eros park track, leaving home at the same time as Jessica went to her classes at around nine thirty and getting back a bit over an hour and a half later. She would rarely meet another walker on the way up but there were people who came up from the other side who circled the hilltop before returning home and who never ventured down to the Crescent. These folk nodded and smiled and Edith acknowledge them in a similar fashion.

This morning was different. Edith heard a voice behind her.

"Great weather for walking don't you think?"

Edith stopped and turned and saw that she was being closely followed by a pleasant looking younger woman, probably in her mid to late twenties.

"Hello! Yes, it's a great day indeed."

The woman came up and stood in front of Edith and smiled as Edith continued. "Do you walk here often? And are you from around here?"

"Yes, and yes. I do walk here often and yes I live down on the Crescent. That is the back of our place there, with the yellow gate, number thirteen. It's called Mount Eros Villa, actually. I sometimes notice you walking past when you take your walk. I'm Chloe by the way. Chloe Leigh. I live with my sister Lottie and an aunt and uncle, Desley and Arnold."

Edith introduced herself and told Chloe where she lived when she was in Sydney and that she was only here for a week each month but was hoping to make it a permanent arrangement soon.

The two continued their walk with Chloe taking the lead. Edith admired the woman's brown shapely legs and her footwear. Unlike the walkers who mostly wore designer gear, Chloe wore very serviceable leather sandals.

"I love your sandals, Chloe." Edith commented when they paused to look across to the first full view of the city.

"Birkenstocks! My third pair. I live in them unless I'm dressing up for a dinner date or other social event."

Chloe and Edith smiled appreciatively at each other.

When they reached the top, Chloe took Edith's hand and lead her over some rock to a secluded spot among the trees with a panoramic view of Sydney.

"This is my favourite spot on a good day and when I'm needing some time out from family and friends."

Both women enjoyed sitting and talking, each telling the other about their lives. Each found the other easy to be with and soon felt free enough to express themselves naturally.

"So is your sister older or younger than you Chloe?"

"Lottie is a couple of years younger. She is much cleverer than I am. She's just become a chartered accountant after years of study. I should mention that she is also physically handicapped as the result of a motoring accident when she was just seventeen. She can walk with a frame or crutches but usually she is in her wheelchair. She has a motorised chair for when she goes into the city. We have a small van-type vehicle fitted to carry the chair. It works well. I should also add that her disability doesn't stop her living a full life in any way."

"Oh, Im so sorry to hear that, Chloe. I would love to meet her one day and I'm sure Jessica, my niece, would like to meet the two of you. And your mum and dad?"

"They died in the same car accident. I wasn't with them on that day. Everyone said I was the lucky one but I sometimes wondered. That was nearly five years ago now and life has moved on and Lottie and I have adjusted to a new life together."

Edith commiserated and in the back of her mind, Edith tried calculating the ages of Chloe and her sister and came up with around twenty-two for Lottie and twenty-seven for Chloe.

"So your aunt and uncle? Did they come to live with you after the accident?"

"Yes, they did. I was in a pretty unhappy state alone in the house to begin with and then needed help when Lottie eventually came home from rehab after a year away. Desley and Arnold are mum's brother and sister. Neither married but later in life moved in together and eventually to us at number thirteen. It works well. It means that Lottie is never really alone in the house. We also have a cook and housekeeper living next door and that works well."

Edith had lots of questions but tried hard not to appear overly inquisitive. She had pieces of the jigsaw still to discover and with Chloe so willing to talk, now was the best time to ask.

"So has the house been in the family for a long time Chloe?"

Chloe looked at Edith and gave a broad grin.

"My great grandmother, Kathleen Mary Leigh bought it. She was a famous brothel owner and supplier of sly grog way back, and became very wealthy. She had plans to open the first high-class brothel, supposedly for well-to-do clients from this side of town who wouldn't visit what they regarded as her more lowly establishments, but she was prevented from opening it by the council.

It was because of this that she commissioned and donated the Eros bronze you can see in the gardens and she also managed to get the Crescent renamed, just too remind the locals of what they were missing out on, but also hoping that she might be allowed to quietly open her exclusive brothel eventually. But it never happened and she eventually died, leaving it to my grandmother who then left it to my father. It now belongs to my sister and myself."

So ended Edith's first encounter with the delightful Chloe. From then on, she and Chloe would meet up for their walk most mornings when Edith visited Sydney and their friendship grew ever stronger.

Wanting to get to know Chloe and her family was yet another small reason for Edith to move permanently to the city. Edith was about to make the decision to leave her husband and their home and when she did, she knew she would never look back.

———

There came a morning when darkening clouds were gathering over the park as Edith walked up the track. She was quite a long way up the track before she heard a familiar voice behind her.

"Edith! Wait for me, please."

It was Chloe, and as Edith turned to welcome her young friend, she felt the first spots of rain and noticed how dark the sky had become.

"It's going to pour with rain Edith. Follow me. We can shelter in my special cave."

Chloe came up close and put her arms around her friend and kissed her on the cheek.

"This way, Edith. Be careful you don't trip on the tree roots."

Holding Edith's hand, Chloe led her off the regular track and through a patch of light woodland until they came up against the rocky cliff face that surrounded the top of the hill.

Heavy rain began to fall as Chloe dragged her friend into a shadowy but spacious cave. The two stood at the entrance and watched as the rain turned into a full blown deluge. Chloe still held Edith's hand but as the two settled in to watch the gathering storm, Chloe slipped her arm around Edith's waist and rested it there.

"This is my hideaway Edith. It's where I come sometimes if I'm feeling blue or just need to be away from the house for a little while. I find it very relaxing."

Edith looked at the young woman's face and saw a fellow soul. Someone wanting to just be themselves without fuss or complications.

Edith reflected on her own life and how things can get complicated and how important it was to make better and more simple decisions. She thought how freer she was now that Jessica and she were lovers and how Rosa gave her great comfort, enjoying each other in a sensual way.

Without thinking about it, Edith slid her arm around her friends waist and gently pulled her closer.

"We never have rain like this where I come from. It is spectacular isn't it?"

Suddenly lightning lit up the sky and shortly after, a clap of thunder sounded directly overhead and the two women pulled each other closer and moved further back into the cave. Chloe turned and looked at Edith intently and Edith looked back at her. Then Chloe leant her head towards her friend, closed her eyes and kissed Edith on the lips.

Edith was confused but for only a second. Then, without thinking about it, she moved her head forward and pushed her lips against Chloe's mouth, wrapping her arms around Chloe's shoulders as she did so. Chloe moved her arms up to hold Edith around the shoulders and pulled her closer. As the two continued with their kiss, Edith let one arm slide down Chloe's back and let her hand rest around her slim waist. Then she felt Chloe's arm and hand follow suit, only in this case, the hand rested directly on Edith's buttocks and moved slowly around, feeling Edith through her shorts.

Passions were slowly rising in both women and anticipation was pushing them together. They unglued their mouths and stared at one another, then each put a hand behind the others head and pulled it forward and their lips met again, and suddenly their tongues was frantically exploring each others warm wet mouth.

Then Edith felt a hand slide down inside the front of her pants and gasped as fingers caressed the hairs on her cunt.

The floor of the cave was carpeted in a thick covering of dry leaves and in just moments Edith and Chloe had slid down, kneeling in the soft carpet while still kissing and gently groping one another.

Chloe made the next move, placing a hand firmly on Edith's crotch then Edith did the same to Chloe and the two pushed enthusiastically against each others hands in celebration of what they would do next.

As the rain hurled down from the heavens, the heaven rose up from the floor of the cave as Edith and Chloe removed each others clothing until they were both totally naked. They laughed and kissed as they divested themselves of their shoes and shorts and panties, then they hugged, rubbing their breasts together while they furtively then energetically fingered each other between their legs. Their sensuous discoveries insured that both were already very moist and a slow gentle caressing of willing vaginas meant that little shudders presaged what was to follow.

This delicious state of affairs continued and the two women languished as they gently explored each others moist lips and special places. Then there came a moment when Edith could no longer refrain from doing that thing she now did regularly with Jessica. She pushed Chloe backwards and stretched the woman out, telling her to lay her arms back above her head. Then Edith mounted Chloe and began a slow but serious masculine thrusting while clenching her lover's buttocks with both hands. But then Edith sped up and pushed hard on Chloe, gasping and whispering as she did so.

Chloe wasn't expecting such violent action. At first she screamed in fear but then, staring into Edith's bright and lustful eyes, she gave herself to her and began uttering a gurgling sound in rhythm with the Edith's strong and rapid movement.

"Oh yes, Edith. Fuck me, fuck me, fuck me! You beautiful woman. You've taken me to where I can give you my cunt. Do whatever you want. Fuck me Edith my darling. All of me is here for you."

Chloe's hands were pulling Edith down onto her and Edith pushed down even harder.

Edith stared down and watched Chloe's eyeballs rolling upwards and her open mouth moving silently and she thought how expressing her desire for this young woman's body was indeed the closest one could ever get to heaven.

Chloe's hands couldn't keep still. Her fingers made patterns on Edith's bottom and delicately explored the crack from her anus to her pussy.

"I'm going to come now, you sexy little bitch." Edith whispered.

Edith's body suddenly stiffened and she arched her back away from between Chloe's legs and yelled and Chloe's body followed her upward, arching up and meeting and coming as Edith came.

"Yes, yes, yes! Oh God! But don't stop. I want to come again."

But Edith wasn't stopping. She wanted to keep fucking Chloe for ever. The woman's reacted to Edith's every move with a noisy response which fed into Edith's lustful desires.

The two continued their wildly energetic sensual dance and twice more, the two orgasmed in unison. Then as Edith slowed and stared down at her new lover, the young woman began to sob, moving her arms up and around Edith's neck and hugging her.

"Say you will make love to me again Edith. You will want more of me, won't you?"

Edith moved her head down and nibbled a nipple and licked the young woman's neck and looked into Chloe's tear filled eyes.

"Yes I will Chloe. I've decided that I will definitely move to live in Sydney. I want you as a lover and we will fuck each other regularly. Is that what you would like, my love?"

Chloe rolled Edith to be beside her, seeking out and nibbling at her breast.

"That is what I want most in the whole world. Thank you, Edith."

The storm had ended and the world outside the cave was silent.

A shaft of sunlight shone through the cave entrance bathing the two lovers in a golden halo, and they were as one.

———

Leaving her husband was the major thing occupying Edith's mind. Having made the decision, it was only hours before she had agreed to take the cottage at the back of Bertie and Rosa's house.

Alice had vacated cottage the week before, to join Freya in her Vaucluse living quarters.

On her first visit to Rosa since they first met and made love some weeks earlier at Maude's party, Rosa had taken Edith out the back to the spare room in the newly vacated two bedroom cottage to show her the flat along with her fantasy dress-up wardrobe and the sex toys and draws full of underwear.

The titillating conversation between the two as Rosa explained the purpose, attributes, and benefits of each toy meant that it wasn't long before the women were giggling between kissing and touching each other. It was their first time together since Rosa seduced Edith and her niece Jessica on that hot afternoon of Maude's housewarming party. Now it was just the two of them and these two sensual women explored each other with 'mature enthusiasm' as Rosa later called it.

Edith was enthralled when confronted with the draws full of sex toys. Edith had never seen a dildo nor a vibrator and while she quickly understood the purpose of those things, she found the butt plugs and the clitoral stimulators beyond the realm of her previous imaginative abilities.

When Rosa explained that butt plugs were for stretching and preparing the anus for sexual adventures, it was all Edith could do not to blurt out that her husband, the Reverend John Cameron was probably acquainted with these things given his relationship with Bernard the church curate and a couple of the choir boys.

Edith pondered what anal sex would be like and made a note to investigate further. She couldn't work out why, but this sexual activity interested her. She decided there and then to check out butt plugs and all things anal at the sex shop.

Rosa sent Edith out of the room while she donned her recently acquired nuns outfit complete with the hidden dildo under her robes.

When she called Edith in from the corridor to meet Sister Carmel, Edith was unable to speak. And when Sister Carmel ordered Edith onto her knees and demanded that she run her hands up sister's legs beneath her robes, the still practising Sunday school teacher thought for just a moment that she was being mightily sacrilegious. But then her fingers touched the tip of the dildo hanging between Sister Carmel's legs and Edith surrendered herself and cried out.

"Oh, Sister Carmel, please show me what you do with this. Please, I really want to know."

Edith hadn't been shagged by a man for fourteen years or more. She had long given up the idea of having a penis inside her ever again. Now she found herself kneeling on the bed with her exposed backside in the air and with a nun putting an oiled dildo into her vagina and with one loving hand exploring her breasts while the other gently touched her clitoris. Edith was suddenly on fire.

"Now young lady, this is what my good girls get as a reward so if you like it, make sure you are always good. Do whatever sister asks and she will give it to you regularly. Now this is called doggy fashion. Do you like it like this? I will turn you over in a little while and give it to you in the missionary position. Now I hope you're ready because I'm about to push in harder. Do you like what Sister Carmel is doing?"

Edith was so excited by what going on inside her vagina and with what Rosa, or rather Sister Carmel was saying. She was experiencing something truly beautiful. The big slippery dildo stretched her but surprisingly fitted her beautifully and the motion of it thrusting into her was heavenly. The nun on the other end of it was on the one hand the epitome of religious piety and on the other, the ultimate provider of sensual and lascivious lust.

"I so love it, Sister Carmel, and I will be happy with whichever position you want to shag me. Please don't stop."

Rosa kept up her rhythmic motion. Then she lent forward and

grabbed a fistful of Edith's hair and pulled her head back while at the same time, pushing the dildo harder into Edith's vagina.

"With bad girls, Sister Carmel is much rougher and she calls them names like dirty little slut or cock loving whores. She also spanks their bottom until they scream and cry for mercy and makes she sometimes makes them wear nipple clamps while she fucks them really hard. And Sister won't let them come until she's ready. Be warned!"

Edith sobbed a little, partly from fear and partly from excitement.

"Now! Sister Carmel is so enjoying fucking her good girl that she is about to cum. Join her if you feel like it."

Both women screamed as each one orgasmed. Then Edith rolled over on top of Rosa and did the thing that she and Jessica now did regularly with each other. She pushed her pussy hard against Rosa's soft mound, rubbing them together in a rough and energetic frenzy, biting Rosa's shoulder as she came again while holding and rubbing the dildo against her own belly. Rosa threw up her abdomen and screamed out 'yes' then fell back, embracing her lover and rolling her over so that Rosa could be on top. Then Rosa lifted Edith's legs up high and pushed the dildo back into her pussy and rode her hard and fast.

Edith was gasping, her eyes were closed and every part of her body sang the same exquisite love song as she released the biggest orgasm she had ever experienced.

Thinking about the positive power of dildos added one more reason to leave her husband. Edith's rescue from a loveless marriage had been helped by something new, something as simple as a piece of moulded rubber and she loved it.

The only questions still on Edith's mind was whether Jessica should or would move in with her? The two were in love but things had moved on and both were now happy to take on other lovers.

Maybe it would be preferable for the two to live separately and enjoy their own private space.

———

Over a most enjoyable Thai meal at their favourite restaurant, Edith and Jessica talked. They needed to sort out their relationship and this was the moment to do it. And it worked out well for both of them.

Edith's pending divorce and her desire to move to Sydney was central to the conversation and it benefitted both that she and Jessica establish early, and without rancour, that each would be better off living alone and independently. They would of course still be a loving couple but agreed in a remarkably frank manner that exclusivity was not a practical option and sharing their lives with others was both desirable and inevitable.

"There are just so many joyful options available to us, darling. So we should enjoy them while also enjoying each other," Edith said as she caressed Jessica's knee under the table.

"Rosa will have women scratching at my wicked aunt's door, I'm sure, not to mention Rosa popping in to Rosa to borrow a cup of sugar."

The two laughed openly about the possible erotic scenarios which might result from Edith's move into the Bennett's cottage.

Clearing the air was like a tonic and both women relaxed and happily held hands and touched each other. They hadn't been a couple for very long, only a few months in fact. But a lot had happened to them emotionally. Coming out as lovers and discovering a new world and ways of living and loving had changed them forever.

As the evening progressed, they even exposed their deeper thoughts and feelings, both freely admitting to feeling more assertive in the way that they wanted to experience their love life.

Edith told Jessica about their neighbour Roger and how she would like to know him better and how she had recently asked him to join her on a walk up the mountain. That triggered Jessica to ask when Edith would arrange for her to meet her new walking friend Chloe and Chloe's sister Lottie who Edith and told her about.

"It seems, dear aunt that you have a more exciting life in your monthly one week visit to Sydney than I do living here all of the time. I just don't seem to socialise enough. Maybe you could give me some tips once you're a permanent independent woman around town."

Edith laughed and said she would. Then the two talked about all sorts of things. During the conversation, Edith said she had discovered that she was about to come into a little bit of money from an unexpected inheritance and that she would like to take Jessica shopping.

"I think its time you had a new wardrobe young lady. I'll transfer some money to your account this week It will be a birthday gift. You can then 'shop till you drop' as the saying goes."

"And does my wicked aunt have suggestions about what apparel this poor penniless student should adorn herself with? Would you like me in crotchless panties and see-through tops? Will I search for slutty shoes and alluring active wear? Will I dress up only for my lover or will I be flaunting myself and casting a wider net?"

Edith stared at Jessica with a bemused look.

"Hmm! Now that you mention it, you have matured noticeably in the past few months. I wonder if it's your sudden discovery of sex? Your bosom has definitely filled out and seems intent on making itself known to the world. It might even be large enough for an elegant little bra. Maybe we could start with lingerie. A set or two of sexy skimpy girly stuff. And a corselette would look nice on that super sexy little body. Your wicked aunt, not to mention most of the rest of the world would find such things most easy on the eye."

The two were enjoying the banter and for once, Jessica wasn't hanging back when confronted with talk about the things that most women were interested in but which she had carefully avoided up until now.

Jessica's skinny body and lack of a bust had meant that she had hidden herself away from girly aspirations. Edith noted that this might be about to change. It also flagged the likelihood of the onset of an interest in boys and Edith was happy about that. She wanted the very best for Jessica and although relationships where fraught with possible difficulties, a woman's desire to have children was likely to come into Jessica's thinking eventually. Attracting a mate at the right time was important.

"We might start with the slutty shoes, darling. Although maybe they won't be too slutty. The sooner you get to practice walking in heels, the easier it will become."

Jessica let out a scream.

"You're really serious about this aren't you. You just want to make me into a bloody lipstick lesbian. I know where this is going."

Edith laughed and rolled her eyes, but Jessica was on a different roll.

"I will titillate you with the tiny lace thong panties with bows that I buy from Victoria's Secret, wicked aunty? And will I use their lip gloss or will a bright red old fashioned lipstick from the chemist do? Oh yes! We are going to have so much fun. I'll be a totally different woman after our shopping expedition. Is that what you want aunty?"

Edith leant forward with her arm under the table and pushed a hand up inside Jessica's shorts and let her fingers gently rub her lovers soft moist pussy. Jessica's draw dropped momentarily and she closed her eyes. Then, in a quiet voice said, "That is definitely cheating and I won't let you get away with it." Jessica slipped her hand up under her aunt's skirt and reciprocated. "Two can play that game, dearest aunt. Which reminds me. I want to talk about sex."

Edith sat with her eyes closed and her mouth slightly open then she refocused. "Yes, a good idea darling. I do too. You go first."

"No! You go first."

The two removed their hands and sat back.

"Anal sex is the subject of my talk today. Please listen carefully."

"Oh wicked aunt. You crack me up sometimes. Me thinks this might have something to do with what I saw in the carry-bag at home this morning. Very suspicious looking things from the sex shop. Is this what you are about to tell me about?"

"Yes! And didn't your mother teach you not to look into peoples shopping bags? Well, those things are butt plugs. You put them up your bum and wear them around the house or whatever, to stretch your anus for when you have anal sex later. I have been thinking about this for a little while and was going to gently introduce the subject at a proper moment. But now you know. I've wanted to try anal for a while now but didn't know how to bring up the subject. It wasn't until my new landlady, Rosa, gave me a tour which included seeing all of her sex toys, that my interest was reignited. So, there! End of story."

Jessica was suddenly the quiet little thing that Edith found so attractive.

"Oh Edith! I so love you. You know how I adore your bottom. I kiss it and lick it often as you know, and you always seem to enjoy it. Does this mean that we will be able to have each others bums as well as our pussies. Can we go home and start wearing the butt plugs now? Please auntie. Say yes. And I promise I'll go shopping if you come with me. I'll even buy heels and lipsticks. And if it makes you feel better, I'll ask doctor Meg to put me on the pill. You both want me on it, I know."

Edith burst out laughing. "You don't have to do anything you don't want to do darling. You know I love you just as you are."

Edith stood up and reached down and took Jessica's hand. "Come along darling. We have an urgent get-together with our derriere's at home. Lets not wait a minute longer."

―――

"Do you remember the Parker twins Jess? It's a long time ago. I taught them at Sunday School."

It was early on a lazy Sunday afternoon and the two women were lying on the bed reading and happily enjoying their newly acquired butt plugs. Jessica turned and stared at Edith.

"Yes, I do auntie. They left years ago and moved to Melbourne with their mother. Why do you ask?"

"Well, they've just enrolled here for elocution and singing classes. They will be living here until they find an apartment according to Maude, so I expect we'll see them. They must be big lads by now. They were well built even back then when they would have been around twelve or thirteen."

Jess continued to stare at her lover lying beside her in her bra and shorts. The two had just returned from a long walk in Eros Park. Edith had arrived for her monthly week-long visit and was looking forward to their time together.

"I didn't question her when she suggested she thought that the lads were bad boys these days. I wonder what she meant?"

The two went back to their magazines. Then Jessica rolled over to face Edith.

"Auntie, there is something I have to tell you about the twins. I want you to know and its best I tell you now incase we suddenly meet up with them."

Edith rolled on her side to face Jessica and looked at her quizzically.

"You make it sound a bit ominous darling. Tell me. And if I'm right, you are blushing which means that it is going to be embarrassing."

Jessica managed to laugh before launching into her story.

"I was almost fourteen and I was with my friend Prue who was already fourteen. It was the term marking day at school so that we pupils had a day off. Prue had called at my place and we were heading over to her house to just muck about, when we met the twins. They were at a loose end so Prue invited them to come home with us. When we got to her house, she suggested we go out the back to the empty granny flat. Her gran had died the year before. Prue's mother was at work.

The twins, Paul and James, would have been around thirteen and were easily influenced by Prue who acted older than she was. Her breasts had also become noticeably large for her age. We both saw how the boys looked at them.

"When we got into the tiny cottage, Prue pulled down the blinds and closed the heavy curtains to keep out the hot sun and darkening all the rooms. Then she looked at me and at the boys and suggested we play hide and seek. She declared that no one was allowed to go outside."

Edith took Jess's hand and looked keenly at her young love. "And how did that go?"

"Paul went 'it' and stood near the front door counting to twenty while the rest of us hid. It all went well and we played for a while. But as we did so, the boys became more cheeky and started trying to put their hands up our skirts to touch our bottoms when they found us or when found by one of us.

"Eventually, Jimmy announced that we should show each other our bottoms to which Prue answered that we would show them our bottoms only if they showed us their willies. I was feeling excited by our games and was carried along with whatever Prue wanted and so agreed to show my bottom on the same condition.

"It was then a matter of who would go first. Prue decided us girls would go first and we lifted our skirts and both turned our backs to face the boys. The twins eagerly reached forward and pulled our knickers down to our knees. Then they slapped our bums quite hard and we yelled.

"Then it was our turn. We slipped our knickers off and faced the boys, letting them see our little pussies. Prue asked them to take their trousers off and with much giggling and protestations, the two dropped their pants leaving them in their underpants. Then Prue and I stepped forward and pulled the boys undies down and off, and suddenly I was looking at my first penis. I was enthralled at what I was seeing. I still can't remember how it happened, but moments later I had Paul's expanding young cock in my hand as Prue took hold of Jimmy's.

"My mind was racing and my heart beat faster, especially when what I was holding quivered and seemed to grow thicker and harder the tighter I held it. It was at that moment we heard Prue's mother calling from outside. Prue jumped up and rushed out the door to greet her and make sure she didn't come in, telling her mother that she was doing homework in grans old place. Her mother unexpectedly kept Prue talking which was to my advantage. As Prue left I reached forward with my other hand and took hold of Jimmy, becoming the proud possessor of two cocks. I was suddenly on fire. Both boys stared at me with their mouths open. Without thinking I moved my head forward and put my mouth over the pink head of Paul's cock and then I swapped and took in Jimmy's. It was so exciting and I was loving it. Then I swapped back again and I found myself doing this constantly as both boys started moving their cocks backwards and forwards, knowing instinctively that something wonderful was happening to them. And I felt so powerful. I seemed to be totally in control of the boys and of the world.

"When Prue came back and saw me sucking both cocks, she grabbed Jimmy's from my hand and confidently engulfed him, rapidly moving her head up and down. Moments later, Jimmy yelled and came in her mouth and I saw her swallow. Then Prue turned and looked hungrily at what I was holding and asked me in a voice that suggested she knew what was required, if I would do it to him or did I want her to.

"I looked up at Paul who looked back at me longingly. Then he leaned forward and took hold of my pony tail and pulled my head forward so that his cock reached into my mouth even further, then I did to him what I'd seen Prue do to Jimmy. I held his cock firmly in between my lips and moved my head rapidly backwards and forwards and moments later he yelled and squirted deep into my throat and suddenly, I was gulping down Paul's cum. Then Prue pulled Paul's cock away from me and swallowed it in an effort to get the last of what was on offer. It was my first sexual experience with a man and my one-and-only blow-job and as you might imagine, it was quite memorable.

"I haven't seen the twins since that day because they moved away the following week which, when I think about it was probably a good thing, as was Prue leaving town with her mum a few weeks later."

Jessica stopped talking and looked at Edith.

"It's been so long that I've forgotten what they look like," muttered her aunt.

"Don't you remember Auntie. Paul was slightly taller than his brother and ..."

"No, darling. I mean cocks."

Jessica was wildly amused.

"Well, they were the only ones I've ever seen so that makes us about even, dear aunt. I guess they would be bigger now."

"Do you mean the twins or their penises?"

Both women were enjoying their silly banter.

"I've told you as I thought you should know auntie, in case we meet up with the twins, I'm pretty sure that when they see me their thoughts will go back to that day and if anything is said, I want to be sure you to understand what might be going on."

Jessica leant forward and kissed Edith. "I hope you are okay with that aunty. I've never mentioned it before. It seemed such a long time ago."

Edith put her arms around Jessica and pulled her close.

"You've made me really horny with that story darling. I'm going to have you right now while thinking of holding and rubbing two happy cocks. What a lucky girl you were. I'm already thinking we should ask the twins to come for afternoon tea. I'm more than happy to take off my knickers and let them spank their Sunday School teacher's bottom and taking anything else they might fancy, in return for a go at their willies. What about you, you cock-sucking little slut? Could you revisit those moments darling? Could you manage the twins for an afternoon snack?"

Jessica had slipped off her pants and was removing her aunties shorts and panties, touching Edith's special places as she did so. Then in her pretend school girl voice she replied.

"If you must invite the twin cocks for a visit, I will do whatever you want me to do and if it makes you happy I will entertain them in any way I can, one at a time or even both together if that would please you, dear wicked aunty."

The two horny women laughed loudly and rolled around on the bed, grinding pussy's together in a randy fit, thinking of stiff young cocks while kissing, licking and putting their fingers inside each other.

———

When the two lovingly lay back and regained their breath, Edith revisited Jessica's story.

"Darlene Higgins, your friend Prue's mum, had to leave town in a hurry because she got into a bit of trouble." You might remember that she was a physical education instructor at a private school.

It appears that Darlene was reported to school authorities for interfering with a student although it was said at the time that there was more than one involved. It was said that Darlene would shower with the girls after playing hockey, at which time she would touch them inappropriately. No charges were laid because the school wanted to avoid that sort of publicity. Darlene was advised to take her daughter and just disappear, and she did, to Sydney I think."

There was silence as they lay thinking about what Edith had just said.

"I wonder if that had anything to do with Prue being the way she was."

"How do you mean, Jessica?"

"Well, it didn't really bother me but a couple of times I heard people say that Prue was very mature for her age. I never thought much about it. She seemed like a good friend, but thinking back to that time with the twins makes me wonder what her relationship with her mother was really like. I guess we'll never know."

Edith looked thoughtful, pondering the situation.

"I should mention that although our association was only to do with church and Sunday school functions, I found Darlene charming and very helpful. But we can never tell what people are really all about, can we darling. Life really does move in mysterious ways."

The women laughed, each thinking about their own situation.

"Now, Jessica. I'm thinking this would be the perfect time to take out our butt plugs and try using the small dildo's. Are you up for it?"

"Oh yes, wicked aunt. I would love that."

Edith turned the girl over onto her stomach and with much giggling mixed with an occasional gasp, she removed Jessica's bright blue plug. Then she reached into the bedside draw and took out a small dildo and a bottle of lubricant. While she was facing the draw, Jessica asked Edith to be still for just a moment while she withdrew the black and silver plug occupying her aunts neat and shapely backside.

"Now it might take a few goes for this to be as good as we would like to think it will be. We will require patience my love. The eight thousand nerve endings of the clitoris are spread all around including around the lower side of the anus. Getting to enjoy some of those thousands might take a little practice, darling. Are you ready. Just tell me to stop if you are not comfortable."

Jessica moved up onto her knees and presented her backside to Edith.

"I'm ready, wicked aunt."

Edith gently ran her hand over Jessica's sweet little bottom. Then she put two fingers into her anus making an opening and squirted lubricant into it. Then she rubbed lubricant onto the end of the dildo and placed the end of it at the intended entry spot.

"Deep breath, darling. Here we come. Relax if you can."

Jessica mumbled a "ready auntie" and Edith slowly pushed the dildo into the girls bottom. Once the nut was in, she stopped and watched how it was being received.

"Keep going auntie. All good so far."

Edith moved the dildo slowly. It was sliding comfortably in to Jessica without any difficulty. Edith stopped for a moment but Jessica said nothing. Edith eased the rubber thingy back a little then forward again to see if there was any negative response, but there wasn't.

"Push it in further please, aunty," were the only words Jessica spoke.

Edith pushed the dildo in, noting that it was in further than she thought. Five inches or maybe six? Then Jessica moaned and whispered, "Move it backwards and forwards, aunty. It's feeling really good so far."

Edith decided that there was no obvious cause for alarm and proceeded to gently shag Jessica's bottom, hoping the girl was going to be okay.

"Oh, aunty, it's wonderful. I love it. I'm already feeling at least half of those eight thousand nerve endings. Push in a little further please."

Cautiously, Edith pushed in, estimating there was now more than three-quarters of the rubber implement inside Jessica's bum.

"Oh, aunty. It's so beautiful. I think I want to cum already. How is that possible? I ... "

Before Jessica could finished, she let out a mighty gasping hoot, first pushing back so that the dildo went all the way in, then arching her back and orgasming before collapsing on to her tummy, sobbing.

Edith gently rubbed Jessica's back and buttocks.

"Well, my beautiful girl. That was impressive. I'll leave our little friend there for you to take out when your ready."

But Jessica had other ideas. She hadn't finished. She pushed back up on to her knees and instructed her lover to move the little thingy backward and forwards again. Edith did as she was asked and Jessica came again, screaming as she did so.

Edith watched Jessica lying silent but with an occasional shudder.

And when Edith gently touched her lovers buttocks, the girl screamed and came again.

———

What Jessica hadn't told her aunt was that she had experienced Prue's mum's interest in young people first hand just a week before Darlene and her daughter disappeared.

Prue had asked Jess to come around to her place on a Saturday afternoon to just hang out. Prue said how her mum had stocked the fridge with tubs of different flavoured ice creams and other great food things in preparation for a friends birthday party the following day.

Prue and Jess were going through a regular girl-on-girl petting stage which didn't bother Jess a bit. She was developing at a rapid rate and loving their kissing and the touching of each others boobs which they had been enjoying over the previous few weeks. So Jess wasn't bothered when Prue took her hand and led her into the little bungalow in the garden and closed the door then pushed her up against it, pushing their mouths together and tonguing each other and with each putting a hand on the others breasts.

On this occasion, Prue went a bit further than she had previously, quickly slipping her hand up Jessica's skirt and feeling her crotch and Jessica excitedly followed suit, finding an already wet patch on Prue's knickers.

It wasn't long before the two were stretched out on the squeaky iron bed removing each others clothes and then giggling about their pubic hair and wondering whether licking a belly button was sexy or not. Soon the two girls were taking turns, frantically rubbing them-selves against each other and rolling over and swapping positions.

It was probably the noise of the squeaky bed that brought Prue's mum into the room and there was a moment of surprise and panic.

Darlene had just returned from speaking at an education conven-tion of some sort and she was dressed up in her smart professional womens clothes. Her red lipstick and her tight skirt and top, her silky black stockinged legs and high heel shoes were like a siren calling out to the world to come and know her better.

Prue and her mum looked at Jessica and both assured her that everything was just fine and when Darlene asked her daughter to move over so that she could put her head between Jessica's legs and her lips on Jessica's pussy, Jess, instead of feeling frightened, felt a moment of extreme excitement, relishing the thought of this voluptuous sexy older woman's big red lips finding her special place and enjoying her.

Then Darlene stood up and asked the two girls to help remove her clothes.

As Prue and Jessica excitedly fumbled with Darlene's zips and garter belt and stylish shoes and her stockings and bra, Prue's mum's hands were busy touching both girls nipples and buttocks and sensitive body places, her big red lips smiling as the two girls giggled and pushed and rubbed themselves against her.

Once naked, Prue's mum positioned herself on top of Jessica, the bright red lips kissing her feverishly, pushing her tongue into Jessica's mouth as she pushed down and rotated her large hairy wet vagina on the excited willing and gasping girl. Then she called on her daughter, Prue to lay down on her back behind her and push her tongue up and into her and Jessica's special places.

Eventually, she asked both girls to lay on their backs with their legs apart. Then she positioned herself in between them and sat back on her legs, staring down at their sweet young faces. Darlene put three fingers in each pussy and a thumb on each girls clitoris and with experienced know-how, masturbated them and the two came almost at the same time.

As the young women lay in a post orgasmic state, Darlene took turns leisurely licking their cunts and pushing her hands up to feel the cracks of their buttocks and fondling their bottoms and generally exploring her two young captives in any way she felt inclined.

Eventually she lay down and drew each one to her, placing their heads where they could each put their mouths on a breast and suck and nibble a nipple.

As Jessica and Prue rallied themselves, they looked down and watched this remarkable lady rubbing her massive sexy cunt. In a frenzy of hand movement, Mrs Higgins exploded, screaming as she came.

This first encounter with an adult was a most significant moment in Jessica's early sexual experience and one she would never forget.

———

It was the weekend after Edith's visit and Jessica was alone in her little flat at nineteen Eros Crescent. Jessica attended classes on week days and walked on the hill or went to movies at the weekends.

In hindsight, she might have remembered that old adage, "be careful what you think of because it might come true".

Returning from her walk in the bright sunlight and entering the dark hallway on her way to her room, a voice called her name.

"Jessica! Is that you darling?"

Jessica turned to see who it was, her eyes adjusting to the gloom. What appeared to be a super attractive older woman was just closing the door of Maude's flat.

"It's me, Darlene. Prue's mother. Do you remember me?"

Jessica's senses came to the fore and in her minds eye she was instantly lying on the old bed with Darlene lying on top of her all those years ago. She felt a deep blushing rising up from her neck to her face and gave thanks to the darkness of the hall.

"Darlene! Of course I remember you." And before Jessica could stop herself, she went on, "How could I ever forget you," realising too late that she had acknowledged that special moment of complicit sexual lust.

Darlene stepped forward with her arms open and embraced Jessica before the girl could do or say another thing. The woman kissed her on the cheek before burying her face in the side of Jessica's neck, kissing her lovingly then whispered, "You haven't forgotten, you sweet girl, I can tell. Lets go in here. Maude is away until tomorrow evening. We won't be disturbed."

Everything was happening so quickly and Jessica hadn't had time to reason with herself about what she should do or say. As Darlene took her hand and led her through the door, Jessica's feelings whirled around and backward and forwards between alarm and sexual excitement. Things were happening so quickly and about to happen even faster.

When the two women were inside the flat, Darlene turned and put her arms around Jessica and smiled that same beautiful lipsticked smile and looked deep into the girls eyes.

"I remember you enjoyed it Jessica and I think you loved it so much that you will be happy for us to do it again, wouldn't you darling. Please, my darling girl. Let me have you again, right now."

Jessica's state of mind was becoming clearer and she realised that she wanted Darlene just as much as the woman wanted her. But now things were different. Jessica was no longer the innocent little thing that Darlene had her way with some six or seven years ago. Jessica was older and her adventures with Rosa and Edith had given birth to a new sort of Jessica, one who knew what she wanted and enjoyed taking it, forcibly if necessary.

Without saying a word, Jessica pushed a surprised Darlene off of her, then she took the woman's hand and led her to Maude's big bed, then turned and pushed Darlene backwards onto the bed, her shapely shiny black stockinged legs and high heels hanging over the edge. Then Jessica lifted Darlene's skirt up far enough to see the tops of her legs and her black silk panties.

"I'm having you Darlene. I'm a big girl now. I must thank you for your attention all those years ago but now, I'm the one in search of your special spots so just lay back. If you are good and do as you are told, I might let you have what you want, later. Are you okay with that darling?"

Darlene was in shock and her face was the picture of surprise. The sexy woman had always been in charge, had always taken the initiative, had always positioned the other person ready for Darlene's usual onslaught. Now she could only lay there, fascinated by what this thin and leggy attractive young woman was doing. Without thinking, Darlene found herself uttering her response in a soft little voice she never knew she had.

"Do anything you want to do to me you gorgeous sexy long-legged bitch. Anything at all. I so want to feel you Jessica. Do anything darling. I will love it. Hurt me if you want to."

Those last words rang bells in Jessica's head. She had discovered a reprint of an old book in Maude's extensive library in the common room and which probably shouldn't have been there. Jessica had found it fascinating. It was called The Pearl: A journal of Facetiae and Voluptuous Reading, first published in the late 1800's. It was an early book of erotica and contained many stories involving disciplining of both women and men. Yes! She did want to discipline Darlene.

Through her recent reading, Jessica had discovered that there was an animal inside her that desperately wanted to express itself and now she had been given this opportunity, she would express herself to her complete satisfaction. The frustration she felt in not yet allowing herself to act the way she wanted to with her aunt, could now be expressed with the super voluptuous and sexual Darlene.

Edith had told Jessica how Maude had shown her around her flat, including opening the wardrobe door to let her see her sex toys and bondage collection, neatly displayed. Edith had mentioned seeing a little leather flagellator and other disciplining toys. Jessica took two steps back and turned and opened the wardrobe door and she saw everything she could possible want for this encounter with her willing older woman, now silently awaiting her fate on Maude's bed.

Jessica turned back to Darlene, lying back with her special place on view, albeit, covered by her silk panties. Jessica lent forward and slid the panties down over Darlene's shapely legs and threw them away. Then she fell onto her knees and pushed her head between the tops of Darlene's legs and when she had had her fill of Darlene's warm wet cunt, she told the resplendent woman to roll over onto her stomach and not move.

Jessica went to the wardrobe and selected a leather spanking paddle and spying an interesting looking strap-on dildo, she carried that back and put them both on top of the bedside cupboard. The hyper-horny young thing removed her own clothing then picked up the dildo and inspected it and licked the end before attaching it to her waist. Now Jessica was both armed and ready to fuck. Darlene lay silently ready and waiting, and breathing heavily.

When Jessica wrought her beast-like passions on the bare flesh of Darlene with the leather paddle, the sexy older woman cried out and shook her body and waved her stockinged legs and heels in the air but she did not call a halt to the things Jessica was doing to her. Then when Jessica pushed the freshly lubricated dildo hard into Darlene's vagina the woman simply screamed. "Oh yes you skinny bitch, don't stop."

Such was the lustful passion felt and enjoyed by both women, Darlene suddenly saw clearly what she had previously avoided thinking about. Her love life had become jaded. So successfully did she hunt down her young prey, seduction had become too easy and predictable and she was now in need of something more. Unexpectedly, Jessica was giving her that something more she would never have guessed would be the ticket to a new world of anticipation and excitement.

Jessica heaved herself at the tangle of black wet curls between Darlene's legs, her mouth and hands working all the time. Sometimes she would stop and pull the big rubber thing out and stare at it and rub it, imagining she was crazed lustful man. Then she she would plunge it back into Darlene and yell and tell her she was a whore and a slut and that she was going to fuck her like this forever

Jessica grabbed Darlene's hand and pushed it between her own legs and made the woman rub her wet cunt, while she rubbed the woman's genitals and her large bottom.

After both women had screamed their orgasms and collapsed on the bed, there was silence only broken by the sound of Darlene sobbing as she lay quivering and shaking on the bed.

Jessica lay still. Her lover's rear remained a prisoner to their latest doggy position activities. Only occasionally did she move the dildo still firmly housed in her new sexy bitch-slave's cunt. Jessica took her in her arms, moving Darlene's face around and looking into her wet eyes and at her smudged lipstick lips and mascara streaked cheeks. Darlene was quiet but not yet finished, twitching and flinching and gasping and enjoying waves of tiny orgasms even as they talked. Darlene sobbed, reaching round and finding Jessica's pussy and clutched it tightly.

"I will want to fuck you like that again Darlene. Will you let me do it again?"

Darlene looked lovingly at Jessica.

"Oh yes, Jessica. And perhaps I can learn how to do it to you. In fact I'm going to buy sex toys immediately. It is time I caught up with the real world. Thank you for showing me, darling."

Jessica laughed at the thought.

"I suppose it's only right that you get the chance for a return match, you incredibly sexy bitch. Do you live far away?"

"Ten minutes on the bus at the most. If you promise me a repeat of today, I'll give you the address."

Jessica promised then said she had questions but only one was nagging her.

"What brings you to Maude's establishment, Darlene? Is Maude a lover?"

Darlene laughed out loud.

"Many years ago we ended up in the same bed while sharing and enjoying an exploit involving her neighbour and the woman's two teenage grand kids. I guess we've been friends ever since. We are not into each other but rather enjoy similar things.

"She contacted me recently to tell me there might be someone staying here that she knew I had known a long time ago. It piqued my interest and she invited me to call over and check them out. As it happens, I found you instead and that has been a wonderful surprise."

"So can I ask who the lucky person might be, if in fact you find them? Who knows? I might have designs on them myself and we will have to share them."

Darlene was amused but suddenly went quiet.

"Well, darling. We are talking about a long time ago."

"Like us, my love?"

"Yes, about the same time, probably. You may well know them. I know that my daughter had a moment with them. Do you remember Paul and James? Well, they are living here until they find an apartment. Now that they are grown up like you are young lady, I thought I'd casually call by and say hello. For old times sake."

Jessica screamed with delight.

"You are a sexy bitch. We've got them on our list. Your daughter introduced me to both of them in your granny flat. I've recently told my lover about the twins incase we are together when we bump into them and knowing that they might act strangely; if they even remember me of course. She got excited when I told her and we are now planning to have them for afternoon tea, so to speak. So there my love. It's a matter of who will get a hold of them first."

"Oh my God! Well, lets hope they are fit and well and have enough to go around. And I guess it will be first in first served."

The two women were now enjoying themselves with stimulating conversation instead of the stimulating of body parts and they were loving it. Then Darlene asked the question that had been running around in her mind for some time.

"So do I know your partner, Jess? From what you are saying, it sounds like it is most likely a woman. Would I know her?"

Jessica suddenly realised that she hadn't once mentioned Edith.

"You do know her and you might be about to get a surprise, Darlene. She is my aunt Edith, until recently the wife of reverend John Campbell but now the ex-wife of the said sad gentleman. We've only been together a couple of months. At the moment she comes to stay here for a week each month but she's just taken a cottage a few doors up and will be moving in next week. There! Surprised?"

Darlene sat up with her mouth wide open.

"Oh my God! I remember her well. She was always so very nice to me. I thought how straight laced she was but liked her more because of it. In fact I thought she might just be hot but repressing it. I'm desperate to know how it all happened with you two but I guess we will have an opportunity to talk again. Now I will go home. I won't go looking for the twins tonight. It's unusual for me to say this but I think I'm satiated for the day, thanks to you.

"Can I meet up with Edith sometime darling? There is something about her which I find very attractive. I'd love it if you both wanted to have me for afternoon tea. Lets see? A jam roll together maybe?"

"Now, before I leave. Will we just leave the twins as open game for whoever gets there first? They will probably be more fun on our own plus I think I'm greedy. Although if you do need any help with them, please feel free to call me."

Jessica looked at Darlene and burst out laughing.

"I should take a picture of you right now and upload it. I guarantee you would get a thousand likes and saves within minutes. You are the sexiest looking sex slave ever."

Darlene was sitting on the edge of the bed, her large shapely breasts and her neck were quite red and glowing and her face was totally smeared with lipstick and mascara and her hair was in a crazy mess. She screamed and ran to the bathroom mirror where she screamed again and burst into laughter.

"Congratulations, darling. Never ever have I achieved this look. It just shows how good you are and how much I enjoyed myself. I would be more than happy if you gave me this look whenever you felt like it, Jessica."

The two tired women chatted while they dressed, enjoying conversations ranging from dress sizes to the price of deodorant. As they parted, they embraced saying how lucky it had been that they had rediscovered each other after all these years.

They swapped addresses and telephone numbers and Jessica said she would invite Darlene for a jam roll when Edith was next in town.

"Oh and Darlene?" called Jess from the front door, "I didn't ask about Prue?"

"A long story darling. I'll tell you next time I see you. Bye."

———

It was a long weekend and one when Edith would not be visiting her in Sydney.

Apart from Jessica, the house at number nineteen was deserted as far as she knew and she marvelled at the silence. Even the owner and music teacher, Maude, had left town and gone to Armidale to visit friends. She had offered to take Jessica with her but Jess was in no hurry to visit her old home town. Edith was there of course, but busy with preparations for leaving her husband and home and Jessica knew her presence would not have been helpful.

Jessica stayed in bed for an hour longer than she would have on a week day when there were classes. She thought about this weekend and what she might do.

Looking out the window provided no clue about the weather

because of the many trees that shaded this side of the building. If it was going to be a dull and cloudy day, she thought she would go and see a movie, maybe even two. And she would spend some time in the big bookshop close by. If it was a bright sunny day she would take a ferry on the harbour to one of her favourite spots and walk one of the beautiful bush tracks that would lead her to the next harbour ferry stop where she would hop on another ferry to another secluded harbour spot where she would find a cafe and have lunch.

Living in Sydney was a joy in every respect.

Stretching and moving her body felt nice and just for a moment, Jessica thought how good it would be if Edith were here and they could make love but she wasn't, so that was that. A movie or a ferry trip were the only things on offer. Then she heard the sound of a vacuum cleaner starting up in the passageway and realised that the cleaning ladies were there as they were every weekend. It might be holiday long weekend but the place still needed cleaning.

Meeting the cleaners when Jessica first arrived had been wonderful. The two well built Russian girls, Yula and Misha had laughingly pointed at her as she wandered down the hallway on her first day, fascinated with her long skinny body. They called out to her and asked her to tell them 'you name?' and when she told them, they argued intently with each other, Yula called out 'Sarai' while Misha shook her head from side to side and in a voice that signified finality, uttered 'Jes-ka'. Misha won the contest since they both now waved and called out Jeska when ever they saw her.

Jessica would dearly have loved to be able to have a conversation with the two women but it was near impossible.

The heavily Russian populated harbour-side suburb of Double Bay from where they came, along with the fact that they could easily get cleaning work meant that there was no great pressure on them to learn english. She guessed that they were somewhere in their early to mid thirties but it was hard to say. Being as large as they were made her think they were older only because Jessica imagined it would take some time to grow to that size, but then their youthful faces suggested a childlike naiveté and in the end Jessica remained confused about their ages.

A leisurely shower set the pace for the day and when she finished that, Jessica put her nighty back on and went to lay on the bed and read.

The sound of vacuuming was now quite close to her room but then it stopped and instead, she heard voices. First there was yelling and a loud woman's voice called out something in Russian.

While Jessica could not understand the words, the sound was one of surprise. Quickly, she rose from the bed and went to the door, but thinking there might be danger, instead of opening it, she peered through the glass of the little spy hole.

It was quite dark in the hallway but Jessica could just see a woman and a man standing and looking as though they were struggling or maybe holding onto each other while two more figures were rolling on the carpet.

Who should she call? Everyone was away and, not only that, she had left her phone on the piano in the music room back in the main part of house.

Jessica looked about, wondering what she should do. Then she saw the breakfast hatch in the wall beside the door. Now rarely used, this hatch was where the staff would leave a breakfast or lunch tray if the occupant had indicated they wanted to eat in their room rather than go to the dining hall. It was similar to the serving hatch still seen in many older motels.

The yelling had ceased but Jessica knew by the muffled sounds she was still hearing that something was happening. Quickly she knelt down and cautiously opened the sliding hatch door, making sure that the little chintz curtain covering the door was now behind her head to stop light from signalling her presence.

Suddenly she could see very clearly what was happening. Only a couple of metres across the hall in an empty carpeted alcove used for suitcases and luggage as people arrived and departed, Jessica could see two men standing in front of Yula and Misha. Each man had a hand holding the hair of the woman in front of them and each of the women had a cock thrusting backwards and forwards in their mouths.

Jessica scrutinised the faces of the men and quickly realised that this was the twins who she once knew, and yes, they were being bad boys.

Jessica had no knowledge of what led up to the scene she was watching. At first she assumed that the two ladies had been forcibly attacked, but first one then other let go of a cock long enough to lift their dresses off over their heads and unclip and remove their brassieres to release their large breasts. Then they reached out and grasped and continued gulping on the twins penises. Jessica was forced to consider the possibility that this was not a rape situation but rather a mutual coming together.

The four figures continued their sexual adventure and Jessica began to feel aroused, putting her hand down between her legs, happily gazing at the scene in front of her. Large ladies happily slurping on large cocks was not something a girl saw every day. And looking at their breasts hanging and swaying backwards and forwards and side to side, Jessica found truly exciting.

Suddenly, Yula let go and swivelled round on her knees and thrust her giant bum in the air while yelling 'fuckie fuckie' and just as quickly Misha did the same and repeated the call 'fuckie fuckie'.

The twins dropped to their knees and as one, pulled down the knickers of each woman, each of whom reached back and divested themselves of the large garments.

A mass of hair, only partially visible to Jessica, confronted each twin as they held their cocks at the ready. Jessica couldn't quite see what the men were seeing, but she got the idea when first one then the other spat between the giant buttocks then planted themselves in where the anus was most likely the target, thrusting forwards whilst slapping the womens' backsides and yelling things which Jessica heard, but recognising only a couple of words, most commonly, 'fucking bitch'.

When the twins first pushed into the two women, Yula and Misha both screamed but after a few moments, they commenced a regular rocking motion suggesting that this was not something new to them. In fact, from where Jessica was situated she now saw that the two were holding hands and smiling at each other, unbeknown to their backend suitors. The two women moved rhythmically to the invading cocks and it wasn't long before the twins yelled and came.

Jessica watched, fascinated as the two men stood up and pulled themselves back into their trousers and then without even looking back at their willing partners, strode forward and out the front door, slamming it behind them.

The two huge and delightful naked women turned and sat back on the carpet then reached out for the other and embraced and began kissing. Then each slipped a hand down between the other woman's legs, while the other hand cupped and lifted a breast to their mouth to lick and bite it.

Jessica was now rubbing herself quite energetically, but then she realised that there was something else she could do.

When Jessica opened her apartment door and stood in front of the naked ladies, the two looked at her and gasped.

"Jeska! Come Jeska," called Misha, in a rich soft Russian voice while gesturing with her hand.

Jessica went and stood in front of them and smiled and waited, knowing that they would want her. And they did.

Four gentle soft hands moved slowly up Jessica's legs sending the first shivers up her spine, then they reached further up under her nightie. She closed her eyes, happy to be the centre of their exploration. Then she lifted her nightie up over her head and suddenly she was naked and being drawn down to the carpet in between two adoring and sensual women. Never had Jessica felt so much soft flesh. First Yula had her way. She stretched a leg across Jessica's body and lay gently on top of her, feeding the young woman with a stiff nipple while she rubbed her cunt against Jessica's.

While she was doing this, Misha went behind her and began licking the crack of Yula's bottom and the sticky little orifice that had only recently been shagged by the twins.

Then the two women sat back and looked down at their long legged skinny sexy friend and smiled. Jessica lifted both arms and fondled each ones breasts causing them to giggle and wriggle their bodies with excitement.

Misha repeated what Yula had already enjoyed, staring down at

Jessica with a loving smile as she shagged her. Jessica came again, just as she had for Yula, arching her back as the large Russian woman lifted herself up to allow her skinny girl to lift her body and scream her pleasure.

Then Jessica indicated that she wanted to bury her head between Yula's legs by pointing first to her own face and mouth and then Yula's mass of pubic hair. Not having the words, she gently pushed Yula backwards then turned herself around to offer her cunt to Yula's face while she explored Yula's sex. Yula happily obliged and parted her thighs. Her cunt was very hairy and very wet and the humid odour was very human and Jessica licked and loved and lost herself in this new and ever-giving and heavenly place.

While in this position, Misha moved around so that she could lick Jessica's bottom, slipping a finger in her little hole and slowly turning it in tiny circles.

Yula's mouth very quickly brought Jessica to orgasm and when that happened, both women groaned and shuddered in response.

After a little while, Yula removed Jessica's head and Misha took her place so that she could have another turn with their long skinny girl, and Jessica was in heaven once more and again orgasmed, screaming and repeating her Russian lovers words 'fuckie fuckie,' and 'yes', as she came.

As things slowed down, Yula and Misha took turns stretching Jessica across their thighs as if she were a baby, kissing her and pushing nipples into her mouth and gently fingering her pussy and sometimes her little anus. Jessica wanted to purr like a kitten thinking that these beautiful ladies were such a joy, and their feelings towards their baby Jeska appeared mutual. And she loved the sound of their voices, "Jeska like Misha's chast", which Jessica understood to be the Russian work for breast.

In the weeks ahead, and on the weekends when Jessica was alone, she would sometimes open her door when she knew that Yula and Misha were just finishing work and she would entice them in with a hand gesture and a smile.

She was excited at the idea of letting them play with the two dildo's that she and Edith had bought. And she was rewarded handsomely.

Fitting on the belts caused much hilarity and the happy ladies giggled and groped each other before shagging Jessica to orgasm and then each other. Then Jessica told them it was her turn and when she was at last let loose on the vaginas of the two incredible Russian ladies, kneeling on the floor with their rear ends wiggling and their buttocks flapping, she went berserk until each one screamed and came, laughing and slapping her and each other.

This was truly a romp to remember and although Jessica eventually told Edith about everything that happened, by then Edith had moved to the cottage behind Rosa's house and Jessica's 'from Russia with Love' ladies were no longer working for Maud.

"Oh I'm so sorry I didn't get a chance to meet them Jessica. I did a couple of years of Russian at university. It would have been such fun. And so educational too, darling."

Jessica laughed at the irony in her aunts comment and prodded her in the ribs.

"I already know a little bit of Russian, dearest wicked aunty.

"Really, Jessica. I'm surprised. It's quite a difficult language. Tell me, sweet heart and I'll see if I know what you are saying."

Jessica stretched and sat up on all fours and pushed her bottom out provocatively towards Edith's face..

"Fuckie, fuckie, Jeska pliz, is all I know."

———

It was a quiet midweek evening when Jessica plucked up courage to go and knock on the door at the end of the corridor. Edith would be arriving on Saturday and Jessica hoped to organise an afternoon tea with the bad-boy twins. She wondered how they would react on seeing her for the first time after all these years. The thought caused a tiny quiver of excitement to run through her.

For just a moment, when no one answered the door, Jessica thought there was no one home, but as she turned to leave, the door opened a young man's head appeared.

"Hello. Can I help you?"

Jessica was surprised. This was not one of the twins. She watched as the door opened further and a second young man stood beside the first.

"Hello! I'm Damian and this is my brother Ashton. You live in number four don't you? We've noticed you. What is your name?"

Jessica realised that things had changed and that the twins were not living here any longer.

"Hi Damian and hello Ashton. Pleased to meet you both. I'm Jessica, and yes I live down the hallway in number four. My aunt Edith comes down from the country and stays with me for a week each month. She's due here on Friday morning. We wondered if we could entice you in for afternoon tea on Saturday afternoon. A sort of welcoming party and a chance to get to know you both. Will you come?"

The two good looking lads smiled at each other and nodded. Ashton, who Jessica thought might be the younger of the two turned and smiled and answered, "We'd love to. What time would suit?"

"Lets say three o'clock? And by the way, what are you studying here?"

"We're both doing music theory and the history of classic composers. Only just started but I'm enjoying it and I think Ashton is too."

Damian looked at his brother then at Jessica.

"Yep! Love it so far."

"Okay then. See you both on Saturday afternoon. Thanks."

———

Edith's arrival was different this time. She was at last in Sydney for good. She had left her husband and her home. Her furniture and possessions were due to arrive at her new home behind the Bennet house at number one Eros Crescent on Monday just after lunch.

Edith was excited to be in Sydney again and hugged Jessica, laughing happily about her new feeling of freedom.

When she had drunk her tea and then cuddled and rolled around with Jessica on the bed, Jessica announced that she had been shopping as a result of their discussion during Edith's previous visit.

"Oh my God! What did you buy? Show me! Did you get the slutty stuff? Did you get the heels? I want to see everything."

Edith was unusually animated in her response to Jessica's announcement.

"Well, wicked aunt. Seeing as you seem genuinely excited, I just hope you won't be disappointed. Yes, I bought two pairs of high heels, the classic plain shiny black pair and a pair of red strappy sandals. And I bought lots of other little bits and pieces which I will reveal to your appreciative gaze later. But first I must mention something that we are doing tomorrow."

Jessica told how she had gone to invite the twins for afternoon tea on Saturday, only to find that they had vacated their apartment and how she had been greeted by two nice young men who were brothers who's ages she guessed at around eighteen and nineteen. She told Edith that, not wanting to tell them that she was actually looking for the previous occupants, she had simply invited them to afternoon tea instead.

"They seem so young. Certainly not the bad boys we had hoped for, wicked aunt. But they seem very nice and we'll all have fun I'm sure."

Edith laughed and looked amused.

"Maybe its an opportunity for you to dress up in your new clothes to get feed back from a younger audience, darling. Seeing a young man's reaction could be fun and it surely won't hurt them. In fact I chould even wear my shortest skirt and stockings and modest heels and provide you with some competition, darling. Who knows what turns young men on these days? An older woman's good legs might just play to their fantasies."

"You are truly a wicked auntie and I'm grateful for that. But be warned that if things suddenly get exciting, it will become each slut for herself; suspenders and sharp heels and bras could become weapons, and may the winner take all."

---

When Edith, wearing her sexy mature woman outfit welcomed Damian and Ashton at the door and introduced herself, the boys stared at her, scanning her from her head to her feet. They seemed very surprised and smiled self-consciously at each other as though they were sharing a secret. And when Jessica called out her hello, the boys simply stared at her long legs, speechless.

Trying to look sophisticated while attempting to walk normally in her new red shoes, caused her pelvis to sway from side to side, exaggerating Jessica's already erotic persona as far as the two boys were concerned, even as she simply felt clumsy and self conscious. But then when she noticed the effect her appearance had on the two young men, she relaxed into the moment, discovering the excitement of being the object of the male gaze and not failing to also notice Edith's gentle smile of approval.

Chocolate cake and glasses of fruit punch made from white wine and lemon and ginger Kombucha fuelled a revelry of sorts with the boys telling stories of growing up in Queensland and attending a Christian Brothers school in Brisbane. But when Edith asked if they thought they would miss anything from their life at home, Damian and Ashton looked at each other then at Edith and smiled sadly.

"We do miss some things," said Damian.

"Special people," echoed his brother.

Edith maintained her loving, almost maternal smile.

"Who do you miss boys? Your school chums? Girlfriends? Do tell us. Jessica and I would love to know."

The lads looked at each other as though they shared a secret.

"We can see by the looks you're giving each other that your missing your girlfriends, can't we Jess," said Edith, teasing while gently laughing.

After a moments silence, Ashton spoke in a subdued voice.

"We are missing aunt Cynthia and our cousin Chelsea. They come to stay at our place to keep an eye on us when mum goes to Sydney to work for a week each month."

Edith saw that the boys were oddly self-conscious about their aunt and cousin in a way that suggested some deeper feelings. Edith noted that during afternoon tea the younger lad when addressing Jessica about something had twice said the name Chelsea before rushing to correct himself. Something about Jess certainly resonated with his memories of his cousin.

The young men had settled comfortably on the settee and with tummies full of sausage rolls and cake and fruit punch, along with enjoyable female company, both were happy to converse on any topic that was raised. And when Jessica and Edith asked questions about girl friends, instead of colouring up and mumbling, the boys laughed and looked at each other and without thinking, Ashton blurted out that they didn't need girlfriends.

Edith thought about what was said then took a punt and asked a question.

"So, you two are obviously close to your aunty and cousin. Are they affectionate and loving women? Do you go out together or do fun things together?"

The slightly tipsy lads smirked at each other and Damian giggled, "They like to play with us."

Edith and Jessica were intrigued and exchanged glances. Jessica responded quickly, "what sort of games do they play with you Damian? Sounds like it could be fun?"

Whether it was Jessica's endearing looks and soft appealing voice or her long stockinged legs or the alcohol in the fruit punch, the two women never knew, but when Damian announced without hesitation, "They make us take our trousers off," Edith and Jessica gasped and his younger brother uttered a loud, "Yes!".

The two women exchanged meaningful looks and nodded to each other.

"Do your aunt and cousin remove any of their clothing?" Edith asked in a quiet and matter-of-fact voice.

"Yes, they take of their skirts and tops."

"And then what do they do, Damian?"

"They tell us that we cannot do anything other than what they tell us to do. Then they hold our cocks and put them in their mouths."

"And do you both like having your cocks in your aunt and your cousins mouths, boys?"

"Oh yes, we love it. That's what we are missing most."

Edith and Jessica looked at each other and smiled, then Jessica volunteered a suggestion.

"Auntie, I'd like to help Damian and Ashton get over their sense of loss, wouldn't you?"

The two lads watched as Edith reached out and took Jessica in her arms and kissed her passionately and letting one hand slide over Jessica's breast while sliding the other hand up under her dress. Jessica pushed her legs wide apart and stared into her lovers eyes. It was a spontaneous show for their young visitors, staged to let them know that their hosts were into the loving things that some people enjoyed. Then both women turned and stared at the boys.

"We want to help you both get over missing your aunt Cynthia and cousin Chelsea. Jessica and I would love to be your pretend auntie and cousin while you are here in Sydney. Take off your trousers right now and we will take off our skirts and tops and carry on from where Cynthia and Chelsea left off. Lets do it right now, boys?"

It took only moments for Edith's offer to register. Both boys speedily dropped their trousers to the floor. Then they watched dumbfounded, as Jessica stood up and lifted her dress up over her head and dropped it onto a chair while Edith unzipped her skirt and stepped out of it then removed her blouse.

What a sight it was for two young hormonally charged men. Edith in her cream-coloured corselet and with her suspenders reaching down over the tops of her bare legs to hold up her tan stockings. And then Jessica's amazing long skinny legs in girly white stockings with lacy thigh-hugging elasticised frills around the tops and her tiny panties and matching red bra

"Now, boys. The rules are the same as Cynthia's. No touching us unless we tell you what we want. Okay? And it's okay for you to call me aunty and Jessica probably won't mind if you call her Chelsea. Is that okay with you, Jessica? Now, are we ready?"

Edith reached forward and pulled down and removed Damian's underpants and Jessica immediately repeated the action with Ashton. Two rapidly rising pink cocks greeted them and the two women looked hungrily at them and each reached forward and grasped one.

Edith and Jessica each held one gently in their hand then turned and smiled at each other.

"It's so nice that we can help these boys out in their hour of need isn't it Jessica?"

But Jessica couldn't reply. She had already placed the head of Ashton's cock in her mouth and was gently running her tongue around the head of it. Edith looked at the beautiful Jessica kneeling on the carpet in her skimpy underwear and holding a cock in her hand and mouth and with her eyes closed, and rejoiced that her lover was enjoying a man for a change.

Edith did the same to Damian and the two young men watched through glazed eyes.

The two women with cocks in their mouths and savouring the soft but firm flesh of healthy penises were in no hurry to move on. But then Edith thinking of her responsibilities, as she chose to regard them, looked up at the two happy lads and spoke. She continued holding Damian's cock with one hand while gently caressing his scrotum with the other.

"At some time in the not too distant future, when you are with a girlfriend in this situation, you need to remember that for her to be happy, things need to move slowly, at least in the beginning. Once she has your cock in her hand, let her set the pace so that she gets to enjoy it. If you do that, you will be well rewarded by her enthusiasm for what you both do later. If you always put your girlfriend first, you will enjoy the best of times."

Edith fed the now rigid cock back into her mouth and continued her revelry. Having this situation suddenly happening to her was another milestone in her move towards freedom. Edith had not handled a man in this way in more than fourteen years and nerve endings all over her body rejoiced. Jessica slipped a hand over and caressed Edith's leg just above her stocking, taking Ashton's cock out long enough to murmur to her lover, "I'm loving this, aunty. I just want to suck cocks for ever."

Edith smiled as Jessica slipped him back into her mouth, her fingers now touching and rubbing the young mans testicles. "I think you are going to get as much as you want from now on darling. Now, just for fun, shall we swap?"

The two women looked up and smiled at the Ashton and Damian, then they swapped places and each took a new cock into their mouths and continued as before.

"You lads might like to feel our tities. Jessica and I are just removing our bras. Now the important thing with breasts is to be gentle with them. Rarely, if ever, does a woman appreciate being mauled with groping hands. If you have groping inclinations, which is natural in most men and many women, then learn to grope gently and probably a girls bottom is a good place to start. You could occasionally nip a nipple between thumb and finger or playfully stretch them gently away from her breast, but the general rule must always be to be gentle."

Jessica had listened to her aunts wise instructions and had quickly removed her bra exposing her small but cute rounded breasts and nipples and Damian was already there with a hand on each one. Edith had removed her bra and her adequate bosom was now being lifted and fondled enthusiastically by both hands of the young Ashton.

After a good ten minutes of cock sucking and breast fondling, Edith figured she should offer the young men the next moment of enjoyment. She knew that however much girls liked sucking, it could become boring for a man if it goes on for too long and given that most men were generally ready to always move on to the next thing.

Edith touched Jessica so that she stopped sucking and looked up at her aunt. Edith pointed to her mouth and puckered up and Jessica obeyed, leaning over for a kiss. Then Edith whispered her instructions.

"I think we should let the boys cum soon. Are you happy to get vigorous, darling? When he is ready to cum, aim him at your mouth or your breasts or you can suck him off in the final moments if you prefer. Please yourself. Oh yes, and look lovingly up at their faces and make eye contact if possible. It makes a difference. Oh, and Jess? I think we should let them go a little further with us next week maybe. Think about it. We can talk about what we'd like later."

Jessica smiled and went back to Damian's cock and made slurping noises just for the fun of it as she dragged him into her mouth as far as she could.

"Now lads, we think its time you both came. Cynthia and Chelsea will masturbate you and you can cum on our faces or in our mouths or on our breasts. Whatever! Ready?"

The two women began to handle the cocks with a much tighter grip and faster movement and it wasn't long before both boys groaned and yelled.

When the moment came for her cock to explode, Jessica pulled Damian right into her mouth and wouldn't let him go as he spurted his copious offering down her throat.

Edith spread the young Ashton's amazing torrent all over her breasts as she beamed a beautiful smile up at his glazed eyes.

Four bodies lay about the floor. Jessica rubbed her pussy and licked cum from her aunt's chest while sharing her with Ashton who was fascinated with Edith's nipples. All four were at peace with the world.

"Well, I think we all enjoyed that. Will you boys make yourselves available next Saturday? If so. get yourselves scrubbed up and over here at lets say, six thirty. We'll order in a pizza."

"We will definitely be here aunty, that's for sure. Oh my God! Quick Ashton! Mum's ringing us on the land line in our room at 8pm. We've gotta go. Thanks Jessica and Edith. That was fantastic. Just what we needed."

In moments the two lads had gone and Edith and Jessica closed the door and then collapsed onto the bed.

"Yes, it was just what we needed wasn't it, my dearest wicked aunty."

"Yes, you sexy cock sucking slut, but now I need you to suck me."

Within moments the two women were rolling and kissing and biting each other on the bed.

"I don't want to be groped gently aunty. I want you to tear me to pieces and eat me all up."

———

Edith had asked Jessica earlier for ideas about what they should do with the lads this time. Last week they had sucked the boys cocks and made them cum.

"Well, wicked aunt, I will be guided by you. Personally, I just love sucking their cocks. In fact now that I think about it, when I grow up I wouldn't mind becoming a professional cock sucker.

Edith giggled and slipped a hand up Jessica's skirt.

"Not wanting to rain on your parade, darling, but may I suggest you complete your music studies as planned. I'm sure you will find time to follow both passions. The world is not going to run out of cocks anytime soon. Just take your time and you can have all of them."

Jessica smiled and said she hoped that was true.

Damian and his brother Ashton arrived at exactly six-thirty the following Saturday. Both were eager for their next session and lesson with Jessica and Edith. The two women welcomed them and when the pizza was delivered just moments later, they all sat and enjoyed a meal together.

"Well, boys, are you ready for a little bit of learning fun? We hope you are. Jessica and I have a new activity for you which we feel sure you will enjoy. So come and stand in front of us and take off your pants. We'll start with a sucking session just to warm us all up."

Edith and Jessica made themselves comfortable on the settee while the boys divested themselves of their trousers and underpants. Then they stood in front of the two women with their rapidly rising cocks waving happily in anticipation of what was about to happen to them.

Jessica was in such a hurry to get Ashton into her mouth that she forgot to open her blouse. Then she saw Edith removing her top and undoing her bra so she followed suit, managing to do the same without letting go of him.

Jessica revelled in what she was doing, sometimes holding Damian's penis in her hand while she licked it up and down and over the hood. Then she would pop him back in and slide him deep into her throat, vividly recalling the week before when he shot his bolt down her throat. All the time she made slurping and sucking noises. Occasionally she would pop her head down lower and kiss and lick his balls, before returning to the main course.

Next to her, Edith was happily sliding Ashton's member around in her mouth and licking him and fingering the slippery looking head so that he trembled and breathed deeply.

After a little while, the two women moved the boys, making them swap places so that each could try the other.

"Now boys, this week we are going to put your cocks in our pussy's or perhaps we should call them our vaginas. But before we do this we must do one important thing. We live at a time, unfortunately, when it is not uncommon to catch some sort of unpleasant complaint from having unprotected sex, even if it is with someone who you know very well. So what should we do?

"Wear a rubber, aunty?"

"Well done, Ashton. Yes, we must wear a condom. So I have them here and Jessica and I will put them on for you. Secondly, you may well tell your girlfriend that you will not cum in her pussy, but she should still not allow you in unless you are wearing a condom.

The other thing worth remembering is that if a younger woman is in love with you, it is possible - though it rarely happens - that she will tell you that she is on the contraceptive pill when she isn't. This is called entrapment; when a woman traps a man by getting pregnant to him."

There were a few giggles and comments as Jessica and Edith rolled a condom onto each boys penis. Then the women ran their hands up and down the newly dressed dicks to "iron out the wrinkles" as Edith laughingly commented.

"Now, boys. Before we pop you in, you need to know that whoever you are popping it into, will want to feel ready, and ready means among other things, wet or lubricated. Never try to enter a dry vagina, for both her sake and yours. There is a lubricating gel that is easily bought at the chemist if you need it. Now, are you both ready?"

The boys nodded enthusiastically and stared as the two women took off the skirts and pulled down their knickers and threw them onto a chair across the room.

"Now there are two main positions that people like for having sex, missionary position and the doggy position. We will start you off with the missionary position. We will lay down with our legs apart and you two should position yourselves by kneeling between our legs."

Jessica laid back on the carpet, her long legs opened out in a welcoming fashion. Then Edith did the same and the two bent their legs at the knees and asked the boy to bring their cocks up close to the bushy places in front of them.

Then both women reached out and each drew a cock up to the entrance of their vaginas and with a little bit of rubbing up and down, slid the boys in.

"There, boys. Well done! Now push your cocks in as far as you can. We will tell you if there is anything wrong."

Jessica was lying with her eyes closed. This was the first real cock she had ever had inside her. Many times Edith had taken her with a dildo, but now, this was the real thing and she secretly hoped it would be as good.

"Now boys, you can do what ever you would like to do now. Gentle is always good but we won't mind if you get vigorous. And whenever you're ready, ask us to roll over so that we can show you the doggy position."

The boys took control and shagged away in the women's special place. Then first Ashton then Damian asked for the women to roll over and get up on their knees, and the two discovered the wonders of the doggy position and the excitement of being able to look down on that other interesting place nestled between the buttocks.

---

When the boys had left and gone across the hallway to their own unit, the two women flopped onto the bed and sighed.

"Well, wicked aunty. I enjoyed that boy thingy. He managed to cum at long last. I enjoyed that moment the most. Really cool! I guess they will get the hang of things as they go along."

"Yes, darling. I'd quite forgotten that it was your first real dick. So glad it worked out for you. Did you notice the difference?"

"Well, Edith my dearest. So much depends on who's doing things and what they are feeling, I guess. You are a wiz on the rubber cock and so I'm spoilt I suppose.

Having feelings for someone or feeling that someone is really into you and that you had excited them, would obviously decide how things work out. I suspect that what we had tonight was a bit clinical. I certainly wasn't carried away. And I think that the boys were so busy working things out that they didn't manage to get emotionally or properly lustfully involved in any way. Never mind.

Now if you've got the energy, wicked auntie, put Rupert Rubber on and give it to me like it matters. Fuck me please, Edith. Make me cum. I'll do anything you want.

It wasn't long before Edith had strapped Rupert on and was straddling Jessica who reached her legs high into the air and screamed. "Yes please, aunty! Don't stop!"

## 3

# BUSH HOLIDAYS

DARLENE HAD ALREADY BEEN for her meeting with Edith some weeks earlier, when Jessica had arranged afternoon tea so that the two could meet up again after a gap of more than ten years.

The meeting had been memorable for the loving way the two eventually kissed and fingered each other and excitedly made love, inviting Jessica to join them.

The wonderful conversation they then had about their lives in Armidale and so many people, some who Jessica knew and other she'd had never heard of. There was sadness and scandal and gossip and the two older women confessed that it had been wonderful and that seeing each other again after all those years had been most cathartic.

"So lets invite Darlene over for her birthday, Edith announced one evening. It's the weekend after this. Are you happy with that Jess?"

"Sure, Edith. She's such good fun and her more than adequate sexy body offers so much to touch and play with, and you two already act like you are old friends. Yes, call her now, wicked aunt, before she gets a better offer.

Darlene answered "yes please, I would love that."

"Great! Lets get a Thai takeaway and I'll make a birthday cake. I won best cake twice in high school so trust me aunty."

All was settled but when the two were reading in bed later, Edith suddenly said, "I think I'll plan something a bit special for her birthday, Jess. Let me tell you and you can tell me what you think."

———

Jessica's birthday cake was a great success and Darlene and Edith had second helpings. Darlene looked sexy as she always managed to do. It was partly what was going on inside her mind, Jessica mused as she blatantly stared at the woman's legs and shoes and her tight skirt and tight blouse. It seemed every part of Darlene was available for sensual adventures, especially her willing attitude.

After dinner Edith dimmed the lights and she and Darlene settled on the sofa, while Jessica cleared away the food and dishes. When Darlene offered to help Jess answered with a slight mocking tone.

"It's your birthday celebration, Darlene. Sit back and Edith will look after your every need. In fact I think she's planning something special. Is that right, darling?"

Darlene beamed and her big bright red lips opened as she laughed and replied. "Just so long as it involves being touched, I will welcome anything on offer. You know that I'm just a slut. So what am I about to get, Edith my darling."

There was suddenly a knock on the door. Edith called out to Jessica in the kitchen.

"I think there is a delivery at the door, Jessica. Would you get it please."

Edith went back to what she was about to do which was to slide a hand up Darlene's leg and under her skirt.

"Who is it, darling?"

"It's our neighbours, Edith. They want to wish our visitor a happy birthday and to say goodnight."

"Bring them in. I'm sure Darlene would love to meet them."

With that, Jessica came in leading two slightly embarrassed young men in their pyjamas. Damian and Ashton stared at Darlene in all her sexy finery like she was a gift from heaven. Then they walked over and stood in front of her and Darlene stared in amazement as the lads pulled their semi erect cocks from the fly in their PJ's and pointed them at her. Then in awkward voices, they managed to sing the first few lines of Happy Birthday.

"Boys? This is our very good friend, Darlene. Darlene, these lovely young men are our neighbours, Ashton and Damian. They are often visiting us on a Saturday night when Jessica and I read them bedtime stories."

Jessica watched as the super sexy woman first looked at Edith and then, smiling with her radiant sexy smile, reached out with both hands and grasped a cock in each.

"Oh my God, this is the most amazing present ever. So please to meet you Ashton and Damian. Am I allowed to suck you?"

The boys murmured their consent. Then Ashton asked Darlene if she would mind if they touched her breasts.

"I would love you to touch me anywhere you feel like touching. Edith and Jessica will both tell you how I love to be touched. Do whatever you want. Will it help if I take off my skirt?"

Damian nodded and said it would help a lot and in no time at all, Darlene's substantial stockinged legs were available as were here beautiful tits.

Darlene drew the two cocks to her and began to suck them. Then she looked at Edith who was happily staring at what was going on beside her.

"Darling, help me with one these please, at least until I get going, then I might want it back."

Edith moved up closer to Darlene and willingly took one of the boys in hand.

Jessica had no intention of returning to the kitchen while this super hot scene was happening in front of her. Instead, she plonked herself on the arm chair opposite and removed her panties and began to play with herself while watching the boys four hands exploring Darlene's super body and Darlene and Edith's heads moving backwards and forwards. She admired Darlene's large red lips and and her outstanding nipples.

Darlene uttered noises of satisfaction and excitement and she slid herself downwards and opened her legs wide showing that she didn't wear panties and that all that a man or woman could want was available at the top of her large stockinged legs.

Edith's lad retrieved his cock, politely muttering, "Excuse me for a moment please." Then he buried his head between Darlene's legs to explore her cunt with his mouth.

Edith took the opportunity to lean in and whisper to Darlene that she and Jessica had only last week, taught the boys why and how they should use condoms. She said she's mentioning it just so that Darlene can reassure them that it's okay not to if she's okay with it and wants them to shag her.

Darlene smiled lovingly at Edith and mouthed the words "Thank you."

The sucking and licking and groping went on for some time and then Darlene announced in a quiet voice.

"I would love you both to put your cocks in my pussy. It's okay. You won't need a condom."

The lads wrestled briefly for first position.

Ashton was invited to be first and was guided into Darlene's wet cunt. She lifted her legs up and they hung in the air like waving flags of celebration as the lad pushed into her. Only moments later, he came along with a lot of verbal utterances, and then as he withdrew his brother presented himself to the beautiful smiling woman who quickly slipped him in to a very slippery heavens gate and very soon, he too was relieved of his load.

Not long after, and each carrying a plate of cakes, the boys said their farewells and headed out the door.

Jessica immediately moved over to the settee and pushed her face in between Darlene's legs, intent on licking up what the boys had left behind, licking and swallowing their with gusto.

"Willful waste makes woeful want." Jessica whispered, licking her lips with a satisfied smile.

Edith looked at Jessica quizzically. "Should I worry about this girl, Darlene?"

"Well, darling, we all think a hearty appetite is a good thing, don't we. From more cocks than I can ever remember, I've guzzled a lot of it and I've always found it to be good for my complexion. No wrinkles yet."

––––––

Darlene lay on the settee in a languid state of undress, one hand fingering a breast and the other between her legs rubbing her newly saturated pussy and smiling as Jessica brought out coffee and the remains of the cake.

"I don't know how to thank you sexy bitches for that wonderful birthday present. It was truly awesome. Who would have believed it could have happened just like that."

"Well, Darlene. Just so long as you are happy for us both to molest you on a regular basis, then no thanks is necessary. But we are both very glad you enjoyed it. We were a bit nervous when we first thought about it but then we just said, what the hell."

The three enjoyed their coffee and cake and talked about various things. But then Darlene looked across at Jessica.

"I keep forgetting to tell you, Jessica. Prue has said on the phone, how much she would like to see you. She lives with my mad sister Annabella and her husband Brendan on their sheep property thirty kilometres west of Goulburn."

"I should tell you that Prudence got into a mess in her late teens. She started living with a drug dealer and had only just started using heroin when the man was arrested and sent to jail. She was cautioned and had counselling and fortunately, being essentially a sensible woman, she saw how important it was for her to get away from Sydney.

"She's been living on the farm with Bella and Bren for over two years now and she loves it. And she has made a lot of friends there, too.

"Anyway, I was thinking that with holidays coming up and me due for a visit, you might like to consider coming with me and although I'll only stay a couple of days, you would be very welcome to stay longer. When you are ready to come back, there is an evening bus from Goulburn that gets to Sydney around eight o'clock. What do you think? And Edith, what are your thoughts?"

Edith answered first.

"Well, I was only thinking about the school holidays yesterday. My solicitor wants me to go back to Armidale for a few days to make an inventory of my stuff and I want to arrange for a carrier to bring some of the stuff to Sydney. I hadn't mentioned it to Jess as yet as I was waiting to get more details from the solicitor before committing to a date. May I suggest that a trip to Goulburn might be a better idea than an as yet unconfirmed trip to Armidale? But what do you want to do Jess?"

Jess looked at each in turn and smiled.

"Hmm! Rarely does a gal get this much choice. I had planned a shopping trip to New York or maybe Paris but now I think about it, counting sheep in Goulburn sounds far more exciting, even better than counting knives and forks and spoons in Armidale. I'll go with the sheep option if that is okay with you Edith. But if you need me to come with you, just say."

"No, sweetheart, I'd prefer you went with the sheep option to be honest. I can't guarantee that there won't be hostilities with the ex while I'm up in Armidale. And you definitely don't need that.

It was decided there and then that Jessica would travel with Darlene in a fortnights time.

"I suppose I should get dressed and move my lazy self," Darlene announced.

Everyone agreed that the birthday party had been a cock-up in the most splendid way, and the ladies ended their night with kisses and touchy goodbyes.

———

Darlene collected Jessica mid morning for their trip to Goulburn. It was a beautiful early spring day and they both rejoiced that they were leaving the city and going on an adventure.

Jessica was intrigued by Darlene's move into a spring time wardrobe, a relaxed floral dress and low sandals and a linen jacket was about it although there was obviously a large bra beneath the dress. Her deep cleavage and shapely arse were the only signs of her innate sexuality.

"Well, Jessica. I hope you are ready for a country style adventure."

Jessica thought for a moment then wondered what sort of adventure Darlene was referring to.

"You make it sound slightly mysterious, Darlene. Is there anything I should know about before we get there?"

They had just left the Western Freeway and were heading directly west towards Goulburn.

Darlene gave a low chuckle.

"Muta East Station is a very large sheep and grain property of around sixty-thousand hectares. As well as that, Brendon and Annabella along with Brendan's brother Gary, own a second even bigger place over near Cobar where the country is drier. There they run mainly cattle. This means that they have a very large permanent staff. Add to that the contractors who come and go; shearers, shed hands and harvesting contractors, etcetera. All in all, there are always at least fifty or sixty people at Muta East at any time. It is like a small village."

Jessica was impressed. She had never suspected that farms could ever be that large.

"So I guess they are just men there, or are there woman farm workers too?"

"Oh there are plenty of girls. There are women who work in the shearing sheds sorting fleeces and stuff, there are women who work in the kitchens and help maintain the living quarters and tourist accomodation, and there are Jillaroos as well as Jackaroos although they are mainly at Cobar, at Muta West.

"But I guess I should tell you a few other important things before you get there, Jess, just so you won't get too shocked or confused. Because I know everyone and have visited over the years, I've grown accustomed to, shall we say, the eccentricities of the locals.

"Out in the country, people have to make their own entertainment. Even though they now have satellite TV and Netflix, they still need to interact with one another or at least tolerate each other. The significant thing about country folk is that they tend to be more accepting of odd behaviours and even start to see some of them as normal, simply accepting people for who they are, not what they should be."

Jessica stared at Darlene. She noted that the woman still wore the bright red lipstick she wore when she was dressed in her seductive city evening wear.

"Well, Darlene. You've got me interested. What strange behaviours will I need to watch out for. Sounds quite exciting. Please tell."

Darlene was busy thinking about what to tell Jessica and what not to tell. Somethings she could be left to her to just find out about on her own, probably after Darlene had left.

"Well, Jessica. You've obviously noticed what I am like and how I am what some people would label highly sexed, or in the old language, a nymphonmaniac."

Jessica interrupted, laughingly saying that she really hadn't noticed but now that Darlene had mentioned it, she did recall moments when she had observed certain exciting behaviours.

"So, I'm forty-nine and my sister Annabella is forty-seven. If I tell you that Bella is at least twice as sexually active as me and, some would say, totally mad, would you therefore assume that my sister could lead a very interesting life?"

"Wow! I certainly would, Darlene. But if she lives out of town and helps her husband run the property, how does she manage to have two separate lives? I mean you, her big sister, doesn't have to consider a husband when planning your fun, do you? So how can she manage affairs and such?"

"The clue to all of it is that Brendan accepts her for who she is. Not only does he accept her, he encourages her to do anything she wants. We're talking sexual things here. In fact Brendan enjoys watching Bella with another man and sometimes with more than one man. He's not gay or bisexual, just very happily in love with her and accepting of whatever she does."

Jessica sat staring at the woman, her mouth open in obvious amazement.

"So just let me get this straight. Brendan will happily watch your sister having sex with one or more other men? And what about him? Does Brendan have relationships with other women?"

Darlene waited for a moment to reply.

"A couple or three years back, they joined a swingers club in Goulburn. I think they are still members. It changed both their lives.

"Bella gets quite turned on watching Brendan fuck other women just as he likes watching her with other men. I should also mention here that Brendan is very well endowed, his cock being bigger and more beautiful than most. Not only that, he is a good and sensitive lover and enjoys pleasuring women. The upshot has been that Brendan will sometimes get a call from a female that they both met at the swingers club who will say that she is feeling lonely and could they meet up? And most often they do, usually at the farm and with Bella's approval.

"Bella will sometimes join them, usually over in the old disused Creamery, a nearby building which has been turned into an unofficial bonking venue, complete with mattresses and cushions. Knowing each other means that Bella has probably been with that woman's husband at the monthly swingers get together.

Jessica was fascinated with what Darlene was telling her. Could this possibly be true? Jessica tried to understand it all but found it difficult. Meanwhile, a tiny separate voice at the back of her mind kept wondering how Darlene knew so much about Brendan's penis.

"And then there is Gary, Brendan's younger brother. He manages Muta West but spends quite a bit of time with the rest of them at Muta East. Along with Brendan, he is a trained pilot so he fly's the company plane between the two properties carrying freight and staff to Cobar when needed.

"Gary has a girlfriend here at Muta East, Gina, who is also Bella's best friend. She manages the kitchen and domestic staff. Gary and Gina follow much the same rules as his brother and Bella and so the two are quite happy to watch each other having sex with someone else. I sometimes think that Gina is even more active than Bella, if that were possible.

"There darling. I think I've covered most of the more blatant behavioural oddities of the people you are going to spend a bit of time with. Just don't be too shocked if you see odd things happening with other folk, too."

Jessica commented how Darlene's story had been truly amazing and that now she didn't know whether to be frightened or excited. Then Jessica asked about the women who worked at Muta.

"Probably around a quarter to a third of the staff are women. All sorts; from girly girls to downright scary looking ones. But as to their sexual preferences, one could never be sure. A sweet girly girl university student and from the landed gentry could be a hardcore lesbian who wants to take you to her room and show you her perfect body, while the one with pink, green and blue cropped hair and heavy metal tattoos could be heterosexual and intent on finding the man of her dreams amongst the shearers and settle down and raise a family. There are all sorts.

Jessica commented quietly that that all sounded most interesting.

"By the way, Darlene, how does Prue fit into all of this. Is she settled and happy?"

"Yes, I meant to tell you. She is in a relationship with a much older woman named Ida, a very similar situation to you and Edith, I guess. I've met Ida and we got on really well. They are both free spirits and have given permission to each other to enjoy other people should the occasion arise. It seems to be working.

Then Jessica asked about the sorts of men she might meet.

"And I take it that there is an interesting cross section of males working there, Darlene, or haven't you noticed?"

Darlene let out a sigh then she giggled.

"You will find whatever takes your fancy, Jess, and it won't take long. You will only have to stroll around the property once with your long legs and you will immediately have your hands full, literally.

"I'm very much hoping to reconnect with two brothers, older men who took me to their cabin when I was there the year before last. They are itinerant shearers and spend two months working at the farm. I just missed them last year. Because of the unseasonably wet weather, they left early to work in another State."

Jessica felt a flush of excitement.

"Tell me why they were memorable, Darlene? They obviously floated your boat."

Darlene giggled again, self-consciously.

"They were probably in their late fifties or early sixties and both gentle giants; around six foot three I'd say. They laughingly told me that they hadn't seen such a good quality beast with an arse like mine since they last sheared on a property in Queensland. Not to be outdone, I answered that I hoped they'd done the right thing by the creature, to which they replied, that they would happily show me what they had done, just to get my expert opinion.

"By then I was charmed by their looks and their physique and good humour and I happily offered to judge their style. They took me home to their cabin and proceeded to fuck me silly right through the night. Their stamina was extraordinary and there being two of them, meant that as one came in me and finished, the other would take his brothers place and keep giving it to me like I was the last whore on earth. But not only that, both men recovered quickly so that with only a short rest between bouts, they would be on me again. And so it went, right through the night. It was then that I understood the meaning of a certain naughty term; cum bucket. I surely was one bu next morning.

"They were also very gentle and caring as well as being strong and demonstrative. I can tell you, Jess that a girl couldn't have wanted for more."

Jessica rubbed her crotch and felt the knickers beneath her denim jeans getting wet.

"Oh, Darlene. That sounded so wonderful. That story has made me horny. What were there names, I'll try and find them before you do."

"It sounds crazy Jessica, but I never did get their names, and that could make tracking them down a little difficult but hopefully, not impossible.

When they reached Goulburn, Darlene parked in front a chemist in the main street, and when she returned minutes later she passed one of two bags to Jessica.

"There darling. A present. I don't want you to miss out on

anything at the farm. I have a strong premonition that your cock fantasies are going come all at once, if you will pardon the pun. In the bag is the active girls essentials collection. Just three items. Condoms, lube and wet wipes, oh yes, and little bags for rubbish, if you know what I mean. I think you will enjoy them far more than chocolates."

Jessica screamed her delight and put her arms around Darlene and kissed her.

"Thank you so much, Darlene," then with a mischievous smile, she said, "Every time I use anything in this bag I will think of you, you darling woman."

Darlene drove the car out of the parking bay and continued the journey westward.

"Not long to go now, Jess. We'll be there in around half an hour. And I so hope you are ready to settle in to cock heaven, darling. I'm thinking when you head out for a walk the boys there just won't know what hit them. Come to think of it, nor will the girls."

———

Jessica couldn't help thinking that she was on one of those amazing film sets where everything was enormous and the activities most varied. Not that there was a lot of activity at the moment of their arrival. It was just that getting there after traversing the wide flat empty plains seemed surreal. It was like a town in the middle of a desert. What appeared to be accomodation in the form of cabins, spread along the road in either direction, and there were two large buildings at the end of the cabins. Jessica caught a glimpse between the cabins of another row of cabins at the back.

"Girls to the left and boys to the right is how it generally works. And there are married quarters hidden away at the back. Two cabins on each side of the homestead are reserved for the owners' visitors. The two larger buildings at each end are staff dining rooms. Only one is used except when there are events like open days or sales or when they open up during the tourism season."

The main homestead was at the point of where buildings ran in either direction at an angle. Opposite the homestead was a woodland

and a small lake with a boat shed and two small ornamental shelter sheds where swimmers and picnickers could escape from the sun or heavy rain. There was also a lovely old brick building beneath a giant Peppercorn tree and which Jessica thought could be the Creamery.

Visitors and workers didn't just park their vehicles outside the main buildings. Except for people who were quartered in the house or cabins, the workers were all required to park in the large carpark when they arrived at the end of the two kilometre drive-in from the main highway. There were at least twenty cars there and room for twice as many more.

A second and larger empty car park could be seen further over and Darlene explained that this was mainly used for visitors attending the twice yearly stud stock sales as was the aircraft landing strip further out.

A young man and a young woman were unloading supplies from a delivery van but other than that, the street was nearly deserted. Darlene explained that there was shearing being done at the shearing sheds a couple of kilometres away and more than half of the residents would be there. She said another group of men would be working on harvesting equipment in the huge hanger out near the air strip and most of the other residents would be working in the big kitchen next to the first of the workers dining room.

As they drew close to the house, three girls on horses wandered past heading in the other direction. Jessica was excited to see young women riding and commented that she wondered if they learnt when they arrive here or did they already know how to ride.

"Many of the young women are the daughters of farmers and are already experienced with horses. Some attend university then take a year off to do this. Others are usually less educated country girls looking for a better life away from their small communities. In short, being somewhere where their mums and dads can't watch over them."

Jessica was most amused and, thinking of her own situation, commented that she thought that made perfect sense.

Jessica was watching the three riders in the rear vision mirror. She was attracted to the tall thin one with the long pony tail who had returned Jessica's stare when they passed each other. The riders had stopped a little way back and the tall girl sat on her horse and stared back at the car, obviously waiting to see who got out.

Darlene didn't miss Jessica's noticing the lanky ponytailed pretty girl.

"I think you are going to have a good time, Jessica. Most of the girls here swing both ways so be ready for anything."

Darlene parked outside the homestead alongside half a dozen vehicles, a late model luxury people mover, and an older Mercedes Benz, a smaller runabout and three utilities, one quite old and the other two very new.

The front door opened as they approached and three women and two men came out to greet them.

"Jessica," called a familiar voice from long ago.

"Prue! It's been such a long time. Feels like a lifetime. So good to see you.

The two friends from school embraced and then stood back to look at each other.

"You're filling out at last", laughed Prue, looking at Jessica's bosom. "I guess we've both moved on as well. Maybe we've grown up at long last."

Darlene called out a happy hello to her daughter and embraced her, then she introduced Jessica to her sister and brother-in-law and to his brother and his partner. Both the men and the women looked at Jessica closely then at each other and smiled and nodded.

"Well, will we offer her job at Muta and try to talk her into staying", asked Annabelle, smiling knowingly at the other three.

"Not sure, yet darling. We'd best check what she can do first before any decision is made. She might be too straight or maybe too much of a handful. Wouldn't want to cause any disruption around the place."

They all laughed and Jessica grinned and went very red.

Darlene came to her aid, "Don't mind them Jessica, they are just trying to frighten you. Mind you, best keep your wits about you. Unexpected things can have a habit of happening here.

Jessica and Darlene where each given a cabin next door to the main house. The little homes were cute and functional and had a double bed and single bunks in an adjacent room. A kitchen and a bathroom made up the rest.

Prue knocked on the door just as Jessica finished hanging her clothes in the wardrobe and when she came in, the two women embraced and unlike all those years back, it was Jessica who pushed Prue up against the wall and put her hand inside the girls pants. The two kissed and then Prue pulled away gently and told Jessica that they must save themselves for later. And when Jessica asked why, Prue told her that it was for two reasons.

Prue told Jessica that tonight was the staff monthly barbecue when everybody got out and had a good time. Then Jessica asked Prue what the second reason was.

"My good friend Mandy texted me and asked if she could meet the new hot chick that arrived this afternoon. Mandy doesn't miss much. She and two friends were riding up the street when mum and you arrived. Mandy said she got the hots for you straight away."

Jessica coloured up and looked abashed.

"Well, if she was the tall skinny one with the pony tail, I'm up for it."

Prue laughed and slipped a hand into Jessica's little bra.

"Randy Mandy is quite a gal. She loves gals and guys and she puts herself out there. She's also got a little slave, Cindy who follows her around and does her bidding, getting Mandy anything she asks for, even blokes. Actually, given half a chance, Cindy is a little performer, too.

"So tonight I'll call for you at around seven-thirty and we'll start by strutting our stuff at the barbecue and hook you up with Randy Mandy. You will love her, I'm sure. I'm meeting up with Ida a little later so forgive me if I just dump you with Mandy and Cindy.

"We will no doubt see the others but mum is on a mission to find two shearers she enjoyed the year before last, so she could well disappear. I hope she finds them.

"Oh yes. Did mum talk to you about aunt Bella? I hope she did. Don't be shocked if you suddenly see Bella behind a tree dressed up in her finery with something in her mouth and something else in her hand. They won't be barbecued chops either, although they will doubtless be meaty and juicy.

"You are in for a good time, Jessica. Now, I've given you my number. Call or text if you are having any problems or need advice. Any questions?"

Jessica was excited by what Prue was telling her and her thoughts were going wild trying to work out the evening ahead.

"Just one question, Prue. What are Brendan, Gary and Gina likely to be doing. Do they get to strut their stuff tonight?"

"Good question. Brendan is very popular with some of the girls here and it's likely that a few couples from their swinging group will turn up. The old Creamery just up on the other side of the road will be unlocked and there are mattresses and cushions on the floor there. Bella will often rendezvous with some of the older shearers there, later in the night. Those men like a bit of comfort.

"Gary and Gina some times swap partners with a couple of the married women that Gina works with in the kitchen and sometimes Gina will hook up with one or a pair of the contracting itinerants and go and have them in their cabins. Gina is as active as Bella and on rare occasions the two will compete for a cock that they both want to try but then they will simply end up sharing it.

"Gary has a penchant for older women and some of the young women here who are from local families, will sometimes introduce him to their mothers or aunts. Like his brother Brendan, he's well liked and seems to be well catered for."

Jessica thanked Prue and they kissed and agreed to see each other later.

Jessica welcomed having time to herself for the first time and discovered that there was a proper bath in the bathroom with a continuous supply of hot water, fed by the nearby Wollondilly river. She bathed in a deep bath, soaking herself in nice smelly bath salts, closing her eyes and dreaming of sucking real men's cocks for the first time, instead of the nice young boys back home. Jessica fantasised and got very excited and played with herself with a bar of soap, "Oh, this is all so wonderful," Jessica whispered as she shuddered.

Prue knocked on the cabin door and collected Jessica and the two wandered across to the barbecue area under the trees on the other side of the roadway. It was late afternoon and sunny but there was already quite a crowd, most of them older shearers and mechanics and contractors, hungry and looking for a feed. Prue said that the younger ones usually appeared a little later when they could more easily be silly or sexy under the cover of darkness.

A voice called out and suddenly the tall skinny Mandy was standing in front of Jessica with her little side-kick, Cindy just two steps behind her. Prue proceeded to introduce them.

"Jessica, this is Mandy and this is her friend Cindy. Mandy and Cindy, meet Jessica. I'm off to town to collect Ida. We'll be back later so we might see you all then."

Jessica and Mandy stood staring at each other defiantly. Both were around the same height and build and both immediately looked forward to physically dominating the other.

Cindy watched excitedly, knowing that this could end either in a hair pulling fight or a screaming explosion of sexual energy. She would be excited either way, knowing that after her idol had a fight with another girl, she would fuck Cindy long and hard with a dildo. And if the encounter with the other woman ended in a sexual encounter, she would benefit just by laying naked alongside the two of them and letting them play with her, if and when they felt like it.

"Lets go for a walk down to the lake."

Mandy turned away and headed off through the trees with Cindy trailing after her but then Cindy turned, beckoning to Jessica to follow.

They had barely left the barbecue area and were passing through the bushy area that surrounded the lake when Mandy turned and grabbed Jessica by the arm and pushed her up against the smooth trunk of a large gum tree. She kissed Jessica forcibly and pushed a hand roughly up the leg of Jessica's tiny shorts. Then she gasped in surprise as Jessica threw her arms around her and swung Mandy against the tree and put her hand up the girls short skirt, fingering her madly as Mandy sagged and surrendered herself, shocked and excited.

"You fucking mad skinny slut. Come with me."

Mandy took Jessica by the hand and they all but ran to the little swimming shack beside the lake. Inside, mattresses lay on the wood floor and big candles sat on saucers on wooden boxes and Jessica saw that it was another place where lovers came.

In seconds, Jessica was on her back with Randy Mandy on top of her.

"Pull her fucking shorts off, Cindy."

Cindy moved in and deftly unbuttoned and removed Jessica's shorts and her panties.

"Now bitch. Give it to me."

Mandy ground her lower body hard against Jessica and probably because the two were already in a heightened state of excitement, both women came, screaming expletives along with many repeated mentions of the word "yes".

Cindy lay close by. She had pulled off her jeans and knickers and was rubbing herself as she watched. Then she gasped and orgasmed and then she leant over to lightly touch the two lovers.

Jessica and Mandy lay in each others arms, staring into each others eyes. They were in love. They kissed gently and slipped their tongues into each others mouths. Peace prevailed.

Suddenly, Mandy jumped up and reached for her phone.

"Whose for some cock? I'll order a take away."

Jessica watched, amazed as her new lady love texted while laughingly saying to the two women laying prone on the mattresses that it was a good time of day to get cock, and that the males were just heading out on the prowl.

A few minutes later, Mandy's phone beeped and she looked and laughed and passed the phone to Jessica.

"It's on the way darling. Us sluts never had it so good. Do you like it?"

Jessica stared at the picture of a large erection and underneath, the words 'On my way. Three more in ten minutes'. Jessica turned and stared at Mandy and smiled.

"Can I lick your phone, you beautiful bitch?"

Three excited women laughed and groped each other.

"You will have the real thing in your sexy mouth in just a few minutes, my love. Then, when the others arrive, you can suck yourself silly. And Cindy and I will too, won't we Cindy?"

"Ooh yes," replied Cindy in an excited voice.

A shadow filled the entrance and a young man in his mid twenties came in beaming a wonderful friendly smile.

"Here I am and I'm here to help."

"Jessica, this is Paul and Paul this is Jessica. She's visiting for the week."

The two smiled and nodded to each other.

"Who else is coming, Paul? I hope we got in early enough given how many horny women seem to have arrived in Muta for the barbecue."

"George is coming and he's bringing a new guy, a visitor who I haven't met yet. His name is Giovani and his from Sydney. Oh yes! Harry is coming and he might be with his shearer mate, Alec. So is five enough?"

Paul laughed and looked appreciatively at Jessica.

"Well, I guess that will get us girls started. Does it sound okay to you two?"

Jessica and Cindy both laughed and said they agreed that it was a start.

Then suddenly the doorway darkened and there were people everywhere. Jessica remembers Paul taking her hand and putting it on his newly exposed erection and moments later she had her biggest cock ever and her first real cock, she thought, well housed in her hungry mouth, kicking off an evening of cock sucking bliss.

The last spoken words Jessica remembered was Mandy calling out that Cindy was in charge of the box of condoms and would happily put the condoms on cocks for those who were too dumb to do it themselves.

Jessica felt Pauls hand gently fingering her pussy, and she blissfully cupped and fondled his balls with both hands and sucked on regardless.

Jessica made a point of occasionally looking across at Mandy and Cindy.

Things were happening very quickly, particularly as far as Cindy was concerned. She was on her knees with a cock in her mouth and a man behind her had his member somewhere between her legs.

Mandy had a cock in her mouth and another in her hand. Her long legs where spread wide apart and swaying in the air and hands were groping her breasts and her pussy. There was a lot of frivolity amongst the men but the girls, for obvious reasons, made few sounds other than sucking noises.

Suddenly, Jessica was shaken from her revelry when Paul gently removed his cock and moved away. For a moment Jessica was confused but then suddenly she looked up at the smiling face of a beautiful swarthy man who was offering her his very large member.

"My name is Giovani. What is yours?"

"I'm Jessica. Pleased to meet you."

The ridiculous formality of their introduction went unnoticed as Giovani offered Jessica his erection and which she accepted with unabashed enthusiasm.

A sudden scream signalled Cindy's orgasm and this is probably what reminded the males that there was more on offer than just being sucked and they took turns getting a condom fitted by the dazed Cindy, who nevertheless, still managed to swallow each cock for a few moments before she deftly fitted a rubber sheath.

Giovani interrupted the daydreaming Jessica and with a purring sexy accent asked her if he might fuck her.

"Oh please do, Giovani," she replied sleepily, happy for lovely man to do anything he pleased.

Giovani went over to Cindy and smiled his beautiful smile and before he could say hello is cock was first licked then swallowed by the excited young woman and only when he took her head in his hand and removed his cock from her mouth did she cover his manhood with a condom.

Then Giovani returned to Jessica and lifted her legs and lent between them and kissed her and told her how beautiful she was and Jessica sighed and mumbled coyly how beautiful he was. Then he put his fingers to her pussy and opened it gently and rested the head of his cock against it.

Jessica shuddered and she felt her wetness looking for him. Then he arrived slowly, moving the bulbous end of his cock backwards and forwards at her entrance. Jessica gasped and reached up and pulled his head down to kiss him and Giovani pushed his tongue into her mouth and moved it gently around. Then he pushed into her and Jessica felt the full force of his giant penis reaching up to touch her womb and moments later and being already in a heightened stated of excitement, she had the first of the evenings many orgasms.

Jessica would not let Giovani leave her. Not that he wanted to, but when he looked deep into her eyes and asked if she had had enough of him and would she like someone else to visit her, she pulled him tightly to her and told him that he must stay inside her all night and that he was not allowed to leave.

Giovani smiled down at her and said he would like to stay right where he was forever, and the sound of his voice and what he said and what was inside her cunt caused Jessica to cum a half dozen times over the next five minutes, each time, shrieking and pulling him down onto her.

When Giovani eventually came, and he filled his condom, the two entwined bodies parted and they looked around. The place was deserted. Everyone had left. Slowly, he lifted Jessica up and asked her if she would like to join him at the barbecue for something to eat. Jessica said that she would and quickly found her clothes and got dressed.

As they ate their steak and onions from paper plates and drank their cokes and coffee, the two kissed and touched each other. And when it was getting on for midnight and Giovani said that he thought he should let her get on with her evening, Jessica looked at him and pointed to the front door of her cabin on the other side of the road and asked him if her would like to spend the night with her. Giovani readily accepted the offer.

The two showered and laughed and got to know each other as best they could in the short time they had together. Giovani said that he had to leave in the morning but how he wished he could stay longer.

Then they snuggled into the big bed and cuddled up. Jessica

immediately felt Giovani's huge erection looking for her beneath the bed clothes and rejoiced. And after she had put a condom on him, Giovani fucked her over the next hour or more, resting sometimes to kiss and talk. Then after her many orgasm and his giant explosion, they settled down and slept.

In the early hours, Jessica awoke to find Giovani's cock rubbing against her belly once more and she knew what she wanted next. Jessica moved down in the bed and took him in her mouth and licked and sucked and then using her mouth and her hands she brought him to the boil, letting him almost drown her as he shot his huge load down her willing throat. Jessica had to remind herself that she wasn't dreaming. Happiness was very real today.

———

It was at a midday lunch in the main house the day after the barbecue. Darlene was there looking sleepy but very happy. And Bella was in a good mood, laughing about the night before and how she'd managed very nicely in the bushes, commenting that there was strong competition at times and on one occasion she'd had to share someone with a slightly tipsy jillaroo who kept saying how she wanted to ride Bella in preference to her favourite mare.

"I told her she could saddle me up anytime she felt the urge. I wonder if she'll try to take me up on my offer. Come to think of it, I remember who she was. I might ask her if she'd like a ride."

Everyone laughed and her sister-in law Gina told her she was a lucky bitch.

"By the way, Bella, I was wondering if I could borrow Brendon on Sunday night. You mentioned that you had something else on in town and because Gary is leaving this afternoon to go to Cobar, I would very much like someone to take me dogging. What do you think. I could go on my own but that is not as much fun."

Bella looked across to where Brendan and Gary were standing talking near the doorway. Bella called out to them.

"Brendan and Gary?"

The two men heard her and looked over.

"Gina wants to go dogging tomorrow and was asking if Brendon could take her. She knows I've got something else on. Is that okay with both of you? Gary? Are you okay with that?"

The brothers looked at each other and smiled.

"Fine by me, Bella as long as Gina is happy," Gary answered.

"I'm fine with it but you will have to take the ute, darling. Gina and I will need the van because it looks like there could be a shower or two.

"Okay Gina. It's settled. Just make sure he doesn't get into any trouble and that you bring him back with all of his bits."

Jessica had been watching and listening to this conversation with interest. She turned to Darlene and asked her in a low voice, what on earth were they talking about?

Darlene looked a little confused, not sure how to answer the question. Then she told Jessica about dogging and watched as Jessica's face too on a look of amazement.

Darlene explained that the name didn't come from the doggy, girl-on-her-knees love-making position but from men telling their wives they were taking the dog for a walk, it being an excuse for going to a public space where certain things were going on. As it was currently practiced at dogging events around the country, it was in no way woman friendly. Darlene said she identify with the theory, that some women might enjoy getting physical attention from more than one man at a time and how they might be turned on by doing things publicly and in front of an audience. But then she went in to say that in many instances that she had heard about, women seem to be coerced by their partners into partaking in a very uncaring and unsatisfying sexual adventure.

"I'm given to understand by Bella, though, that this group is totally different and the people who show up are a more exclusive and selective and caring crowd. They meet under the pine trees at a disused church half way between here and town. It's on private property so that the public doesn't have access. The people are mostly from town, professional people and business folk along with a few wealthy farmers. A few of them are in Bella and Brendon's swinger group. The people are all older, some are widows and widowers, and there are a lot of single men who have never married, usually farmers. And there are a couple of single women who have never been married and who apparently are comfortable interacting with men or women.

"If they were dogging any where else, say at any old public dogging venue, a woman would generally want a man with her as protection, but because this venue is like a gated community with most of the people knowing each other, Bella said quite a lot of women feel comfortable coming on their own if they are single or their husbands are not feeling up to it or are doing something else.

"Some women will come together in the one vehicle apparently, which sounds sensible and possibly even more fun.

"I really must go along one day. It would be interesting to see women honestly enjoying themselves and not there because their husbands pushed them into it. I suppose that in this instance it is really just like the swingers club but with fewer inhibitions."

Jessica looked at Darlene's fat red sexy lips.

"So have you tried it, Darlene?"

"Not here, unfortunately, but a couple of years ago, a man I was friendly with invited me to go dogging with him one night to a park in the eastern suburbs of Sydney. It was quite an eye-opener, I must say, and yes, after the first half an hour or so, I actually began to see how I might enjoy it if it wasn't so grubby. It depends a lot on the people that turn up whether or not you have a good time. I would love to go to this one but I'm leaving in the morning so won't be able to."

Jess continued to stare at Darlene's sexy lips.

"I'm still not understanding how things work, if you know what I mean. How do things get started and where?"

Darlene thought for a moment, eyeing Jessica carefully.

"Well, it began in Briton, probably starting when a couple were making out in their car in a carpark one evening and discovered that they were being watched through the car windows by what seemed like some pervy men, some of whom were exposing and playing with themselves.

"Instead of asking the men to go away, the couple began doing more sexual things together, partly as a joke and then simply to entertain the onlookers. From there it moved on to lowering the window so that men could put a hand in and touch the woman's breasts and from there, it wasn't long before women were enjoying touching the mens cocks. So now dogging sort of follows that historic format. Entertaining an audience outside the car and then, depending on circumstance, allowing them to participate in the action.

"Any questions, darling? Fire away. I'm getting fired up thinking about it.

Jessica laughingly whispered that that was enough to wet everything including her appetite, and that she was already in full dogging mode.

"You might like to ask if you could go along just for the experience. It's a wonderful opportunity to see it happening in a safe environment. And you only have to watch Gina. She is always so enthusiastic about anything she does. Seeing her having fun would be a turn on I'm sure.

"Because you are so much younger than the women who attend you probably won't be expected to participate. Unless you wanted too, of course. You would certainly command an enthusiastic line up at the car window if you did. I guess you could claim to be a university student working on a project on sexuality in older people, or something. "

With those last few words, she looked closely at Jessica with a bemused smile.

The two women laughed and Jessica found herself thinking about it, a bit more than she would have expected.

As the Saturday morning get-together came to an end, Jessica nervously approached Gina who was talking to Brendan. The two looked up at Jessica and smiled. Gina spoke first.

"Hope you had a good night last night Jessica. Heard you hung out with Randy Mandy and Cindy. Great gals. They would have kept you busy, I bet."

Gina glanced down at the lower half of Jessica's body appreciatively, and quietly commented that she hoped she had been appreciated by the local lads.

Jessica coloured up and replied that she had had a great night and had no regrets.

"I just wanted to ask you both if it would be possible for me to come with you tomorrow night. Darlene has been telling me about dogging and now I desperately want to know more. I thought that, if needs be, I could say I was a university student working on a project about sexuality in older Australians, or something. But would it be rude to go along as just an observer? Please be honest. I don't want to cause any trouble or difficulties."

Brendan spoke first.

"Well, I'm okay with it but I think it's really up to Gina. She'll be holding centre stage so she should be the one making the decision. What do you think, Gina?"

Once again Gina gave Jessica the once over, and smiled warmly.

"I think we could take her. She might have to wear a poncho for a while, to hide her charms and not be competition for me. But I can handle that. Yes, come along and extend your education sweetie. And if you want to join in, well I won't get upset. I'll probably just grab you like I will be doing to everyone else."

Everyone laughed and Jessica thanked them.

"We'll be leaving from out the front at eight-a-clock. You will be in the passenger seat as Gina will be in the back seat. Okay with that, Gina? Is there anything else we should tell Jessica?"

"Only that it looks like it will be a warm night but bring a jacket in case it turns chilly. And finally, if you don't think you are up for joining in then best not to dress up too much. Not that it really matters except heels and stockings will quickly get the men going, and if you are not interested in getting involved, you might regret having worn them.

"And if you do find yourself getting excited and you want to join in, we're there for you."

———

Jessica decided to have an early night and was the first to say her farewells as dinner came to a close.

The crowd at the table had been jovial and raucous and she had very much enjoyed their company.

She and Prue sat together along with Prue's partner Ida, and Jessica couldn't help but notice how the older Ida so reminded her of her own partner, Edith, and she wondered about how Prue's situation had come about, given the unusual circumstances surrounding her and Edith's discovery of each other.

She would inquire about it later when she and Prue were alone together.

Sunday dawned and Jessica showered and went off to the lake for a walk.

A mist rose off the water and cockatoos and galahs screamed from the gum trees. It was truly a beautiful time of day and Jessica wondered what it must be like living here. Then she reminded herself that every place was wonderful but the longer one stayed the more every day seemed like a day anywhere, regardless of the attractions.

She recalled the wonder of her first few months living in Sydney, and whilst she still loved it very much, Jessica rarely awoke with the same excited feeling of expectation she had when she first arrived there.

Then Jessica started to sort things through in her head; the adventure she was going to have this evening, then a brief moment of thinking about the lovely Giovani followed by another sudden vision, this time of Mandy's legs wide apart and waving in the air.

But mostly Jessica's mind focused on what she had learnt about dogging. Scary as it might seem, many men exposing their cocks to her through the window of a car couldn't help but make her want to touch herself. Then Jessica revisited that glimpse of Gina looking at her and the attractive woman's smile of appreciation as she scanned Jessica's long body. The thought that Gina wanted her, unexpectedly excited her and she thought about the woman and her comely body and that delicious smile radiating above the woman's alluring cleavage.

The saying that you get what you think about repeated itself again when there was a knock on the door in the early afternoon. "Come in," Jessica called out.

Gina came in and, smiling, walked over to her and without saying a word, took Jessica in her arms and kissed her. Jessica responded, putting her arms around the well built, almost maternal figure. Then to Gina's surprise and before the woman could make a move, Jessica slid a hand up inside Gina's blouse that hung loosely over her jeans, discovering to her surprise, that Gina's huge bosom was being held up by a bra that had holes for her nipples to protrude from. And protrude they did, standing out like little thumbs.

"Oh God! You are the horny little creature I'd picked you for," uttered Gina, gasping from the feeling of Jessica's fingers on her nipples.

Jessica lifted the blouse and looked at the amazing bust and the even more amazing brasier.

"Gina! I so love your bra. How magnificent your tits look. That is so exciting."

Gina laughed out loud and pushed Jessica backwards so that she could see her face.

"These are the latest thing for some of our ladies at dogging. Delvene at the lingerie shop in Goulburn got them for us.

"The larger ladies with big tits are all a bit self-conscious when they see themselves hanging down or swinging about when they are being energetically exercised at the club. Delvene looked into it and came up with these. The ladies love them and so do their men. The girls show them off to each other sometimes when they arrive at the venue. And some have said that they wear them at home because the bra is a turn on for their husbands resulting in them getting much more attention.

"Delvene has also said that she had something else on order for us to check out. Butt lifter crotchless pants. Now how exciting is that?"

Jessica put her mouth over a nipple and Gina squirmed.

"Now, Jessica. You've made my visit a lot easier. Thank you. I came to ask if you would ride in the back of the van with me on the way to dogging tonight, instead of in the front with Brendan.

"Normally, when Gary takes me, I sit in the front on the way there and unzip him and play with him. It warm me up and makes me hot to trot as soon as I get there. It makes it so much better if you're wet already. I haven't been able to stop thinking about you since we met, and if you would be so kind as to ride in the back with me until we got there, I'm sure that would properly warm me up so that I'd be well and truly ready for my first cock when we arrived. Then you can just hop into the front passenger seat before anyone came over, and hide under the poncho if you need to. Will you do that, Jessica?"

It was a no brainer and Jessica laughed and said how she would be honoured to have the opportunity to warm Gina up. The two laughed and kissed some more and Gina couldn't resist running her hand up Jessica's legs and groping her small and perfect bum.

"You are so beautiful Jess."

Jessica slipped a hand down over Gina backside, appreciating the size and feel of her large firm buttocks.

"Can I ask you something, Gina?"

"Anything you want Jess. Fire away."

The two women sat on the edge of the bed and held hands.

"Well. I've only recently sucked off a my first couple of cocks and I did enjoy it. I experienced a thrill of a sort which I can't explain to myself. It got me wondering what you feel when your are sucking all those cocks at a dogging event. I'm in two minds about it. On the one hand I'm horrified at the idea and on the other, I'm intrigued and realise that you must be doing it for a reason. Can you help me with this, Gina? Can you tell me what it really is that makes you want to do it? Am I too inexperienced to understand it yet?"

Gina stared into space, obviously trying to think through what Jessica had asked.

"You probably know, Jessica, that what you see of a woman's clitoris is really only a tiny part of a huge web of nerves running all over the place, even up to the anus. Ask any woman who enjoys anal sex.

Scientists say that a woman's genitals are home to more than eight thousand nerve endings.

"There is the belief that women crave many cocks for a variety of reasons, be it an unhappy childhood, bad self-esteem, or in the case of dogging, because they are at heart, exhibitionists who get a thrill from being watched by other people while having sex.

"I can't speak for any of those reasons specifically but there is a common thread running through the swinging and dogging community and that is that men, despite claiming that they don't get enough, are in fact far less sexual than women. Once a man as ejaculated, he's finished, at least for quite a while and not only physically. He losses emotional interest entirely, avoiding any sort of touching or intimacy until the next time he wants sexual release.

"Women are totally different physiologically. They are sensitive to erotic feelings for a much longer period and this can often give them pleasure in many parts of the body simply by touching.

"That pleasure, a sort of sustained mini orgasm can, in my opinion, be even more enjoyed as the result of sucking a man off.

"In my experience, sucking and tossing off a man provides a sort of sexual transference from the man to the woman. When I'm holding and tossing off a cock I will automatically sense when the man is about to cum and knowing this, feelings begin to act on my genitals so that at the moment of his orgasm, I get an intense feeling deep down resulting in a chain reaction of continuous euphoric sensations.

"Does that make sense, darling?"

Jessica stared at Gina with adoring eyes.

"Oh yes, Gina."

Then Jessica pushed Gina back on the bed and climbed on top of her and did her violent shagging movement, taking the two to lovers heaven.

Gina lay back, her eyes ablaze.

"You are definitely warming me up tonight, Jessica, and those poor men will wonder what's got into this ravenous creature with the extraordinary bra."

Brendan wasn't really surprised when, on opening the passenger door for Jessica, Gina called out.

"No Brendan. Pop her in here. Jessica's warming me up tonight."

Over the twenty minute drive to the old church, Gina showed Jessica what she was wearing under her full length coat.

Oh you are truly beautiful, gasped Jessica, looking at Gina in her corselet, suspenders and stocking and high heeled shoes. And then there was the black bra with the large holes displaying not just her nipples but also the large chocolate areola that surrounded them.

Jessica immediately thought of a chocolate ice-cream topped with a large treat of some kind.

The two women kissed and fondled one another and in what seemed only minutes, Brendan announced their arrival.

Gina gave Jessica one last kiss, then she lifted her legs and removed her panties.

"A girl is not dogging until she removes her knickers."

And with much laughter and a final kiss, Jessica got out and moved into the passenger seat in the front. She looked at Brendan and he leant across and pulled a clear plastic poncho over Jessica's head to help hide her and it was just as he did that and Jessica bent her head, she looked down and was shocked to see that he had his cock out of his trousers and it was standing very stiff.

Brendan suddenly realised that he was exposed to someone who was new to dogging.

"Sorry, Jessica. Blokes have to warm up too. I would have been in the back but you were there, so I had to do it on my own."

Brendan moved to put his cock away but before he could manage it, Jessica had reached out and was clasping it tightly.

"Would you mind if I helped you warm up just a little bit more, Brendan?" Jessica whispered.

Then a laugh from the back and Gina commented.

"Well, Jessica. You managed to get hold of one before me. Well done."

Then in a different voice, the lady in the back announced that her first customer had arrived and Jessica just heard the electric window going down.

"Hello, Harry! Have your brought me something. Oh yes, I can see you certainly have. It's looking very appetising too. Come a bit closer love."

Jessica's head was full of swirling images. She now had a hand on Brendan's cock and Gina was about to enjoy Harry, whoever Harry was, through the back window. She needed to make sense of things; to work out what she was going to do with all that was going on.

Brendan looked at Jessica with a loving smile.

"I'll have to leave you shortly, Jessica. Not that I don't want to be with you but I do have an appointment somewhere else which I must attend to."

A voice came from the back seat.

"That'll be with that randy Daphne. Don't think I don't know Bren. She's got a soft spot for you. Have fun."

Then Jessica heard a more muted voice from the backseat, "I think we're nearly there Harry. Are you ready?"

And then only moments later, after Harry had yelled "Yes", Gina with a new voice spoke again.

"Hello Tom. Don't go away love. You're next."

When Brendan left the car, Jessica could hardly wait to look between the seats to the back, at what was going on there. She heard a man groan and saw Gina thrusting his cock down her throat and she saw the man's mask-like face as he came. Within seconds, Gina had reached out to another stiff cock nearby and was drawing it in towards her.

Jessica was excited beyond belief. She'd had a cock in her hand just a moment ago but it had got away. Now she desperately wanted another one. She leaned over the back of the seat. Gina already had a second cock in her other hand which she stroked lovingly.

"Gina? I want to put my window down too. Is that all right with you. Just say if it's not."

Jessica heard a stifled sound then Gina's voice.

"Go for it girl. There is plenty around tonight. I'm going to open the door on the other side shortly anyway. I need to offer my other end. The boys deserve the full menu."

Jessica absorbed what Gina had said and then she thought about what the woman had said earlier.

"A girl is not dogging until she removes her knickers."

Jessica lifted her backside off the seat and slipped her panties off. And yes, the minute she did that she felt different. Then she removed herself from the poncho. Then she heard Gina's muffled voice again.

"Show your tits darling. That will bring them closer."

Obeying her dogging guru was now the order of the day and Jessica pulled the tiny straps down over her shoulders, and let her cotton dress drop to her belly and leaving her small tight pointy breasts on display to the world.

Then that quiet voice came from behind came again.

"Let the back of your seat down a bit so that you can lean back to show off."

Then the voice was gone leaving just the sounds of Gina sucking and gurgling.

With the back of the seat adjusted, Jessica nestled back and glanced down at her breasts. Then, out of the corner of her eye she noticed something moving. Two stiff cocks were swaying and lifting up and down beside her, against the passenger door window and a little voice inside Jessica screamed with delight.

As Jessica was about to press the button to let down the window, Gina's voice spoke again.

"Don't rush darling. Tease them a bit. You will enjoy it and they'll get even stiffer."

The message made Jessica slow down. She smiled sweetly at the two cocks and the faces above them. Then she pressed the button and let the window down about a third of the way.

A hand and arm came through and began to caress Jessica's breasts and she closed her eyes to savour the moment when she made her first dogging contact. Then a second hand came in and tried to reach down to lift the hem of her dress but couldn't quite reach.

Jessica opened her eyes and looked at the arms and hands reaching out for her.

Gina had said to tease them and Jessica was excited about that. She slowly put a hand down and lifted the hem of her frock up over her belly. Her small matt of auburn hair covering her pussy was now on display and she sensed the excitement outside the window. Jessica glanced through the window and was shocked to see five or more cocks attempting to get her attention. This was a lot more than she had envisaged and she wasn't sure what to do.

"Hold and suck one while you hold and rub another. Don't try to do too much. Just finish off one at a time."

Jessica realised that she was in love with Gina. How could she not be. With a slight feeling of trepidation, Jessica lowered the window to that she could reach the men. In just moments, there was a hand on her pussy and she found herself pushing against a man's inserted fingers and with her legs wide open.

Then she made a move. Jessica reached out and took the closest cock into her hand and began to rub it. Then she took another one with her other hand and suddenly she was rubbing two big stiff cocks and admiring each one for its colour and shape. The first stuck straight out while the second had a definite bend upwards. And the purple veins that ran around each were pulsating and calling to her.

Jessica became aware that Gina had opened the other side door, and taking time out for a cursory look behind showed her that Gina was on her knees and a gentleman was kneeling behind her waving his cock. Jessica couldn't help but hear the conversations, especially the low reassuring voice of Gina.

"Just pop it in Henry. You know how I love to have you in my pussy. And go as hard as want lover boy. I'm hungry for it. And the condoms are where they always are, in that box on the floor."

And then to someone in front of her, "Hello Bernie. Got something for me I hope? How is Mildred? Is she back home yet. Dreadful business. Now we just need to get you relaxed and wanting to give me that little present you know I love. Lets just tickle you under here. Would you like that?"

Jessica found herself smiling and appreciating this amazing woman's easy going but supper sexy manner. She wondered if she could ever be like Gina.

Jessica was brought back to her situation when she suddenly realised that the cock in her mouth was about to cum. And then she felt it. That tingling feeling in her pussy and elsewhere as the man pushed in to her mouth and shot his semen down Jessica's throat. Then he was gone and the cock in her other hand was pushing itself towards her mouth and feeling quite ready to cum and suddenly and just in time, Jessica took another load of cum into her, tingling all the way down and around her genitals.

And the cocks kept coming. By the time Brendan returned and Gina had said her goodnights and closed her doors, Jessica figured that she had sucked at least a dozen cocks and felt a similar number of different hands on her tits and between her legs.

Gina pushed her head between the seats and kissed Jessica on the cheek.

"Well done, darling. I got the feeling that you might have enjoyed it. Am I right?"

Jessica lifted a hand to Gina's face and caressed her cheek.

"Yes I did, Gina. And I even felt what you had described earlier. Thank you."

Brendan arrived and got into the drivers seat.

"Everyone okay? Ready to head home?"

Gina reached a hand through and felt Brendan's trouser front.

"Yes, yes! It's still there. By the time we get home and you've had a shower I'll be ready to finish you off, Gina, I promise."

Gina smiled in the darkness then spoke.

"I can't really speak for Jessica but she has been busy while you were away having yourself some fun. She might like to be finished off, too.

"It happens a lot, Jessica. Bella and I, like most women, enjoy being properly shagged when we get home. Our finishing off as we call it. Do you have thoughts about having something like that, darling. An optional extra, I call it."

Jessica smiled and remembered Brendan's lovely cock that she had in her hand only momentarily earlier in the evening.

"If there is enough to go round, I'd love to be finished off."

Brendan and Gina laughed heartily.

"Make that two finishing offs, please driver."

"Certainly, Madam. My pleasure."

———

It was a late Friday afternoon as Brendan delivered Jessica to the bus station at Goulburn. She had said her teary goodbyes to everyone and promised to come back again soon. Even Mandy had shed a tear, calling her a bloody slut who should live here with people who understood her.

Prue said she would be in Sydney in a few weeks to stay with her mum and that it would be nice to catch up then. And Gina winked and whispered that she would miss her and made her promise that she would go dogging with them again and do her the favour of warming her up beforehand. Jessica, hugged her and told her she would and thanked her for showing her the way forward.

"I will never forget what you've taught me, Gina. Thank you."

Whether it was that last moment with Gina or something else, Jessica put on her 'finery' as Bella called it, her stockings and high heels and her very short skirt and happily jumped into the utility when Brendan tooted from outside her cabin.

"Wow! Is there something going on that I haven't been told about? Brendan said, looking at Jessica appreciatively.

Jessica leant across and kissed him on the cheek.

"If there was, Brendan, I'd make sure that you were the first to know."

The quick ride into the bus station was very pleasant. Brendan talked about the farm and how managing during the drought had been extremely difficult. And when Jessica enquired about the swingers club, Brendan talked about how he and Annabella had decided to join the club some three years back and how that had impacted on their lives. He said how it had brought them closer together and how that now they watched out for each others emotional needs much more than they had before.

"It's so enriched our lives," he said. He went on to tell how both he and Annabella shared thoughts about other people and potential lovers. Each wanted to see the other enhance their lives and that making love to other people did just that.

At the bus terminal, the big coach was already sitting with its motor ticking over and most of the passengers had already found seats. Jessica farewelled Brendan in the half light of early evening and as they hugged, she said how she had enjoyed her visit far beyond her expectations.

Jessica climbed aboard the luxury coach and presented her ticket to the driver. Then she wandered along the aisle until she found a seat towards the back. The window seat was occupied by what appeared to be a priest or vicar in black clothing and with a white dog collar. He looked up and smiled and Jessica thought how handsome he was and put the man's age in the early to mid thirties.

Jessica deliberately turned her back towards the man and bent over pretending to look for something in her bag before sitting down, hoping that he had taken the opportunity to look at her long legs and appreciate her tight short skirt.

As Jessica settled in to the soft padded seat and started to roll the images of the past week through her mind she was suddenly amused when it occurred to her that if she had been a catholic and the man next to her was a priest, he might have enjoyed listening to her confession.

With an almost silent purr, the coach moved off, the bus interior lights were dimmed evening and Jessica watched the last moments of the setting sun across the vast empty plains.

After about twenty minutes, when Jessica was sitting with her eyes closed and playing out a scene in her mind of Mandy with her legs in the air, she felt a gentle touch on her knee. The initial shock was immediately followed by her sharp sucking in of breath, the sound of which Jessica managed to stifle. Then she allowed herself the thrill of accepting that the priest was interested in getting to know her better, and remembering that it was only recently she had come to under-stand the excited feeling she got in her head and her groin when men wanted her, when they longed to touch her. Jessica was soon on fire.

Then Jessica remembered the wise words of her teacher, Gina, when they were in the car dogging and Jessica was staring through the car door window at her first line-up of cocks. "Don't rush darling. Tease them a bit. You will enjoy it and they will get even stiffer."

Jessica looked down in the dim light of the bus and could just make out the priests fingers lightly touching her leg and moving slowly up towards the hem of her skirt, and she smiled inside, knowing she had a man all to her self for the next couple of hours.

Jessica sat back and savoured the moment. The man's fingers softly rubbing her stockinged legs felt so beautiful. Then Jessica thought about the situation and realised that, while the journey was going to take another couple of hours, she couldn't be sure how far her admirer would go. She decided that she had time to wait a little while before responding and noted how his fingers were already up under her skirt, softly rubbing and pushing down between her inner thighs.

Jessica wondered what he would think when her groper discovered that she wasn't wearing knickers, and she smiled at the thought; that was if he could get past just wanting to play with her suspenders. Men totally love suspenders according to her sex guru, Gina.

Two fingers reached her crotch, and met a little bush of hair and stopped. Then they moved down to discover Jessica's already very wet vagina and two fingers slipped inside her.

It was time for Jessica to make a move. It must be obvious to the man that Jessica was happy with what he was doing, she reasoned. Now it was her turn.

Jessica half turned and moved an arm across and placed her hand on the priests trousers, finding a sturdy lump which moved violently when she touched the spot where it was buried.

Not to be backward in coming forward, Jessica moved her second hand down to where the man was feeling her pussy and she pressed him in further, signalling her approval of his wanton but much appreciated action.

A hand removed Jessica's hand from her spot on the trousers and she sensed a flurry of activity in the semi-darkness as the priest extricated his member. Then he reached over and took Jessica's hand and placed it on his liberated cock and Jessica rejoiced, knowing that her quiet time on the bus was going to be well spent.

Jessica pulled her hand upward and gently massaged the head of the priests cock with her finger tips. She was in no hurry. Jessica listened as the thousands of nerve endings in her genitals celebrated the actions and she shivered with the intense excitement she felt at the proposition of sucking the priest off.

Her man of the cloth, having received confirmation of Jessica's approval of his actions was now enlivened and he rubbed her pussy enthusiastically. Jessica responded and rewarded him by slightly lifting her abdomen and thrusting it forward onto his fingers. She even put her hand down onto his and took another finger and put it herself to join the other two. Three fingers is the best number, Darlene had once told her.

Jessica felt the cock in her hand throb and it suddenly felt bigger and stiffer and she felt saliva trickling into her mouth in preparation for her feast.

When Jessica at last got up on the seat on her knees and put her head down and took the priest into her mouth, the man sighed and stroked the back of her head.

Jessica was impressed with her new acquisition. The cock was not long but it was impressive in its thickness. She lovingly worked her tongue around it, lifting her mouth off of it before plunging it back into her mouth and swallowing it again.

Jessica thought how heavenly this cock felt then found herself smiling at the idea of the priest taking her to heaven. She slid her hand down and rubbed the man's testicles and she heard his soft groan.

While Jessica pushed her lips and mouth all over his cock, the priest was now able to reach over the kneeling woman and pull up her skirt and run his hand over her bottom. He touched her anus and rubbed a finger up and down that little valley that joined her anus and Jessica's vagina and for just a moment, Jessica thought how good it would be if the priest could fuck her. But that wasn't possible and in any case, she was having such a good time with what was already available to her.

Jessica had been sucking and rubbing the priest for almost an hour. His fingers in her cunt had afforded her a few mini orgasms and now, she reasoned, it was probably time to relieve the man of his load. She removed her mouth and began to rub him more vigorously and the priest sensed where she was going and pushed his cock upward in anticipation.

Then came the time when Jessica knew that the man was about to cum and the host of nerve endings excitedly urged her on. Jessica told herself that she should be ready in about thirty seconds and sure enough, the priest gave up his holy message with great force while he clutched Jessica's head so that she could not get away.

Jessica had no desire to escape and lovingly slurped the exhausted member, licking everything and sucking gently while feeling the heavenly cock slowly subside.

Jessica lifted her head and smiled at the man through the darkness and murmured, "Thank you. I really enjoyed that."

That the priest appreciated Jessica's comment was made clear when he leant forward and kissed her on the lips.

"Thank you, you beautiful girl. I will remember this moment."

When the coach arrived in the Sydney depot, the lights went on and everyone rose to leave. Jessica and the priest looked at each other and Jessica felt herself blushing. Jessica made an effort to speak.

"Are you visiting Sydney or do you live here?" she asked, not really knowing what to say.

The handsome priest swung his small suit case from the rack above and smiled.

"I'm just here for a visit. I'm going to a fancy dress party tonight. The theme is Changing Ones Occupation. What do you think? Do I look convincing?"

# 4

# THE CLUB

It was Maria's cleaning day and Roger made sure he was up and shaved and dressed and presentable before heading downstairs for his first coffee of the day.

As usual, Maria was looking attractive and Roger appreciated both her looks and her energy. For the umpteenth time, Roger thought about if and when he would make it known to Maria that he knew about her secret morning visits to his bed when he was in a deep sleep and how much he enjoyed her sucking his cock. With Caroline in London, now was probably a good time to do it and even perhaps move things along even further and seduce the woman. He was ready to confront Maria but when he said her name as she folded clean tea towels on the kitchen table, Maria got in first.

"Roger, I have one thing to tell you and one thing to ask you. Is now a good time?"

Maria's smile was irresistible and Roger indicated that he wanted to hear what she wanted to tell him. He assumed that they would be about the house and working. He was in for a shock.

"Please! No time like the present as they say in cheap novels."

Maria fixed him with a look that foretold that a secret was about to be divulged.

"As you know, I do housework and sometimes cooking for a number of wealthy clients here in the Western suburbs. One of my customers is a woman named Desley who is the daughter of the long dead but well known brothel keeper, Kathleen Mary Leigh. Kathleen Leigh famously bought the house near by and she was instrumental in naming this crescent Eros Crescent. Mount Eros is the name of their house; number thirteen, on the other side of the track leading up the mountain."

Roger smiled and said how he knew the name and had read the inscription on the plaque at the edge of the park.

"Well, a couple of months ago, Desley opened a club. She runs a charity for older and out of work prostitutes, so she thought what better way to raise money than exploiting an activity she knows a lot about. She has slowly built the reputation of the club so that now it is so popular, she has been forced to limit membership and stop accepting new enrolments, unless of course, another member leaves. But she now has plans to open second club on the other side of the harbour, probably at Neutral Bay or somewhere on that side of the bridge, anyway."

Roger put up his hand.

"Before you go on, Maria, just fill me in on what is special about The Club?"

Maria laughed and for a moment Roger thought he saw her blush.

"It's basically a sex club. It shows end-to-end blue movies for the six hours it is open on six days of the week. But before you say that it sounds sordid or creepy, I should tell you more about it.

"Desley went to a lot of effort to set the place up. It is beautifully designed and very functional. But what makes it unique is that it is female friendly. She thinks it is the first of its kind and she thinks she will eventually be able to sell the concept around the world.

This leads me to why I'm telling you about it. Desley is looking for a person to write up the story of The Club and what she has achieved. She wants something in print that properly describes the club, the way it functions and how it is used. She also wants something that can be used as a prospectus for likely overseas clients.

I told her that I thought I knew someone who would be good for the job and who might be interested. I lent her a copy of your previous book and she loved it and enthusiastically said she wanted to meet you.

Roger looked at Maria intently, digesting what she was telling him. His first reaction was of disbelief that such a place could exist.

"I've visited sex shop movie theatres in New York and in Amsterdam. I can't see how they could possibly be restructured to provide enticing entertainment for anyone other than the most desperate people, mostly male and very rarely, female.

Have you been to the club Maria? And if so, what was it like? From a woman's point of view."

Roger watched as Maria coloured up again.

"Well, yes I have, Roger. I have long enjoyed an active sex life, both with men and with women and Desley knows that. Desley gave me a free membership to The Club and I can only report that so far, I've loved it. It does it for me and from what I observe, it does it for all the other women I see there. And the men seem very happy too."

Roger was in a sort of shock. The sad pervy men attempting to grope the unattractive and equally sad women who he had observed in adult theatres overseas could never fit with what Maria was telling him.

"Desley said she would be happy to pay a considerable sum of money for the story and hoped I would be able to interest you in the project.

"There is one other thing though, before you meet her. I am allowed to take a visitor to the club. It's all part of the membership. Three visitor tickets a year. She insists that I take you along to see the place working prior to her meeting you. She acknowledges that, having had that experience, you might not want to take on the job. I think she is right. You need to see it working.

"I suggest we go early one afternoon. You can accompany me and meet my friend Veronica. We mostly sit together. Then you can wander off and explore the club and we can see each other back here if we don't catch up at The Club at the end of the day. How does that sound, Roger?"

Roger was thinking fast. His natural interest in human behaviour was being teased out in a way that was hard to switch off. There was also an erotic component that could not be ignored. But his answer was swift.

"How could I not want to take up your offer, Maria? You might or might not have noticed that I have always acted appropriately in your company but I should put you on notice that this could change the instant we arrive at the club."

Maria laughed sympathetically and stared at him defiantly.

"Why would you wait until you were somewhere where there was likely to be stiff opposition, Roger? But perhaps a visit to The Club will encourage inappropriate behaviour in the future. We'll see."

Roger was immediately excited by Maria's suggestive stance. But he had questions.

"Maria? What would you say was the thing that made The Club experience so appealing to women? I can easily understand men being drawn towards interactions with women but I really do want to know what is the appeal for the ladies?"

Suddenly, Maria took on a different persona, showing an intellectual interest in what I had asked her.

"I'd put uncertainty and anticipation at the head of the list. The uncertainty coupled with the expectation and excitement of receiving unsolicited sexual attention, i.e., "Will someone I do not know, try to do something sexual to me when I wasn't expecting it?"

"The second thing, strangely enough, is the feeling of empowerment. A woman at The Club knows that ultimately she is safe but like all good stories, the opportunity is offered whereby the woman can suspend disbelief. She can pretend for just a short time, pretend that she will be surprised by titillating things that might happen to her, sexual things that she does not normally experience in her daily life.

"And thirdly, wanting to be adored is a natural trait of all women, even if it might be only temporarily. How much a man adores her is demonstrated by his persistence in wooing her despite the difficulties she might put in his way. She is in a position to reward or reject her would-be lover; or most likely, tease him and enjoy his tortured persistence.

"I love to have my boobs displayed and played with, but a man must work hard to persuade me before his fingers touch my nipples."

Roger eyed Maria and her bust, with more than intellectual appreciation.

"Tell me where to meet you and when, Maria, and I'll be there."

Maria smiled a wicked and beautiful smile. Then she reached forward and her hand closed over the bulge in Roger's pants. With her other hand, she unbuttoned her blouse exposing a low-cut bra.

"Bare my breasts Roger, please. I don't want to wait any longer. We've waited too long already."

A beautiful boob in each hand and a willing woman on the end of his penis while her legs waved wildly in the air, cleared all thoughts of anything else from Roger's head and he melted into the moment and between Maria's thighs.

This had been a long-time coming, and yes, he would tell Caroline, eventually.

————

Roger was very surprised to discover the location of The Club. Only a short walk from his own house and he'd never suspected that it was there.

He met Maria in what was originally intended as a car park, many years back, but which was now just a large flattened expanse of land that lay at the foot of the mount and stretched behind both numbers thirteen and eleven Eros Crescent.

Marie looked extraordinary. She was not wearing her usual black skirt and top but instead, a very short red miniskirt and a light cream coloured blouse with a frilly low neckline. Her bright red lipstick and her red high heels and white stockings pushed her appearance over the top. She took his hand and looked into Roger's eyes.

"Sorry about this outfit Roger, but it is the second Tuesday of the month. It's when Veronica and I meet two older lesbian ladies who we both happen to work for. They are super rich and live in big houses next door to each other in Vaucluse. They love to come over here once a month and have us together and wanting us to look as slutty as we can make ourselves without getting arrested. Interestingly, of the things that some women regret not doing in their younger days, dressing as sluts is one of them, although they will never admit it. If you sat close by and watched, you would be amazed at how many women approach us when we look like this. Far more interest from women than men."

Roger thanked Maria for her explanation saying that he was a little taken aback when he first saw her.

"I do hope today is going to work for you Roger. And can I say quickly, that when you wander off to see the sights, feel free to come back to me if I'm around. I will always be more than willing to bare myself to you. And Vickie will want you as well, I know what she likes. Mind you, though. today we might look just bit too slutty for your more refined taste."

Roger laughed and took Marie's hand and squeezed it.

"I just hope I can make myself ignore you both. Just for research purposes of course."

Marie burst out laughing.

"Now while I'm thinking about it, tell me about the films, Maria. The few I've seen in porn cinemas were often violent. How are the films here selected."

"Oh yes! I was going to mention that and then forgot. Desley's brother, Arnold has worked in the sex industry all his working life and is an authority on blue movies. He has selected an extensive range for viewing at the Club and all of them he and his sister have judged as female friendly or at least, close to. No rape or violence apart from the occasional bit of slap and tickle. The female club members seem to love them and can happily just sit and watch a movie with their skirts pulled up and their legs apart and their fingers busy. Seeing and watching them playing with themselves is one of the little known delights of being a member.

Alvie at the front desk even has a list of favourite movies that women clients would like to view again. Interestingly, the number one favourite is called Debt Collectors and depicts a woman being told by three gangsters that because her husband can't pay his debts, she will have to pay them for him, in kind. You can imagine what follows."

Roger stopped walking and took hold of the beautiful Maria and kissed her. When he thought he should stop, she wouldn't let him go and pressed her hand on his crotch.

"So looking this slutty hasn't put you off Roger. You must promise me that you will act inappropriately at your house whenever the idea enters your head. I will love it."

They were inside the door now and Roger looked around.

At reception, Maria flashed her membership card on the electronic reader and pointed to Roger.

"My guest, Alvie."

The older woman looked at Roger and smiled.

Alvie reached over and fastened a small tag to Roger's shirt showing the number 28.

"This must be your first visit? Haven't noticed you here before."

For just a moment, Roger felt like a naughty boy who'd been caught looking at a copy of a lad magazine.

"Yes! I'm looking forward to it."

"I'm sure you will enjoy yourself, love. Just remember the first rule, Slow and Gentle. That way no woman will ever disappoint you."

Maria beamed at Alvie and then at Roger.

"Let me know if you want to practice either or both of those things, Roger. Happy to give you a lesson if you think you need it."

Roger and Alvie laughed, enjoying Maria's innuendo. Alvie handed Roger a brochure entitled The Club Rules: Advice for New Members.

"Just in case you enjoy yourself so much that you decide to put your name down for membership, Roger.

---

Roger was impressed from the very beginning. The Club entrance area was bright and airy with white walls and brightly coloured doors and woodwork, and signage was clear and tasteful.

A small counter offered peppermints and jelly beans and chocolate almonds along with condoms and wet wipes, and lubricants in a range of perfumed and non perfumed products in squeegee bottles.

This small foyer area which led to the entrance to the cinema, was flanked by male and female bathrooms on either side, and signs pointed the way to two other venues. Signposts pointed to the Home Deliveries room and to Gals Only, and The Parlour seemed self-evident. Well, sort of. Roger had no trouble guessing the purpose of the Gals Only room but the Home Deliveries did not translate into something he could immediately identify and The Parlour, well that could be anything.

"Ready, Roger?"

Roger looked at Maria and smiled.

"Definitely ready, Maria."

It took only a few moments for Roger's eyes to adjust to the dim theatre lighting provided by the cinema screen. A movie played and provided gentle narration of a sexual encounter and with the voice of a woman screaming yes, yes, in the background.

The floor sloped down quite significantly allowing easy viewing over other patrons heads.

As he slowly adjusted his eyes to the dim light and took in the scene, Roger was again impressed by the design and layout. Each row of wide, red vinyl covered seats, contained four sets of four seats leaving a wider access aisle up the middle as well as those on either side. He counted twelve rows. There was a wide walkway at the very back where people could stand or another row of seating could be installed. Another wide walkway divided the front three rows from the rest. A quick calculation showed that the theatre could seat one hundred and ninety patrons.

People were scattered around the theatre, some alone, some as couples and there was at least two sets of three people.

Maria pointed out to him that that the three front rows were off limits to men unless they were with a consenting female partner. These front rows catered for couples and women on their own who did not want to be approached by other members.

Lone women would go there to simply watch the movie and likely touch themselves if so inclined. Occasionally - according to Maria - two women in a row might exchange glances and indicate that they would be happy to enjoy the other's company for mutual touching and kissing in which case, one or the other would get up and move next to her newly found friend.

Maria took Roger's hand and led him along one side to a row half-way down. Then she whispered, "Veronica will find us when she gets here shortly."

On the screen, two women were now laying on a bed kissing, each fully clothed but obviously interested in slowly removing bits of the others apparel. Close by, a semi-clothed man sat exposing himself on the bed and holding himself at the ready, awaiting the call.

Maria took Rogers hand and lent towards him and whispered. "Once your eyes have adjusted, feel free to wander off and check every-thing. I would suggest you start at the back wall where most men hang around while working out their next move and who they might approach. Your learning starts now, Roger. Best of luck."

Roger gave Maria a peck on the cheek then rose and turned to walk to the back. But he couldn't help noticing a woman two rows back. She was not alone. She stared straight ahead, stoney faced and completely absorbed in the movie, seemingly oblivious to the two men who sat either side of her gently groping her fully exposed, neat womanly breasts.

But then Roger saw that wasn't all that was going on. The woman had an arm stretched out on either side of her with each hand holding and slowly rubbing a man's fully erect cock. This was bordering on the erotic existential moments of 1920s Paris and Berlin that Roger had studies some years ago. He wanted to stop and watch but thought it would be rude to be a gawker, and moved on.

Roger couldn't help but wonder what was going on in the woman's head. Was she excited? Was she getting what she came for? Then he remembered Maria's explanation: "She can pretend for just a short time, pretend that she will be surprised by titillating things that might happen to her, sexual things that she does not normally experience in her daily life."

So this really is a properly functioning porn cinema, Roger murmured to himself.

Sometimes in life, things happen really quickly, no matter how prepared you thought you were for sudden shocks.

An arm shot out and grabbed Roger's arm and suddenly a tall thin elegant woman was by his side.

"We are just what you are looking for, darling."

The woman dragged Roger in to where she was sitting alongside her more substantially built lady friend. Before he could say a word, the woman put her hand behind his head and dragged it down between her companions large stocking-clad thighs and ordered him to "lick my friends pussy." But she didn't stop there. As Roger's face drowned in a beautiful tangle of wet and perfumed pubic hair, he felt his trousers being removed and suddenly his member was first in the hands of the thin lady and then in her mouth.

But then Roger had an epiphany. It was an extraordinary moment. He was transported to a time when he was sixteen-year-old and on holidays at his aunt Ella's sheep property.

There was a moment during the dinner commemorating his late uncles birthday, when the slightly tipsy Ella had asked Roger to get down under the dinner table and retrieve her serviette. It was there that he had discovered a pair of magnificent stockinged legs spread wide apart and, due to the randy aunt's lack of knickers, Roger found himself looking at a very large hairy pussy while in the background he heard his aunt call out, "take your time darling, have whatever you want."

But the epiphany didn't stop there. Aunt Ella's housekeeper, the thin and delightful Sheila, when later helping Roger get his now fully inebriated aunt to bed, had looked into his eyes then grabbed him and removed his trousers and her own clothing and dragged him down onto the bed beside his now sleeping aunt. Then she provided him with such a fucking as had not been matched since that day. This memory of his first sexual experience had propelled him forward in life to a rich and energetic love life. That first encounter with raw woman-hood helped add sensual substance to both his personal life and to his work as a writer.

Roger now found himself again in that moment. The thin lady who had grabbed him and removed his trousers now hung onto his cock with her mouth as though she wanted to become a part of him, just as Sheila had done all those years ago. And the aunt Ella lady was squirming beneath his cunnilingus assault on her giant vagina.

At an appropriate moment, Roger chanced a glance upwards to see what was happing topside.

The view was erotic to say the least. Two fully exposed mammoth white mammarys floated on a body that laid back in the seat. The woman's head was pushed over the back of the seat by a hand on her neck. A mouth sucked a breast and Rogers proxy aunt Ella was taking turns at sucking the two cocks being offered by men standing on either side of her head and behind her. But Roger's efforts won the day and the big lady threw up her body and came with a violent scream before pulling Roger's head further in between her legs.

Now it was the thin ladies turn and she wasn't going to miss out.

Dragging Roger's head from between her friends legs she stared into the darkness where she thought his eyes were.

"Give me what you gave her, you beautiful man."

Suddenly the lady was laying flat on the floor with her legs waving in the air and wide apart and a hand held Roger's face against her comparatively tiny wet pussy.

Roger didn't hesitate, moving straight into a repeat of the professional cunnilingus mode he had learnt from the lovely Italian ladies in Positano.

When the skinny Sheila substitute lady arched her back and screamed, Roger moved forward and plunged his cock into her willing wet vagina. She screamed again and bit him fiercely on his chest.

"Stay in me, lovely man. I'm coming again."

Roger rewarded her and himself by pushing in even harder. Then he exercised his preferred penis move, one taught him by those same experienced older ladies on the Amalfi coast. He pushed in hard, then, when the root end of his member was hard up against the woman's pelvic bone, Roger maintained the pressure against her clitoral area so that she could not move away from him. The effect was dramatic. The woman screamed once and came and then screamed again and came again and kept on repeating the happy event.

Roger knew that by not letting her back away, she would probably just keep orgasming again and again until she pleaded with him to stop. But the lovely lady couldn't bring herself to give up the magic of what Roger's cock was providing. In the end, she just stopped moving her body and began to sob. Only then did he pull back. He touched her face gently and cupped her mouth in his hand and kissed her. The effect was that she orgasmed once again. Then she slumped into a sleeping position and gently moaned.

The multiple cock sucking Ella lady above him suddenly came to life again and Roger felt a hand trying to pull him up by his shirt collar.

"Am I too late for some more?" came the voice of aunt Ella's double.

"Yes, you are," answered a dozy voice. "Sorry about that, darling, but we can find him again. He is a visitor and I've noted his visitor number. I think the club should offer him free membership. Never had anything like this before."

————

When Maria called on Roger the morning after their visit to the Club, she announced that she had both bad news and some good news.

"Desley is away, overseas for three weeks, unfortunately, so she won't be able to see you yet."

Roger looked at Maria in her regular black outfit and found it difficult to remember her as the slut who took him to The Club the day before.

"And the good news?"

Maria bathed Roger with her most radiant smile.

"I can take you to the club again, but only if you want to go, Roger. I heard you had a good time with the lady mayor and her assistant. At least, they had a good time with you, or so the rumour goes."

Roger's face took on the amazed look of someone being told an impossible tale.

"They did? I didn't know who they were. Which one was the mayor? Oh, but no! Don't tell me. Better I don't know in case I meet either of them socially one day."

Now Maria couldn't believe what she was hearing.

"You didn't know who it was? I suppose that's possible. If you didn't already know them and it was your first visit to the Club. How funny is that? I can't wait to tell Veronica. She'll become hysterical and start rubbing herself. I can see her now."

Roger was thinking through the various scenarios that tried to answer the questions flooding into his brain. What was the Mayoress doing there anyway?

"Charlotte O'Connor has been a member of the club from the very beginning, as have a number of city councillors. It has been very good for Desley's project, helping her get through the various planning permissions and red tape and so on.

"So, are you up for another visit, Roger."

Roger was still busy thinking through his epiphany moments of yesterday, when vivid memories of his first ever sexual experiences had suddenly come to the fore and expressed themselves vividly when he made love with the two ladies. Surely that was a one-off event. He couldn't count on an epiphany event each time he fronted up to a lady. Maybe he just wasn't cut out for The Club. But then he remembered something he wanted to ask Maria about.

"Maria? I noticed a blond woman yesterday at the club. She was sitting alone down at the front. From my brief observations, she stayed on her own for the whole time. Don't suppose you know anything about her?"

Roger's brain had moved on, seduced by the image of the solitary female who had caught his eye. In truth, for some reason she reminded him of Agnes, his librarian lover he'd met at a book signing at Self-ridges, many years back. Well dressed and demure. And those horn rimmed glasses helped too.

"Oh, Roger, you are funny. Yes, I do know who you mean. That was Yvette. It is well known that she has never been seen interacting with anyone at the club, male or female. In fact she never even talks to people there. Rumour has it that she is highly intelligent and an academic who, at a party a few years back was attracted to a man and ended up in bed with him and immediately fell pregnant. It turned out that the man was gay and this was really an accident from his point of view, and there was no way that he would enter into a relationship.

Roger raised his hand.

"Stop there, Maria. How do you know all this given that you have already said that Yvette is not forthcoming with any conversation. This must all surely be rumour and I'm a little suspicious of rumour. Enlighten me, please."

"Well, Roger, you already know that I do house work for a number of wealthy women. One of them knows Yvette and her parents so she is my prime source of information. Yvette lives with her three-year-old daughter in her parents house in Vaucluse. The parents and a house-keeper look after the child while Yvette is at work at Sydney University. I think I even know what faculty she's in. English Literature, I think. Don't know how I know that. I think that is what it is.

"So Roger, will you be my guest again at The Club? I'm sure there is still a lot there for you to learn about before you get to meet Desley. Do you have any questions at all? Now is the time to ask."

Roger already knew his answer.

"Yes, Maria, I would love to be your guest again and yes I have a couple of questions. Well, probably a lot of questions but most can wait.

"The first one is probably obvious but I don't get it. What happens in the room labelled Home Deliveries. There are three doors, each named after a plant or flower, I think, but they were all locked. What happens in those rooms, Maria."

Maria's face looked a bit sheepish and she seemed uncertain how to answer, staring up to the ceiling while she formulated a reply.

"Ok! More and more of the female members are using the Home Deliveries booths although a number of members still don't really approve of it. There is a sort of stigma attached to the concept. It's seen by those members who consider themselves more superior, as a British working-class activity which is beyond the pale.

Others have got over the shock and even if they don't yet use the rooms, they can appreciate the activity for those in need of it. By the way, those three booths are each named after a flower, Tulip, Buttercup and Primrose."

"Christ, Maria,for God's sake tell me what happens in the rooms. The suspense is driving me mad."

Maria giggled like a schoolgirl.

"Well, have you heard of dogging, Roger?"

Roger's mind took a sharp about face to accomodate what Maria had just said. Yes, he had heard of dogging.

"Are you serious, Maria? Do some members actually participate in this behaviour?"

"Oh yes, Roger, only the female members initiate it of course. But at the club, the activity is very different and we would never use the term dogging.

"Many women share the fantasy of being made love to - fucked, I suppose I should say - by more than one lover at the one time. The difference here is that the male suiters are club members and therefore "approved and certified" so to speak; not a load of stray smelly pervy types normally associated with dogging overseas.

"Not everyone uses the rooms, but more are enjoying it and dare I say that I can sort of understand why. We could perhaps discuss this at another time. Even I am a bit embarrassed thinking about it while talking to you. Somethings in life you just do things, but which you don't talk about Roger, I'm sure you understand that, you being a writer and all.

"But now that you know what the rooms are for, let me tell you how it works.

"If a woman wishes to avail herself of Home Deliveries, she makes a booking at the office when she first arrives and she is allocated a time slot, usually a two hour period to allow time for getting things sorted, along with the name of her room. By the way, she also nominates her preferred number of delivery boys; two, three or a maximum of four.

"The arrival of swipe plastic key cards has made life much easier. Her booking time and details are logged into the system and a message is sent to her mobile approving her so that she can use her card as an access key. Her access, by the way, is via doors in the Gals Only room."

Roger continued staring at Maria.

"So how are men selected to become the lucky delivery boys?"

"Well, again, the computer and magic swipe card takes care of everything.

"Men who have checked in to The Club that day, receive a message on their phones telling them that a female member has made a booking at Home Deliveries for a certain time and in a particular room. A man simply needs to send back a Yes if he is interested. A half hour before the start time, men are advised whether or not they have been allocated a delivery slot by the system's algorithm and if they have, the room name and the time.

"There is more. When more than one woman has booked in, and there could be a number during the day given that there are three booths and quite a few two-hour slots, details of all bookings are sent out to checked-in male members.

"Many men will reply Yes to all of them, improving their chances of getting selected for one. They cannot attend more than one each day. The computer analyses the data and sends out a confirmation to those selected a half-hour before the event is due to begin. There is an option for the men to cancel if they suddenly find themselves otherwise occupied. This enables the computer to issue another person with an invitation and issue the first man with another invitation if another Home Delivery event is available.

"It has all worked very well, so far.

"Does that help, Roger? Any questions?"

Roger was staring at Maria in wonder. Then Maria smiled and answered the look on Rogers face.

"Oh yes, of course there is. Maria laughed, self-consciously, "And the answer is yes, Roger. Twice in fact, and I must say that on both occasions, it was just what I needed. I'm sure more women would do it if only they knew how cathartic it can be.

"Some women I've spoken to think that they need it most at certain times of the month. This might be true."

With his brain in overload, Roger managed to look into Maria's eyes.

"I want to come to The Club with you Maria. Can we go on a Tuesday? I liked Tuesday's at The Club."

Maria took Roger's hand and leant forward and kissed him gently on the lips.

"Tuesday it is. And best of luck with Yvette. You will have to be really good to get that gorgeous creature to speak to you, let alone open her legs.

"And Roger! If all else fails and you can see that me and Veronica are not entertaining anyone, please feel free to come and bother us. I promise we'll do a good job of resisting your advances until we know we must surrender to you. That slut Veronica has already indicated that she wants your cock in her hand and her mouth and in other places too."

Maria started to leave, then stopped and said, "There are still a few things for you to learn about the club, Roger. I've just thought of a couple more.

"There is an unstated code of how the cinema is laid out and used by club members. I've already mentioned how the men hang around at the back and take up the first two rows of seats; rows one and two. Women never choose to sit in those rows.

"Rows ten, eleven and twelve at the front, you know about, and eight and nine are where women go who would prefer to be approached by women. This is not exclusively so, but it is what generally happens and it works very well. Veronica and I often sit in them when we are simply horny for some girl time.

"Rows four and five are known as Shy Way One and Two. They get their name from the fact that this is where the shy men sit. It is interesting how many men are nervous about approaching women and so this is where they sit. Some of them might be self conscious of their bodies, their weight for instance or think their penis is too small. And some might just prefer to be dominated.

"These rows are more popular with woman than one might think.

"The men sit in every other seat, where possible, leaving an empty seat on either side. A woman will cast her eye over the line-up and then go and sit beside the man of her choice and immediately open his fly if it isn't already open, and fondle him. She then either gets him off with her hand or mouth or sits on his cock and rides him. Neighbouring men will often join the couple, opening her bra and baring her breasts and groping her.

"For the woman in a hurry, it certainly beats waiting to be approached.

"Rows six and seven are multi purpose where anyone can approach anyone else. This is probably where the bulk of interactions take place.

"This brings me to the row some members call the Jungle, row three. You probably thought I'd missed it. Firstly, there is a walkway between row three and four, just as there is between rows nine and ten."

Roger took a deep breath, "My goodness, Maria. This is all fascinating information and it would take anthropologists years to document this level of detail while studying primitive peoples. But I'm interrupting, just as you sound as though you're getting to the good bit. Tell me about row three, Maria"

"I will paint you picture, Roger.

"I mentioned earlier that a number of a particular kind of women members looked down on the Home Deliveries booths. We might say that they are generally the wealthier and can I say, snobbier ones.

"We'll call them ladies, I'm sure they would like that. Anyway, imagine a couple of these ladies meeting for lunch and then wandering off to shop at designer shops and exclusive boutiques or visit their hairdresser. Later they pop home to their large houses with their shopping to hang it in her already extensively stocked walk-in wardrobe.

"The woman then removes her one-off designer clothes and showers and puts on a pleasant relatively inexpensive off-the-shelf outfit and drives back to her friends place. There they enjoy an hour or two of sitting beside the pool, nibbling hors d'oeuvres and drinking champagne.

"At around 3.30 they drive to the club in search of that little something they feel they need, to finish off the day. A bit of fun before dinner, telling each other that a girl needs a little fun, that something that they consider is missing in their life."

Roger found Maria's story wonderful, something he could never have written. It was a woman's point of view and he was loving it.

"The two happy ladies, thin and elegant in their light floral frocks and fancy frilly topped light coloured stockings and absurdly high-heeled sandals, enter the cinema hand in hand and then, after parading up and down the aisle like models on a cat-walk in a way that couldn't fail to get them noticed, they settle in seats two and three in row three. The Jungle row.

"One could probably hear the murmur of mens voices and feel the excitement in the air.

Maria looked at Roger and smiled, "Finding this yarn a bit of a turn-on Roger? I admit that I do."

"You bet I am Maria, so please don't stop."

Maria put her hand out and gently touched the lump in Roger's trousers and smiled her angelic smile.

"I think I better shorten the story, Roger.

"It is only moments before a hoard of males move in on the ladies. Very soon, their clothes have been removed and they are kneeling on their seats, minus their cheap skimpy underwear and with four men standing in the walkway taking turns with the rear ends of each of the women. The cock hungry ladies suck the juices from a half a dozen men facing them from behind their seats in row two who are happily groping the women's breasts while the ladies are swallowing their cum with great delight.

"Then two men will wriggle in under the women and the ladies will lower themselves onto stiff cocks while a man behind places his cock in the same stretched cunt or in between the cheeks of their elegant ladylike derrieres, looking for that other welcoming spot. Everything is performed in such a ladylike manner. Even their screams are ladylike, Roger."

Roger and Maria came together spontaneously, fucking like it was their first time.

"I'm happy to be your elegant lady bitch anytime, Roger. We don't need the Jungle. And I hope you will you have enough left to fuck my derriere, darling man? I would so enjoy that."

When the two stopped and laid back, happy and satisfied, Maria finished her story.

"So the ladies who decry the Home Deliveries as lower class dogging, do in fact go dogging themselves, only in a slightly different way. But then, each to their own, I say."

Roger and Maria held each other close and caressed each other's bodies.

"I love making love with you Roger. Make love to me and Veronica together, soon please. I'm sure you will enjoy a threesome. I know we would."

Roger laughed and slapped Maria lovingly on her rear.

"How could a man refuse two such elegant ladies."

"I think I should go to the kitchen and make us a sandwich, Roger. You've made me hungry."

———

Roger was excited about his second visit to The Club. It wasn't just the thought of having an opportunity to communicate with Yvette. That was a challenge that he looked forward to. No! It was something else and he at last admitted to himself that he was at heart, a voyeur.

Watching people doing things that normally they would never do in public was sexually appealing and he accepted that there was an intellectual component although that would be hard to defend. A bit like saying you only looked at men's magazines for the articles.

On his first visit to The Club, Roger was slightly embarrassed to look closely at what was going on. It all seemed so personal and private. But now he realised that everyone in the movie theatre, both men and women, were there for pretty much the same reasons and that what one person was enjoying could be happily observed and even sometimes shared by anyone. Roger was ready for an adventure.

And of course there was the intellectual side of things. Watching something as rare as both sexes encouraging each other to display their base instincts was a very unusual event in our culture. In the past, only anthropologists had observed and written about these sort of behaviours in so called primitive peoples. Now Roger could see it at work in the comfort of a nearby mansion, just walking distance from his house.

Alvie at the front desk, welcomed Roger back.

"Well, young man. Rumour has it that you were a great success on your first visit; not naming names of course. Let's hope this week will be as successful."

Alvie pinned Roger's visitor number on his shirt, taking time to affectionately fiddle with his buttons and straighten his collar.

"Now if there is anything you need, just pop back out here to the kiosk, love. I'm here all day."

As Roger and Maria walked towards the cinema door, Veronica arrived. Roger hadn't really met her properly last week and it was in the dark, so it was a surprise to meet a very slim small youthful looking woman in a very tight fitting skirt and top along with the obligatory stockings with seams, and high heeled shoes. In different clothing she could easily have passed for a university student.

"Pleased to meet you properly, Roger. Maria will try to keep us apart. Selfish bitch! But feel free to sit beside me any time you need a break from your activities. Smaller bites of someone special like me can be just what you need when the bigger girls on offer become over-whelming.

"And you can simply be with me and rest if you want. Just so long as you hold my hand."

Roger enjoyed the woman's wit and, looking at the grinning Maria, replied enthusiastically that he looked forward to such an opportunity.

Roger found Veronica's face especially appealing. While everything about her was fine and petite, Veronica's large brown googly eyes and her wide permanently open mouth displaying two rows of big bright white teeth and framed by her huge stretched-out cupid lips was a siren calling from the shore.

Roger could see that Yvette was not in the theatre, at least not yet, but looking around, he could see that things were starting to happen.

A couple of rows back, a man already had his hand inside a woman's wide open blouse and, without even glancing at him, she unbuttoned herself and lowered her bra to expose her nipples for him. At the same time, she wriggled her backside as she lifted her skirt and reached up and pulled down her knickers. At least, that's what Roger thought he would be seeing if he was closer. Bad light and his rampant imagination could well be robbing him of the true situation, but he didn't mind one bit. He decided to take a closer look.

Roger nodded goodbye to his two lovely companions.

"Don't get into trouble Roger. Come back here for that."

Roger moved leisurely up the aisle, noticing other things happening in almost every row.

In one row close by, two women had uncovered their breasts and each was busily licking and sucking the other. Both were in the act of lifting their legs and pulling up their skirts to provide each other with even greater access to the more intimate parts of their hungry bodies; and their mutual heavy breathing and gasping was audible and, Roger thought, strangely reassuring.

Roger reached the row of seats where the activity that had first drawn his attention was in progress. The couple occupied seats two and three leaving one seat at each end of the row, empty. Roger sat down beside the woman, who, sensing his arrival looked across at him and smiled. Then Roger felt her hand on his trousers and he knew he was now part of the game.

Roger lifted himself up and pushed his trousers and underpants down around his knees, letting his penis stand up, seemingly searching around in the dim light to discover its whereabouts. A hand came and took his hand and placed it on a breast and rubbed the breast with it gently. Then the woman's head turned and looked down at Roger's lap and she immediately reached out and took hold of his penis and began to rub it up and down lovingly.

The man on the other side, let go and raised himself to also drop his trousers and pants to his knees, exposing himself as Roger had done and almost immediately, the lovely lady took hold of him. Then she turned to Roger and leant towards him and whispered, "Kiss me like you love me."

Roger put his spare hand behind the woman's head and pulled her gently to him and kissed her, at first most softly but then, as she responded, the two mouths opened to each other and their passion burst forth.

"Oh, my God. Kiss me like that again."

The woman grasped Roger's penis with a stronger grip. Then she let go of the other man and pulled up her skirt to display a neat little tuft of pubic hair. Then she rubbed herself and in a hushed sexy voice said, "Tell me how much you want to fuck me. You do want to fuck me don't you? You want to very much I know. Say it!"

Roger had no difficulty telling her that fucking her beautiful pussy was the thing he most wanted to do in life which he honestly felt to be true at that moment. At that point, the woman had shuddered, leaving his mouth just long enough to groan before fastening her mouth back on his.

"Come and do it to me now. Put your beautiful cock in my cunt. And don't stop kissing me, you beautiful bastard."

Roger suddenly noticed that another woman had arrived and seated herself at the other end and in just moments she had stolen the other fellows cock and was unbuttoning her shirt and dragging his hand to her breasts.

"All's fair in love and war." Roger thought as he moved down between his lovers stockinged legs. He deliberated about what he would do and what she expected him to do. If she was wanting a cock inside her then cunnilingus was probably not where he should go right now. He slid his cock into her moist vagina and the woman wriggled around.

"Bang me hard my darling. And don't stop kissing me till I cum."

Roger decided that given how she was already hot and excited, he would exercise his usual cock hard in and then hold his end tightly up against her pubic bone, not letting her move away from it. If she was already in a state of excitement similar to what results from cunnilingus, then all should work out to both their satisfaction. And it did.

With their mouths still locked in a never ending kiss, the woman came and then came again. And when she thought she should move back to let him thrust, he wouldn't let her move, and to her great surprise and great happiness, she came again and then again and just kept coming and in the end Roger heard her final exclamation of a great outcry of "Oh Yes!".

Their kissing ended and the woman slumped back in her seat. She gasp and then spoke.

"Oh yes! You really loved me, didn't you, you sexy bastard. Promise you will find me again. My name is Jasmine and I'm here on Tuesday's and Wednesdays. Thank you. That was truly beautiful."

Jasmine rested her hand on Roger face and happily held his still monumental cock.

"You are beautiful Jasmine," replied Roger, purposely forgetting to offer his name. But then he noticed her looking at his visitor number.

"I will remember you number twenty-eight, and I will make sure that you and I go to heaven again. Thank you."

———

Roger had not really looked at the male members of The Club. This might have been because, as a boy one didn't look at the other boys when they were in the changing room after sports. To do so would have attracted unkind comments and elicit aspersions about ones masculinity. And given that most of the men here at The Club had their cocks in their hands as they fiddled around working out what to do next, to look too closely at them could have been embarrassing for both parties.

Two things set the men apart from the average collection of blokes. The first thing was that they were all well dressed and seemingly well off. The second thing was that they were all older men. Even though the joining age for men had been lowered to forty-five, men below sixty were not much in evidence. Roger noted that these older men looked very fit. Most looked as though they exercised regularly and most appeared sun tanned.

Roger guessed that the lack of younger men could be because they were at work during the week, not yet having retired from their jobs. Given that The Club was open every day except Sunday, he wondered if Saturday was when younger men showed up.

There seemed to always be a few men standing up at the back or spread out on the back two rows of seats who seemed happy to just be rubbing their cocks while watching the movie and Roger wondered if, and at what point any of them chose to interact with the horny ladies in the rows further down.

Roger sauntered back down to where Maria and Veronica where sitting, realising as he approached that the two women were not alone. What appeared to be the same two women that Roger had observed making love further up the aisle earlier, had now moved to be on their knees in front of Maria and Veronica. His friends lay back with their eyes closed and their lovely breasts on display. They held their beautiful legs up and wide apart and bent at the knees. Two heads were moving rhythmically between their legs, totally absorbed and slurping with great enthusiasm.

Veronica sensed Roger's presence and opened her eyes and looked up at him and smiled lazily.

"Show me your cock, Roger. I was just dreaming about you. Let me suck you."

Roger undid his belt and let his trousers drop to the floor and then he pushed down his underpants to join them. His cock was still rampant and Veronica's mouth dropped open.

"Oh Roger. You've been a naughty boy haven't you. Where has this been, I wonder. I can smell something nice. What a lucky lady; but she didn't finish you off, Roger?"

Veronica reached out and took Roger's cock in her hand.

"You distinctly told me, Veronica. Don't get into trouble. Come back here for that."

The two laughed, enjoying the gentle joke.

"Oh Roger, you are such a darling. May I finish you off now? I think I should before you get into any more trouble."

Maria opened her eyes and looked across at the two beside her, saw what they were doing and smiled.

"Oh you lucky slut, Veronica, he came back just for you. I'm very jealous."

Roger felt the small hand of Veronica and moments later, she opened her bright red lips and her mouth took charge. Her mouth movements were divine and it wasn't long before Roger erupted deep in her throat.

Veronica's big eyes smiled loving up at him as she gulped and then she held and lovingly licked his cock. As she did so, her flashing eyes moved back under her eyelids and her body stiffened and she gasped as the woman between her legs reached that certain point of no return. Veronica came and Maria came moments later, and the two ladies who had given them both such happiness, clasped each other and fell back on the floor, rubbing each other and calling out.

Veronica came out of her orgasmic trance and looked up at Roger.

"Promise me we'll do that again, Roger. I could happily suck your cock for ever. You are definitely the man I've been looking for."

———

Desley had arrived home from her overseas business trip. She contacted Maria and asked her to arrange for Roger to come and see her. She said that Saturday morning at around eleven would be a good time.

Roger thought about The Club membership. With huge numbers of women working, it was likely that many now worked five days a week right into their later years, but Roger wasn't drawing any conclusions about the age spread just yet. It also occurred to him that quite a number of the wealthy sun tanned older men he'd seen on his earlier visits might be spending time on yachts in Sydney harbour, either their own or a friends.

Roger was a half hour early and the friendly smile from Alvie in the office was welcoming.

"Busy day, Saturdays. I hope you can find something to your liking."

Alvie giggled as she pinned his number onto his shirt. She stared at Roger and Roger wondered what this woman did when she wasn't working. Did she have a husband, perhaps?

Roger wandered into the cinema. Most of the seats were taken and it was soon apparent that some of those who could only comfortably get to The Club on a Saturday, were making up for their lack of access during the week.

Womens heads were bobbing up and down or backwards and forwards while other's had their legs waving in the air while their breasts were being groped and their mouth were sucking on cocks offered to them from the rows behind, their free hands rubbed the cocks of those sitting either side of them. One knelt on her seat as a man shafted her from the back while she rubbed and sucked the two men standing at the back of the seat.

There was a buzz of activity and Roger thought how much it reminded him of when the honey-flow happened in the huge gum tree at his front gate.

There was much more action today compared to what Roger had witnessed on his previous week-day visits. He thought how much more active the women were and noted that they all seemed to be happily engaged, much more noticeably than what he had observed on week days. He pondered if this might be an example of presence of younger members or was it herd mentality, where once a certain number were doing something, then everyone runs off in the same direction, or in this case, everyone rushes to open their bras and their legs.

Roger scanned the cinema for Yvette and it was only at the last moment he spied her and his heart gave a little thump. But then he realised that, firstly, he was on his way to a meeting, and secondly Yvette was sitting in the second row from the front meaning she had placed herself off limits. But then he was happy about where she was sitting.

Roger then wandered up to the entrance door but he still had about fifteen minutes before his interview with Desley, so he turned right and headed towards the room signposted as The Parlour. The room was beautifully furnished and provided six cubicles, each with a large sofa bed along with small fine touches such as a vase of fresh flowers and jugs of fresh water with fresh cut lemons floating in it, glasses. There was a black and white framed print on each cubicle wall. Roger noted that each print was from a collection he had seen in a large volume of work entitled 'Erotic Art From the 17th to the 20th Century', and collected for an exhibition in Frankfurt in 1995.

Each room had its own door and blinds making it totally private. Roger heard loving sounds coming from one cubicle that had its door shut and he thought that this would be the place where he would like to bring Yvette.

———

Meeting Desley was a great pleasure. The very fine looking older woman smiled at Roger and began by congratulating him on 'a certain successful interaction with one of our most respected members".

Roger murmured something about it being his pleasure and he was glad the client had enjoyed it too.

As the two talked, Desley sat behind her large wooden desk holding a pen and occasionally writing on a pad. Maria had told Roger that Desley was in her mid sixties but she could very easily pass for someone at least ten years younger.

"Now, Roger, I've read your book and I've heard a little about your recent exploits and so far, I'd say that you seem to tick all the boxes that will lead to me offering you the job of writing up the story of The Club. I assume we should start with you asking me questions. Is that what you would want, Roger?"

"Yes, Desley, we can start there. We should start by being brief, at least me in my questioning. We can expand on things later. And the first question must be what led you to want to start a female-friendly adult cinema club?"

"Well, Maria might have told you that I run a charity for older and unemployed, pre pension age sex workers. Raising money is not that easy. It's not a cause you can easily sell raffle tickets for or advertise. There isn't a strong sympathetic public to exploit.

"I was looking for something new, then I remembered visiting a porn cinema in London many years ago and being shocked at how awful it was even though at the same time, I was intrigued. It was just a place for desperado's and lonely pervs and the few women that I saw visiting were indeed a sad lot.

"I forgot about it for a long time, then one day I was talking to my brother Arnold who reminded me that he had the finest collection of blue movies on the planet, completely catalogued and cross-reference every which way, and how it was a pity we couldn't capitalise on them.

"It was then that the idea was born. And it fitted in nicely with the philosophy that I was developing regarding womens empowerment. As you know I've always been close to what is generally known as the sex industry but which I prefer to label "essential personal needs services".

Roger watched the relaxed woman, enjoying her facial expressions and easy movements.

"So, Desley, if I might interrupt. In trying to understand the essence of things, what I most want to know is what motivates women to join The Club. In other words, what is on offer that they haven't had access to previously.

And I have a second part of the same question, namely, if - and I emphasise the word if - the excitement for a woman derives from anticipation of something pleasurable but unexpected happening, this means that such events cannot be prearranged because they only work if they are spontaneous.

Roger paused and looked at Desley.

"Well done Roger. You are right on the mark with your question and the answers are not simple but have their roots in an amalgam of elements.

"Firstly, lets talk about the movies. A woman visits The Club knowing that she can sit for as long as she like in complete comfort watching erotic movies. In itself, this is exciting for a woman. She can watch other women be a part of a narrative that, while it is usually predictable, still offers a female viewer the excitement of illicit and taboo action in a darkened room where, if she is so inclined, she can entertain herself with her hands and fingers. I should add that a number of female members never want anything more than to come to watch the movies, ignoring or rebutting moves by males and females to involve them in anything else.

"This is why I instigated the women and couples only front three rows.

"So that is number one.

"Secondly, a woman wants to be wanted and also adored. If being wanted coincides with her already feeling horny from watching a movie, and then being surprised by a would-be suitor touching her arm, then she is given an opportunity to play a game. We could say it's a version of flirting. Resisting the persistent male until he either leaves or triggers a positive response whereby she accepts, in part, some of his or in some cases, her advances. Punishing or encouraging her suitor to make him even more interested is historically part of a woman's game play. It provides proof of the man's serious intent."

Roger moved forward on his chair.

"Let me interrupt you there for a moment. I hear what you say but I can't help feeling that at The Club, there must eventually be an "Oh, not you again," moment as the women confront their suiters.

"I'd like you to address that, Desley."

"Your point was definitely something I worried about a lot when we started and fortunately, the growth of membership has helped considerably. But your question is still valid and I can only give you the answer I came up with.

"Remembering that my interest is in making a place for women to enjoy helps to understand that I am not too fussed about how men react. Not that I don't want the men to enjoy themselves. It's simply that men have a different take on things entirely because of the way their bodies work. They will do whatever it takes to satisfy themselves and not necessarily at The Club. Their drive is simply to touch a female's private parts or be touched by her.

"Coming back to your question, you might not know this but there are twice as many male members of The Club than females. However, the men are restricted to alternate days access which switches each week. For example, if you were rostered for Monday, Wednesday and Friday this week, you are rostered on for Tuesday, Thursday and Saturday the following week.

"This not only provides a much greater number of males for the women to choose from, rotating them means they also know that a man they saw at The Club last Wednesday won't be back there at least until Wednesday fortnight. Women can to a certain degree avoid a person or seek him out. Whatever their intent. So far this has worked well but I'm for ever watching how we can improve things."

This was new to Roger and he was impressed.

"Wow! No, I didn't know that and it certainly sounds like a practical solution to a number of possible hiccups that I can now stop worrying about.

"So now, let me ask about the age of club members. I understand it is currently fifty for women and forty-five for men. So should I presume that the lower age for men is to offset the likely reduced physicality of the older males? Or have I got it wrong? By the way, I have already ascertained that many of the men are taking one of the erection enhancement drugs prior to their visit to the club.

Desley looked kindly at Roger and smiled her wonderful older women-come-motherly smile that so easily excited Roger.

"Yes. Libido is something that we have only limited control of. In fact we have no control other than providing the various enhancements at the kiosk along with a range of dildos in the Gals Room and Parlour.

"Just as an aside, in the early days, we considered putting in a Glory Hole facility. You can probably quickly foresee the problems. A plentiful supply of volunteering strong large cocks would be needed which would require younger men, and given The Club's membership age range, this just wasn't going to happen.

"In some ways, the Home Deliveries room has provided a sort if alternative to the Glory Hole. It's appeal fits a similar group of enthusiasts. The room is slowly becoming more popular but the stigma of what goes on there is probably going to last for some time. On the bright side, it means that we are catering for a wider audience which must, in the end, be a good thing."

Roger chuckled and Desley looked at him quizzically, and asked what was amusing.

"Well I've heard that some woman now refer to it as The Bitchery, partly due to the idea of bitches coming on season, which goes a tiny way towards getting rid of the old connotation of "rough trade".

"It was also mentioned that observations suggested that some women following a monthly cycle in their usage which fitted the in-season concept. Not sure why I'm telling you this but I thought it was interesting.

Desley laughed heartily.

"Well, that's new to me and I do appreciate you telling me. It's amazing what you can miss if you are away for a while.

"I've just being going through the letters in the suggestion box. I sometimes think it was a mistake putting it there at the front counter, but never mind.

It seems from the letters, that a number of female members would like a service that offered them a cock in a private location so that they could satisfy their cock sucking desires. There are some of them, apparently, who would like to meet up with a man who was happy to volunteer to be sucked for at least a good half hour or more. Some men, it seems are in too much of a hurry. They say that getting a good suck is difficult in the theatre and ideally there would be a service that the computer could administer, similar to Home Deliveries.

As it happens, we do have an unused spare room so I'll think about it.

Now, next question, Roger?"

"Right! Now I've read the Guidelines for Membership and found them both comprehensive and impressive. All of the points are made clearly and I have no questions arising from them.

"So for the moment, you have satisfied both my curiosity and my need for information. My suggestion is that I take the outline of what you want me to write and come back to you with a point-by-point outline of what I believe I should write.

"While writing the article looks straight forward, I think we might have to talk through some of the sociological or psychological questions - particularly about women - that we've touched on, just to be sure we both understand what we are wanting to convey.

There are a couple of deep philosophical questions regarding human behaviour that are worth discussing even though no conclusions can be made, nor could references to the studies be mentioned. I refer to recent works on the social lives of the Bonobo monkeys who live under a matriarchal system, and how one can draw parallels with human female behaviour and the Bonobos.

If you are interested, I could drop some reading matter in to you. I would love to hear your thoughts on the subject.

"So! Why don't I come back to you with something this time next week, Desley. And after you've looked at it, you can decide if you think I'm the person for the job."

The beautiful Desley smiled broadly at Roger and stood up and came around to his side of the desk.

"I think I've already decided that you are the one, Roger. But yes, come back next week and we can discuss things, including your payment."

Desley came close to Roger and put a hand on his arm and stared into his eyes.

"The Mayoress said you were a wonderful kisser, Roger. Because of my work and position I have very little opportunity for any sort of social life on the side, so to speak, and I do miss some things. I would appreciate it if you kissed me Roger. And I promise that if you can't do that, it will not affect our business relationship."

Roger was unprepared for this moment and he wasn't really sure how much kissing Desley's words implied. But he responded as was befitting a younger man being invited to attend a special party.

Roger put his arms gently around the well built Desley and drew her to him, all the time looking into her smiling eyes. Roger put his hand behind the woman's head placed his lips on hers and in moments Desley opened up her mouth and the two tongued each other.

Then Desley took Rodger's hands and slid them down over her tight skirt and her very large buttocks. Then she pulled his head down and thrust it into the cleavage Roger had tried desperately not to stare at during their meeting. Roger could smell apples and peaches, and Disney's breasts felt just like ripe peaches as he ventured to touch them with his tongue.

Roger could feel the woman's solid buttocks through her dress and moments later he felt her hands rubbing the very large lump in his trousers. The two clung on to each other and groped one another for some time. Desley sometimes pulled back her head and gasped then quickly sought out Roger's mouth for more kissing.

Roger was about to start unbuttoning Desley skirt but the woman called a halt to their adventure, putting her finger to his lips and nodding her head from side to side.

"We will have a relaxed time together later, you beautiful man. My voluptuous body is wanting to be your stairway to heaven Roger, and I promise it will. Don't forget me."

———

Desley had given Roger full visiting rights for The Club. She smilingly suggested that she wouldn't like to think he was missing out on any of life's essential nourishments. While doing his research he would have every opportunity for erotic dalliances and she said that she expected him to sample them all. Only for his research of course.

It was only to be expected that Roger's erotic disposition would be heightened when he wandered around The Club. He was still trying to answer the question definitively what excited women and drew them to use The Club. In particular what attracted them to accept the advances of men they'd never met before. Men's motivation was an open book. They were driven by mother natures simple programming that ensured that eggs got fertilised, regardless. Women on the other hand, were expected to treat the fertilisation of their eggs with greater thought and responsibility. But then perhaps modernity had changed women's perception of their sexual role? And of course, older women need not play by those rules. More questions than answers seemed to be the proper take on this topic.

Roger reasoned that he needed to put himself into the situation where a woman - any woman - would either reject or accept him. He needed to go in cold and attempt to seduce someone. He smiled to himself as he heard himself say "for research purposes, of course".

It was mid-afternoon and the cinema was quite busy. Men populated the back rows, some holding their exposed cocks and watching the movie whilst also keeping an eye on the activities of the women in the rows in front.

Roger stood at the back and surveyed the scene. A voice inside him barked instructions. It told him to just get on with it and walk down and approach the first woman who was alone. In the end, Roger did just that.

Sitting beside a woman wearing a buttoned-up rain coat wasn't difficult. But what next? As Roger lowered himself into the seat beside her, the woman glanced across at him but gave no acknowledgement, no hint of a smile or even a nod. Then she turned back to continue staring at the cinema screen.

Roger put the woman's age at between fifty-five and sixty. She was thin and her face had that hint of someone who regularly enjoyed a drink or maybe two or three in the evening before bed. Roger believed that whatever people might say, women who drink regularly are more likely to show a deterioration of their body and particularly their facial features than do men; and there was also a cigarette smoke odour, which to his mind wasn't conducive to love-making.

Roger settled into his seat, noticing the thin shiny stockinged legs and the high heeled shoes, showing below the woman's coat. He could smell a perfume mixed in with the cigarette smell which was not unpleasant. Roger ventured a quick glance and he saw that her small mouth was tight and her lips were thin.

Roger waited, wondering what length of time would be appropriate before he made a first move. After what he thought was an acceptable passage of time, Roger put his hand across and touched and gently rubbed the woman's upper arm. He expected an initial rebuff but that didn't happen. Instead, a few moments later, the woman slowly reached up and begun to unbutton her rain coat, her bejewelled fingers flashing as her rings caught the light from the cinema screen. When she stopped, Roger looked and saw that she had exposed a black bra covering a pair of small breasts. Then the woman turned her head and with a stony look at Roger, seemed to indicate that she had made him an offer he couldn't refuse.

Roger hesitated but then he responded. He leant over and began unbuttoning the rest of the woman's coat as the she continued to stare ahead of her. Then Roger pulled back the raincoat to expose her fully, not expecting to discover that the women was wearing neither a skirt nor panties, seeing just a suspender belt and her stockings.

Wondering what the woman would like him to do next or what she expected him to do, occupied Roger's mind for just a moment. Then he reminded himself that to make this totally real, he should be asking himself what he wanted and not be too concerned about her choices. She would express herself in whatever way she felt inclined too.

He placed a hand on a bra cup and rubbed gently, feeling a nipple beneath the satin. Then, with a bent index finger, Roger pulled the bra down on both sides and exposed two upright nipples on tiny flat breasts and instinctively he leant over and took each in turn into his mouth and sucked and nibbled them.

His attention to her nipples seemed not to register with the woman. She remained stony faced and staring at the screen. Roger wondered if he should kiss her but wasn't drawn to the idea for some reason. Her unresponsive manner and his own lack of desperation seemed to add up to a complete non event. Not that Roger thought that his activities so far had been especially romantic or erotically motivating.

Various scenarios crossed Roger's mind as he pondered the situation. Was he already sexually too well nourished? Was he being too stereotypical in his approach? Was the chemistry between them simply wrong? Was he just not showing signs of needing her attention? Suddenly, all was revealed.

Another male arrived and sat on the other side of the woman. His fly was open and his cock was upright and waving about. He placed his lips on hers and his hand plunged in between her legs. The woman reached for the man's cock and rubbed it vigorously and just moments later she pulled him over in between her legs and fed him into her vagina. Then she began to heave her backside up and forward to meet his frantic thrusting and in a few moment, the man erupted and moments later he had disappeared.

All that Roger had witnessed had happened very quickly. Just as he was reviewing his situation, another man arrived with his cock waving in the air. And again, the woman took hold of it and rubbed it vigorously then pulled it down in between her legs and the same scenario was repeated. As the man was about to leave, he announced in a low voice that he would "See you in the Primrose room shortly, Lola"

As Roger moved slowly up the aisle, the woman he had just been with, pushed past him and he watched as she disappeared headed towards the Gals Only room. Roger knew that Lola was heading off to meet her delivery boys and he couldn't help wondering how many there would be.

A voice from not far away called out "Go Lola," and the tone suggested that the caller knew the woman intimately.

Roger decided that this was not his finest hour. He was out of his league and that it would be wise to move away, shouldering the brutal image of his failure.

In many ways, Roger felt relieved. Maybe he hadn't failed after all. Rather he just hadn't succeeded where in fact he should never have been in the first place. He was never going to be enough for Lola. She obviously knew what erotic experiences she wanted and it definitely included nothing like what Roger was fumbling around with. Roger had to admit, he just wasn't hardcore enough.

———

Roger had risen earlier than usual. He had things to do other than continue to outline his fourth novel. That was already coming together, partly in his notebooks but still mostly in his head.

As happened on most morning before rising, Roger's catalogue of important reference points cycled through his brain like an old black and white move.

Firstly, Caroline was going to become a mother in just a couple more months. That could be life changing.

Secondly, he had a deep down and unsettling yearning for the lovely Alice's delightful body probably only because she had called him recently to say that all was good and she was happily looking forward to having his baby. When they had almost finished the call, her voice changed to one he could only describe longing, as she whispered "how nice it was to hear your voice, Roger" before she hung up. He could never get away from the image of her dressed to look like his old lover, Agnes when she came to him for their one and only baby making session.

They had made love as prearranged as part of the baby making agreement. A second meeting was arranged but then interrupted by the virus lockdown, but as it happened, all went well and Alice became pregnant as a result of the three heavy sessions on the day of their first get together.

This yearning was to be ignored and got rid of as it was unlikely to happen now that Alice was with child and Caroline was home. Not that Caroline would object, Roger thought, and she would most likely want to be the third party in the bed.

Thirdly, until lockdown and in the first few weeks of the opening of The Club, Roger had enjoyed the company of the hired help, Maria along with her clubbing friend Veronica. Being at The Club had been invigorating to say the least.

Roger discovered the voyeur in himself and as well, was just beginning to vent the inner sexual adventurer persona that he had no idea was a part of his make up.

Roger stopped running the film. It could go on forever. There were so many delectable moments in the recent past that he knew he should just let go of and get on with what had to be done.

Caroline came in to his tiny office, now moved from the main house to the second bedroom of the cottage.

"Hello darling. I'm sure I've felt the baby moving this morning, so there really is three of us. I guess we had better be careful and not swear or say naughty things or get angry or anything. Do you agree daddy-to-be?"

Roger smiled lovingly at Caroline and beckoned to her to come around the desk and sit on his knee. Caroline sat and put her arm around Roger's neck and rested her head against his.

"You can feel me up a little bit darling, if you feel you'd like to."

Roger laughed and put his arm around her waist and pulled her close. Then he put his other hand on her knee and slid it up under her skirt and quickly found an already damp and welcoming spot between the tops of her legs.

"What more could a man want. A sexy bitch who can also make a pavlova."

Caroline squirmed joyfully on Roger's trouser front.

"If you would like to show a girl your cock, fine sir, she would happily cover it with her wet pussy. And if you did that and she was of a mind to, she would then go and make sir a pavlova."

In just moments, Roger's cock was firmly planted in Caroline's special place and the two wriggled gently around kissing and sighing.

Then Caroline turned and looked lovingly into Roger's eyes.

"I came to tell you that me and the baby are going out in about an hour with Jackie and Miranda. Jackie has booked us in for a pandering session at a beauty parlour in the city. After that we are going for a late lunch and probably some shopping. Is that okay with you, darling?

"Oh yes. I've tried to call Helen in case she wanted to come but there was no answer. If she comes by looking for me, tell her I'm sorry I missed her but I'll be back at around three or four o'clock."

Then Caroline gave Roger an odd look.

"You might not have noticed but Helen and Frederico are going through a bit of a thing, partly because of Sofi and Freya's wanting to see more of Freddy now they are going to have his babies.

"We talked about it and she said she hoped this jealousy thing she was feeling wasn't going to happen with me and Alice.

"I told her that so far, Alice hasn't acted in any way that seemed remotely possessive. I also said that if she did, it might be different for us because she and I are closer in age than Helen and the two girls.

"I'm mentioning it so that if she shows up, you won't be too blokesy. Bye darling!"

Caroline turned back to look at Roger. She was very relaxed, but offered him an odd look and then smiled.

"Come to think of it, Roger, if she does happen to call in, I'm certain that it would be much appreciated by her and me if you were able to be especially nice to her, seeing how lonely she's feeling. You get my drift, don't you darling. Just a last minuted thought. See you later in the day, sweetheart. I'll try to think of something special to bring home."

Caroline blew Roger a kiss and disappeared.

———

Roger had just returned to his desk with his cup of coffee when there was a knock at the door and Helen's voice called out.

"Can I come in?"

Roger heard the door close.

"I'm in here, Helen. Come through."

Helen appeared at the door of his office come spare bedroom.

"Hi Roger. It's so lovely and warm in here. Is the girl around?"

Roger looked up and was immediately smitten yet again with the beautiful wife of his best friend, Frederico. This mature woman ticked more of his boxes than he ever thought possible.

A smiling Helen stood in the doorway dressed in a heavy jumper under a see-through poncho. He noticed her tweed skirt and heavy brown stockings and practical brown walking shoes. Her medium length brown hair had been messed up by the violent winds blowing outside.

"You've missed the girls. They've gone of to do pampering or some such thing that men don't really understand. Caroline told me to pass on that she had tried to contact you but without success."

Helen stared at Roger as though trying to read his inner thoughts.

"Never mind. I'll go and put the heater on in my studio and try to get creative. Looks like you are pretty busy, Roger, so I won't interrupt you."

Roger's response was very quick.

"I'd love you to stay, Helen, that's if you would like to. I'm just going through stuff that Desley gave me. She wants me to comment on the things people have left in the suggestion boxes at the club and report back with my thoughts. It could be fun. You might help me, perhaps.

"After that, I'm about to restart a major project for her that stopped because of lockdown, but I'm putting that off for a couple of days until I get more information.

"Please stay. It's warm here and there are comfy chairs and even a bed if you get tired and need to take a snooze. And I will even attempt to make you a perfect coffee if you so desire."

Roger was aware that he was selfishly wanting Helen to be here with him while at the same time, attempting to fulfil Carolin's wish that he be especially nice to her girl friend.

Helen's stare softened and she agreed that his office was probably the right place to be given how cold and windy it was outside.

Helen came in and walked over to the armchair at the end of Roger's desk, and made herself comfortable, laying her arms on the soft chair arms and crossing her legs.

"Have you and Caroline sorted out your wedding arrangements,

Roger? The last time I saw the two of you together, she was telling you to sod off. I get the feeling that that is well behind you now."

Roger's face made a tight lipped grimace.

"A man never really know where he stands with a woman. But to answer your question, yes, I think our betrothal will happen in the spring, complete with a full lesbian ceremony and service.

"I suspect I'll be the only man there. Oh no. Freddy will have to be best man of course. I haven't asked him yet. I hope he'll be up for it."

Helen seemed to stiffen in her chair.

"You might like to consider a plan B, Roger. Freddy is preoccupied with his other wives to the point of not having time for anything else."

Roger reminded himself that Caroline had told him that Helen was in a difficult space at the moment. He looked at Helen and smiled.

"Thank you Helen. I'll remember that."

He removed the two clips holding the mens and womens notes from the suggestion boxes at The Club.

"Okay, Helen. Are you ready? I'm going to start by just reading quickly through all of them, then we can go back and address each question in detail.

"These are from the mens suggestion box.

"Note one: 'Why can't we have erotic pictures on the walls in the wash rooms instead of large coloured pictures of Bondi Beach, brawny life savers or Uluru?' Signed: Naughty is nice.

"Note two: The mechanism on the toilet paper dispensers is faulty. Please consider another manufacturer. Signed: Fumblefingers

"Note three: My gay brother and his boyfriends would love to join the club but say that have been refused membership by The Club management. Are these grounds for a law suite? Signed: Equality for all.

"Note four: I've heard that queers are trying to join the club. Is this true? If it is, we should all be informed before decisions are made one way or the other. Signed: No way

"Note five: Why do we need bidets in an Australian wash room? We are not French. Signed: Frognot

"Well thank God that's it. I think Desney is right. She should not have installed the boxes in the first place.

"Lets see if the women's suggestions are more edifying."

Helen had responded to the humour of the moment and laughed loudly which encouraged Roger to think that she was likely to relax and enjoy her visit and maybe his company.

Helen got up and came over and stood beside Roger enthusiastically urging him to let her see, "what the girls have to say."

"From the ladies suggestions box, we have;

"Note one: Do condoms get recycled and if so what do they end up as? Signed: Stickyfingers

"Note two: Could we please have deodorant available for sale at the kiosk, particularly men's deodorant? Signed: Nosegay Gertie

"Note three: Could we have a service via the smart card where a woman can book a man for a long session of cock sucking. Men generally are in too much of a hurry to move on to the next bit. Signed: The Pointer Sisters

"That sounds reasonable," Roger mumbled.

"Note four: One man and one woman for extended anal sex sessions in private. Signed: Bottom Draw

"Oh wow! How do I find this woman? My fantasy could be fulfilled after all these years."

Roger heard Helen gasp and looked up at her. Helen was staring at the last entry and then she looked at Roger. She seemed as though she was trying to sort something out in her head. Then she reached down and took Roger's hand in hers and looked at him strangely.

"Is everything all right, Helen?

Roger held onto her hand and looked up at her, waiting for her response.

"I wrote that last one, Roger. I went for a pee just before we left The Club the other day and just couldn't resist adding a suggestion."

The two stared at each other as though they were about to go through a door to an unknown land.

Roger found himself reaching out with his other hand to Helen's leg standing beside his chair. He touched her on her calf and felt the excitement of gently rubbing her stocking covered leg.

Helen let go of Roger's hand and touched his face and looked longingly at him.

"Is that suggestion really what you would like, Helen."

"Oh yes Roger. Oh yes, it really is."

Helen clasped the sitting Roger's head to her bosom as Roger's hand moved slowly up her leg. He didn't want to frighten her or for her to think he was just making out for the sake of it.

"Roger?"

"Yes, Helen?"

"If it is true that we both want the same thing, then I should tell you that at the moment, no matter what I want, I'm feeling quite fragile and vulnerable and could find it difficult to respond to you in the way we both would want. One thing that would help me would be for you to just kissed me, Roger.

"Stand up and kiss me please Roger. I need to sort out my emotions and kissing will do it for me."

Roger stood up and put his arms around Helen, feeling her collapse into him. Then he felt her trembling and heard her sobbing and he pulled her closer. She lifted her head and her eyes shone and she put her mouth on his and the two melted into one another.

After trembling for some time whilst still managing to kiss Roger, Helen moved her head back so that she could look at him.

"I must warn you that I won't be able to stop once we start, Roger. Once I give you my rear you will have me forever. I will want you there and you will want to be there, be it for just ten minutes or for hours on end. If you can give me what I crave then you will never get rid of me."

Helen felt Roger's cock growing in his pants against her belly and she relaxed and smiled and went back to kissing him.

Roger ventured to put a hand down over Helen's thick skirt and massage her backside. Then he lifted her big woollen sweater up to her neck and looked down at her beautiful chest, slowly heaving with emotion. Helen breathed deeply and he noticed she'd stopped trembling. She reached up and moved his head so that she could put her lips back on his and they tongued each other.

"I'm ready, Roger," Helen whispered. "Before you take me anally you will have to fuck me a little bit. It will get things wet for me and I so love to be wet."

Roger heard what Helen said. He didn't want to let her go but he knew he would have to. He wanted what she wanted and they both wanted it now.

Roger reached behind Helen and unzipped her skirt and it fell to the floor. Then Roger held her hand while he stood back to look at her. She was a vision splendid. He turned her around and looked at her backside. Roger was looking at his ideal woman.

Roger knew that he wanted to move on with Helen. He unzipped his pants and removed them along with his boxer shorts and his member stood up tall and straight and Helen stared at it.

"I'm feeling better every moment, Roger. And I can see you are serious. Take off my undies and inspect and touch my rear, Roger. I'm desperate for you to feel me."

Helen reached out and took hold of Roger's cock and whispered to it.

"You are going to heaven and taking me with you. You will become mine and I will become yours."

Helen looked deep into Roger's eyes then she slipped a hand into her knickers and rubbed herself.

"My activities in recent years have only been with women, Roger. This feels very much like my first time and I'm nervous.

"Women accept other womens bodies and behaviour quite easily. So if I tell you that I have a very hairy vagina and that I often make a lot of noise during sex and I sometimes bite people, will that put you off me? Before I can relax, I need to feel secure, Roger. Help me feel secure, you lovely man."

Roger stepped back a little and looked down at Helen's beautiful body. He stared at her strong stockinged legs then with one hand he pushed down Helen's knickers to her knees and uncovered her hairy crotch and with the other he felt her between the legs, bunching her ample bush in his palm.

"How beautiful you are, Helen. And I love your hairy pussy. You know that I've had two years in Italy where hair down here is worshipped, so believe me when I say I will happily worship you. And I should confess that I can be noisey too."

Helen gave a little start and Roger felt her hand grasp him more tightly, and his cock jumped in appreciation.

Helen put her other hand up to his head and pulled his face to hers and opened her mouth and engulfed Roger's lips, then pushed her tongue into him. As she did so she let go of his member and reached down and removed her panties.

"Fuck my bushy cunt first, please Roger. Then you may take my other spot. I want you to fuck it for ever."

Roger moved Helen over to the bed and lowered her, all without letting go of her sweet spot. Then he pushed her legs apart and removed her hand and nestled the end of his prick in her now very wet hairy vagina, and slowly moved it right in. Helen orgasmed immediately murmuring "Already? Oh God!"

The two bodies clasped each other tightly and tongued each other and Helen's body shook regularly with tiny orgasms that she was prone to when excitement overwhelmed her, and which she hadn't experienced for a very long time.

Helen removed her mouth from Roger's. "Oh Roger, this might end up killing me. This is so beautiful I will never want it to end. Spoil me more Roger and tell me that you love me. I promise I won't hold you to anything you say. Tell me you love me and that you love being in my hairy cunt."

Roger needed little prompting.

"How could I not love you, you beautiful sexy bitch? My cock is in paradise. How will I be able to leave it for that other spot at the back. You will still want me in the back, won't you?"

Helen swung her legs around Roger's waist and pulled him into her, then gave a little laugh.

"Oh Roger. You are such a joy. I want you everywhere all at once. But having you in my arse should settle me down. Take it whenever you wish, my darling. Your cock is nice and wet now and my bum is already screaming out for your attention.

"And Roger. If Caroline comes home and finds us like this, don't worry. She put me up to it. She said she was so fed up with seeing me miserable that she insisted that I have you. I love her so much."

Roger had actually suspected something when Caroline had looked at him as she was leaving and how she had commented that she would like him to be especially nice to Helen. "Well, if she does find us, then she will just have to join in," Roger mused.

Roger slowly removed himself from the hairy heaven. Then he kissed Helen lovingly, and lifted up her legs and backside to make her arse easily accessible.

"I want you this way, Helen. I'll role you over later."

Helen wriggled to position herself in readiness, "Yes, sweetheart. I'm ready. Which ever way is fine."

Roger kissed and licked Helen's anus then inserted two fingers and moved them about. Then with both hands, he opened her hole and stretched it a little and peered inside the pink tunnel. Then he entered her, gently at first and then more assertively.

"Oh God! Yes, yes, yes!"

Helen was happy and so was Roger. The tunnel felt wonderful on his cock and he knew that he could spend a long time there, quietly moving his dagger or stiletto as his Italian twins had tutored him.

Roger looked down at Helen's smiling face, both rejoicing in their erotic pleasure.

The two shagged on through the early afternoon with intermittent kissing and shouting. The they rested and Roger brought his new love, cake and ginger beer. Then they looked at each other and Helen rolled over onto her knees again both nodded indicating it was time for more shagging.

"Oh Roger. This is so beautiful. I just want you to shag me forever. Your big cock feels so wonderful. I just want to cry."

Roger rolled Helen over and pulled her up onto her knees and entered her from behind.

Suddenly, Helen burst into tears and sobbed, her body shaking in unison with Roger's shagging motions.

Then Caroline walked through the door.

"Oh my God. How beautiful you both look. But why is Helen crying?"

Helen looked around at Caroline and put a hand out towards her and Caroline responded. She dragged her thick jumper off over her head, unbuttoned her blouse and threw herself on the bed beside her female idol. As she did so, Helen orgasmed for the umpteenth time, dragging Caroline to her and raining tears and saliva on Caroline's bosom.

"I'm so happy, Caroline. Thank you so much. I won't let Roger stop. I hope you don't mind. I hadn't realised how much I needed this moment. He has been so wonderful and I can't stop shagging him. Why don't you lie beneath me and share. I could lick you and you could play with me and him. I would so love that."

Caroline kissed Helen energetically.

"Oh my dearest Helen. Yes please. Let's do that."

Helen pushed her legs apart far enough for Caroline to squeeze between them, then, as Caroline gently fingered Helen's cunt, Helen reciprocated, fastening her mouth on Caroline wet and fluffy special place.

Caroline put her head to one side so that she could peer up at Roger while at the same time, she took his testicles in her other hand. "Love you darling", she called. Then in a semi jocular voice loud enough for Helen to hear, she called out.

"Fuck the sexy bitch, you wonderful man. I can feel you, and it feels as though you are fucking me too. I love it!

"I think you two are cock-in-the arse loving sluts. I think Helen will want this at least once a fortnight. Am I right Helen? Don't bother answering. I know I'm right. We'll arrange it."

Then Caroline arched her back and enjoyed a very strong orgasm triggering the same thing in Helen causing her to give way to her final surrender as she collapsed on top of Caroline, and leaving Roger sitting back with a still hungry cock.

"Sorry, Roger."

Caroline seized the opportunity and rolled herself out and around and pulled her lover on top of her and, gripping Roger's cock firmly in one hand, she led him to her own little door to heaven nestled between her buttocks, and fed him in.

"Finish yourself off there please darling, as hard and as soon as you like. You deserve it, sweetheart. Thank you. I love you."

It was only moments later that Roger orgasmed inside his lover who lifted her body to meet him and cum with him. And Helen added a small scream and her body shook violently in unison with her two loves.

So ended Helen's first of many loving moments with Roger.

———

Helen had become very excited watching Roger bugger Caroline who had only recently discovered the joys of anal sex and of course the two women would share their orgasms and Roger in the ultimate loving relationship.

Helen loved to touch the two of them when they were making love, Caroline's clitoris and Roger's testicles being much favoured along with breasts and buttocks.

Arrangements were made for Helen to come and stay over on those nights when her husband, Frederico was with either of the two pregnant ladies, Sophie and Freya.

Sometimes Helen and Roger would be given space in the afternoon to be alone but often they would invite Caroline along for the ride and the three would shag for a whole afternoon.

And whilst the double bed was fine for three people making love, after a night of excitement, Roger would remove himself and cross the room to sleep in the single bed leaving the two women cuddled up in their post orgasmic slumber.

Who ever woke up first, went and made and delivered a tray of hot drinks then Roger would join the two women and they would all cuddle up and most times they would fall into a second slumber.

———

Rogers life had definitely become more hectic since accepting the job of writing up The Club prospectus.

Life at home had become second to the new writing task and even the moments with Caroline on Skype seemed remote to his senses. Caroline said that her belly was now a noticeable bump but that she was feeling super healthy. She was due back in Australia in about a month and laughingly suggested that she would be well and truly ready for his cock, or daddy-thing as she was now calling it, when she arrived home.

Roger hoped to have The Club project totally off his plate by then. Desley was happy with the finished manuscript suggesting only a few minor adjustments which he had done. The typesetting had been completed except for the corrections and the interesting collection of photos had been strategically placed through the text.

Arnold had been put in charge of processing and enhancing the pictures a few of which were taken surreptitiously by Desley inside a porn bookshop cinema in Brixton. It showed the abject horror of that level of adult entertainment, contrasting it with coloured photographs of the beautiful interior of The Club.

As a document that Desley wanted to use to sell the concept to franchisee's around the globe, it contained enough to wet appetites but not the full details of the management structure. Those details would be available to people who bought a franchise along with her and Arnold's personal attention where needed.

Caroline had asked Roger on Skype, how he was going with the project. He had mentioned it to her after they had had a conversation about money when he wanted to let her know that he did get other work apart from the books he'd had published. However, he'd thought twice about telling her everything about The Club, only that it was an expensive private club. Roger was pleased that she hadn't bothered to ask for more details.

The day came when Desley called Roger to say that she had a cheque for him and that she wanted to give it to him in person at The Club on the upcoming Sunday afternoon. They would have the place entirely to themselves, she said.

"I've long wanted to play out the part of a club member, she said over the phone in her seductive mellow voice. I hope you will indulge me, Roger. In fact, it would be the perfect time to play out a fantasy from your second novel that got me so excited."

Roger thought for a moment. He guessed what Desley was referring to. That was the bit he had had a bit of bother with his editor over
the subject of incest but by making the protagonists very distant relatives helped get it through.

Suddenly, the idea appealed to Roger although he wasn't certain
why. Was it for the right or wrong reasons, he wondered. Followed by,
but what were the right reasons?

"Let me guess which part, Desley. You would like me to play uncle
Luigi and you be Carlotta?"

"Yes!" came back Desley's emphatic reply. Would you do that for
your little university student five-times removed niece? She so
wants it."

"We don't have her two wicked aunts to hold her down on that
first occasion that her uncle does naughty things to her,
unfortunately."

"Just talk me through it when the time comes you dunderhead,
laughed the now excited voice at the other end of the phone. And by
the way, will Luigi be happy to cope with a much larger uni student I
wonder?"

"I'm sure he will welcome a size increase, dear lady. I just happen
to know that he would."

Desley giggled excitedly down the phone.

"Can we say three o'clock on Sunday afternoon. I'll leave the main
door open and you can lock it from the inside. I'll be in the cinema
down in row four. See you then, uncle Luigi."

———

When Roger walked into The Club on Sunday afternoon, he noted
how eerily quiet it was. The hushed tension and hint of excitement
that permeated the place when you came in on other days was missing.
But that didn't matter. Roger knew where to find what he was looking
for.

What no one but Roger knew about the Luigi and Carlotta inci-
dent - even his editor - was that it was based on an event that really
happened to him when he was in Italy.

Loving exploits with older Italian ladies in black and organised by his delightful older woman friend and lover Martina, in Positano, had included monthly visits to the Rossi sisters, Giulia and Arianna. Giulia and Arianna were in their mid fifties and were of independent means, owning quite a number of cottages and two trattoria and a ristorante in the region. Neither had felt any need to . Their strong female bodies enjoyed whoever they selected to bring home, be they a man or a woman.

The Rossi sisters made quite a fuss of Martina's friend Roger when he came to visit and he occasionally wondered whether he had the stamina to keep going, swapping between the two pairs of legs waving at him from on high, beating the air in anticipation while the two excitedly called out who-knows-what in Italian. But Roger had quite early in life, learnt to forego his own orgasms in favour a yogic withholding strategy, giving him the opportunity of being able to enjoy lovemaking for an extended period and this ability served him well when he visited the sisters.

One day when Roger arrived at the Rossi house for a weekend visit, he was pleasantly surprised to find that a young woman was staying with them. The constantly smiling girl was a student at the University of Salerno at Fisciano and she was the daughter of a distant relative of the Rossi family. She was a big well-built girl who hadn't learnt about the pitfalls of eating too much pasta, nor the difficulties of fitting into her blue and white check student skirt and long white socks; and her bulging blouse verged on the indecent, or at least that is how Roger saw it, or perhaps one should say, appreciated it.

Roger was introduced to the young woman by the sisters in very broken english but fortunately, the young Carlotta spoke perfect english and immediately took over proceedings. Carlotta listened to her aunts enthusiastic commentary then looked at Roger.

"My aunts speak very highly of you, sir," Then the young woman coloured up and grinned as she decoded the aunts' ongoing discussion.

"What are they saying, Carlotta?"

The red faced young woman lowered her eyes to the floor then murmured that she preferred not to say because she thought it was too personal.

That evening at dinner, the Sangiovese flowed and the housekeeper served a sumptuous meal and all were merry and bright.

The women had dressed up in their finery and Giulia and Arianna seemed intent on impressing on their young visitor the forbidden carnal delights that a grown-up woman deserved to enjoy. At least that is what Roger seemed to pick up from the raucous laughter and banter and the fact that Carlotta's face was bright red most of the time and that the large girl - bulging in her tight clothing - seemed never sure whether to laugh or cry.

It was later in the evening, when the dishes had been cleared away, and when Arianna came around to Roger and made him move his chair out from the table before putting her hand on his trousers, that things began to hot up. Giulia followed, dragging a protesting Carlotta with her.

Roger admitted to himself that he had drunk more than he had planned. He seemed to find himself grinning stupidly at all three ladies and moments later he looked down to see Arianna holding his cock and waving it at the confused Carlotta who had been pushed down to kneel with her head close to Rogers proudly waving member.

The wild-eyed Carlotta and her aunt Giulia watched as Arianna put Roger into her mouth and sucked him. Then the two pulled Carlotta's head over him and Arianna pulled Roger's cock up to touch Carlotta's lips while Giulia held the girls head firmly in position to complete the task at hand. Roger felt Carlotta's lips open and her mouth slowly take him in and then the two tipsy sisters cheered and congratulated Carlotta on her first cock sucking adventure.

The Rossi sisters moved away to find and refresh their glasses and Roger stared down at the source of the beautiful feeling on his cock. Then he felt the young woman's mouth let go and she lifted her head and looked up at him with her pretty face smiling coyly and whispered, "Am I doing it right, Roger?"

Roger assured Carlotta that what she was doing was indeed being done right. "You are sucking me beautifully, Carlotta. I love it," he whispered back. Carlotta smile broadened and she went back to her sucking, even venturing to run an exploratory hand under his testicles and lovingly rub his balls.

It was only a short time before the sisters returned. They stood and smiled at the now enthusiastic girl's head moving rhythmically up and down. Then they looked at Roger and one said, "Is good? Si?" Then they whispered in Carlotta's ear and the girl stopped sucking and stood up and smiled lovingly down at Roger.

"I think we are expected on their bed, Roger. I will if you will?"

As the sisters marched Carlotta down the passage way to the bedroom, Roger lifted himself up onto his feet and followed. He attempted to think about what was happening but didn't get very far.

Giulia appeared and took his hand and led him to the bedroom. Arianna lay on the bed holding Carlotta's head between her legs. The young woman seemed to be enjoying herself and Giulia left Roger and joined them. First she removed the kneeling Carlotta's blue and white check skirt and her knickers, displaying the girls very large and beautiful rear end including her near-hairless pussy. Then she pushed her face into the girls vey slippery looking vagina and ravished her with her mouth.

Roger stood at the side of the bed desperately trying to focus. The only part of him that seemed to function was his stiff penis which, unusually, seemed impervious to the effects of the alcohol. He thought he felt hands guiding him onto the bed but that was definitely the last thing he recalled.

When Roger woke in the early hours, he found himself in the bed and cuddled up to the gorgeous soft body of the naked Carlotta. The young woman was sleeping soundly while holding Roger's half erect cock with one hand while the other propped up a large breast near Rogers lips.

A gentle exploration with his hand discovered that one of the sisters had a hand between Carlotta's plump thighs and the other was holding one of her sisters breasts. All were happily sleeping.

Roger had obviously passed out and missed the party.

Roger yawned and lamented his absence from whatever happened. Then he smiled and reasoned that if the women had enjoyed their time with him when he wasn't really there, then it was likely that they would all be happy to do it again, even if only to show him what he had missed.

And things turned out exactly as he had thought and that evening the performance had been repeated only with Roger definitely less inebriated and fully awake.

Before Carlotta left a couple of days later, and when the sisters had taken a trip to the shops, the young woman came up close and said to Roger that, while they were alone and because she was leaving that afternoon, would he please fuck her. She said she wanted it without the assistance or interference of the sisters to which he replied in the affirmative as he took the earnest young woman's hand and led her to the bed.

First Roger enjoyed exploring Carlotta's delightful body. There wasn't a spot where he wouldn't have been happy just rubbing himself against her. And he delighted in licking those chubby and prominent parts surrounding her pussy. But he knew the two had only a limited window of opportunity and he led the charge with his cunnilingus act, watching the flesh on her delightful big body roll around. He followed with his hard-in penis finale. Carlotta screamed and threw herself about as she experienced a series of multiple orgasms.

When they had finished and were lying back on the sisters' big bed, Carlotta announced that she was going to come down and visit regularly. But then she was silent for a moment. Then she asked Roger where he lived. And when he gave his address at Positano, she excitedly turned to him and asked if she could come and fuck him there at the weekends, to which he replied that much as he loved the idea, he was only there for another three weeks as he was returning to London. Carlotta was at first devastated but then she laughingly commented that maybe her aunts would find her another nice cock like his. Then, as she pondered all the options, Carlotta announced, "And in the meantime, we can do a lot in three weeks."

Roger grudgingly confessed that her getting introduced to another nice cock by her aunts was all very likely, and that three weekends of fucking the large young woman would suit him just fine.

———

When Roger walked down the aisle to be with Desley, he couldn't have imagined how things would be.

Laying back in her seat, Desley was a picture of Roger's erstwhile dreams of Carlotta.

Desley had pulled up her blue and white check skirt displaying her large white legs and her cotton tails, the crotch of which her hand was gently massaging. Her white blouse was unbuttoned and pulled right back displaying her giant breasts standing like vanilla blancmanges and displaying a pair of nipples that were set in a large circle of pinky-brown flesh that called out for Roger's mouth.

Desley looked up at Roger lovingly.

"I've even shaved my pussy, uncle Luigi."

Roger looked down on the scene and, as had happened to him in the recent past, he slipped happily into another epiphanous moment and believed he was really with the now carnally enlightened Carlotta.

"Well, Carlotta. What will uncle Luigi do first to his beautiful girl? Maybe he should kiss her."

Roger's time in Italy had provided him with a believable Italian accent

Roger bent over Desley and found her willing mouth and they tongued each other, passionately, just as Carlotta had kissed him after she had discovered how much she had enjoyed his cock for the first time. As he did so, each hand took hold of a nipple and tugged them upwards then he took turns sucking on them.

"Oh, uncle. I'm feeling strange all over. Will you show me your cock, please uncle?"

Roger unzipped his trousers and removed them. Then he took hold of Desley's hand and wrapped her fingers around his member, feeling her tremble and gasp with excitement.

"Now uncle Luigi wants Carlotta's beautiful pussy."

Roger knelt down between Desley's legs and did his cunnilingus thing. Unconsciously, he wasn't expecting a big reaction, considering Desley's age and likely vast experience, but her large body began to heave and tremble and suddenly she pushed herself up against his face and came, yelling, "Oh yes, uncle. Yes!".

"What a darling girl you are, Carlotta. Uncle wants to fuck your pussy now, you beautiful little slut."

Roger removed his cock from Desley's hand and slipped it inside her welcoming cunt. He looked at her beautiful countenance and thought how peaceful she appeared, her eyes were closed and her mouth was slightly open, breathing in and out as he slowly shagged her.

"Give me a nipple you naughty girl. I want to bite you."

Immediately, Desley thrust a giant nipple at his mouth and Roger gorged on it. Roger slowed and then did his hard fuck trick, holding his member hard up against the top of Desley's large hairless mons and not letting her back off. Desley squirmed and tried to get away, but then she let out a scream.

"Oh, uncle Luigi. You are fucking me to heaven. Don't stop."

Desley pulled her breast from Roger's mouth and pulled his head to hers and smothered him with wet kisses.

"Oh, God! This is so beautiful uncle. Tell me you will want to fuck your little slut again like this. Say it, Uncle Luigi."

Roger waited a few moments. Then speaking as uncle Luigi, he answered.

"If, when I roll you over and fuck your beautiful arse Carlotta, and you tell me that you love it, then I will decide if we should do this again."

Desley shook with excitement, "Oh my goodness, I soo love this."

Roger waited a little longer, letting Desley cum again from his hard-in shagging. Then he made his next move.

"Now you horny little bitch, let uncle roll you over and sample your other wares. His cock is hungry for what you are hiding from him between your beautiful buttocks. Tell him you want it. Go on, say it."

Desley was squirming, torn between wanting a final orgasm before Roger withdrew, and the excitement that uncle Luigi was suggesting he wanted to do to her bottom.

Carlotta squeaked her reply.

"Oh, yes please uncle. I've been dreaming of you fucking my big lonely bottom. Do it to me, uncle Luigi."

Roger looked down on the totally enraptured woman and he leant forward and kissed her passionately. Desley groaned and thrust her tongue into his mouth. But then he let her go and rolled her gently over onto her tummy and then he lifted her so that her knees where on the floor and her backside looked up at the ceiling.

Roger looked down on a backside like no other he'd seen since Carlotta's.

Even at her age, Desley had managed to keep her body in very good shape and her rear-end was flawless. He was about to reach for his trousers and the tiny bottle of lubricant, but then, when he parted Disney's buttocks he saw that the shiny pink anus had already had a visit from a lubricating squeegee.

Roger rubbed his cock up and down the crack between Disney's buttock cheeks while at the same time, reaching right round the large woman's hips to cup her chubby pussy in his hand. He fondled it gently and gently bit into Disney's neck. The woman shuddered and moaned and muttered something but he couldn't make out what. Then she called out.

"Oh uncle Luigi! I love you so much. Please put your tongue in where you want to put your cock and make me a very happy girl. Oh yes, uncle, give me more please."

Roger obliged, licking Desley beautiful anus and dribbling saliva into it.

"Now, Carlotta. Uncle's Luigi is having your backside. Are you ready?"

"Oh yes, uncle. Do it to me, please."

Roger's cock slipped easily into the cavernous backside doorway. It briefly crossed his mind that he was traveling down a well-worn tunnel and that Desley had enjoyed anal sex for a very long time.

Roger had been happily having his way in Disney's secret place, almost forgetting he was uncle Luigi. Then came Carlotta's voice.

"Uncle Luigi?"

Roger took his time inside Desley arse. It was a truly wonderful place to be and he really would have liked to stay there for longer.

"Yes Carlotta. What is it?"

"I want to get you off uncle. Please let me."

There was a silence as Roger considered the offer. He would be happy to cum here in her beautiful backside but he knew he shouldn't be selfish.

"Yes. All right Carlotta. Are you ready for it?"

"Oh yes, uncle Luigi. I'm very ready."

Roger moved back so that Desley could roll back over and when she did so, he couldn't resist pushing his face into her vagina and giving her another orgasm. Then he pulled out and waved his penis at her.

"Here, Carlotta. Here is a present for being such a good girl."

Desley took hold of Roger's cock and pulled it up to her mouth and began to suck him off.

The two gazed into each others eyes, contentedly knowing that these two adults had enjoyed a fantasy together and that it could quite likely happen again.

———

Roger had savoured a number of beautiful backsides during his time in Italy where, after he'd shagged them in his special ways and they had orgasmed, his ladies in black would turn and look at him with their special beautiful smiles and utter the word 'Culo', rolling over on their stomachs and pushing themselves up on their knees and presenting Roger with a perfect view of their naked rear ends, their arses and their loving fluffy triangles.

Never did he disappoint them and over time and with a sometimes difficult instruction process because of language differences, the ladies educated Roger in the preferred ways of pointing his dagger, or stiletto, when once he'd entered that other special place that women have to offer a man.

———

It was some weeks later, at the end of a business meeting with Desley late one Sunday afternoon, and when they were discussing many things, Roger had somehow let slip his intense enjoyment of that moment in Desley's backside. To his amazement and pleasure, the delightful woman walked around to him and put her arms around him and kissed him passionately. Then she bent over the end her desk and lifted her skirt. Roger's eyes feasted on her silk covered legs, the suspenders and the black knickers with the lacy trim.

"Pull down my knickers, Roger. I would love you in my arse right now, please. In fact I'd love it if you fucked my arse as often as you liked. Don't forget me. Anytime I'm free I'll be more than happily to bend over and make my derriere available for our mutual pleasure."

Roger and Desley shared their anal play with enthusiasm, both giving an occasional shudder as each experienced those special feelings that people who know how these things work can really enjoy.

———

It was the end of June and in a meeting with Desley, owner of The Club, Roger had been asked to proceed with the preparation of a similar booklet to the one he had written for The Club at the end of the previous year. This new booklet would be for The Dunking venue in which Desley had a small financial interest.

The Dunking was the first ever known commercial gated dogging community as far as anyone knew. It was designed and opened by Sally Bloomingdale, a friend of Desley's who had visited a semi-private dogging community event in the grounds of an old church just west of Goulburn.

Sally's late husband was a property developer. Claude Bloomingdale had purchased a large open span warehouse at low price thinking he'd sell it on when the time was right. He then came up with idea of turning it into the first ever indoor camping venue. He began to develop the idea until his grown up children explained to him the real reasons that people went camping, at which time, coincidently, Claude suddenly took ill and died in hospital of a heart attack.

When Sally eventually visited the site with the solicitors working on the disposal of the Bloomingdale company assets, she was suddenly inspired by memories of her visit to the dogging event in Goulburn and immediately had a vision of what was to become The Dunking.

The Dunking had opened on only three occasions prior to the lockdown as a result of corona virus, but was now scheduled to reopen in July.

Sally Bloomingdale approached the owner of The Club via a mutual friend and she and Desley got on very well. Sally was looking for advice, in particular, how to attract more men so as to make it sufficiently interesting for women.

It was a marriage made in heaven. In return for a stake in the venture and the assurance that the opening hours of The Dunking would not conflict with those of The Club, Desley provided free tickets for two visits to The Dunking to all of The Club members. There was also an offer of a discount on a first year's subscription to The Dunking. The response was overwhelmingly successful and on the third and last week of being open, The Dunking enjoyed a massive increase of visitors, many of whom then applied and paid for membership.

This was Roger and Desley Leigh's first get together in eight or nine weeks. The last time was when he and Desley enjoyed themselves acting out two characters from Roger's last published book in a steamy get together one Sunday afternoon at the club.

"Whilst I believe The Club will always be the better money spinner, I do believe that Sally's idea will be popular and could easily become a successful franchise proposition.

"Now as well as that job Roger, I wondered if you wouldn't mind taking these notes from the suggestion boxes at The Club and having a think about them. As you know, there is a box in each of the male and female wash rooms. In hindsight, I'm not sure that they were a good idea but anyway, we are stuck with them for now. And in fact there are a couple in there which I will think about seriously."

Desley handed Roger a large manila envelope containing the messages.

"Happy to do that, dear lady. Will that be all, Desley?'

Desley looked at Roger with her wicked smile she saved only for moments like this.

"Well of course there is, Roger. But I have another meeting in fifteen minutes so we don't have time. But I'll make sure that we do on our next catch up."

The two stood up and Roger decided that he could happily give Desley a kiss on the cheek at least, and stepped forward and smiled.

"May I at least kiss you please madam?"

Desley put her arms around Roger and pulled him to her and pushed his head down into her cleavage.

"Of course you can, you randy bastard. You know damn well I'm up for it."

Then she lifted Roger's head and the two tongued each other while he rubbed her backside and she lovingly massaged the front of his trousers.

"Until next time, then. Desley?"

"Yes. Sooner rather than later, I hope."

———

"There are challenges involved in getting The Dunking project up and running that we hadn't foreseen."

Roger was in the first meeting with Desney since he had taken himself and Maria on a dogging expedition to The Dunking in preparation for writing up a promotional booklet for the venue.

"Wild dogging is what I will call straight dogging in public places. We know that this activity has some undesirable features, at least to the more sensitively inclined. Private dogging, or dunking, needs to confront and remove the not so nice aspects of the activity to make it universally attractive. I really mean simply an activity that every one can at least understand even if they choose not to be a participant.

"The most obvious shortcomings are the lack of choices for women. From the little I know, Wild doesn't take what women might want or like, into account. Often there is either a degree of coercion by male partners or if not, it attracts a particular type of woman to whom most other women would not seek to identify with.

So what are the obvious changes required to make private dogging acceptable to a wider audience.

I'll list them only briefly now but for wider discussion later.

The first must be the choice to have or not have, an interaction with somebody. Being able to easily and comfortably refuse a proposition. This is catered for at The Club by the rule of denying someone access three times.

The second is the option for interactions by women with bisexual women. This is well catered for at The Club.

These two items are probably the most important. If the private dogging community is to succeed, it must address the two issues ahead of any others.

Taking everything into account, I can't recommend The Dunking for you to invest in. Perhaps things will sort themselves out but it will take time.

In the meantime, I do have a couple of suggestions. The first is that The Dunking offers one night a week to the Lesbian community and one night to the Gay community. Depending on the response, another night could be for all who identify with the LBGTQI set.

A second suggestion is that on general public nights, a smaller area is fenced off with a gate that can only be opened by a female member's card. On that side, women can park alone or with female friends; no males allowed. Women who arrive in the larger general area with a male partner can sneak off and have access to the female area if they suddenly have an inclination to do so.

# 5

## LOVE OR LUST

MARY AWOKE TO A DIFFERENT WORLD. She felt different. Hungry!
At first she thought she was simply hungry for food but then she had
another thought. She wasn't hungry for food, Mary wanted something
else, something she could touch and feel. Mary wanted to feel another
body. And the feeling was really intense.

Mary touched herself, her breasts her thighs, her sex. Then she
thought about her new medication. Her doctor had prescribed a
course of hormone replacement therapy when Mary went to her a
week ago and said that she was feeling a bit run down and out of sorts.

Doctor Meg had smiled and written a prescription and told her to
get straight back to her if Mary thought that the dosage was not right.

It wasn't as though the world had really changed. Yes, Sophie was
pregnant and this was now a factor in their relationship. The two
women were still lovers but less often did they roll around in the bed
together. They were indeed now living like an older married couple.
Both women were handling it quite well. Neither complained about
not getting what they used to have and they both still cared very much
for each other.

Mary was also aware that things had change for Sophie since her encounter with Frederico in Helen's studio when Freddy was on his way home from giving Mary her sexy birthday present.

From being a twenty something year old woman who had never been with a man, Sophie was now carrying Freddy's baby from that once chance accidental hook-up and now Mary sensed that Sophie was in love with Freddie and thought about him constantly.

Mary wondered if Helen realised how deeply Sophie was in love with Freddy and did Freya also know how Sophie felt about the man who was also fathering her future child. Did Freya also carry these loving feelings for Freddy? Had Helen omitted to consider the emotional consequences of what had happened?

All this was vitally important but in the short term, Mary's day to day emotional and physical needs were rising up and likely to take over.

Mary feeling so horny was now a thing she could no longer ignore.

Other things had changed recently, too, although in this instance Mary regarded it as a positive rather than a negative. Her long time friend Janice was now permanently employed at a a nursing home and so the timing of their usual morning coffee and their loving romp on the bed had necessarily moved to a different day. But it wasn't just the timing that had changed. Janice's new job had made her a different person in the bedroom. She was no longer simply the compliant receiver of Mary's lustful advances. Janice now asserted her self in many different ways, bringing home her experiences with her lesbian boss and her many adoring nursing aids.

Janice brought unwashed stockings, still bearing the perfume of her little nursing aids creaming on her legs, and rubbed them against Mary's face while recounting in vivid detail how she made the girls cum on her.

Everyone knew her as Sister Janice and thought she had been a nun and this ruse had been the reason for many of her sexual encounters.

Mary was now also the recipient of a number of semi-violent manoeuvres that Janice brought from her encounters with her boss. Janice tied Mary up with silk chords and plugged both of Mary's orifices at the same time as she whipped her with a small flagellator.

Mary screamed and threw herself about but when it was all over, she melted into Janice's arms, sucking the woman's tiny breasts while sobbing happily while her genitals still throbbed as she enjoying the aftermath.

Mary made changes too. Janice had always refused to try anal sex, but now that she was experiencing more erotic experiences, she found herself encouraging Mary who was now at last able to let herself go mad on and in her lovers magnificent bubble-butt derriere.

"Oh, Janice, you beautiful slut. I want to ride you like this forever."

"Ride me like this for as long as you like Mary. I'm converted and I want more. Fuck my arse hard you big bitch."

Janice and Mary now seemed closer than they had ever been and over cups of tea and coffee, Janice told how her subterfuge as an innocent nun had begun when she was at Mary's birthday party and jokingly suggested it to Maria and Serina who were both most attentive. Going home with the two women and having a sexual fantasy moment with the hot mother and daughter, pretending she was one of their naughty convent school nuns led eventually to Janice getting the job at the old priests' home.

Mary swore to keep this information secret, especially as she was now the beneficiary of Janice's ever expanding sex life.

So what was this hunger? Mary had her suspicions. It wasn't just the new medication but rather the new more passionate and daring responses she and Janice were exploring. Mary's sexual emotions where being slowly drawn towards a more animal lust where anticipation and not knowing what would happen next, could cause excitement. Mary wanted surprises in her sex life.

------

Maude had hired Mary to look after the daily running of the music school premises for the four days that she was going to be away. There wasn't a lot to do other than make sure that the current nine residents' coming and going went smoothly. Someone needed to be there in case of an emergency. Plus there were occasional inquiries by phone or mail to which Mary would respond with a mailing piece and friendly conversation or simply provide information by email.

There was a note saying that a new person might be checking in. Carmela Russo was a young singer from Griffith in central New South Wales. She would be delivered by a friend sometime over the weekend and most likely in the early afternoon. Carmela was training to sing opera and was already a well known teenage performer in her Italian community back home in that now famous fruit growing region south-west of the Blue Mountains.

————

Mary wandered into the shady hallway of number nineteen. She thought she was alone but then the door of number one opened and the friendly face of Maria appeared.

"Hi, Mary. Just finishing up before I head off to another job. I'll be away only a couple of hours then I'll come back here. Grandpa Aldo and his friend Giorgio are working in Maude's garden today so I need to keep an eye on them. Italy is going soccer crazy at the moment because of the European cup. The Juventus versus Real Madrid match is all the men talk about. I just need to make sure that they work as well as talk football.

"Mary, you look a bit down. Are you okay?"

While Mary knew Maria and Serina quite well, they had never had intimate conversations. There was no reason. It just hadn't happened. Mary only recently became aware from a conversation with Janice that there was more to the two women than she had ever imagined, interestingly, in a sexual context.

"I've just started hormone replacement therapy, Maria, and I'm not sure whether or not the dosage is right. I feel a little bit agitated, Maria, or more truthfully I should say that I feel decidedly horny."

Maria's smiling face looked at Mary intently.

"That is interesting Mary. Damn! I forgot to water Maude's potted palm. Follow me in here for a moment Mary while I fix it."

The two women moved back into the room and Maria filled a

watering can from the bathroom. Then on the way back she went up to Mary and put her face close to Mary's.

"More often than not, these things can have a simple solution, Mary."

She continued staring intently at Mary then turned slowly and moved over towards the potted plant.

"I find that when I feel like you are feeling Mary, I make myself reach out for what I want."

Mary listened as she watched Maria bending over in front of her to water the plant, noticing the woman's neat and shapely figure.

"I think if you see something that grabs your attention and you know that you want it then its best to just take it while you can, Mary."

Maria placed the watering can down on the carpet and while still bent over, then took hold of the hem of her skirt and lifted it up and back to display her perfect bottom to Mary.

"You are more than welcome to put your hands anywhere you want Mary. I know I would love it. I'm horny most of the time dear lady so you can please me as well as yourself."

Mary gasped and she stared at the vision in front of her. Maria's backside was beautiful. Without a second thought, Mary moved forward and placed both hands on the waiting woman.

"Oh, Maria, you are such a darling. Oh, my God, yes. This is exactly what I need." The feeling of Maria's naked bottom on the palms of her hands was electrifying.

Maria wriggled and rotated her bottom slowly in a show of appreciation while Mary fondled and groped her

"I will have to leave you in a few minutes darling. But I will come back with more if you would like me two. Or maybe to your house later?"

Mary was rubbing Maria's beautiful posterior and licking her shiny firm buttocks.

"Mary?"

"Yes, Maria?"

"Just quickly, please pull down your knickers and rub yourself pubs against me. Then finger me between my legs. That will keep me wet for the a while."

All too soon the woman were forced to stop so that they could get on with their duties

"Now Mary, there is something I should warn you about regarding our soccer crazed gardeners."

"Warn me about? What do I need to worry about, Maria."

"I suspect it's only a Sicilian thing but I should tell you in case something happens while I'm away. Those two reprobates in the garden are great fun and the truth is Mary, I let each of them get between my legs, quite often, as does Serena. They both have magnificent cocks."

Mary stared at the beautiful woman in awe.

"Maria? I'm shocked and intrigued? Tell me more."

"Well, you being a new female wandering about coupled with them both being so excited about the match, well, they are likely to open their pants and display their cocks."

"Good heavens, Marie, what do I need to do?"

Maria eyed Mary with amusement.

"It is up to you darling woman. Respond as you feel the need. Maybe as you did to me a moment ago? They are both rough diamonds but they have good hearts and would never hurt anyone. Now I must go. Best of luck if it happens.

"One last thought. Before we had our moment together just now, I was considering leading Giorgio down between the runner beans and the snow peas when I got back this afternoon. That way I could have him doggy style while I was happily eating fresh peas. I can usually get at least four orgasms out of Giorgio before he comes. By the way, Giorgio prefers pussy where grandpa has a penchant for both pussy and a willing arse."

Maria reached out and pulled Mary close to her, slipping her hand into Mary's pants for a final tiny loving squeeze.

"Stay moist, Mary. For a woman, it's the answer to all of life's problems."

Mary stood and watched Maria disappear through the door while noting that the longing in her excited pussy was demanding her attention. Mary moved towards Maude's bed and fell back. With firm stroking while reviewing images of Maria's beautiful rear end in her mind's eye, she came and the release was sublime. And moments later, she was thinking of those gardeners who she might meet later in the day.

Maria's advice urging Mary to stay moist might not be a problem after all.

———

Mary was suddenly brought back to the present when the phone rang in the office. It was a wrong number but the interruption served to bring her focus back to her administrative duties, and for a while she was able to forget about her hormones and her symptoms.

The diary said that the accountant, Giovanni Romano would be calling in at around two o'clock to go through the monthly accounts. Mary had already met this handsome man who was purportedly a singer of opera and she thought how he seemed like a thorough gentleman.

Mary busied herself with catching up with the filing of correspondence, something Maude avoided on the pretence she would need to look at a letter again soon. Then Mary printed out mailing labels in readiness for next months newsletter posting.

In between times, Mary made a cup of tea and ate the slice of fruit cake she'd brought from home.

At noon, Mary tok her sandwich and went out into the garden to sit in the old summerhouse near the vegetable garden, and enjoy the sun, her summer dress moving in the light summer breeze.

As Mary moved down the garden path and came nearer to the summerhouse, the sound of mens voices calling out reminded Mary of Maria's warning. Was this Georgio and Aldo carrying on about the World Cup? And what had Maria said they might do? Surely she was making those things up. Mary smiled at the thought of the two men being as outrageous as Maria suggested they might be. Then Mary turned the corner and saw that it was true. Both men were sitting on the summerhouse steps happily eating their sandwiches and drinking their vino; and yes, the two mens' trousers were open, and yes, two cocks stood at half-mast.

A radio played quietly close by and Mary heard the roar of a crowd and cheering. Then grandpa Aldo and Giorgio spotted Mary and called out and beckoned her to come and join them. The men were excited by the soccer match and even more so when they realised they had company.

Aldo patted the step in between them and invited Mary to join sit, smiling and calling out 'Juventus' and 'Italia'.

Maria felt a little apprehensive as she seated herself between the two men, but she was feeling something else as well, something akin to her recent hunger feelings.

She tried not looking at the mens genitals and pretended she hadn't noticed them. Grandpa Aldo poured Mary a beaker of wine and passed it to her, speaking to her softly in Italian but finishing with her name in English. He remembered her name from the time he met her at the house warming party Maude had given more than a month ago.

Mary remembered that Aldo had overtly ogled her, putting his hand on her rear and moving her around, obviously impressed with her backside.

Mary turned and looked at Giorgio, nodding and smiling and acknowledging his presence. The two men then continued what seemed like an ongoing conversation about the football match.

Mary sat back and got comfortable, happy that they were relaxed enough in her presence to continue simply talking to each other, and probably much as they had been doing before she'd arrived.

While the two men carried on, Mary observed each of them out the corners of her eyes. Was what Maria said, true. Did she really let these men have her?

Mary could see the attraction. The simple manliness of the two characters was a lot different to most of the men Mary knew. They seemed so self-assured and comfortable in their honest interactions with their world. But then Mary was alerted to something that was happening and she felt a moment of panic.

Aldo had put a hand on Mary's thigh and moments later, Giorgio put his hand on her other thigh. She glanced at the faces of the two men, both of whom were happily smiling at her. Then Mary glanced down and got a bigger shock. Both mens cocks had grown to be very large and stood tall between their legs and if that wasn't surprising enough, when each man took one of Mary's hands and wrapped her fingers around their erections, Mary experienced a moment of grave fear mixed with a strange counter emotion of excitement.

When the men let go of Mary's hands, they watched her face to see her reaction. She looked from one to the other, stoney faced, not knowing what she should do. But then something happened. Mary suddenly felt a wetness in her vagina and she heard Maria's final words from earlier in the day, "Stay moist, Mary. For a woman, it's the answer to all of life's problems."

Mary offered the men just a hint of a smile, but then she tightened her grip on their cocks and their already happy smiles broadened.

Aldo lent across and lifted the hem of Mary's frock, pulling it back so that her large thighs were adequately displayed

The two men continued their animated conversations about soccer, leaving Mary alone with her thoughts and her feelings. She loved it that their cocks felt welcoming to her touch and loved the excitement her body felt when one cock or the other pulsated or throbbed in response to Mary moving her hands.

Mary's hunger was being nourished in a way she would never have expected. Womanly erotic feelings floated joyously to the fore and Mary fantasised unabashedly about what she had in her hands. She began to gently move her hands up and down on each penis, relishing the feeling and intrigued at each ones ability to grow even bigger and harder.

Sitting like this in the sun with her eyes closed and happily holding on to two manhoods was beginning to have an effect on Mary. Loving things as they were was fine, but having got to this point, what should she think about doing next. Could she suck each of them in turn? Would they want to fuck her as a result?

That decision was made for her by what happened next.

"Can I join you?" A deep gentle male voice came from just in front of Mary, startling her and she opened her eyes.

"Mr Romano! I wasn't expecting you for a while yet. These two are celebrating the soccer. I'm sure they would love to include you too,"

Mary was confused. She knew she should have let go of the two men but the unexpected suddenness of Mr Romano's arrival made that seem pointless. Perhaps he would understand how the celebrations were progressing, him being Italian as well.

"Call me Giovanni, Mary. It's you I would like to join."

Mary stared and watched totally dumfounded as Mr Romano unzipped his trousers and dropped them around his knees. Then he pushed down his boxer shorts and produced something extraordinary.

Set amid more pubic hair than she ever imagined anyone having, an already large penis was stretching up and expanding rapidly and what's more, it was pointed directly at Mary.

Aldo and Giorgio laughed and yelled appreciatively, and Mary gasped.

Giovanni stepped closer so that the head of his now enormous cock waved gently in front of Mary's mouth.

"Open your mouth, Mary. This is for you."

The gentlemanly Giovanni reached forward and put a hand behind Mary's head and slowly moved it towards him.

Mary couldn't refuse. His cock was beautiful and like nothing she'd ever seen before. She first licked the head of it and then she began to take it into her mouth. It was so big and hard that she wondered whether she would be able to manage it. But then Giovanni held back a little, happy to just rock his cock backwards and forwards in between Mary's lips and her teeth.

Mary became aware of something else happening. Aldo was reaching his hand up between her legs and she felt two large rough fingers slide into her very wet cunt. Mary's glazed eyes tried to focus but the feelings in her cunt and in her mouth were so wonderful, she didn't want to think about anything more. Everything was so very wonderful. Mary's hunger was being properly fed at last.

Mary had no idea how long she had been enjoying herself, but suddenly, woman's voice invaded Mary's revelry.

"You lucky slut, Mary. I'm so happy that you found a way to keep wet."

Mary opened her eyes and looked at the beaming Maria.

Maria looked up at Giovanni and smiled, "Beautiful cock Mr Romano. I can see why Maude likes it so much. Make sure it does the right thing by my friend Mary. She deserves a proper shagging. And maybe you'd like to try me one day? Or Mary and I can arrange a double act if you're interested."

The energetic Maria smiled at Mary and leant and kissed her on the forehead.

"Just came to take Giorgio for a ride in the vegetable patch."

Maria removed Mary's hand that was still attached to Giorgio's cock and wrapped her own fingers around it.

"Come along dearest man. Let me take you for a walk. Avanti! Venire!"

When Maria spoke to him in Italian he quickly rose and followed the amazing woman around the corner to fulfil his obligations.

After Maria and Giorgio had left, it wasn't long before Aldo and Giovanni lifted Mary up off the step and moved her onto the carpet inside the summerhouse. The two men removed her dress and her bra and pants and then commenced a most serious shagging threesome and one that Mary would never forget.

First Giovanni laid her on her back and held up her legs and fed his enormous cock into her welcoming cunt. Then after shagging her to orgasm, he let Aldo have his way.

Giovanni laid on his back and Aldo helped Mary to first kneel and then to climb on top of Giovanni, feeding the man's cock back into her. When that was accomplished, Aldo moved up behind Mary and placed his cock between her large buttocks and it was only moments before Mary had enthusiastically opened her back door to him and welcomed Aldo to the party.

All three lovers rhythmically danced a sexual ritual that had been played out over the centuries. Two men and a woman embedded in a heavenly tryst. What more could Mary want.

———

Maria called on Mary one afternoon after Maria had finished work.

She had phoned ahead and said that she had things to tell Mary which she thought might interest her.

After Mary had made love to Aldo and Giovanni the week before, instead of being more settled in herself, her sexual hunger had increased and she was wanting even more sex. Mary expressed these thoughts to Maria when they ran into each other at the local shopping centre.

"I just don't understand," Mary told Maria on the telephone. "The doctor assures me that the medication I'm taking is fine. So I've no idea why I'm in what seems like a permanent state of lust."

When Maria arrived at the house, she quickly assured Mary that she wasn't bringing bad news and that there was nothing wrong and that her visit was about things which were good and might help Mary.

"There are women like us, Mary, who just need to make love more often. Actually, I would put the number like us at around seventy-percent of women except many don't know and will probably never know what ails them.

"Staying healthy and happy demands that we live our lives fully and without too many restraints. I'm here because I believe I can offer you a solution, an answer to a horny woman's every fantasy."

Mary giggled and topped up Maria's coffee cup.

"Forgive me, Maria but you do sound as though you've taken on the local Tuppa Ware agency. Should I be worried?"

Maria laughed. "Now that you mention, I do, don't I? But no, I'm here to tell you a story and you can tell me when I've finished, what you think. It will take a little while to tell, so please bear with me. But do interrupt at any time if you have a question.

Without saying where it was, Maria began to tell Mary about The Club.

"Imagine a place that is super safe, clean and well run and comfortable, where women can go to interact with men or women in order to enjoy a wide range of mutually agreed upon sexual exploits. I'm here to tell you that there is now such a place and I want to tell you about it.

Over the next forty minutes, Maria provided details of the organisation of The Club and the required code of behaviour. She thought it best to begin with what happens at the club because that was really what people want to know most and what Mary would be most interested in asking questions about.

And ask questions, she did.

By the time Maria had completed her discourse, Mary was truly excited. Maria asked her to repeat some of the things she'd said just to be sure that she had understood the main points.

"So, Maria. I go to The Club and I'm wanting to meet a man, or as you've pointed out, maybe more than one man. I find a seat anywhere in rows six or seven, and settle back to watch the movie.

After just a short wait, a man will come and sit beside me and after a few minutes he will attempt to touch me, most likely on a leg or a breast or an arm. Then its up to me how I respond, encouraging him or discouraging him. If you want to make him work for his grope, refuse him a couple of times, three max, otherwise he will assume your not up for it. To get of rid of him, four rebuttals should do or just keep moving his hand away.

Meanwhile a second or even a third man might turn up and suddenly I've got more than I can safely handle."

Maria laughed at Mary's childlike enthusiasm.

"You've got it Mary."

"If I'm not getting any takers in sex or seven, I can go and pick a shy bloke from rows four or five and do whatever I like with him.

"And if I want to meet up with a woman, I go and sit in rows eight and nine. In those rows we approach each other with signals - smiles and hand gestures. Sensitive touching and groping, and kissing and licking coming a few minutes later.

And if I'm with someone and we don't want to be interrupted by another horny person, we sit in rows ten, eleven or twelve. We also sit in those rows if we simply want to be alone and watch the movie and play with ourselves.

And finally, if I want to get ravaged, I go and park myself in row three where, in just a few moments I will be deluged with gropers and cock wavers prancing around in front and behind me.

The two woman laughed and Maria commented that she would

love to make a movie of Mary on her first visits and how it could be hilarious.

"Now do you remember what other stuff is on offer, Mary?"

"Yep! Haven't forgotten a thing. The Gals Only room is where you can go with girlfriends to canoodle more comfortably, and you will also find dildo's there in two sizes. You can also have a wee and powder your nose. You can even use it as a bolt hole to escape from over zealous blokes.

"The Parlour is like the Gals Only room but it caters for both sex couples.

"Lastly, Home Deliveries sounds like the stand out! The sin-bin. Girls can make a booking and say how many blokes they would like to entertain. Allowable numbers are two, three and four."

"How am I doing, Maria, and where the bloody hell can I find this place?"

"Just tell me a couple of the rules Mary. I need to know that you know the rules."

"Easy, Maria, and number one, don't give anyone your name, phone number or address or any information that will allow them to find you anywhere other than at The Club.

"Arrive at The Club clean and properly clothed. I guess that means not covered in shit, and naked.

"Oh yes, important! Avoid getting into conversations. Talking is anathema to fulfilling your lustful desires. We all remember the visual hunk on sporting TV who made the mistake of trying to talk? And the same goes for women."

"So, my love. Just one more question. Would you like to come along as my guest next Tuesday afternoon. If you enjoy it, I'm allowed three visitor passes a year so that you can come with me again. So Mary? Are you game? Can you face all those horny men and women?"

Mary's face became very serious as she murmured, "Yes please Maria. I would love that."

———

Mary's had a lot of trouble accepting that The Club was within walking distance of her house. This seemed so ridiculous as to bring Maria's whole story into question. It wasn't until she was safely in the door and facing the wonderful Alvie, as she attached her visitor number, that Mary begin to think the story was true.

"There you go love. Come back and see me if you have any problems."

"I told you how I would be meeting a girlfriend here didn't I? Veronica and I have known each other for years and we work together sometimes. She and I usually sit in rows eight or nine, mainly to meet girls, but occasionally we hook up with a bloke or two. And if we are fishing for a man, we'll move back a couple of rows. You can sit with us while you're settling in and then wander off to explore and see the sights. You might be shocked."

Mary looked around, wide-eyed.

"It is so beautifully designed, isn't it."

"Wait until you've seen the cinema, Mary. That is the centre of this world."

Veronica called out as she arrived through the front door and the two waited for her to join them. Maria introduced them.

"I've already filled Veronica in on who you are Mary. She said she was excited for you and wished it was her first time. But that is what we always say about anything, isn't it."

The three entered the dimly lit cinema and Maria pointed out that Mary's eyes would soon adjust so that she would be able to see everything going on around her, to which Veronica responded with, "but she really only wants to see the hot bits, like the rest of us."

Tuesday was just another normal day at The Club and as with every other day, activity hotted up a bit an hour or so after The Club opened.

Maria and Veronica stood each side of Mary and each took a hand so that she didn't fall down.

"A lot of people in heels topple over in the isles because of the steep slope and the dim lighting."

Mary suddenly found herself staring down at the movie screen watching as a woman attempted to swallow a very large penis while making sucking noises. She wanted to keep watching but her friends wanted to move her on.

"You said I could just come and sit in the front row and watch the movie, didn't you, Maria?"

"Yes, darling, but surely you wouldn't deny all the other people access to your delightful self. What a waste of a body that would be."

"She will probably never look at the screen again, once she gets active, don't you think, Veronica?"

Mary suddenly stopped in her tracks. "Oh my God, I've just noticed something."

Maria and Veronica laughed and Veronica said, "Well thank God for that. And do you like what you are seeing, Mary?"

Maria and Veronica smiled at each other in the dim light and glanced over to where Mary was staring. A few seats up and across the other side of the next isle, a woman was on her knees on her seat and a man behind her had just pulled down her panties and was feeling between her legs. In front of the woman, another man was holding out his erection towards her face as an offering.

Mary gazed at the scene in silence. She was mesmerised.

Maria noticed a woman heading slowly up towards the threesome.

"Mary? Just watch that woman approaching the people who you are looking at. She is coming towards them from the other side of the row. I think she's moving in to try and get some of the action."

Mary looked and gasped. "My God you're right. Look! She's got her hands on the cock of the man at the back and she's helping him put it into the lady without knickers. And look, another man is arriving and he's pulling up the dress of the woman who has just arrived. This is incredible."

Veronica giggled, "They must be early starters. There's not usually that much action until a bit later.

Maria agreed, "She is obviously a morning person."

"Welcome to The Club, Mary. Veronica and I hope you will enjoy yourself."

Maria and Veronica looked at each other and smiled. Then they moved as one, leading Mary to a seat in row seven and each took a seat on either side of her. Then Veronica turned and smiled at Mary and reached down and lifted Mary's skirt and stared excitedly at her substantial blue stockinged legs while Maria unbuttoned Mary's top, releasing her huge bust. Then Maria pulled down the bra straps and eased two big beautiful bosoms from their cups and rubbed her fingers on a nipple.

Veronica reached under Mary's backside and found the top of her knickers and slowly pulled them down and over her knees while Maria licked and kissed Mary's massive breasts.

Mary had initially made noises of protest, but not for long. She had wanted to watch the couple up further, but she realised that what she had here was much better.

Veronica began to kiss Mary on the lips while gently caressing her large bare thighs above her stockings and this quickly turned into a passionate exchange. Mary turned and embraced Veronica around the shoulders and wanted to completely devour the small woman. Veronica responded and took Mary's hand and guided it up under her short skirt and whispered to Mary, "Please feel me up, Mary. Finger me you beautiful woman."

This first time with the girls was getting Mary's juices running as they hadn't for a very long time. It suddenly reminded her of Helen's seduction of her the year before. It felt almost similarly religious which sounded silly. But having her hands busily discovering the small delicate woman's special places was amazing.

"Oh Veronica, you little darling. I just want to fuck your beautiful little pussy."

Maria likewise dragged Mary's other hand up under her skirt and pressed her fingers to her vagina. But then the women were suddenly interrupted.

Another woman joined them and was kissing Maria while removing her own top and exposing her bosom. Maria responded quickly, dragging the stranger's top off and then sucking her breasts. Moments later, a man arrived and touched both women's breasts while his erection stood waving in the air.

The newly arrived woman stopped and looked at it then took hold of it and sucked it briefly before looking around at everyone before asking if any of them needed a cock in their cunt.

To Mary's surprise, Veronica called out. "Yes please. Come around to this side and I'll have it, thanks."

Veronica turned and looked lovingly at Mary.

"You've made my pussy feel really good Mary so I'll have some cock to go with it. I can usually come in a very short time when I get fucked. You will enjoy it too, my love. I'll make sure of that.

The man made his way around to the other side and parked himself next to Veronica.

"Mary, darling. Will you give him a suck and a rub and make him wet while I position myself to climb onto him."

Mary did as she was asked, reaching her head down and taking hold of the gentleman's quite large cock. She lovingly tugged at it then she leant over and put her mouth over it and slurped saliva on him.

Moments later, Veronica lifted herself up and impaled the man's member in her tiny pussy. Then she jiggled up and down energetically and in no time, she gurgled and moaned and twitched and came. Then she removed him and suddenly she was back kissing Mary like she'd never left.

It all happened so quickly and Mary found that she had loved the whole event, so much so that she was now totally in love with the doll-like Veronica.

The man disappeared and then Mary heard Maria scream and looked down to see her thrusting her cunt hard agains the mouth of the unknown woman and it seemed that the woman was coming at the same time and just a few moments later the two were enjoying celebratory kissing. Mary heard Maria whisper, "Thank you", and the woman replying "my pleasure". Then the visitor was gone.

Maria reached across Mary and slipped a hand into Veronica's tiny bra.

"I love you two horny bitches. You are the best!"

If Mary thought the party was over, she was wrong.

"I need a pee," announced Veronica as she adjusted her clothing.

"I'm taking Mary to the Gals Room. We'll take a booth and relax. We so want to eat each other out, don't we my darling?" Veronica looked lovingly at Mary.

"Hope that's okay with you Maria. I'll catch you tomorrow if you're not here when we come out."

Maria looked at Mary and reached out and took her hand and smiled wickedly.

"You might be about to have the best moments of your visit, Mary. Just do whatever Veronica tells you and enjoy yourself."

Veronica led the way back up the aisle, walking slowly so that Mary could look around at what other folk were up to. Mary was still partly dazed from recent events plus she was excitedly attempting to foresee her upcoming moments with Veronica.

Mary was torn between staring at the beautiful apparition of Veronica's perfect little body swaying from side to side in front of her, and perving on the club members activities on either side.

For her benefit, Veronica would stop when she thought Mary might be interested to gaze on a particular exchange of sexual favours happening close by.

Each time she did this, she would kiss Mary on her cheek and fondle her buttocks and nod her head towards what she had noticed and while Mary watched with fascination as one woman helped another by dragging a cock she was sucking, over to perform in between her friends legs, Veronica continued to run a hand over Mary's posterior. And when Mary stared at a woman who was pretending to be oblivious to the fact that her naked breasts were being gently groped by a man sitting behind her, Veronica nibbled Mary's ear and whispered endearing messages, telling her what she wanted Mary to do to her once they were alone.

As the two neared the top of the aisle, Veronica stopped and nodded towards what was happening in the notorious row three, known to some as The Jungle and to others as Gang-bang Alley.

"This is where you come for something fast and furious, Mary. Maria occasionally likes to park herself there but I make her do it without me. I'm not against it and I would like to try it one day, but not yet. I think it's because I'm so small and I'm frightened it might be too rough. Besides, there are more than enough nice and more gentle things to do here."

Mary's mouth dropped and she whispered, "Oh my God!", staring at what was happening in row three.

Two near naked women were kneeling on their seats, side by side and with their rear ends thrust upwards and slowly wriggling to entice the half-a-dozen men who stood behind them taking turns filling their cunts and arses. The womens heads were resting on the backs of the seats and their mouths were being fed by a platoon of penises. As one cock was being sucked, the woman's hands would be tugging on two others.

Every so often one of the two women would scream loudly and it would rise above the hubbub of the cinema.

"I'd guess that those two are friends and they came here either as a dare or to celebrate something; a divorce maybe. Row three doesn't get a lot of visitors so your quite privileged to see this rare event."

Mary was dumfounded and deep down, she was sexually aroused by what she was watching.

Then Veronica turned Mary's head and kissed her.

"Come along darling. The Gals Room is just here. I want you."

While Veronica went into the toilet for a pee, Mary surveyed the Gals Only room. It was tastefully furnished with a low table, arm chairs and two sofa's. A huge vase of fresh flowers adorned the table and jugs of water and glasses sat on a side cupboard and etchings of erotic artworks hung on the walls. There were six doors which opened on to private booths and four were ajar and when Mary peeped into one, she could see that these too, had vases of flowers and water jugs and artworks on the walls as well as two armchairs and a bed on which lay pillows and bolsters.

Mary could hear happy giggles and squeals and moaning coming from the two booths where the doors were closed. One door showed a red engaged sign but the second showed green meaning it wasn't locked. The other difference was that the first had the curtains pulled completely across but the windows on the second occupied booth were only partly closed, allowing anyone to peep in.

Veronica later told Mary that partly drawn curtains and a green door sign signalled that the occupants would be happy to receive visitors.

Mary would have liked to peep but then Veronica re-appeared and took Mary's hand and led her to a booth and they went in. She locked the door and pulled across the curtains then turned and took Mary in her arms and reached up on her toes and the two kissed.

Both women were excited to be alone together and Mary nervously watched as Veronica dropped her skirt to the floor and stepped out of it, displaying her perfect little body. Mary stared at this most youthful looking fifty-something year-old and a part of her cried out, wanting to devour Veronica or even to be Veronica, standing there in her red stockings and suspender belt and red stilettos and her naughty little red bra that only just reached above her nipples. Veronica's straight black bobbed hair framed her beautiful face and accentuated the wide always open smiling mouth and big cupid lips and emphasised the tiny doll's big angelic brown eyes.

Veronica bent down and lifted the hem of Mary's dress, lifting it up and over her head and dropping it on a chair nearby. Then she stood back and stared at the full-bodied Mary in her blue lace-up bodice corselet and her blue stockings and high heels.

Mary stood still for Veronica's slow inspection. First the woman put her fingers on the white flesh just above Mary's stockings. She seemed intent on the spot where Mary's thigh bulged slightly above the patterned stocking top where the suspender curved around.

Then Veronica lifted Mary's left arm and pushed her face into her armpit and inhaled. Then she licked just below the arm before moving her face to be in front of Mary's breasts.

Veronica small stature meant that, in her high heels, her face was inline with Mary's chest. She lifted one hand and her fingers took hold of and fondled a nipple.

Then she took Mary's hand and led her to the bed.

The two hugged and kissed. Both loved kissing and agreed that proper passionate kissing was the key to making love.

"Mary, my sweet darling, I must tell you first that I am blessed with that rare ability to cum pretty much whenever I want to. Right now I really want to sit on your face and cum on your mouth. Can I do that, please? And Mary, I want you to treat me like your sex doll.

Anything you want is all right by me. Don't hold back. Let us be lovers to the full. I desperately want to cum all over you."

Mary listened to what Veronica said and joyfully stared at the petite doll-like sex toy nestled in her arms and mentally drooled as she considered just a few of the things she could imagine doing to Veronica.

And, almost as if Veronica had read Mary's mind, the sex doll spoke in a quiet and reassuring voice.

"Oh yes, I forgot to mention that there are sex toys in that draw, dildos large and small. And yes, Mary my love I intend to use them on you and would love you to use them with me. Feel free to shag me with them and send me to heaven, Mary. And it might surprise you, but even my tiny bottom will welcome your attention.

"And Mary, you will be my sex doll to love and to hold.

It wasn't long before Veronica lifted herself up and swung a leg over Mary's chest. She looked down at Mary lovingly as she moved her perfect little bottom backwards and forwards and side to side over Mary's large bosom. Then she put Mary's arms down beside her and moved up and hovered her little vagina over Mary's mouth. Mary gasped and felt a quiver in her groin.

"Now, my darling. I can cum quickly or slowly and right now I think I want to come slowly. I'm going to rub my wet pussy all over your face. You can lick me and push your tongue or nose into me and when I decide to orgasm, I'll tell my sex slave so that she can grasp me tight and hold me. I would love that.

———

Jessica was asked by Maude if she would help out with a couple of the pre Christmas musical commitments that the school had made.

The school choir leader and one of the music teachers had the bright idea that it would be good for students to perform in front of an audience to get experience. Jessica was to join two other students to visit retirement villages and give a concert during the late afternoon after residents had had their nap.

Their first gig was at The Willows, a village for wealthy retirees, situated on the coast just below Bondi. The residents loved what the students did which was a medley of songs from the 40's and 50's and everyone applauded and asked for more.

When the trio finished, the boy and girl who were a couple, downed their soft-drinks and cake and left as quickly as they could, citing another engagement further down the coast.

As Jessica finished her slice of apple cake, a couple of residents who were still at the table smiled at her and the well groomed woman with bright eyes asked Jessica if she would come to their unit for dinner the night after next. With nothing planned and not giving things much thought, Jessica agreed and when she asked what she could bring to the meal, the woman assured her that just bringing herself, would be quite sufficient.

Jessica made the short bus trip to a stop near The Willows and when she arrived, her hosts, Angela and Craig, said how very pleased they were that she had found her way there and how excited they were to see her. The unit was very beautiful and much bigger than Jessica had anticipated, boasting three bedrooms and a study as well as the lounge and a large dining alcove.

The good looking couple must have been in their mid sixty's or a little older. He was partially deaf and when his wife asked him why he wasn't wearing his hearing aids, he just answered that he couldn't find them. As a result, Craig didn't have a lot to say because he wasn't able to follow the conversation.

Jessica at first felt a little self-conscious, intending to dress more casually, she ended up confused and settled for smart conservative in a tight black skirt with a white blouse, tan stocking and standard shiny black low heels. Angela was also smartly dressed in fashionable clothes including black stockings and low heels.

The meal was excellent and Jessica enjoyed the opportunity to relax in pleasant company and enjoy a glass of wine; a white sauterne which went well with the poached fish.

When they eventually moved back into the softer light of the lounge room and sat back on the sofa and arm chairs, they swapped stories about family and their childhood upbringing and then slowly moved on to talk about their daily lives.

Craig must have realised that he was missing out on most of what was being said and rose, and excused himself, announcing that he was going in search of his missing hearing aids.

Jessica smiled at him and wished him luck, thinking what a fit and good looking couple these two older folk were.

"I would assume that an attractive young woman like yourself would have a boyfriend?" asked Angela with a knowing smile when they were suddenly alone.

Jessica laughed and replied that, no she hadn't settled on the right man or woman yet and was very happily enjoying herself and playing the field.

Angela looked happily surprised and smiled and looked at Jessica closely, then chose her words carefully.

"Can I confide in you Jessica?"

Jessica was slightly taken aback, wondering what Angela, a mature woman, had to confide to a very young woman.

"Of course you can, Angela, but I'm not sure whether I'm a person who can be of much help. I'll soon let you know if I can or can't."

At that moment, Craig came back into the lounge room.

"Found them! Now I'm just popping up to the corner shop for more wine, darling. We're out of everything and we'll need some for tomorrow when the kids come for lunch. See you both shortly."

The two women farewelled him and Angela told him not to get lost, fixing him with a stern stare.

"I have a feeling that Craig is spending time with another woman, darling. I know I shouldn't burden you with this but I really don't have anyone outside the family or neighbours to talk to and the subject is too delicate anyway."

Angela asked Jessica to come over and join her on the sofa. Then she took Jessica's hands in hers and looked deep into her eyes.

"There's a new woman at number forty-nine. Robyn is her name. She is quite a hit with the men in the street and I'm sure some of the other wives are having the same trouble as me.

"Robyn has a woman friend visit her regularly and the two of them seem to attract the men like flies to a honey-pot. I don't know what they all get up to but it certainly keeps the men knocking on her door."

Jessica noticed that Angela had moved one of her hands onto Jessica's knee and was absentmindedly caressing it with her finger tips, as she spoke. It felt very nice. Jessica decided to take a risk.

"Have you ever been with a woman, Angela? I have a woman lover as well as male friends. I find being with a woman is emotionally very rewarding."

Angela's jaw dropped as she thought through what Jessica had just said. Then she rallied herself and with her eyes downcast, she whispered that she hadn't ever been with a woman in that way but it was something she had thought about often over the years. Angela looked up as Jessica replied.

"I find you very attractive, Angela. Would you let me kiss you? It's all right to say no. Its just that I love everything about you. Just one kiss will do?"

Angela was flustered and didn't know where to look. She put her other hand on Jessica's thigh. Then she rallied, made the decision and looked at Jessica.

"We will have to be quick, before Craig gets home," then she closed her eyes and lent forward.

Jessica smiled and before she moved in to kiss Angela, said. "From what you have told me, I suspect your husband might enjoy seeing two women kissing.

Angela's lips touched Jessica's and the woman sat frozen in time. Then Jessica moved her lips around a little, trying to encourage Angela to participate. Then she took Angela's hand from her thigh and lifted it and put it on a breast, rotating it gently. Finally, she moved the hand on her knee up under her skirt until it touched the soft flesh above her stockings. It was then that Angela pushed her mouth against Jessica's and pushed her tongue in between Jessica's lips, making little breathless sounds indicating her excitement.

"We have lift off," Jess thought as she moved her own hand up under Angela's skirt and felt a warm spot at the top of her legs buried beneath Angela's tights.

Angela was enlivened, throwing her arms around Jessica and falling backwards and pulling the young woman on top of her. Then just as quickly, she unbuttoned her blouse, pulled her breasts out from her bra, and pushed Jessica's head down to suck her nipples.

"Oh Jessica this is wonderful and you are wonderful. Please keep kissing me."

"Yes, this is wonderful Angela. I'm so loving it, too."

Jessica felt Angela's hand unzipping the back of her skirt and smiled when the woman's fingers found the crack in her buttocks. Angela's hand didn't stop there. It slid down to the back of her legs then pushed forward gently and discovering Jessica's wet pussy.

Angela sighed and pushed her lips hard against Jessica's and joined the young woman in a tongue dance. Jessica remembered that she had an urgent question for Angela and pulled her head up and looked at her.

"I do just have one important question relating to your husband, though, Angela. Tell me, do you ever suck his penis?

Jessica looked down at Angela's face with a look of amazement.

"Well no, I don't. My mother taught all four daughters never to touch a man there because it wasn't a nice thing to do. Strangely, whilst it's crossed my mind on occasion, I haven't had the courage to go against my mothers advice. Why do you ask?"

"It's one of the main things that women can do to keep their husbands from going elsewhere."

Jessica listened for an answer and in response to Angela's silence, except for her heavy breathing, went back to kissing her breasts while at the same time pushing her hand up hard against Angela's vagina, sheltering behind the crotch of her tights and underpants.

"I really want to taste you between your legs, Angela. I'm taking off your tights. Okay?"

"Please do, Jessica. This is all like a dream. I love it."

Jessica first removed her own skirt and then lifted Angela up and began to drag her tights down over her legs. It was when she had them down around the woman's knees, that she heard voices. It was far too late for a cover up.

Craig had brought two mates home for a drink and a supper snack and to meet their nice young visitor. He'd met the men in the street on his way home from the shops and when the men were just arriving home from golf. One was a married man who's wife happened to be away for a week, visiting one of her children. The other was a widower. All played golf together and as it happened, all visited the new woman, Robyn, at number forty-nine.

When Craig and his friends looked at what was happening on the sofa, none could believe their eyes, especially, Craig.

Angela looked up at the shocked faces of the men and found herself smiling. She had been liberated from so much in just such a short time by Jessica's loving touch, and without stopping to think, Angela called out, "We're having a party if any of you gentlemen would like to join us."

The three men stared at the two women. Angela had her breasts on show and her legs were together to facilitate her tights being removed.

"This lovely lady, gentlemen, is Jessica. As you can see, we are quite busy, but don't think you have to leave. We will happily deal with you all in a little while. Is that right Jessica? And Jessica, the good looking one in the blue trousers is Norman and the other good looking one is Matt. The other good looking one is my husband who you've already met."

Jessica turned and looked at the three well dressed and fit looking older men.

"Hello everyone. Pleased to meet you. Angela and I will certainly be happy for you to join in our fun. Why don't you all get your cocks out and warm up? We won't be too long and we are happy for you to watch."

Jessica returned to what she was doing and finished pulling off Angela's tights. Then she reached up and removed the woman's panties, deliberately throwing them towards her husband, Craig.

Jessica now buried her head between the top of Angela's legs and licked the woman and nibbled at her clitoris. Angela sighed and closed her eyes and pushed herself up towards Jessica's face while rubbing her breasts.

Loud whispering ensued as the men excitedly talked among themselves while staring at the wondrous scene in front of them, and one by one they took surrendered to Jessica's suggestion and got out their penises and began stroking them.

Jessica lifted herself up and moved up and laid on Angela and looked lovingly into the woman's smiling eyes. Angela looked back and puckered up and the two kissed.

"In a few minutes, Angela, I'm going to let you watch me suck cock. Later, you might like to forget the one piece of bad advice your mother ever gave you, and join me.

"Cock sucking is one of my favourite hobbies Angela, and it's very healthy for girl, for both the mind and her body. I won't mind if you don't suck them. You can just play with them and rub them if you like. But watch me anyway, and see what I do. Is that okay, you sexy woman?"

Angela laughed. "Sounds wonderful, Jessica. I'm desperate to learn more."

"Oh yes, there is just one more thing Angela. These gentlemen will probably want more than me sucking them and will probably want to put their cocks between both our legs.

"Are you okay with me letting Craig pop his member into me, Angela? Just say if you're not and I'll make sure he doesn't. Hopefully your Craig will soon learn the benefits of being at home with his newly liberated woman. What you do with any of other two is your call."

Angela hugged Jessica tightly then ran her hands gently over her body. "God, you sexy little bitch. I want everything. Now! And in answer to your question, do whatever you want to with Craig. I'm sure I will love watching you."

Jessica felt hands on her buttocks and experienced the thrill she always felt when touched ahead of a sexual encounter, instinctively knowing that things were about to happen. She turned her head and saw three erections standing in a row in front of the sofa. Jessica whispered to Angela that she should put her arm out and grab the nearest one and not worry about who it was attached to. Then she continued, "I'm greedy so I'll have two."

Angela giggled at Jessica's comments and immediately pushed her arm out and took a cock in her hand. Then, as Jessica moved away to sit up, Angela swung herself round to a sitting position and looked up to see who lived on the end of what she was holding, and Jessica heard an excited and breathless little voice.

"Hello Norman. You won't mind if I have a play with this, will you?"

"Well done Angela," thought Jessica. "You're on your way."

Jessica looked up at Craig who seemed confused, staring first at Jessica and then at his wife and what she was doing with Norman.

Jessica looked up at Matt, the widower, whose cock seemed the most impressive by size.

"Lovely cocks, gentlemen. I'd love to get to know them better. I hope you won't object if I do."

Jessica looked up at the two men with her sweet coy and oh-so-innocent smile. Then she a visualised a memorable scene; that moment not long ago when her first two stiff cocks presented themselves, swaying and lifting up and down beside her just outside the passenger door window at her first dogging session. And that same little voice inside Jessica screamed with delight.

Jessica reached out and took hold of Craig's cock. It instinctively jumped up and down in her hand and she fondled lovingly.

"A girl just can't help herself at a moment like this, Craig. I might get carried away and lick and suck you both. Is that okay? Tell me to stop if you want."

As she spoke her words caused the two cocks to jump upwards. With her other hand Jessica took hold of Matt and she began a slow rubbing motion on the two of them.

Jessica played with her two cocks for a just a few moments rubbing her fingers over their hoods and tickling their testicles, then one after the other she took turns feeding them in between her lips and slowly licking and sucking them. Jessica chanced a look over at Angela and discovered that the woman had indeed watched Jessica and was now busily sucking Norman whose face showed a level of ecstasy that Jessica hadn't seen in a man for a long time.

Angela looked as though she was truly enjoying herself and Jessica recalled the first time that she and Edith and Rosa had laid on the bed in a cool room on a hot summers day and discovered one another, and how the world had been the better for it ever since.

Jessica was loving having access to cocks again. It had only been a couple of weeks since her wonderful sex filled holiday at Goulburn but she still felt as though she hadn't had a proper cock for in ages.

Jessica had still to experience being fucked and enjoying it with as much pleasure as her sucking provided. But she did like it and was aware that fucking was what men ultimately felt was their reason for being. For that reason she considered it important to make it available to them. It was important for her not to be selfish.

Encouraging men to have their way was a form of insurance. Being certain that they would be happy to be sucked again was assured when they knew they would be the beneficiaries of a full service afterwards.

Jessica remembered that thing that Gina had said the evening they were dogging in Goulburn. "I'm going to open the door on the other side shortly. I need to offer my other end. The boys deserve the full menu."

After quite sometime in cock play, Jessica decided it was time to move on to fucking mode. But before she did, she wanted to do one thing.

"Angela? Can I have a turn with Norman please? Lets swap places. Angela nodded her agreement without letting go of Norman's cock and Jessica stood up and walked around the back of her two men and behind Norman, and Angela moved over. Within moments, Angela had a two cocks to deal with, one being her husbands. Without missing a beat, she smiled up at Craig and Matt and took turns feeding them into her mouth, slurping generously on both of them.

Around ten or fifteen minutes after the change over, Jessica whispered as best she could to Angela that she was about to get onto her knees and show the boys what she was offering next on the menu. Angela almost choked laughing. "I'll watch and then I might do the same," she replied.

Jessica stopped sucking Norman and looked up at him.

"I fancy you in a different spot now, Norman. Hope you will be happy with it."

Then Jessica stood and turned around and knelt on the sofa, displaying her backside and vagina.

All the men looked at Jessica's rear end, and as they did so, Angela took the opportunity to do what Jessica had just done. She turned and perched on the edge of the sofa on her knees. Jessica noticed and instructed the men accordingly.

"We are offering unrestricted access here today. Please enjoy yourselves, gentlemen. We certainly will."

There was a sudden rush. Three cocks and only two pussies.

Craig plunged his member into his wife without further ado and Norman took a slow easy approach to pussy poking at Jessica's already wet rear end.

Angela kindly called to Matt to come and sit beside her so that she could rub and play with him to which he acted swiftly, accepting her kind offer.

Having her husband shagging her, excited Angela for some reason she couldn't quite understand. Was it to do with her sudden arrival into a world of more honest interactions. Was him fucking her in this situation like what it was going to be for them both from now on. Was she conscious that this was likely to be the successful way of weaning him away from that tart up the road? She did love him, and hoped all of these things were true. Then she smiled to herself and the new Angela thought how nice it would be to fuck his two friends before the night was over. Other mens cocks were probably the last essential ingredient in her liberation.

Jessica had considered the lack of condoms but dismissed it as a concern, telling herself that these men were probably clean and she had been for a check-up this week and was fine.

Funny how we tell ourselves reassuring things when it suits us, she mused.

Craig came quite quickly and Angela felt a huge load slipping around in her and she also experienced small orgasmic tremors in her genitals. He bellowed like a bull and everyone smiled.

As her husband left her, she looked up and smiled and blew him a kiss. Then she turned to Matt.

"I'd would love it if you fucked me too, Matt. But only if you want to."

Matt was up and at her in just moments, and Craig turned and watched in awe.

"Oh, Matt, how kind of you. Give it to me like it's your last one ever, Matt, and I'll make you your favourite chocolate cake tomorrow."

What more of an incentive could a man ask for, Jessica smiled to herself, overhearing Angela's offer. Then she thought about not having made a chocolate cake for ages and that she, being the top cake maker of her final school year, should surprise Edith with one next week.

Norman came with a bleating sound accompanied by what sounded like a last gasp.

"Thank you Norman. Craig? You've given it all to that other slut. But perhaps you could manage to give me a little touch up, please?"

Craig stepped forward and put his hand between Jessica's legs and fingered her very wet pussy. She returned the favour by gently rubbing his balls. Then she took his hand in hers and pushed three of his fingers into her vagina really hard and moved them vigorously, in and out. Then Jessica uttered a little scream and came on Craig's hand.

"Thank you Craig. Just what I needed."

The men stood or sat around, a little dazed and unsure themselves, like boys thinking they were still about to get into trouble for what they had been doing. But then Angela put her arms around her husband who sat on the floor in front of her, and nibbled his ear.

"Thank you darling. What a wonderful husband you are. Hope you liked it. Just ask when you want some more."

Jessica laughed and looked at the other two men and said how she thought that they were pretty good too.

There wasn't a lot to chat about at that moment, so Jessica thought she should say something.

"Thank you all. I really enjoyed your company tonight and want to thank Angela for making it possible. At the risk of looking stupid, would you raise your hands if you feel you would like to do it all again sometime. If Angela and Craig were willing of course, I'd happily come over to their house again for another romp."

Everyone put their hand up then Jessica looked at Angela.

"I look forward to hearing from you, Angela."

When the men had shuffled off home, or in Craig's case, farewelling Jessica and excused himself and headed off to bed, the two women reached out for each other and kissed then rolled onto the sofa together.

"Oh my God, Jessica. Life will never be the same again, thanks to you."

Jessica moved quickly, put her head down between Angela's legs and began to slurp up what two lovely men had left behind and was now dribbling from her new love. This was nectar to the extraordinary cock loving Jessica. Then just as she was finishing and about to take her mouth away, she felt Angela stiffen and realised that the woman's pussy was looking for more.

With three deft fingers and a thumb, Jessica gave Angela her first proper orgasm in a long time, enjoying the moment when Angela arched her back and screamed out. Then she held her in her arms while the newly liberated lovely lady sobbed and placed sloppy kisses all over any part of Jessica she could reach.

The two settled down and rested in each others arms.

"Angela?"

"Yes, Jessica?"

"Did you like sucking cock, darling?"

"Loved it!"

"And being fucked by other cocks?"

"Loved it!"

———

Jessica visited her new friends, Angela and husband Craig, every six or eight week at their unit at The Willows, a retirement village for well off retirees. It wasn't that she wouldn't have liked to see more of them, it was to do with the amount of time available to her, what with study and her other activities.

Enjoying herself at Angela's place was most enjoyable for the good food and company as well as the sex with neighbours, usually the same two men plus Craig.

Jessica was Angela's first female sex partner and her coming out and her liberation meant that she was keen to catch up on those things in life that she thought she had missed out on. So when Angela called her and asked her if she was up for a visit and something a little different, Jessica jumped at the opportunity.

"I hope its still rude, whatever it is, Angela?" Jessica asked, laughingly.

"Definitely!" Angela assured her.

"Are you going to give me a hint, at least, you senior slut?"

Angela laughed. She loved it when Jessica called her her senior slut. It sounded like she was the holder of an important position in life. And Jessica assured her that indeed, it was very important.

"If I said there would be a lot more cocks and probably extra women, would that interest you, my little baby slut?"

Jessica was immediately excited and screamed her answer into the telephone.

"God yes, Angela. I'm looking for my lubricant as we speak. Are the ladies experienced, can I ask, or do we have to introduce them to the better things of life."

Angela screamed back her amusement.

"Well Jessica, it seems that, unknown to me, there are quite a number of swinging residents here at the village and also among other members of Craig's golfing fraternity. He says there are at least half a dozen bringing their partners who will not doubt be expecting to have a good time with other womens husbands.

"Robyn, our honeypot from number 49 wants to join us. She's already visited me during an afternoon when Craig was at golf. If I just tell you that we got on famously, you will get the picture."

Jessica feigned disapproval.

"You slut, you. Do I have to share you now with an experienced bisexual superstar who lives practically on the premises? How will I ever be able to compete?"

"Oh you are a darling. I think you will like her. And if you don't, well you can fight it out between sucking and fucking all the men and women that are coming. Half the golf club apparently, if Craig isn't exaggerating."

"Well, bitch. I'll certainly be there to compete for cocks with the two of you. So watch out!"

———

Jessica made a point of being late. It wasn't something she would normally do but there was method in her madness. She knew that making a late entrance would get her the most attention and dressed in her sluttiest clothes, she knew she would get an interesting reception.

Strangely, it wasn't the men she wanted to impress the most, it was the honeypot woman, Robyn. If it came to a cock sucking stand-off, Jessica wanted to win. Then she reminded herself that she was being foolish; but then reminded herself again that she was going there to have fun, there was nothing worth fighting over.

Angela and Craig's apartment was crowded. Everyone was still going through the niceties of greeting each other and asking after each other health. But a few that had got there early and had a glass of wine, were already showing signs of wanting to try out with someone.

Jessica found Angela and they kissed and then Angela took her and introduced her to Robyn who immediately put an arm around Jessica's waist and pulled her close. Then she kissed her on the lips saying how Angela had told her all about her tall young friend. But there was too much going on and too much noise for anyone to have a proper conversation.

Jessica told her host that she would like to have a little wander about on her own to get the feel of things and Angela smiled and replied that the sooner people started feeling things, the better.

Handsom well dressed men and women were everywhere and Jessica thought how much they reminded her of the crowd at the dunking she had been to with Gina and Darlene.

Not everyone was in the same mould, however. In the kitchen she discovered a huge blond woman in a brightly floral kaftan and with bare feet, wearing her hair braided like she had just got off the plane from Bali.

She wore blue eyeshadow and pink lipstick and her varnished finger and toe nails were pink. She spoke with a Dutch accent and threw her arms around any man that came within touching distance, kissing him passionately and telling him with only a slight slur in her guttural accented voice, that she hoped he would favour her body before the night was out. They each murmured something which Jessica couldn't catch accept the woman's name sounded like Dunya.

"Well, that will be interesting," thought Jessica, looking at the woman. She would surely have been six-foot three or four and had a huge backside and enormous breasts.

In the passageway that led to the toilet, a couple where in each others arms and kissing passionately. In the lounge, men and women were talking and laughing and quite a few men and some women were rubbing someones rear end, affectionately, a preliminary signalling perhaps.

It wasn't until she looked into the first of the dimly lit bedrooms that she saw things we're really starting to get under way.

A good looking well built man was leaning against a wardrobe door with his trousers and pants down around his ankles. Two women knelt in front of him sucking what looked to be a sizeable and happy cock, and passing it backwards and forwards to each other. One woman had a hand between the others legs who in turn was slowly unbuttoning the shirt of the woman feeling her up. Jessica response was to put her own hand down and slide her fingers up under her mini skirt. She would have liked to join in but thought she would keep looking around before making any moves.

As she turned to leave the room, a smiling woman entered followed closely by two men. The woman had a cock in each hand and headed to the double bed. Then she stopped and let their cocks go while she lifted her dress up over her head and then unfastened her bra and let it drop to the floor. Then Jessica heard the woman speak in a low sensuous voice, "Who wants to be first?"

Jessica couldn't help but feel horny. But she was determined to have a good look around. She still had two bedrooms to look in plus the dining room.

In the second bedroom, at first she thought it was empty, but then she heard sounds coming from the carpeted floor on the other side of the bed and tippy-toed across and peeped.

She was surprised but enchanted with the hot scene that confronted her, and what was said was even more exciting.

A woman was on her knees with her bare bum in the air. A second woman wearing a dildo was shagging her vagina energetically, and talking in a breathless voice, "I know you've been fucking him for ages, you bitch. But all along, it was me that you were after, wasn't it? Wasn't it? Bitch? Well, now you've go me and I'll expect more of this, you dirty little husband fucker. From now on you will come to my place once a week and get what I'm giving you now. And you are going to have to fuck me too. Have you got that, slut?"

A weak sobbing voice answered. "Yes, yes, Susan. Oh yes. Just keep shagging me, Susan. Please don't stop. I want it."

Jessica was rubbing herself furiously, wanting to be both the fucker and the fuckee. She made a mental note of the two women incase she ran across them again later.

Bedroom three, and what a scene. Two men were holding a women up off the floor, each with a shapely leg over their respective arms. Her arms held each man by the shoulder. All her clothing had been removed except for her stockings and suspender belt. A third man was fucking her enthusiastically, yelling that he was about to come. The woman screamed her satisfaction then let herself down from the two men while they changed places and the next man fucked her equally enthusiastically. Jessica figured that the woman had probably already had the third man before Jessica arrived.

When this third man finished, the woman let herself down, bent down and picked up her clothes and, without looking at anyone, mumbled something like thanks fellas and walked out.

Jessica saw the same woman a little later in the dining alcove on her hands and knees while three men took turns at her from the rear. And jumping ahead, in the early hours of the morning, when Jessica was being had from behind by a big happy man, the same woman put her head in the door and spoke. "Will you be long Gary? I'd like to go. I'm quite tired and ready for bed."

Such was the world of experienced swingers, apparently, and for some reason, Jessica thought about that moment a lot over the coming weeks.

When Jessica made it back into the lounge room, there were still many people chatting and drinking and she realised that maybe not all of them were intending to make out with someone. Or maybe they just hadn't found anyone they wanted to be with. She was soon to find out.

Jessica suddenly thought of the woman in the kaftan, and wondered how she was getting along and happily wandered to off in search of her. Someone had switched off the bright fluorescent kitchen lights and fetched a beside lamp which was adequate and much nicer.

The Bali braided woman was nowhere in sight. Instead, a naked woman was laying on the kitchen table with a man between her legs and with her ankles on his shoulders. Three other naked men stood around the table with their cocks waving as she attempted to grab and swallow each one. She was very vocal and appeared a little out of control, begging for the men to fuck her non stop while at the same time, chastising them loudly. "One of you bastards hasn't been around to fuck me this month? When I work out which one it is, they'll know about it."

But then Jessica could appreciate the woman's situation and admitted to feeling slightly envious.

Jessica moved out and along through the scullery and looked out through the fly wire door to the back garden. There was the kaftan lady, bent double and swaying gently and totally naked under a full moon; and her suitors where many and not exactly who Jessica would have expected. Jessica counted six men with their cocks at the ready but there were also four women amongst them, brandishing what looked like oversized dildos, strapped to their waists.

There seemed to be an already understood pattern of behaviour and Jessica was mesmerised.

A woman stood in front of Dunya and told her to stand up straight. Then the woman stepped forward and fed her dildo up into the big woman's vagina. Then another woman would step up behind Dunya and feed a dildo in between her huge buttocks. Then men would take it in turns to step forward and shag the two dildo brandishing woman from the rear, the mens movement adding heft, helping push the oversized dildo's into Dunya's enormous vagina and arse. As the men stood around waiting for their turn, the two other women would move amongst them feeling and sucking their cocks to get them hard ahead of their turn with the women and laughingly letting the men handle their heavy sagging dildos.

While Jessica found this interesting, she wasn't sure what was really going on. It wasn't until she was talking to Angela's new friend Sally, in the early hours of the morning after the woman, along with Angela, hunted her down and took her to a little spare bed in the laundry, and smothered Jessica with kisses and wet stuff and took turns heaving themselves joyously into Jessica's vagina and bottom with dildos, that all was made clear.

Jessica surrendered happily to the honeypot from number 49 and said she'd come over again and spend time with just the two of them.

"Dunya loves men but because of her size they are just not big enough to give her what she wants. She happily lets men suck and play with her tits, but she won't let them fuck her. And even though men can use a dildo, Dunya's preference is for a woman to do her. She says they know better what to do and anyway, she loves their female energy.

"Everyone appreciates her predicament and makes a point of giving her what she wants. Doing things this way means that the women can also get all the cocks they want, at the same time."

Mystery solved. But there was more.

"You might or might not have noticed the size of the dildo's. Dunya got them online from a sex toy firm. Apparently they have quite a range including Draft horses and, would you believe, Unicorns. It's true. She showed my them on the internet."

———

Jessica wandered off out of the laundry, leaving Angela and Sally planning their next adventure.

As she was passing by the double doors that led to the little dining area and sun room, she glanced in and saw three men sitting on a sofa. They looked much older than the other men she'd seen so far. They were happily laughing and talking and Jessica thought how relaxed they were and she wanted to know more about them.

"Hello gentlemen. Can I join you?" she ventured as she came close and they looked up at her.

Jessica put them all in their late seventies and thought how she had never seen three men this age together before. They seemed so relaxed and unthreatening and she wanted to know them better.

Three sets of appreciative and smiling eyes stared at Jessica.

"Welcome to the gang of three, dearest lady. You are very beautiful. Please come and sit with us. Move up Henry and let the girl have a seat. That is Colin up that end, Henry in the middle and I'm John. What is your name?"

"I'm Jessica. Pleased to meet you all."

Jessica squeezed in between Henry and John.

"How is it that three fine looking men like you are all alone. Have you finished with all the lovely woman here already? Or have you been told to behave yourselves?"

The three men laughed and John answered. "Well, Jessica. We are all in our mid eighties but we have one other thing in common. All three of us have wives who are much younger than us and as you can imagine, because of our age, the girls are missing out on some of the things we were once keen to share with them. As a result, we like to bring them somewhere where they can meet younger men and get a bit of you-know-what. This means that we can all stay happily married."

Then Colin added his voice to the conversation. "We can get them up but they're just not hard enough anymore, are they boys.

"We love our wives so we are happy that they can get a good stiff cock in them at do's like this. My Mary came past a few minutes ago to see if we were okay and said all three were having a great time and their only worry was that they might be running out of cocks."

John laughed and said how if that was the case, his Maureen would want him to put on the dildo when they got home and he wouldn't get to sleep until the early hours.

Jessica was fascinated by what these jolly men were saying. She wondered if the three men's wives gave their cocks any attention but decided not to ask.

Jessica decided to play the innocent girl. Well, sort of innocent.

She told the three gentlemen about how difficult it was to find men who would just give her a gently touch up and play with her breasts and caress her and talk to her. As she did so, she put a hand on John and Henry's knees and lightly rubbed them.

"That sounds about all we can do, girl. Would you like us to play with you then? We certainly won't hurt you. Why don't you lay yourself across our legs so that we can all have a bit of you. Do that and we'll see how we go. What do you think fella's.

A thrill ran through Jessica's body. She stood up and surveyed the men, then she lifted the hem of her skirt and asked them if she should she lay face up or face down. Two out of three said face down, so the excited girl carefully laid on top of six legs, her shoes touching the arm of the sofa one end her head on John's trousers at the other end.

"That is nice, isn't it fellas? She's quite something isn't she? Look at those legs."

Jessica felt six sets of fingers moving gently up and down on the back of her legs.

"I bet she's got a nice little bum up here somewhere, too."

Jessica felt someone unzipping her skirt and she lifted herself a little bit and put her hand underneath to show them and help whoever it was, wanting to pull the skirt down.

"May as well take it right off, Col."

With her skirt gone, Jessica felt hands on her bottom.

"Take her knickers off, too, Col."

Jessica rejoiced, knowing three sets of eyes were feasting on her bare backside. Then she felt a finger on her little anus, going round and round but not intruding.

"Nice little Poppy's parlour", came the voice of Henry.

"How come you call it that, Henry. Never heard it before."

Jessica felt wonderful. Fingers played gently with her ankles and moved her shoes on and off her feet. She wondered if Collin had a foot or shoe fetish and when he alternated between her two feet, she figured that he had both. She loved it.

"When I was a youngster living in a village in England, the youngest of the girls who lived a couple of doors up from us was named Poppy. You don't hear it these days. I quite liked it and I liked her.

She was a happy girl but some folk thought she wasn't all there, so to speak. She seemed vague at times and you could never be sure what she was thinking or what she would do next. She wasn't subnormal or anything, though some called her one of gods Angels which in those days usually meant mentally handicapped."

Jessica felt John's hands slide under the top of her body and slide beneath her blouse and find her nipples. This was bliss, she thought.

"When I was much older, my mother told me that Poppy's mum, Ivy Gateshead, told my mum something she had told her daughter when she was fourteen.

"She told the young Poppy that as she got older, men would start to give her a lot of attention and that she had to be especially careful what she did with men or they might get her pregnant. She told her that what she had between her legs was called the bedroom, and what she had between the cheeks of her bum was called the parlour. She went on to tell Poppy that she must never let any boy put his willy in her bedroom, and she could only let him into the parlour, just like when they had special visitors at home.

"She told her that one day. when Poppy had a husband, she could let him into the bedroom so that they would be able to make babies."

Jessica thought what a lovely story this was and with all the attention her body was getting from the three mens fingers, she felt that she would happily be the mens Poppy and let any of them into her parlour.

"Poppy developed early and her breasts attracted a lot of attention which excited her. Being so innocent and not wanting to offend, she discovered that by letting boys, and later, men into her parlour, she was suddenly much admired and loved by all. She also discovered that she really liked having someone visit in the parlour and it wasn't long before Poppy's parlour was a euphemism in the village for any girls back entrance."

Jessica was loving this story so much. Then she noticed movement beneath her. It was in John's trousers. He was obviously aroused and she couldn't be sure if it was a reaction to touching her or to his story. She figured it was both.

"What a great story, John. I take it you made visits to the parlour?"

"I did Henry. I was a bit younger than Poppy, but when I was sixteen and she was probably eighteen, I was out walking near the Oak forest just a mile from the village, with my friend, Bernard, when we ran into Polly. She smiled her dreamy far-away-look smile at us then she said she wanted to show us something.

"Poppy led us off the track into the woods a short distance. Then she turned and unbuttoned our trousers and took out our cocks and rubbed and sucked them.

"This was all new to us and very exciting. Then she pulled up her skirt and pulled off her knickers and knelt down on the soft leaves, displaying her backside. Then she looked up at us and said that we had to take turns in putting our cocks into her parlour. She pulled the cheeks of her bum apart and showed us where to put them.

"After a bit of confusion and with Poppy's help, we managed to get into her and happily rode the lady, listening to her moan and groan as though she was unhappy, but then we enquired after her wellbeing she informed us that she was very happy and if we were happy, to keep going in her parlour.

"Over the years Poppy got a reputation and there came a time when there was hardly a man in the village, young or old, who hadn't visited Polly's parlour.

"Then one day she met a young man and they fell in love and got married and she went on to give birth to eight beautiful children.

"A was in my twenties and I accompanied my mother too the wedding. I will always remember her dabbing her eyes as we watched the bride and groom leave the church, and saying, 'She's the only girl in the village that deserves to wear white.'"

———

Jessica could feel the large bump in Johns trousers getting bigger which excited her, and she began to unbutton his fly. She soon had his respectable cock in her hand and shortly after that, in her mouth.

Then with a spare hand, she reached down to where Henry also had a lump in his trousers and Jessica signalled to him that she wanted him to expose his member. Then she rubbed her knee against Colin's crotch and felt movement in his trousers.

Jessica swung herself off the men and kneeled on the floor, sucking John and rubbing Henry. Then Jessica moved to suck Henry leaving both hands free to rub Colin's newly liberated cock while continuing to rub John's.

"By jove, this girl has got what it takes. I think I'm actually going to be able to give her something."

John was about to erupt and Jessica managed to get him in her mouth the moment before it happened.

Just as she was swallowing John's present, Henry began to tremble in that way Jessica knew pre-empted a man's orgasm and she got his contribution without loosing a drop.

As the first two men slumped back and smiled through dreamy eyes at their beautiful liberator, Colin spurted forth into Jessica's loving mouth, then slumped backward alongside the other two.

"What an amazing woman you are, Jessica. I'm sure I can speak for all of us when I say thank you and extend to you our very best wishes," said John, affectionately.

Jessica stood and looked down upon them, regretting it was all over. She felt she could have let them touch and play with her forever.

"Thank you gentlemen. I really enjoyed your company. Can a girl be a bit forward and ask if you would like to see here again and if so, where she might find you all? I loved getting your attention again and I would be happy to be your Poppy and let you visit her parlour, and now, thanks to the contraceptive pill, she could even let you into the bedroom.

"I just love being with you any which way. And sucking you all was a bonus. Are you ever available? Unfortunately I'm at work during the day so it would have to be in the evenings or at the weekends."

The men rallied themselves and looked at each other and nodded. Then John rallied himself.

"Our wives go to the swingers club together on the second Monday night of each month. They get home very late. At around 2 am, usually. We three usually get together for a drink and supper and watch TV or play cards.

"I believe I can safely say that we would much prefer to watch and play with you, Jessica. You could come over after eight o'clock to 89 Seaview Crescent, The Willows. We would love to see you."

———

Jessica was surprised when a call came through one evening from Robyn, the woman her friend Angela called the Honeypot.

Jessica had met Robyn at Angela's swingers night at The Willows retirement village a month or more back. All three women had had a very enjoyable night, both with the lots of horny people who came along and also with each other.

"Hello Robyn. Nice to hear from you. How can I help?"

Jessica listened as Robyn giggled and spluttered and mumbled before answering coherently.

"Well, darling girl. I'm organising a night which I thought you might be interested in attending. It is free to you as I will enjoy having you there as will everyone else, I'm sure.

I've had an evening like this before and I thoroughly enjoyed myself. Actually, it is the niece of a friend who organises things. Sharna works in the admin section at one of the universities. She is a bit older than you, around her late twenties I expect.

"To be brief, the event is really a gang-bang or perhaps a better labeled would be a cock fest, but a clean and friendly one.

"Shana chooses and enlists students who she judges as suitable for the job. She organises a venue quite close to the university, and we simply show up and show ourselves off. The lads do the rest. I pay her a small amount to defray costs and depending on the number of students she's getting in.

"The arrangement naturally includes her in the event. Shana is a very sexual woman and loves to get a go at all the lads.

"So darling, what do you think? I've put in an order for twelve young men to share between the three of us. If you enjoy it, we could always do it again and get more lads if needs be."

Jessica was a little taken aback by Robyn's offer. She didn't know the woman very well. But then they had enjoyed each other very much on the bedroom carpet with Angela later in the evening when they all accepted that they had run out of cocks for the night. Yes, the Honeypot was fun.

"So kind of you to ask me, Robyn, and yes, I will be most happy to accompany you to this exciting event. Text me the details when you're ready."

Jessica was about to hang up, but suddenly thought about something she needed advice about.

"Robyn? Before you go. What should girl wear to something like this?"

More laughter from the other end.

"Well whatever you wear darling, I can guarantee that it won't be on you for very long.

"You looked beautiful and sexy at Angela's swingers night. I so loved your cummerbund suspender belt darling and I'm sure everyone else did too. And lads these days are all looking at porn on the web and most of the women are still wearing what I wear, traditional lingerie, a corselet, a bra, panties, stockings and heels.

"Stick to what you feel good in, darling and you can't go wrong."

Jessica went to bed and dreamed of having many stiff cocks all chasing her down to the little hut beside the lake at the farm near Goulburn where she had enjoyed a wonderful holiday. When she got inside the hut in her dream, she threw herself on the mattress and let them all jump all over her.

———

Jessica wasn't sure that she had the right address as she stared at the old brick warehouse in a backstreet in the inner Sydney suburb of Surry Hills. Then she saw a door open further along the lane and a group of people entered and she headed towards it. A dim yellow light illuminated the door and Jessica pressed the door bell.

A very attractive young woman in a tight shirt and skirt and very high heels greeted her and introduced herself as Sharna and ushered

Jessica through a narrow hallway into a small sparsely furnished room full of smiling young men who hooted and cat called on seeing the leggy Jessica come into view.

"That's enough fellas. Behave please. Show some respect. This is Jessica who looks forward to meeting you all soon. The show doesn't start until you are all here and at the moment there are still two of you missing. Knock on the door when they arrive.

Shana took Jessica's hand and led her down a short passage and through a door into a small sitting room.

"Is Robyn here yet, Sharna?"

Sharna smiled and explained that Robyn had phoned the day before to say she wouldn't make it. She had told Shana that she foolishly went to a surprise swinger event in her street. She said how good it was because there were many more men than women and as a result, she received a lot of attention. This led to her being exceedingly sore the next day and she realised she would have to do without tonights entertainment.

She said she wouldn't call you because you might decided not come and she didn't want you to miss the fun.

"So how many men are coming, Sharna? Can we manage them all between the two of us?

Sharna smiled at Jessica and put a hand out and touched her cheek.

"You are very beautiful, Jessica. Any chance that I will get to kiss you later? Is it something you would do?"

Jessica reached out and put a hand on Sharna's chest and smiled.

"I'd like to kiss you right now, Sharna. May I?"

At that moment, a side door opened and an older woman came in. She smiled a big happy smile.

"This must be Jessica? What a gorgeous young thing. Competing with you two is going to be difficult but I'll settle for a bit less."

Jessica smiled at the attractive slim older woman.

"Jessica, this is Robyn's friend and my aunt, Crystal. She volunteered to help out when she heard that Robyn couldn't get here.

"Crystal? I'm just about to kiss Jessica. I'm sure she would be happy to let you have one too."

Jessica laughed and replied that some attention from both of the women would be welcomed.

Sharna unbuttoned Jessica's blouse and then she and Crystal put their arms around Jessica and took turns kissing her mouth and her breasts while both women slipped their hands up Jessica's short skirt and discovered her already wet little pussy and played with it.

Jessica hungrily put a hand up each of the womens skirts and lovingly palmed their warm moist hairy vaginas.

"Are you looking forward to all those cocks out there, darling?" Sharna murmured.

"Oh yes, Sharna. It is my first time but I think I'll manage. How many will there be?"

"Well it was to be around sixteen but it's now down to around twelve. I hope that will be enough."

All three women laughed and Crystal joked that she would need at least eight of those, "So bad luck to you two".

"Now, Jessica. Make sure you assert yourself when necessary. The lads all know that no means no. And it is understood that you can push a hand away if it is annoying you. This usually only happens when an overzealous fellow wants to maul your pussy or it could be that he is doing something that you are not happy about.

"Another thing I should mention is that I've instructed the lads that there is to be no coming on faces. I told them to simply remember the four b's - breasts, belly, back and butt and unless invited, not to cum anywhere else.

"Now I forgot to check with Robyn what your feelings were about anal? Are you okay with it or not."

Jessica was writhing under the delicious feelings she was getting from the womens' attention and she couldn't help thinking of her dogging guru Gina talking about warming up. Jessica was definitely warming up. She managed to gasp her answer.

"I'm fine with anal, thanks for asking."

There was a knock on the door and a voice called out, "Ready when you are, Sharna."

"I'll just say before we go in, these lads are mostly in their early to mid twenties. From what I know about them, they are usually a polite and caring group, but we know that men can change when confronted with erotic situations and might well act a little differently. I'm confident though, that whatever they get up to, we'll be able to handle it."

The three women stopped feeling each other up and laughed. Then the bright eyed thin and elegantly dressed older Crystal spoke. "Lets go and handle it now. I'm more than ready. But I doubt well get a five tonight but I'm happy with a four."

Jessica asked what she meant.

"One in each hand, one to suck and two between the legs is a five. These lads might be too innocent to make it a five."

The three laughed and Jessica thought how good this all seemed.

"With a bit of luck I'll get a lad who desperately wants to fuck his mother. I can usually pick them. You'd be amazed what I can get in return for the phrase 'mummy would like you to ...'"

The two younger ones yelled and said that gave Crystal an unfair advantage.

"And then what happens when they get home and really start chasing their mothers around the house? Aren't you leading them astray?"

Crystal rolled her eyes, "Lucky mum, is all I can say."

Then Sharna went and got a squeegee bottle from a cupboard.

"Hang on a moment girls. Lift your skirts and pull down your pants and let me squeeze some lubricant into your butts.

"And Jessica, just remember that you are in charge of everything even if you think you're not.

Sharna moved towards the door.

"Give me just a moment while I organise them. I'll knock when they're ready."

Sharna knocked on the door and led Jessica and Crystal along a passageway to a large dimly lit room. It was warm and comfortable. Three mattress on wooden bases were lined up in the middle of the room and fourteen naked young men stood against the wall, most with their hands over their cocks.

Sharna gestured to Jessica to take the far end bed and Crystal to take the middle one. Then Sharna introduced the women by name adding that all were excited to be there to meet the boys. Then she invited them to stroll around and "get to know us". "And don't be shy. We all know why we are here. Lets enjoy ourselves."

———

Jessica couldn't help but feel excited but also nervous. She recalled Gina's wonderful attitude when dealing with the men on their dogging expedition and how she personalised each and every encounter with the men that presented themselves to her. Jessica wanted to be like Gina, but was it possible in this situation?

Jessica kneeled on the bed and spread her hands over the front of her frock and moved them around on her breasts. Suddenly there were two, then three then four men standing beside the bed and she knew that she was required to make the next move.

Jessica could see three cocks pointing in her direction. She put her hand out and took hold of just one and looked up at the face that owned it.

"Hello! What's your name?"

A slightly embarrassed face looked down at Jessica.

"I'm Damian."

"Hello Damian. I'm Jessica. Pleased to meet you."

Introductions over, Jessica took Damian's cock into her mouth and began to lick and suck him, at the same time thinking that this was a most civilised way of doing the thing she loved most. But then things got even better.

Fingers touched an ankle and started to climb up the back of her right leg. Then Jessica felt other fingers, this time on her left leg and behind her knee and they too were on a slow march upwards. Then the hands of a third party lifted her skirt up over her back and Jessica felt palms on each buttock. And as this was happening, a second cock was jostling for position with Damian's, anxiously searching for her response. Jessica kept sucking but stopped touching Damian's balls and took the second cock in hand.

Damian reached a hand forward and slipped it inside the top of Jessica's top and inside her bra and fondled her lovingly.

Jessica removed his Damian's cock and looked up at him.

"Do you want to cum now or later, Damian?"

"Now, please."

Jessica increased pressure with her hand and with her lips and mouth and in no time at all, Damian shot his load down her throat.

Jessica looked up and smiled and nodded a thank you then turned and looked up at who was on the end of her second cock.

"Hello! What's your name?"

A cheerful face looked down at Jessica.

"I'm John."

"Hello John. I'm Jessica. Pleased to meet you."

Jessica took John's cock into her mouth and began to suck him.

The activity at her rear was hotting up in more ways than one and Jessica realised that her skirt had been unzipped and was about to be dragged off over her shoes and her panties were moving down over her stockinged legs close behind, and again Jessica couldn't help but recall Gina's words, "A girl is not dogging until she removes her knickers."

Jessica was suddenly alerted to John's early ejaculation as he poured his contribution into her. As John moved away he was immediately replaced with another person offering a stiff erection, waving it in front of Jessica's happy face.

"Hello! What's your name?"

A nervous looking lad with glasses looked down at Jessica.

"I'm Scot."

"Hello Scot. I'm Jessica. Pleased to meet you."

Introductions over, Jessica took Scots's cock into her mouth and began to suck him.

Jessica closed here eyes, savouring the moment. She couldn't count the number of hands and fingers feasting on her rear and all she knew was that the feeling was exquisite. Her top had been unbuttoned and she moved her arms to let the liberator remove it. Apart from he shoes and stockings and garter belt, Jessica was naked and she rejoiced.

Enjoying the nervous Scot's cock along with the delicious rear action, Jessica took a moment off to glance across and listen to what was happening next door to her. Crystal was on her back with her legs pointing to the ceiling and her feet were pirouetting with excitement.

A young man was energetically exercising her pussy under serious instruction from this mother figure.

"Darling, you can fuck mummy harder than that. You have before, don't you remember? You always managed to give mummy a good fucking when you got home from school on a Friday night when you were hot from feeling up that slutty sixth former, on the school bus, didn't you? Remember? And then mummy would make you a chocolate cake as a reward.

"That's better, darling. Now suck mummy's titties and bite her nipples. Oh yes! Good boy."

Scot yelled and deposited his contribution down Jessica's throat and immediately he moved away, a new penis arrived at the gate.

Jessica's eyes were momentarily closed as she rejoiced in the manhandling she was receiving at the rear. A hand was rubbing her pussy and was immediately followed by a wet sloppy mouth kissing and licking her.

"Hello! What's your name?"

A very happy looking young man with a swarthy look smiled down at the still closed eyes on Jessica's face.

"I'm Brad."

"Hello Brad. I'm Jessica. Pleased to meet you."

Jessica opened her eyes and looked up at the man and couldn't help but be uplifted by his strong looks and his smile. Then she lowered her gaze to look at his cock and was transfixed. Brad's member was very big and healthy and sat in bush of curly hair. She felt as though he were presenting her with a posy of flowers.

Jessica didn't immediately put him in her mouth but instead, stuck out her tongue and circled the tip of Brad's cock in a slow loving movement. This was partly to savour the delights of his member plus she wanted to be able to talk to Brad and if she had managed to get him into her mouth, she would be tongue tied.

"Are you from Sydney, Brad?"

"No, Goulburn, or rather just past Goulburn. The folks have a farm there."

Jessica was intrigued. I have friends just the other side of Goulburn, Brad. They have a property, Muta East. Do you know it?

Jessica was now rubbing Brad's cock and noting how solid it was.

"Our neighbours! I do a bit of work for Brendan and Bella. Wonderful couple and really good property managers. Good friends of mum and dad too."

Jessica was trying hard to concentrate on what Brad was saying. She desperately wanted to know more about him but their was someone attempting to enter her at the back making things a little tricky. Jessica gave a gasp has her suitor finally made his entry, then he settled in to a quiet slow shagging mode which afforded her the opportunity to ask another question.

"What is your surname, Brad. I'll mention I met you but not where I met you."

The two laughed.

"It's Braithwaite and it's probably better that you don't, although to be honest, it wouldn't much matter. Bernie and Mildred are very broad minded. In fact they are members of the same swingers group as Bren and Bella. But I've been in Sydney for a month doing a course and I wouldn't want them thinking I was having too good a time."

Jessica knew that she was running out of time. Things at the back were picking up speed and she couldn't really keep Brad in conversation, especially when he was just out having a good time, although Brad seemed more than happy just to talk. Then Jessica remembered something.

"When I was there, I noticed there was a dogging night at the cemetery. Do you go to that Brad or are you too young?"

"Mum and dad go sometimes, although mum's been crook for a while so I don't think she's been lately. Yes. I'm too young. But that's okay. Us younger set have our own fun at the same cemetery on a Friday night and I sometimes go to that.

"I'll tell you what. The next time your over my way and you feel like a fun night out, give me a call. I'll come and pick you up."

Jessica felt more excited at Brad's invitation than she had been about anything else in recent times. Now she had to cement the friendship.

"Thanks Brad. I'll try and get there for the next holiday fortnight. Now I better check you out properly."

Jessica launched on the most heart-felt sucking episode of her life. She carefully managed to get Brad's enormous cock into her mouth before setting out on a very loving voyage. But it was not a long voyage. Brad stroked Jessica's hair and touched her forehead then removed himself from her mouth.

"Are you moving to the back end, Brad, just as I was really enjoying you here?"

Brad laughed and bent and kissed Jessica's cheek.

"Sorry, Jessica. I've gotta go. I promised Shana that I'd be her fantasy man, Brad the very bad cousin, her 'bastard from the bush' as she wants to call me.

"Make sure you call when you next get to Goulburn."

Jessica would have been devastated at Brad leaving if it wasn't for what was now happening in her pussy and for the fingers gently tugging her nipples. So much was happening and she was loving it, and then there was a new cock waving infant of her face.

"Hello! What's your name?"

A grinning plumpish young man smiled down at her.

"I'm Linton."

"Hello Linton. I'm Jessica. Pleased to meet you."

Linton was a lucky boy. Jessica managed to erase the image of Brad by giving the blow job she'd planned for him, to Linton.

Then Jessica felt her body being lifted and rolled over so that she lay back and across the bed.

She quickly looked down between her legs and saw that three keen cocks were standing to attention, seemingly looking forward to getting into her now very wet vagina. Her legs were quickly lifted into the air at the same moment as one of the cocks rammed into her. She lifted herself to meet him and to give herself and him that little extra pleasure from his energetic ramming.

Jessica put Linton back in her mouth then reached out to two more cocks standing each side of her. In her mind she registered that she was now enjoying a four pointer.

On the next bed, Crystal was kneeling and venting her motherly wrath on the lad attacking her from the back. On either side of him, two lads were holding Crystal's ankles to prevent her moving away.

"Mummy didn't tell you to bring the whole school home, just one of your mates. You're a naughty boy. But now they are here, I hope they can fuck mummy as well as you do, darling. That would be very special for mummy. Now give Jimmy a try and I'll see how good he is then I should give Daryl a go."

Jessica smiled, quite turned on by Crystal's mummy talk. It was obviously working for her so why not keep it going.

The cock in Jessica's cunt suddenly removed itself and she felt a hand touching her.

"Mind if I have a turn? Just in case you don't get to Goulburn or forget me when you do."

Jessica looked down at the radiant face of Brad with a large countryman's hand lifting her red ankle strapped slutty shoes upward.

"Oh Brad. Please have a turn. I was just thinking of you and even planning my visit to Bren and Bella's place.

"But what happened to Sasha? Did she change her mind?"

Brad nuzzled the end of his cock in the lips of Jessica's wet vagina and laughed.

"I must have been too good unless she was still really excited by the bloke who was in her before me. She came really quickly so all I could do was spank her arse which made her cum again, and then I left. Would you prefer it fast or slow? I'm happy with either."

Jessica couldn't believe her luck. This man was ticking boxes faster than she could invent them. To have him back and still unspent was a joy.

"I'm happy with either, Brad. But I like having you here so slow might be better and I can ask you difficult questions."

Brad roared laughing and moved his huge cock slowly in to the place where he and Jessica could enjoy themselves.

Jessica had already decided that she was in the early stages of being besotted with Brad and she told herself that whatever she said to him would not really be detrimental to their relationship in any way. So she kicked off with an obvious question.

"Brad! Question number one. Do you have a wife or a permanent girl friend or even someone you really fancy?"

Brad was concentrating on his cock and the delightful pussy it was enjoying.

Jessica let out a groan and then a gasp as Brad's large member made its presence known.

No to all of those," Brad murmured.

The two enjoyed a quiet moment with their own and each others genitals. Jessica sighed and lifted herself up to meet him then she would back away so that Brad's cock had to follow down her wet tunnel and beg for more. Brad seemed to love that movement.

"Question two, Brad, and don't panic. Its really only a technical question. Other than pregnancy or money, what are the three reasons that you would ask a girl to marry you?"

Brad stopped shagging and Jessica saw him thinking hard, seemingly searching for the right answer. Then he got back on the job and thrust his cock in hard, making her gasp and jerk her body as she felt the beginning of an orgasm.

"Jesus, Jessica! How is a man supposed to answer that. He will know when he finds the right girl. It'll be bloody obvious."

Jessica was now softly panting and closed her eyes, knowing that she was heading towards an almighty orgasm. But she wasn't going to let Brad get away with glib answers. Jessica groaned and stretched her body out and tried to close her legs around Brad's neck and fold them there. Brad saw what she wanted and let her legs go where they wanted. Now she could see her feet and ankles and her slutty shoes swaying behind Brad's head and her excitement doubled.

"That is not a very good answer, Brad." Jessica whispered between her clenched jaws. "Think about it and try again, as though your life depended on it."

Brad was nearing the moment of truth and so was Jessica, and when they both came, miraculously at the same time, Jessica screamed his name and Brad shouted "Fruit cake."

Brad laid on top of Jessica and stared at her gorgeous face. Brad had seen a lot of gorgeous faces in his short life but this one did things for him that the others hadn't.

Jessica stared back at Brad, incredulous that this man had achieved so much with her emotions so quickly. But she was not confused. Far from it.

"Fruit cake? Is that it? I won best fruit cake three years in a row at Armidale Church of England Girls Grammar School, Brad. I'll remember this moment and remember too, that if I'm ever looking for a husband, there is a good chance that my cake making skill will make me potential winner."

Brad reached forward and grinned and put his lips on Jessica's and kissed her gently and lovingly.

"Come to Goulburn and make me a cake, Jessica. And Jessica?"

Suddenly Jessica was doe eyed and emotional.

"Yes Brad?"

"I'm glad we met this way. It's like we cleared two years of potential shit out of a relationship in just a couple of hours.

"I think it wouldn't be hard to be in love with such a beautiful sexy bitch like you, knowing that if we ever needed to, we could both happily go dogging at the old church."

Jessica held Brad tightly to her bosom. She wanted to cry but managed not to.

"Brad?"

"Yes, Jessica?"

"Can people still get married in the dogging church?"

Brad nestled his enormous but softening cock in Jessica's pussy and sighed.

"Well, I reckon it's possible. My family do own it after all."

———

The boys had all left and the three women were in the tea room having a cup of tea and a chocolate biscuit. They were understandable subdued even though they were very happy.

Sasha spoke about her night first.

"I think this was my best night ever. The lads all rallied around and did the right thing by me. There wasn't a slack cock amongst them and I believe they all had a great time. What about you, Crystal?"

Crystal reached for a second biscuit.

"My night was good too. I couldn't believe how well my playing the fantasy mother who wants to be fucked by their son, played with the boys imagination. They all responded really well and now I'm sure there will be a few confused and molested mums when they all get home."

Jessica yelled out her support for Crystal.

"I managed to perv on Crystal a couple of times and I was quite envious. She really had the right words flowing to keep the boys giving her all they could. I'm hoping I can come up with something similar for my next time. Maybe a cousin could get them going? Or how about an old girlfriend who had jilted him?

Sasha laughed then looked closely at Jessica.

"I think you did very well, Jess. From what I saw, you had your hands full along with everything else. You even stole one of my favourites.

"Brad Braithwaite seemed a little less than enthusiastic when he got to me after being with you.

"I know him quite well as does Crystal who comes from near where his family live. We had arranged a fantasy about him being my bad boy cousin but he couldn't do the deed.

"I don't know what happened between you two but I sense he has a soft spot for you. I saw him shortly afterwards giving it to you like he meant it. Best of luck with that, you cousin stealing slut."

They all laughed but Jessica was thinking about what Sasha had said. Was it possible that she was right. Did Brad really have a thing for her? Jessica's heart was pounding as she thought about Brad and how when she held him tight, she felt something she's never felt with man before. Then she smiled, thinking about him and presenting him with a fruit cake.

"What does Brad do? I know that his parents have a farm property. I guess he works on the farm? If so, what is he doing in Sydney?"

Sasha eyed Jessica with amusement.

"Ah ha! Me thinks that maybe the lady is interested?"

Jessica felt herself blushing.

"Brad has been in Sydney for a month studying something to do with his course. He is in his final year at Charles Sturt Veterinary school at Wagga but occasionally he attends short courses at the

Sydney University of Technology. That is how I met him along with some of his mates.

"He's a great bloke and he will make a great vet. I'd let him fix up my pussy anytime. And a woman I spoke to recently commented that in her experience, vets who work with large farm animals are really great at fisting. Go figure, girls."

Much laughter ensued as the three satisfied ladies collected their bits and pieces and headed off. Sasha called out as they stepped out into the warm night air.

"Are you sexy sluts interested in another night if I get one organised?"

Crystal answered first. "Only if they are young enough to play to my mothering fantasies. As someone once said, when you find something that works for you, stay with it."

Jessica said her goodbye's, adding that she would happily present herself for a repeat of this evenings entertainment.

———

When Jessica had showered and slipped into her nightie, she wandered over to the bookshelf. There it was. Grandma's original copy of the Country Womens Association Cookbook.

Fruit cakes were suddenly what Jessica wanted to think about and she smiled to herself.

"I wonder if Brad likes peel or not? You can never be sure with fruit cake. Some people love peel and others don't. Now how can I find out?"

Jessica recalled watching a friend of Prue when they were at school together. Ingrid had sat with them at the table in the common room, picking out every piece of citrus peel in a slice of Jessica's latest fruit cake masterpiece.

Jessica knew that she wanted to get to know Brad better and she knew he liked fruit cake. The more she thought about it the more she was convinced that this man would eat cake with peel or without. She would make her usual cake and that was that.

"Lookout Brad!" she whispered.

# 6

# THE DUNKING

Jessica was surprised one day when her phone rang and she saw who it was.

"Gina! how lovely to hear from you. What brings you to my phone you adorable lady."

Gina giggled and explained that she was in Sydney and staying with their mutual friend, Darlene. Jessica heard a distant voice calling hello to the telephone and she called back, hello Darlene.

I'm here for a function later in the week to which I thought you might like attend with both of us. If you were free tomorrow, we could both call around and tell you all about it.

Jessica asked if they would like to have a pizza when they arrived and Darlene said they would and with a bit of toing and froing with Darlene, gave Jessica their preferred pizza toppings order.

"We'll see you at about five thirty, darling. Bye!"

———

The two larger than life women arrived at Jessica's small flat and made themselves comfortable.

"Oh I do wish I was young and fancy free again, don't you, Darlene?"

Darlene and Jessica laughed and Jessica said it had its advantages but she doubted they made up for the exciting lives that the two women seemed to enjoy.

"She's even got a couple of lads on tap in the flat across the hallway who will appear at her bidding," Darlene whispered loudly, suggesting this was a well kept secret.

Gina looked at Jessica with a glowing smile.

"I will have to visit more often, I can see that."

Jessica coloured up and deflected further comment by asking what event she was being invited too, later in the week.

"Well, darling. Sit back and I'll explain. And I will understand if you choose not to come."

Gina then launched into her story about a woman named Sally who she had known for many years but now only saw occasionally when she visited Goulburn with her husband, Claude. She told how Sally had a brother who farmed near Goulburn and that he and his wife were friends of Annabella and Brendan. These friends were also a part of Bella and Brendan's swinger group and were regular attendee's at the dogging events under the pine trees at the disused church.

Sally's husband, Claude, was a property developer in Sydney.

"A year ago, the husband acquired a very large open-span warehouse that had previously been used as one of those giant budget furniture outlets.

"Claude wasn't quite sure what he was going to do with the property, but it was available at such a low price, he simply bought it, thinking he would work out a use for it later, or simply sell it on at a profit when prices for industrial properties rose.

"Eventually Claude had the sudden idea that he would turn it into an indoor camping site. Inspired, he rushed to put in a pool and a sauna and a playground and he was even planning get some pet wallabies and have avery-bred cockatoos flying around inside the cavernous building.

"It sounded ridiculous at the time but he loved the idea of people being able to camp all the year round and without going very far.

"Claude sealed the whole factory with that soft spongy asphalt stuff we sometimes see on footpaths. He laid out car parking spots, each with a space for a tent and with a small bench and table. All were numbered so that spots could be assigned to a family who joined.

"It was only after his grown-up children took him aside and explained about the real reasons why people went camping, that he changed his ideas.

"He was in the middle of coming up with some other use for the place when he suffered a heart attack and died.

"Sally was eventually face with selling up his properties, but when she visited the warehouse with the accountant and saw how much Claude had done, she knew what to do."

Gina stopped talking to take a deep breath.

"Sally and Claude had, since the very beginning, attended the dogging sessions at our church site near Goulburn and they had loved it.

"Sally suddenly envisaged the warehouse as a gated dogging site and without further ado, threw herself into organising it with the same vigour as Claude had with his camp site plans.

"Everything was going fine, she put in a lighting system that allowed itself to be turned into bright moonlight, and even added clusters of large indoor ferns in huge containers.

"But Sally realised that she had one problem. How to get enough men to make it interesting for the ladies. After all, the whole thing was supposed to be female friendly and she wanted to be certain that their needs would be met.

"The enjoyable experiences she had had at our little dogging sessions at Goulburn where made possible by the fact that we had a large number of widowers and bachelors as members, as well as the women and their husbands.

"Where to get men and more importantly, the right men?"

Gina stopped talking again and rested. Jessica looked at Darlene and smiled and said how exciting Gina's story was and how she so hoped that it would have a happy ending. Darlene laughed and said she thought they would be finding out very soon.

"It was a stroke of luck that Sally was introduced to the owner of

The Club, a female friendly club where men and women, and women and women, could meet up during the day for sexual encounters. I understand that it is located not far from here, Jessica?

"The owner, Desley Leigh had heard about the doggers at Goulburn from the member who introduced her to Sally, and she thought it sounded interesting.

"The upshot of this meeting - and after numerous get togethers between the two women and their accountants - was that Desley would offer her members, both male and female, a voucher giving them two free nights at Sally's new venture which, by the way, she had named The Dunking, a name she chose in an effort to move people away from the original dogging label yet still sound suggestive. She had moments of considering other names, like Donuts & Dunking, but eventually settled for the shorter name after talks with Desley.

"The signed agreement outlined that Sally's business should not compete with The Club so that it should not open before 7 pm in the evenings and never be open during the day.

"This arrangement was agreed to resulting in a trebling of the number of males who turned up at The Dunking's opening and was pivotal to the enormous success which The Dunking now enjoyed."

"Finally, ladies, I have an invitation for myself and two friends to attend The Dunking tomorrow night. So are you both up for it?"

Darlene looked at each of the two women and then back at Jessica.

"I'm definitely up for it. What about you, Jessica?"

"Count me in. I'm already hot just thinking about it."

———

Gina, Darlene and Jessica all agreed that The Dunking venue looked truly amazing. As they stared out of the car windows while lining up to have their credentials checked, they slowly edged forward through the double gates and looked down on a sea of cars and tents.

The time was only seven fifteen. A large sign at the entrance advised that a gong would sound at eight o'clock at which time the lights would be turned down to a bright moonlight level at which point, attendees could begin the fun part of the evening. A second sign cautioned against bringing alcohol or drugs to the venue. It also asked that peoples radios and phones remain switched off until the end. Photographs were forbidden.

The sounding of the gong also signalled that from the that moment on, women were required to be dressed or at least covered with a robe if they were wandering around outside the painted lines marking the perimeter of their allocated campsite. Men were also expected to be modest and keep things inside their trousers when wandering between locations.

People roamed about looking at each other and at the vehicles and various features of the venue. Some were standing at the buffet over at the far wall, enjoying snacks. Others were inspecting the one of the twelve repainted kombi vans that Sally had bought from a wrecking yard and positioned around the place.

As well as being painted in bright colours, the vans had been stripped of their back seats and then carpeted throughout, including the raised engine cover area at the back. The passenger door and drivers door had newly fitted electric windows, replacing the old rusted up manual windows. The front seats had been recovered and the long upright gearstick removed.

The kombis' were placed within the boundaries of a dozen numbered sites and were available for hire by those who wanted more room.

As Gina drove into the assigned parking space she announced that she had rented the kombi van parked beside them.

Jessica screamed with excitement.

"It has always been a big regret that I was born to late to rumble in a kombi. Now my prayers have been answered. Oh God, I'm warming up already."

The two older women laughed, enjoying Jessica's enthusiasm.

"Well, darling. You might have to share it with two experienced kombi ladies. What do you think, Gina? Will we let her put her lovely body on the floor of the van with us?"

"Of course Darlene, just so long as she shares her suitors with us if we're not getting enough attention."

Much laughing ensued and Jessica called them rude names.

"I'm so young and I have much to catch up on to catch up to you two. It would help me if you left my conquests alone so that I could get a full experience. You wouldn't want me to have less than a proper education, would you?"

Everyone got out of Gina's large people carrier to look around. The place really was like a camping ground.

Smiling women and men passed by, looking closely at the three newcomers.

The crowd seemed so clean and middle class and a woman could be forgiven for thinking that these men could never act in a demonstrative and sexy manner.

Perhaps she would find them boring, thought Jessica.

"Only five minutes to go girls. Are we just about ready?"

Gina went and stepped into the open double doors of the yellow, green, and orange kombi. First she laid down on the carpeted floor. Then she got up and turned and leant over the raised carpeted motor cover at the back of the van. She lifted her skirt and called out.

"How do I look, girls."

The two women stared at Gina's brazen display, appreciating her delightful rear end and Darlene clapped. Then Jessica remembered Gina's advise to her when they were dogging in Goulburn.

"I was once told by an expert that a girl is not dunking until she removes her knickers, Gina."

As Jessica finished speaking, a loud gong sounded and the lights dimmed. And in the new soft light, Gina laughed and slipped her knickers off.

"Everybody to their positions. Time to go and enjoy ourselves girls. Best of luck."

Darlene looked at Jessica.

"I fancy the back seat of the van we came in, Jessica. I need to spread myself. Is that okay with you?"

"Sure thing. I'm going to start where I finished up on my first time; the front seat of the van. Okay with you, Darlene?"

The two took their positions and looked out at the still milling crowd.

"Knickers off then, Jessica?"

"That would be a start, Darlene. Plus the other thing Gina told me."

"What was that, darling?"

"Show your tits darling. That will bring them closer."

Darlene laughed and said what good advice that was. She laid back on the wide back seat and unbuttoned her blouse, displaying her big breasts held in by an enormous lacy bra, and then she lifted the hem of her skirt to display her stocking tops and suspenders.

Jessica pulled down the long rear vision mirror that Brendan had installed - his perving mirror he called it - so that she could occasionally check on Darlene. She saw her friend laid out in all her finery.

"Oh Darlene, I think I want to join you, you sexy bitch."

Jessica unbuttoned her top and looked down at her small shapely breasts.

Suddenly both women had other things to think about and Jessica heard Darlene's soft voice from the back of the van.

"Cock alert, darling."

At that moment, Jessica realised that she had not thought as much about sucking cocks over the past twenty-four hours as she would have normally. It was now a topic close to her heart and a day would rarely pass that she didn't slip into a semi daydream state and imagine herself with her mouth around a fully erect penis.

Since her dogging event at Goulburn, Jessica had come to understand a bit more about a man's magic phallus. She now understood how enjoyable it was to hold the covering skin tightly between her lips while they were stretched over her teeth, and moving his skin covering around and rotate it like a sleeve or a glove, independent of the flesh and muscle that it covered.

Just as Jessica felt herself drifting into her dream state, a sound beside her brought her back to the present. There was a light tapping on the window and outside, two big red cocks were peering at her through the glass, lifting themselves up and down and sometimes wagging from side to side.

Again, Gina's voice echoed in Jessica's head, "Don't rush darling. Tease them a bit. You will enjoy it and they'll get even stiffer."

Jessica looked above the cocks into the eyes of the neatly dressed men they belonged to. Accountants or middle management she mused. She smiled, and rubbed her hands over her breasts and pushed them out provocatively, then she lifted the hem of her skirt and palmed her pussy then lifted herself up off the seat, wriggling her naked abdomen and her small tuft of hair up close to the window.

The cocks lifted and wagged with excitement and Jessica wanted to purr like a cat. And just like a cat, Jessica wanted to play with these cocks and taunt them until they begged for release.

And who were these men, anyway? And were their partners here too? Were their wives semi naked in a cars here, touching themselves between their legs while at this very moment, looking at cocks through the window and for the same excitement Jessica was looking for?

Jessica dropped the window so that she could reach out and take a cock in her hand. Two hands dived into the car, one went to her breast and the other between her legs.

As her hand closed around a warm welcoming penis, Jessica felt that magic feeling as the thousands of nerve endings she'd learnt lived in that area around her genitals, rejoiced.

And while gently directing the first willing penis towards her mouth, Jessica chanced a look into the kombi next door.

Gina was kneeling in front of two men. She had a cock in each hand while at her rear end two other men were taking it in turns to shag her most energetically. Gina was very busy.

And in the back of the car she heard Darlene voice and glanced up at the long rear vision mirror. Darlene also had a cock in each hand, sucking each in turn. But she had stopped for a moment to speak to a man who had just arrived between her legs.

"If you want to go there, you'll have to lick me first. It needs to be properly lubricated. Condoms are in the box on the floor."

Jessica smiled and leant her head toward the open window, then she opened her mouth wide and fed that first stiff member down into her throat, rejoicing in the moment. With her other hand, she reached across and took hold of the other cock, running her fingers up and down to reassure it that it hadn't been forgotten.

Liquid soon surged down Jessica's throat and she smiled inside. She murmured a thank-you as the man moved away. Then she turned and smiled at the eyes above the cock she was holding, noticing as she did so that more men were lining up nearby.

One after another, penises kept coming, literally. Another surge of liquid and another happy man moved off. How many had that been, Jessica thought to herself.

As time went on, Jessica found herself thinking all sorts of crazy things. One thought was about the partner of whoever she was fucking at that moment. Who was fucking his wife, she wondered. And then who was fucking the wife of the man fucking the wife of the man fucking Jessica?

Across in the kombi, Gina's lovely legs and her high-heels where pointing skyward, held by firm hands as still another man came inside her, dropping his filled condom in the ice cream container outside the door as he withdrew and moved on, and then another pair of hands kept Gina's legs in the air and still another cock took possession of her.

In the mirror above the dashboard, Jessica looked at what Darlene was up to in the back of the van. Again, there was the vision of legs stretched upwards. But Jessica noticed with fascination that a man was stretched out beneath Darlene and his cock was firmly planted in her backside, while a second man was right up tight in her vagina and moving backwards and forwards. As if that wasn't enough, Darlene held a cock in her hand close to her mouth, sucking it with a generous amount of slurping, making noises that signalled her multiple pleasure's.

Jessica wondered if she should try fucking. So far, she had only a small amount of experience; with the boys at home and then with the two young men at the farm when she was down in the little house beside the lake with Mandy and Cindy. Then there was the three men at The Willows retirement village.

All her experiences had been enjoyable but Jessica still didn't know if penetration could ever compare with the super wonderful feelings she felt as a result of sucking a cock.

Feeling so turned on by her sucking and looking at Gina and Darlene enjoying themselves, Jessica decided that one way or another, she would take a cock in her pussy. She first thought that the best way to do it would be to get out of the car, and play it by ear, as some would say. Then she looked at the half a dozen men standing waiting for her and thought better of it.

Under some circumstance, being manhandled might be fun but this didn't seem to be the right time.

Then Jessica remembered what seemed like an obvious solution that she'd seen on the one dogging night she had attended, and decided that was the way to go.

Jessica recalled looking across at the car parked next to theirs which, on arrival, she noticed contained two women. The back right side door and the front passenger doors were open. Jessica could really only properly see the back open door and a couple of times the group of men moved so that she glimpsed the rear end of a woman kneeling on the seat. And at another moment, she glimpsed the face of a woman staring through the drivers window and seemingly doing the same thing in the front seat but on the other side of the car.

―――――

Jessica smiled through the window at the three men standing awaiting their turn and indicated to them that she was about to open the door and that she would like them to move back a little. But first she turned and knelt on the seat, facing away from the men outside. Then, when she felt comfortable and in control, Jessica turned and opened the door. The moment had arrived.

With the door open, Jessica walked herself backwards on her knees to bring her rear end level with the door. Her long stockinged legs stuck out of the door and her red stiletto heels were like sentries on duty that a man would need to watch out for if he was to stand between them and claim his rewarded. But then any man would happily risk death to own that beautiful moon shaped vision with the red suspenders and the tiny tuft of hair.

The men standing at the open door couldn't believe that what they were looking at was really on offer. The perfect bottom on perfect thighs and legs and framing a perfect pussy was a rare sight.

All around and in vehicles everywhere, there were exciting and sexy sights, large women and small ones, and in different shapes and wearing a scanty uniform that called out to onlookers to "come and try me". But Jessica rated a 10 and her admirers where in awe of her.

Then a gentlemanly voice spoke in a whisper, "You are truly beautiful. Let me introduce myself."

Jessica felt the first of what would turn out to be many entries into her vagina that day.

Occasionally a man would forget to put on a condom and would fill her with cum but before that could begin to trickle out, another solid cock would have moved in to the newly lubricated magic tunnel.

Jessica felt calm and at the same time excited. She decided she liked being fucked like this.

Dunking in the doggy position quickly became something she felt good about as well as her becoming good at it.

With interest, she noted how all those little nerve endings would celebrate more with some cocks and less with others. The sheer weight of cock numbers gave Jessica the opportunity to find out what cock activity caused the most excitement and she began to experiment, manoeuvring the inside of her cunt to bring about a better outcome.

Using her long fingers added to Jessica's enjoyment. Early on, she discovered that reaching back between her legs and touching the mens scrotums added to their enjoyment and to hers.

Sometimes she would rest the balls in her palm and jiggle them up and down. At other times, her fingers and her finger tips would surround the man's balls at the very top as though she were about to pick a pear from a branch. Another favourite was to encircle the cods at the top and pretend to milk them like the teat on a cow's udder.

Performing these movements delighted and entertained Jessica and they obviously enhanced the owners experiences too. And Jessica benefitted greatly from the mens added enthusiasm.

Darlene had mentioned how men like women to make noises and this pleased Jessica very much. She was forever wanting to sound off when she felt the need.

Sucking cock wasn't really conducive to making sounds other than wet slurpy noises. Now, as she felt each cock rocking gently or rampaging inside her, Jessica found a variety of non verbal gurgling and groaning sounds to add to the vocal expressions of her excitement, interspersing the calling out of "yes" and "harder" and "more please". And all this served to urge on the fortunate happy fellow between her legs whilst also exciting those in the line behind who could hear her.

Jessica had at last discovered that she could enjoy entertaining many cocks in the activity that they were designed for, and amidst the smell of soaps and deodorants and even the occasional whiff of cosmetics and body smells from other women, and even a hint of dry-cleaning fluid, Jessica languished in cock heaven.

The sound of the gong signalled that all activity must end in half-an-hour. A quick glance backwards told Jessica that there were still at least four men waiting and she realised that she had been on her knees accepting cocks for well over an hour. And what's more, she knew that she would be happy to accept many more.

When all was finished and the sound of car engines preparing to leave drowned out the soft background music, Gina and Darlene sat back in their own van and looked at Jessica.

"From my occasional observations, I think it would be safe to say that Jess, enjoyed coming to The Dunking. What do you think, Darlene?"

"Well, she certainly didn't travel far from her front seat. And she never seemed to send a man away who wasn't satisfied. Was it okay for you, Jessica? Did you enjoy yourself?"

Jessica looked at her lady friends with a smile and with her eyes still half closed.

"Oh God, yes. I loved it. When can we come again, please?"

———

Jackie and Miranda arrived in Australia a month before Christmas. Roger and Caroline welcomed them home and the night after they got back, entertained the two over dinner at the cottage next door. Roger made his one main dish, pan fried fish, a dish he enjoyed so much during his time in Italy.

"So you two are really getting married? We are not sure how it happened, but weirdly, it sounds sort of right, doesn't it Miranda."

The betrothed looked at each other and smiled.

"It was a decision we came to so that Caroline could be a member of a club that I belong to. It was nothing really romantic."

Caroline punched Roger's arm.

"That is not quite true. Roger persuaded me - on his knees, mind you - that for our babies sake, it would be better if we got hitched. Some of the private schools require parents to be married apparently, so just in case we go down that track for junior's education, we thought it best to be able to tick all the boxes.

As all three women had gone to private schools, they didn't need convincing but Roger wasn't done.

"I'm just glad we don't allow polygamy in this country. Imagine having all of one's wives turning up to a man's clubs. And how many teacher-parent nights would he need to go to?"

Jackie looked at him with a wicked smile.

"Just because we are not getting married, Roger, doesn't mean that I won't be expecting you to take an interest in our child."

Roger remembered too late that he was to father Jacki's baby. Not only that, tentative plans were afoot for him to impregnate Miranda, although the two had yet to talk that through.

"So what was the club you wanted to be a member of, Caroline."

Miranda was usually the quiet one of the two, but she was obviously intrigued to know what it was that so interested Caroline that she would consider getting married to be a part a of it.

Caroline and Roger looked at each other, both wondering whether to talk about The Club or, because it would need quite a bit of detailed explaining, should they leave it for another time.

With a nod from Caroline, Roger began to tell the two about The Club. Caroline went and got copies of the booklet Roger had prepared and handed them around so that the two could scan them while he talked.

Jackie and Miranda would occasionally gasp or utter a "my goodness" or similar phrase as Roger, with help from Caroline, painted the picture and gave details of the structure of The Club.

Caroline finished Roger's monologue by saying how Roger had taken both her and their neighbour Helen and that both of them had very much enjoyed the experience.

"Well! I'm not sure what to say. We've planned a big party here for early February. A mix of house warming and Meet and Greet for friends. Perhaps we could arrange to hire The Club instead of having the party here? It sounds much more than what we had already planned for our friends."

Everyone looked at Jackie and laughed.

Caroline rose and asked if everyone would like desert. "Pavlova and cream with passion fruit of course. What could be more Australian to welcome you home."

Jackie looked at Roger and smiled lovingly.

"We are so happy to be here, Roger. We'll spend the next few days catching up with friends, in between sorting stuff and arranging the last-minute renovations and the curtaining requirements.

"And, Roger, Miranda will look for a moment of your time to have a chat about those things we've already discussed. Is that right, Miranda?"

The shy dark haired beauty coloured up a little and smiled, "Yes Roger. Are you still able to offer your services? I will understand if you're now thinking that two children are enough. I'm sure you would agree that if you have any reservations it would be better to say something now rather than later."

Caroline arrived with desert and busied herself with setting out plates and serving portions. Roger watched, thinking how wonderful it was that he'd met a woman with the ability to turn out sweet things in the blink of an eye.

"I certainly have no reservations whatsoever, Miranda. I think that things couldn't really be any better suited to bringing up kids than what we all enjoy here. I'll be guided by you. And yes, just let me know when you would like to talk things through."

Caroline had picked up on the conversation and laughed and commented.

"Children's bedtime stories will never be the same again; Whose Been Sleeping in My Bed, and Roger And The Beanstalk, and a whole lot more."

Everyone laughed and tucked in to desert and sipped their champagne or red wine, and toasted each other and said how they felt blessed to be living here in Oz.

Jackie talked about the housewarming party that she and Miranda were planning for the first weekend in February.

"It will be really big and for girls only. Sorry, Roger, we might find you a position in the kitchen but you will have to wear a wig and a kilt so as not to frighten our really hard-line lesbian friends."

They had mentioned the party often over the recent months on Skype but now it was looking more real. And they had invited friends from London and Los Angeles and a few other places.

"So it's a Meet and Greet party? Are people coming who have never met each other before?" asked Roger.

One of Roger's great passions was human behaviour and he liked the idea of strangers catching up in foreign places. So much could happen.

Jackie looked at Miranda and then at Roger, and laughed.

"Yes, a couple of them have never met, and of course the Aussie contingent haven't met the folk from overseas. Certain people might prefer to call it a Kiss and Lick party, Roger. You would no doubt have that already noted in your encyclopaedic catalogue of human exchange?"

Roger was very amused and replied that it wasn't a term he had been familiar with, but having just learned it, he would be sure to consider it in future writing.

Then the topic turned, as it so often did, to the house and the renovations and Natalie's name was mentioned, the interior decorator who had had her way with both Roger and Jackie the day she finished working on the house and a few days before she went off to Italy.

"Natalie is calling around later in the week for a social visit but also to see how the place is looking now that the curtains are up and all the furniture is in place.

"I will invite her to the party. She also would like to meet Caroline and Miranda and catch up with Roger if he's around."

Caroline smirked at Roger from across the room.

"This is the woman you think I would like to meet about refurbishing the cottage, isn't it darling. I understand she was very forth-coming in helping you refurbish our bed while I was away

"Im very much looking forward to meeting her. Given that I apparently now suffer from mood swings because of being pregnant, I'll enjoy either tearing her eyes out or dragging her into the bedroom. Whichever way it will be fun, I'm sure."

Jackie looked at the two with fond admiration. She was now in love with Roger and so pleased to be home at last.

"She's also dying to meet Miranda as well so it could be an explosive time. The more I think about it the more I'm thinking we should simply invite her for the weekend and be done with it."

"What a good idea, Jackie and we can make sure that she goes home totally exhausted. What fun! A pity she's not a bit younger so that Roger could get her pregnant too. I think you need five children to be able to start a child minding centre."

Roger smiled and eyed his new wife wondering if she was really emotionally affected by being pregnant. So much to consider when you are a novelist.

# 7

# GOODBYE AND GOOD LUCK

No one on Eros Crescent remembers exactly the moment when the words COVID-19 or Corona virus were first uttered in their houses. Needless to say, it would first have been heard on a television report and the importance of the message would have taken a few days to sink in.

The world suddenly changed. Words and phrases like lockdown and self-isolation and social distancing were suddenly in the forefront of all conversations as people enacted the requests of government and the nation to act responsibly to assist in the national objective to achieve what quickly became known as flattening the curve.

---

For Roger, life couldn't have been less effected. His daily routines required only that he rose from his bed, showered and shaved, ate his breakfast, went for a walk, and made sure he had sufficient pens and paper. Although it did impinge on his new paying project.

He had been asked by Desley to write another booklet similar to the one he'd written for The Club, only this was to be for The Dunking, a venue he had not yet visited or, until now even heard of. Desley explained that it was planned as a female friendly dogging site which she had been offered the opportunity to take a financial interest in.

When Desley explained the concept and related what the setting inside the warehouse was like, she also told him that he was to accompany Alvie, the older woman from the The Club front office. On hearing this, Roger was doubly keen to get started given how he found Alvie most appealing. But the arrival of the virus put an end to that project, at least until further notice.

———

For Caroline and Jackie and Miranda, staying at home was what they enjoyed anyway, that is when they weren't travelling abroad or window shopping or having coffee in cafe's.

All three women had worked in executive positions in London, but moving overseas brought that era to a close, although they had been invited to join similar companies in Australia.

A top of the range coffee making machine was promptly ordered along with a supply of fair trade East Timorese Maubisse, medium blend. Browsing online shops became the new window shopping.

Instagram took on a new importance as the pandemic took hold around the world. Stories and pictures of people in isolation doing amazing and sometime ridiculous things became the rage. Jackie uploaded hundreds of images of the inside and outside of the newly renovated house, earning the praise of interior designers and architects.

———

Helen and her husband Frederico were effected in so far as Freddy's job as a flight controller at the airport was soon to be reduced in the number of hours he worked. However, there was no threat to his income as he was on standby as an essential service. But Helen's work as a freelance Human Resources consultant to industry came to a sudden halt. She embraced online conferencing on Zoom but this was no substitute for real hands-on consulting.

Helen had also become somewhat restricted in her love life, already reduced as a result of her husbands responsibilities to Helen's two lovers, Freya and Sophie who had inadvertently become pregnant to Frederico.

Sophie and Freya had each been granted a night each week with Freddy. Unable to visit or have visits from her own lovers, Polly or Celia Ashbee because of the virus, Helen would just have to manage with her next-door neighbour, Mary, especially as what looked like the answer to a maiden's - or in this instance a neglected wife's - prayer, The Club had been forced to close.

But then there came an answer to her prayers when her lover Caroline, offered her partner, Roger to Helen. This was so well received by all when Helen and Roger discovered that their mutual sexual fantasies involved anal sex. It was immediately arranged that Helen would stay over on the nights her husband was providing emotional and physical support to Freya and Sophie.

———

Mary's only loss of employment was her volunteer job at the Salvation Army Opportunity Shop which she would miss very much. She would also miss her sensual workout with her close friend Janice. But most of all, she would miss her newly found excitement at The Club which she had only recently discovered and joined.

Her niece and housemate, Sophie, worked at a horse stud and accepted reduced hours and looked forward to doing baby things at home. Because she and Mary lived next door to Helen and Freddy, the two households would have access to each other when needed. And of course, Freddy was to be the father of Sophie's unborn child.

———

Alice and Frey both lamented the loss of work in their jobs as school counsellors. They both loved their jobs. Both were pregnant and accepted they would be forced to spend more time at home together.

Like most of the others, they had their favourite sex toys for when they weren't knitting baby clothes or doing jigsaw puzzles. And like so many women in lockdown, they visited female friendly porn sites online. The two decided that they would always share these internet session and happily parked themselves on the sofa, transmitting the websites from their phones to the giant television set via a magic little box. This meant that the images were so big that they felt they were in the same room and this proved most enjoyable on many occasions. When the virus hit, both women took advantage of offers by both Helen and Caroline to move into their homes to be with each of the men who would father their children. Alice took the second bedroom at the cottage and Freya did the same at Helen and Freddy's house.

———

Bertie and Rosa were the older folk who were most vulnerable to the virus. They were happy to be isolated although Bertie complained that he would miss his fortnightly get together for coffee and cake with Freddy and Roger.

Bertie complained that he still had much to say on the subject of breaking down the worlds dependance on the "couples model" as he called it.

"Nothing good will happen while we maintain this ridiculous habit of pairing off for life." Firstly, in over half the cases, it doesn't work and people separated or divorced.

"Secondly, it was obvious that people who stayed in these relationships were deeply frustrated by the repressive demands on them of constantly answering to another person.

"Thirdly, paternity and property ownership where the only reasons this system was maintained and with the likely end of democracy as we know it looming, house prices and pension funds and equity investments were likely to collapse.

"And I haven't even mentioned the problems of religion and religious wars."

Rosa looked at him. She loved him dearly but managed always to call him out.

"You haven't mentioned love once."

"Sex and love are two seperate things, my dear. We both know that."

Most of the close friends and relatives knew that Rosa and Bertie had broken up years ago and taken lovers. Rosa entered relationships with her close girl friends and occasionally, a man.

Sometime later, she and Bertie got back together as a couple, but both maintained their freedom to embark on other relationships if they so chose, and this arrangement worked very well. It wasn't that they were desperate to take on other romantic adventures, but just knowing that they were free to do so, made the difference. They broke up after almost twenty years and had now been together for nearly fifty years.

"It was a necessary pause," agreed the two of them, lovingly.

Footnote: Freddy set up a Zoom facility on Bertie's and Roger's computers and they met each week at a certain time bringing their cups of coffee with them. Bertie was unhappy because he wasn't able to steal cake from the plates of the other two.

———

The two people that were originally going to be living together but in the end chose not too, were Edith and Jessica. But living at different ends of the same street meant that they would not need to forego their times together. And they, like Maude and the others living in number nineteen, had each other for company if and whenever they wanted.

Edith and Jessica had the boys on hand and could also still get a pizza delivered, although it sometimes took a little longer.

But then they learnt that they would now be sharing the boys with the very sexually active Maude and possibly with the two new girls who moved in to number eleven just before the lock down.

Jessica and Edith's plans to invite the new girls in for a pizza, were in hand and soon resulted in very fulfilling sexual exploits, sometimes with just the girls and on some occasions, with the boys and girls together. Maude was invited when she wasn't away as she often was. When Maude was present, the evening soon moved to the status of an orgy with all seven people happily exhausting themselves and each other.

———

Edith still went for her walk on Mount Eros on most mornings where she usually met her friend Chloe and the two, more than not, would spend loving time together in Chloe's secret cave.

It was thanks to the lockdown, that Jessica met Chloe. Edith had long wanted the two to meet so when Jessica was unable to attend classes she accompanied Edith on her walks.

Jessica and Chloe were instantly attracted to each other and become friends. Both knew that the other understood Chloe's relationship with Edith. And when the rain fortuitously arrived on their first walk together, all three made haste to the hidden cave and it was only a few minutes before Jessica had Chloe underneath her on the carpet of leaves with Edith dragging first Jessica's then Chloe's shorts and panties off before sitting beside them with her bare breasts available for the occasional grope from both girls.

It wasn't long before Jessica and Chloe discovered they had the same sexual fantasies and the two began to scour the mostly secret grassy spots on Mount Eros for anyone that might be up for a sexual encounter. Often it was a couple who were making out and who welcomed two gorgeous young women to share their blanket and their lovemaking. Occasionally they would find two or three healthy young men exercising their bodies on the steep slopes and the girls soon found ways to let them exercise other parts of their bodies. "Exercising with benefits", Jessica called it.

———

It was Desley who had the most to lose but she wasn't particularly put out. The Club had to close only two short months after opening and only a few weeks after Desley had been offered a partnership with her friend Sally who had opened The Dunking venue. The Dunking was closed too as a result of the pandemic.

Desley welcomed the opportunity to take a rest and review every-thing about the club and the new venture and be ready to make any necessary changes or recommendations to Sally when they eventually reopened.

She and her partner Alvie, lived on the premises. Alvie knew about Desley's dalliances with Roger who she said she also had a soft spot for.

Desley had laughed, saying that now that they had so much time on their hands, she would endeavour to entice Roger to pop in for a threesome if Alvie didn't mind sharing. To which Alvie replied that she wanted first go.

But then Desley decided to let Alvie go with Roger to their first dogging session at The Dunking, just for research purposes she laugh-ingly told Alvie. But Alvie's excitement was soon dashed when the The Dunking was also forced to close.

———

Maria and her daughter Serina were at first, forced to stay home with grandfather Aldo and the boarder, Giorgio. They mostly worked for older people as cooks and housekeepers in the stately home of Vaucluse and Woollahra.

They successfully applied for positions with the council as carers so that they could continue working.

They both had each other and the two live-in men to play with when they felt like it plus a range of toys they enjoyed.

It wasn't long in their positions as carers before they both found relief with willing sexual partners, albeit older and less energetic than they would have preferred. But as Maria told her daughter, a bird in the hand is worth more than nothing in your hand.

———

Maud, the owner of the music school and owner of the property at nineteen Eros Crescent though isolation would be difficult and severely limit her adventures although she had managed to entertain herself with young Ashton and Damian discovering the two had became suddenly sexually aware after falling prey to pizza nights with Jessica and Edith. Maude soon had a set of testicles in each hand and a cock in her mouth and even though she liked something bigger, she made do with them taking turns between her giant buttocks.

And Sylvia and Stella, the two girl who she had enjoyed briefly when they stayed over on the night of her house warming party, seducing Maude with the help their bunny outfits, had booked in for music classes and accomodation the week before lockdown. Maud reasoned that maybe life wouldn't be too bad after all.

———

Peoples attitudes were changed in part by the arrival of the pandemic. Australia was fortunate that it could close its borders and clamp down easily on travel.

Europe was badly affected and Britain failed in the early stages to take action which might have prevented many of the casualties they suffered.

The USA continued to be the sad case that it had slowly become over the last fifty or so years.

Big enough to make loud noises but also it seemed, too big to be able to maintain good democratic government.

It was presided over by a man who couldn't cope with an enemy he couldn't see and he couldn't lash out at nor verbally deride.

The arrival of the invisible virus was likely to prove to be his undoing.

———

Life on Eros Crescent went on. The residents continued to love each other in many different ways and despite the sudden disruption of the pandemic, there was a feeling of optimism in the air.

Babies were on the way and new life called out for new ideas. And new ideas about how society worked were desperately needed.

Cross your sanitised fingers everyone, and hope.

# FIND US

Publisher or review enquiries should include your full name and details
in all correspondence.

Email address:
*admin@richardlee.biz*

# RICHARD LEE PUBLISHING

**Erotic Fiction**

*The Eros Crescent trilogy in separate volumes:*

The Fifi Code

ISBN - 978-0-909431-02-0

Eros Crescent

ISBN - 978-0-909431-05-1

Mount Eros

ISBN - 978-0-909431-08-2

———

*Excerpts from the Eros Crescent series:*

Janice: A sexual enigma

ISBN - 978-0-909431-10-5

Jessica: A young woman's journey

ISBN - 978-0-909431-13-6

Helen: Enough is not enough

ISBN - 978-0-909431-14-3

Maria: Always available

ISBN - 978-0-909431-15-0

Mary: Catching up

ISBN - 978-0-909431-11-2

The Club: Ladies love it!

ISBN - 978-0-909431-11-2

———

**Literary Fiction**

Australian Short Stories
ISBN - 978-0-909431-00-6

Restless: A novel about two young men growing up
in Australia between 1900 and 1936 (Publication date not set.)

———

**Out of Print Titles**

Mathematics for Young Children by Helen Western
*ISBN - 978-0-909431-01-3*

Currajong: For Those Whom Schools Have Failed
by Bruce Wicking
*ISBN - 978-0-909431-03-7*

The Puppetry Handbook by Anita Sinclair
*ISBN - 978-0-909431-04-4*

Wordswork by Chris Davidson & Bruce Wicking
*ISBN - 978-0-909431-06-8*

Sheep Production by Murray Elliott
*ISBN - 978-0-909431-07-5*

Ducks for Starters: A Practical Guide to
Backyard Duck Keeping by Bruce Wicking
*ISBN - 978-1-875207-00-8*

Sweethearts by Colin Talbot
*ISBN - 978-1-875207-02-2*